CODE WORD: PANDORA

AN INTERNATIONAL THRILLER

5/17/18

For Paul and Nancy, with many thanks for your friendship and your support of the Code Word series.

Doug

DOUG NORTON

Code Word: Pandora

First Edition: November 2017

First published by Magothy River Press
1236 River Bay Road
Annapolis, Maryland, 21409

ISBN Print: 978-0-9994976-0-9

Printed in the United States of America

Do not be overcome by evil, but overcome evil with good.

—*Book of Romans 12:21*

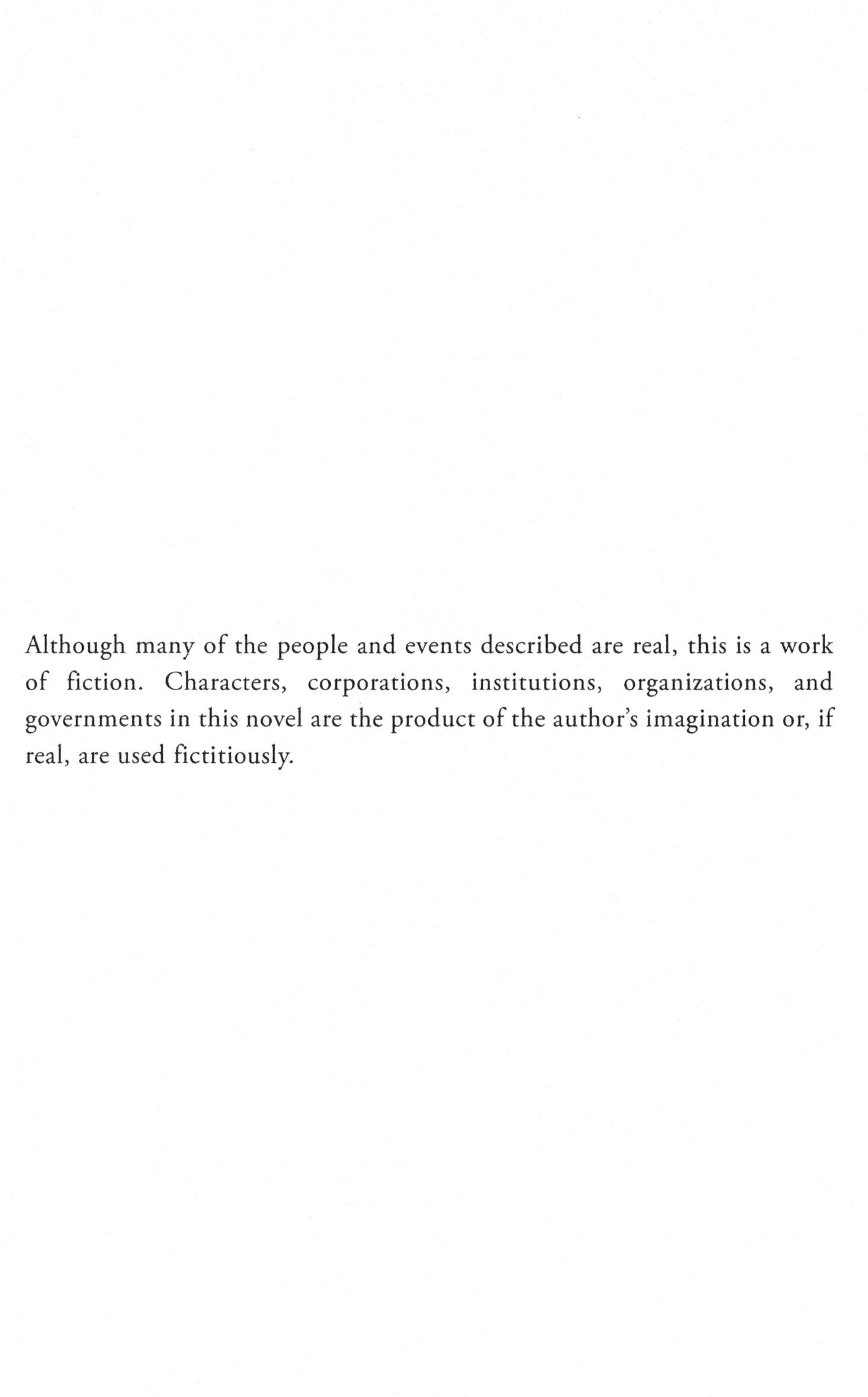

Although many of the people and events described are real, this is a work of fiction. Characters, corporations, institutions, organizations, and governments in this novel are the product of the author's imagination or, if real, are used fictitiously.

Abbreviations and Terms

AOR	Area of operations, the region within the purview of a military commander
CAP	Combat Air Patrol
CCP	Chinese Communist Party
DHS	Department of Homeland Security
DIA	Defense Intelligence Agency
DNI	Director of National Intelligence
DOJ	Department of Justice
DPRK	Democratic People's Republic of Korea (North Korea)
EOD	Explosive Ordnance Disposal
Gitmo	Military slang for the U.S. military prison located at Guantanamo Bay, Cuba
Guard	243.0 MHz, the radio frequency designated for military air distress use. All U.S. military aircraft monitor (i.e., "guard") this frequency in flight.
HRT	Hostage Rescue Team, an elite unit of the FBI
HUD	Head Up Display, a cockpit system that projects information on a transparent panel at eye level. The pilot can remain head up, observing outside the cockpit while monitoring cockpit instruments.
IED	Improvised Explosive Device

IOC	Initial Operational Capability, the date when a new weapon is ready and available for use by military forces
JAGM	Joint Air-to-Ground Missile, a U.S. military program to develop a new air-to-surface missile
KCIA	South Korea's CIA
KSM	Khalid Sheikh Mohammed, mastermind of the Nine-eleven attacks
PAX River	Military abbreviation for Naval Air Station Patuxent River, Maryland
PDIB	President's Daily Intelligence Briefing
PLA	People's Liberation Army
PRC	People's Republic of China
ROE	Rules of Engagement, guidance on use of force
ROK	Republic of Korea (South Korea)
RPG	Rocket Propelled Grenade
SAR	Search and Rescue
SCI, SCIF	Sensitive Compartmented Information Facility (SCIF), a secure facility, commonly called a "skif", where the most sensitive classified information, designated Sensitive Compartmented Information (SCI), is available to particular individuals who are specifically cleared for access to that information.
SIOP	Single Integrated Operations Plan, the list of options a president has for using U.S. nuclear weapons.
Sivitz	Slang for "Secure Video Teleconference"
STE	Secure Terminal Equipment, the U.S. government encrypted landline telephone
Stryker	An eight-wheeled armored fighting vehicle used by the U.S. Army
UAV	Unmanned Aerial Vehicle (a drone)

Prologue

Coronado, California

ALTHOUGH IT WAS RISKY, THE wiry man riding a blue bicycle wanted to see for himself. This one was unique. He wouldn't take the chance of doing it personally or even being in San Diego when it happened, but he needed today's physical connection to reach closure.

Today was his fourth ride-by of the Naval Amphibious Base at Coronado, California. It was also his fourth bicycle rental, each from a different shop, and his fourth change of clothes. And he was far from alone—this bike path that paralleled four-lane State Highway 75 was a popular ride. The marine layer of overcast was a threadbare gray blanket over Coronado that failed to cover the sky's blue promise; a steady sea breeze from the right felt chilly. The path and highway stretched before him, blacktop with yellow center striping appearing straight as a plumb line, interrupted at intervals by cross streets controlled by traffic lights. Here and there, ice plants' green, yellow, and magenta fingers reached upward alongside the paving. As he pedaled, the north-south sprawl of the Naval Amphibious Base was easily visible to his left and right; the highway actually cleaved the military reservation like a river. The base stretched from the high-rise condos of Coronado Shores southeast toward Mexico for perhaps a mile and a half of sand dunes and surf.

Although most visitors' attention was drawn to a huge American flag billowing above the left-hand section of the navy base, he was much more interested in the collection of one – and two-story tan stucco buildings to his right guarded by a heavy iron fence. Definitely scalable, but without cover.

Just before he reached the intersection ahead, the traffic light at Tarawa

Road turned against him, allowing a squad of would-be SEALs to trot across the highway. Clad in olive drab, collars buttoned to the neck, the helmeted trainees looked straight ahead as they hustled to their next event under the proprietary gaze of a man wearing a desert camouflage uniform displaying the unmistakable insignia of a SEAL. Muttering a short prayer of thanks at this unremarkable reason for halting, the nondescript cyclist slid from his seat, straddled the bike's low frame, and pulled out a water bottle. He stood immediately across the highway from the sole entrance to the compound he had come to observe. He experienced a moment of satisfaction as he realized this group presented an ideal opportunity for the spectacle he intended. But his pleasure vanished as he realized the timing of such movements was unpredictable. No, this wasn't the setup he sought.

Swilling water, the cyclist glanced casually across the street, noting the substantially built guard post in the center of the narrow entrance road, barely wide enough for the eighteen-wheeler he saw struggling to make the tight ninety-degree turn into the compound.

Not so good for a truck bomb, he thought. Possible, but the setup lacks the space for a high-speed approach that would burst through the guard post and reach the large building set back from it.

He stretched ostentatiously, torso twisting and eyes scanning, counting five security cameras covering the highway, Tarawa Avenue, and the area immediately inside the guard post. If the two sentries followed protocol, one of them would always be observing the security cameras. There was little prospect of an attacker sneaking close to them.

The light changed and he pedaled onwards. A little south of the compound entrance was an odd tower about fifty feet high, a cylindrical tube wrapped in an exterior staircase, with a small rectangular room perched atop. He noted a low building nearby that was clearly an area of higher security because coils of razor wire barred access to its low roof. Probably the armory, he thought. Next in line was a building lettered across its portico, "Phil H. Bucklew Center for Naval Special Warfare."

Pumping south from that building, the cyclist rolled past the terminus of the fenced area, observing men on rappelling towers and others climbing walls as still more ran an obstacle course set among dunes. Southward beyond that was just dunes, a broad beach, and surf. The sandy strip was featureless except for scattered patches of ice plant, the occasional pair of colorful rectangular panels clinging to metal posts, and "Keep Out" signs facing the public highway.

As he pedaled, the rider digested his findings. Although he had seen groups of SEALs occasionally, this was not an inviting area for his purpose. The men were always at least a hundred yards from the bicycle path, and there was frequently a strong gusty crosswind. Other than the bike path, this was not a public place. He wanted many people to see the act and recoil in horror. He had encountered cyclists who appeared to be SEALs on their way to and from the installation, but once again the probability of having an audience for the spectacle he planned was low.

The cyclist's concentration was broken by the need to thread his way past a family of four, dawdling along ahead of him, spread across the bicycle path. He slalomed slowly among them, smiling and excusing himself.

Back on pace, he decided the act must occur in Coronado itself. That would ensure an audience. It would also ensure the warrior could not escape, so he needed to be positive that one would be martyred, even if it meant shooting himself. Since the Americans had given up torture, he didn't believe a captive would betray the group, but why leave anything to chance? He had not survived ten years of building what the crusaders called IEDs by leaving things to chance. He had not destroyed an American city by leaving things to chance.

That satisfying thought was followed by anger. He had not gained the fame he deserved for striking the greatest blow ever against the main enemy, America. The higher purpose was served by letting the infidels think the "perp," as they said, had died in the act. There was no evidence incriminating the Umma, the community of believers. That was a wise strategy, and it had spared the Umma tens of thousands of deaths from the Americans' response, but it deprived him of his due rank among jihadis—which was even greater than that of Sheikh Osama.

He heard the whining growl of jet engines, but not those of a navy helicopter heading for the nearby airfield called North Island. This came from the beach across the highway.

As he pedaled southward, the sound grew louder. Soon the source of the noise appeared: a large, haze-gray craft he had never before seen. It was roughly oval in shape, perhaps twenty-five meters long. At one end was an enclosed cockpit, its windows reflecting the sun's glare; near the other end were two propellers, rippling and blowing the sand, even at idle speed. Two armed men in blue and gray mottled coveralls provided security for the gray beast, whatever it was. When he drew even with the strange machine, he stopped, feeling freed to do so by a similar curiosity rooting other cyclists in place.

At some invisible signal the guards left their posts, jogging toward the gawkers. The jihadi's stomach knotted. How could they know? He tensed for flight, then realized that would only make him a target. A moment later he registered the sound of engines revving and realized the guards were simply scampering clear of the sandstorm springing up around the odd contraption.

Levitating noisily, the oddity rose; as it did, he recognized it as a hovercraft, although unlike those he had ridden across the channel between his native England and France.

Now a foot or so above the sands of the Silver Strand peninsula, the hovercraft twisted ponderously through about ninety degrees, pointing its blunt snout seaward. It threaded its way among the rise and dip of small sand dunes in its path and trundled to the ocean, where it threw spray in all directions, but especially behind. The beast stopped for perhaps ten seconds, seeming to get its sea legs, then accelerated toward the horizon, supported on a cushion of air from powerful fans and thrust along by the two propellers at its stern.

The small cluster of spectators resumed their journeys. Accelerating clear of the clot of other riders, the man considered options. A few questions, ones the merchants and bartenders had heard many times from hero-worshiping tourists, had revealed that the SEALs favored several burger joints and coffee shops on Orange Avenue. In the evenings, there were usually some at a bar called McP's.

Because SEALs had martyred the Sheikh, it was crucial they be among the first Americans to feel the next wave of the Umma's rage. Allah decreed it. And he—known here in the crusader homeland as Al Hassan, known to his Palestinian parents in England as Fahim al-Wasari, and to his jihadi brothers as abu Shaheed—would see to that.

* * *

Yasukuni Shrine, Tokyo, Japan

At six in the morning, the Pilgrim was alone, as he always wished to be when his soul required connection with this great congregation of heroes. Buses did not yet fill the parking lots; other visitors did not yet wander, gawking and chattering. Short-legged and compact, he nonetheless moved rapidly, marching through the first gate and then the second with a precise stride and serious bearing, a confident man in a dark blue suit, crisp white shirt, and regimental-striped tie. Approaching the main gate, he halted his advance, pausing to purify himself.

Through the main gate, its green roof tiles glistening with dew, he turned sharply right and advanced across a courtyard with its cherry trees and small theater. Leaving behind heroic statues on his left, he turned right again and entered the museum. Threading his way between exhibit cases, the lone man halted before a wall of posed photos of men and of women, most of the men in military garb. It was as if thousands of homes had offered their displays of family and comrades to sanctify this spot.

The Pilgrim's eyes roamed the wall of faces, most of them young. He opened his mind to their voices and heard their stories. His heart was lifted, as it always was, by their eagerness for battle and by the undaunted spirits with which they faced death for Nippon.

I honor you, he thought, and when I have done what I must, your warrior spirits will rejoice. Power and respect will again distinguish the country you died for. Betrayals will be avenged.

After glancing at his watch, the Pilgrim bowed and left through a door opening to a roofed courtyard that shielded a gathering of mid-twentieth-century military equipment in pristine condition. The Pilgrim snapped a salute to a young man, in a pilot's uniform with an insouciant grin on his bronze lips, cast with hands on hips and scarf streaming as if he were minutes from takeoff in the lithe fighter nearby.

Hurrying back through the cherry trees, the Pilgrim turned right, passed through a gate, and halted before the worship hall, an open-sided structure with a green tile roof that swooped in graceful curves and rose to sharp peaks. He clapped his hands twice, gently, and bowed twice. He paused before the heroic spirits, palms pressed together in front of his breastbone, then turned and launched himself down the long, straight walkway, through the gates, past the early visitors, and into another day of his mission of restoration.

PART ONE

In a time near at hand

Chapter 1

Rock Creek Park, Washington, DC

HEAVY FOOTFALLS TRAMPLED THE DAWN silence, scattering sparrows from their feast of soggy popcorn beside the trail. The watcher glanced toward her wrist, shifted her feet, and looked left. The man she awaited was a little early, but she had prepared for that. She'd been observing him long enough to know both his routine and its variations.

Ray Morales picked up his running pace, enjoying his body's response to his mind's challenge. His shoulders and chest were scarcely contained by a white tank top sporting a Marine Corps globe and anchor insignia that the watcher thought was a perfect aiming point. After Morales bulled his way past, the watcher spoke into her radio: "He just passed Echo, a little early."

"OK, Foxtrot's got him," replied the final watcher.

Others converged on that watcher, and the drivers of three carefully positioned Chevrolet Suburbans with darkened windows surged from relaxed to alert as if someone had dialed up a dimmer switch.

Morales heard ragged breathing behind him and picked up his pace. Spying the trail out of the ravine in Rock Creek Park, he lunged to his right and chugged upward toward Connecticut Avenue, hairy, thick legs driving his bulk forward. Exploding over the crest, Morales sensed movement to his right, glanced, and saw a silvery cylinder spiraling toward him.

Catching it one-handed, he flipped open the top, sucked water, swirled it, and spat, all the while trotting toward one of the three Suburbans.

Ray Morales—formerly General Morales, USMC; chairman of the Joint Chiefs of Staff; later congressman from Texas's twenty-first district; and now secretary of homeland security—settled on a plastic-draped section of the middle Suburban's back seat. He wiped his face with the towel hanging over the grab bar to his right, swaying slightly as the vehicle accelerated.

"Morning, Andy. So you lost the shake today and have to ride to the office with the sweat hog, huh?" Nose wrinkling, Morales mimed sniffing his left armpit.

Looking over his left shoulder, the buzz-cut man riding shotgun said, "Coulda been worse, sir. I coulda had to run with you."

Morales grinned. "Sucking up will get you nowhere. I know you security guys huff and puff along behind just to make me feel good."

Ray Morales's face was more round than oval and it fronted a head set atop a thick neck. From shoulders up his appearance evoked a battering ram. In repose his lips naturally turned down, giving the misimpression of perpetual displeasure. He knew that and, when he remembered, he maneuvered his mouth into a slight smile. It was an action he had tried to make as automatic as his military bearing but somehow he hadn't succeeded.

Scooping his iPhone from the seat, he clicked the Twitter icon.

> Ray Morales,
> Here's what's trending on Twitter today
> The New York Times @nytimes
> Martin Campaign Blitz in Cal http://nyti.ms/179KNMM
>
> North Korea Seeks More Aid to Rebuild Nuke-Ravaged City
> Chinese President to Visit Pyongyang Next Month
> Las Vegas Bomber—Three Years On and Still At Large

Morales's blunt index finger brushed the phone's screen to pull up the article.

> Las Vegas Bomber—Three Years On and Still At Large. FBI investigators believe the terrorist who detonated the North Korean nuclear weapon in Las Vegas nearly three years ago is likely still in the United States.

Morales raised his gaze from the iPhone and looked straight ahead, considering something beyond Andy's broad shoulders and stumpy neck. The fleshy lips below Morales's broad nose compressed, and his black eyes narrowed. His jaw muscles flexed as he gritted his teeth. Though Ray had been leading DHS for less than a year of the unidentified mass murderer's three-year run as the world's most wanted terrorist, the monster's continued evasion was a parasite gnawing at his gut.

Someday, you bastard! You'll make a mistake. Or I'll get lucky. Or the thousands of men and women looking for you will pick up your trail. And when that happens you'll go down like bin Laden and I'll piss on your grave.

* * *

Aboard Air Force One

"Sir, the Las Vegas Special Zone will be coming up in about a minute on the starboard side."

President Rick Martin looked up from a document. "Thanks, Sergeant."

The president had an athletic build that evoked swimming or distance running. He wore a white pinpoint oxford shirt with a button-down collar now open and displaying a solid burgundy tie at half-mast.

Air Force One, deviating from its transcontinental flight path and descending to ten thousand feet, bumped slightly in an updraft. Within the president's office the sounds of flight and the hum of a fluorescent light were faintly noticeable.

Graciella Dominguez Martin caught her husband's abrupt mood shift. That's like something out of *1984,* she thought. Calling this place a "Special Zone." It bleeds the emotion from it, and, of course, that's why. The first lady brushed back her shoulder-length black hair, tucking it behind her ears. She wore a light blue pantsuit, the lapels of which were modestly high cut, revealing only a necklace of off-white textured beads pleasingly set off by the brownish tint of her skin.

His shoulders tense, Rick gazed intently as the irregular, mottled brown he saw through the cabin windows became the straight lines and angles that mark human order. As they flew over the city, he saw heavy equipment—scavenging beetles on a carcass—and vehicles patrolling a fenced perimeter.

"Ella" Martin moved to the seat beside her husband and took his hand. She saw the deep lines in his face, the gray in his hair that hadn't been there before. *Before* is how most of us see time these days, she thought. Before what everyone calls simply "Six-thirteen." She and Rick lived in the *after* and that shaped everything.

Especially Rick, she thought. He had both a strength and a sadness about him now. Gone was the boundless optimism and confidence that he could solve any problem through the force of his intelligence and personality. In its place was a sober acknowledgment that evil was real and that some humans were animated by undying, unreasoning hatred and could not be stopped short of death. She had known that since she was, oh, seven or eight, had heard the shattering gunfire and the shattering grief of those deprived of a spouse or child or parent by the killers fighting for control of the drug trade with *El Norte*.

"Two and a half years after," said Rick, squeezing his wife's hand. "I need to be reminded. I need to be reminded that I had to do it. That in the end there was no other way."

Ella's dark eyes flashed, and she squeezed back sharply. "Rick, we both know you tried every other way! In fact, I still think you tried too long—American society nearly unraveled. Bruce Griffith is a jerk, but he was right about that."

Rick winced at his wife's characteristic fierceness and certainty, but he knew it balanced his own cerebral nature, something she had once described as obscene rationality.

Air Force One began a gentle starboard turn, the view of Las Vegas spinning slowly as the aircraft's nose pivoted in response to the pilot's control movements.

"Bruce is a patriot," said Rick, continuing to look out the window. "And yes, he's ambitious, but so is every vice president. Why take the job unless you expect to leverage it into the presidency? I know you want me to take him off the ticket, but that would turn him loose, maybe to run against us—although I don't think he'd dare—but certainly to live on the talk shows, maybe even have his own show, and roast us. God, he's hard enough to control now, as my running mate!"

"Well, I'm just glad you've taken back the powers you gave him," said Ella. "You know, I think somewhere in that reptilian brain of his he thought he could use his control of internal security to take over. If Ray hadn't told him to stuff it, he might have tried something worse than encouraging your impeachment."

As always, when Ella spoke of Secretary of Homeland Security Ray Morales—now a mutual friend but once her lover—Rick felt a pang. He and Ray had become close, welded by the heat of a duty that nearly destroyed him. Rick knew Ella loved him and was committed to him by their history and their two children, but he couldn't banish the thought that if she had it to do again, she would follow Ray to Quantico and the Marines after leaving Princeton rather than going to Columbia Law.

"Ella, Las Vegas below means I don't have much time left to work on tonight's speech." Rick gave her a peck on the cheek and returned to his seat.

I'm losing my husband, thought Ella, feeling the aircraft's climb to cruising altitude press her a bit more firmly into her chair. Actually, it had begun years ago and now was an accomplished fact. Face it, once the campaign began, he was pulled away from you like a swimmer in a riptide. And like some swimmers, he put himself in the riptide, choosing to plunge into the surf despite its danger.

I lost him to The Machine.

The Machine had hit them like a massive wave, crashing over them, choking them, shoving them where *it* wanted them, except *it* didn't really know where to go and so would push them one way at breakfast and another way by bedtime. Advisors, drivers, consultants on everything from rhetoric to facial control, beauticians, gophers, pilots, videographers, his-and-hers valets, personal shoppers, and trainers—and that was just the staff, the people working to get them elected. Then there were the campaign contributors, the bundlers and high-net-worth folks who demanded personal attention in every major city.

And the press. My God, the never-ending demands of smart, shallow, conniving, frenzied journalists! Never mind that the proposal you made last week to deal with X was correct and hasn't been factually challenged, *that was last week.* And, last and least, there's the voting public, always to be kept at an intellectual distance, to be lectured to, manipulated, smiled at, gripped and patted alongside rope lines, and heard only through the reports of pollsters.

During their first campaign Ella's image of The Machine hadn't been this massive object moving inexorably forward to victory. No, her image was a surrounding mob of pygmies with whips and goads, constantly giving contradictory commands and lashing out when they were not obeyed. And as much as she tried, she could not stay with Rick. The pygmies surged between them, would not allow her to touch him. He was *theirs*.

The presidency was far worse. At least during the first campaign they had had a few moments together when they laughed at the absolute nuttiness of it all, its incredible lack of substance, the unbelievable presumption of some donors. But in the White House the number of people who did nothing but attempt to anticipate Rick's every need and meet it before he asked was at a new level. And The Machine had changed. Gone were the sometimes-comical pygmies. The Machine now subsumed all the resources of the executive branch of government. *This* Machine was a huge, streamlined object moving inexorably toward A Second Term; the campaign didn't stop for governing. Anything in the way was crushed, unless she or Rick happened to see it in time and made a great deal of noise.

The Machine had been halted by the horror of Las Vegas and by the brutal duty it imposed on Rick. During those months they had been close. They had loved and fought and laughed and cried together, had reasoned with and shouted at each other. And in the end, she had seen a new side of Rick, a grim, responsible determination to do his duty and accept its personal price, and she loved him the more for it.

But when the dead, the dying, and the grief-stricken had disappeared from the world's video screens and the governments of the major powers made fulsome promises of peace and cooperation and never again, and the nations of the UN began to listen seriously to Rick's proposals, The Machine was resurrected.

I've lost him, she thought. Because of his reelection campaign. Because he's bought into "second term at any cost" and tuned me out.

I feel betrayed.

Chapter 2

Tokyo, Japan

ISOROKU KIMURA PUSHED BACK FROM his neatly organized desktop and lit up. Calling to his secretary, he dropped the burnt match into an ashtray. He leaned back and took a deep, satisfying drag. He was addicted, he knew, but it was an addiction that gave him strength by allowing him to order his mind and think in the abstract. He could strategize and see connections between events that others missed. If it eventually killed him, he would die of cancer with a samurai's smile on his lips, as he would have done had he been a young man during the Greater East Asia War.

His secretary was suddenly in front of him. "*Hai*, Senmu-sama," she said with a slight, graceful bow, eyes downcast.

Startled from his reverie, he thought: she seems to materialize rather than walk in here. How does she do that?

"Tanaka-san, I am leaving now. I will not return tomorrow until ten. That's not a problem for my schedule, is it?"

"No, Senmu-sama, it is not. You have no morning appointments."

Later, after shouldering his way through other commuters flooding from Tokyo's Akihabara district and pushing his way aboard a Japan Rail Blue Line car, Kimura felt the mass of passengers sway as the powerful engine accelerated on its journey to Yokohama.

Forty-five minutes had elapsed when Kimura slid open the door of his home, paused briefly to switch his street shoes for tabi, clapped and nodded toward the family shrine, and exited to a courtyard soothed by the soft sounds of pigeons. He gazed into their cote, then gave a grunt of satisfaction. Reaching the pigeon he had spotted, he removed a packet from its leg, stroked it for a moment, and returned inside.

Placing the packet on a large rolltop desk, the only Western furniture in his house, Kimura set about making dinner. He prepared and served steamed rice, soup, and fish, then poured sake for two. After placing one sake and a small offering of rice at the shrine, he sat on the tatami and ate slowly, deep in thought.

The Chinese are so arrogant. They act as if they are still the Inner Kingdom, taking as if by right anything they want. They simply say, "It has been ours since ancient times," as if that should be enough. The Senkaku Islands, for instance. The Chinese had put soldiers ashore briefly on several of them, and his own government, the rightful sovereign of the Senkakus, had done nothing!

Well, actually they had done *something*, but it had been calculated to avoid encounters between Japanese and Chinese soldiers. There is now a permanent Japanese presence in the Senkakus, but it is the coast guard, not the navy or marines.

That, of course, is due to American pressure. They are committed to defending Japan, but have no stomach for doing so. We must stop depending on them!

And just last week the Chinese intercepted a Nippon Air flight, en route from Sasebo to Hong Kong, when its path—a scheduled flight within an international airway—took it inside their so-called Air Defense Identification Zone. Frightened Japanese citizens spent twenty minutes gazing at Chinese fighters flying near the wings of their A-320 airbus. The Japanese pilots' calls for assistance went unanswered. Despite F-15 Eagles based within range, the Chinese were allowed to bully these helpless civilians in an airliner proceeding on a flight path established by the International Civil Aviation Organization.

It makes me ashamed to be Japanese!

Downing his sake and pouring another, Kimura seated himself at the desk. Although it was Western, he had paid a great deal to own this particular rolltop because it had once belonged to one of his heroes, the samurai who had humiliated the American Navy at Pearl Harbor, Admiral Isoroku Yamamoto.

He held the packet the pigeon had brought, a smile playing on his lips.

Often the old ways are the best, he thought. Just as pigeons had faithfully served the Imperial Army in the twentieth century, they served his group in the twenty-first.

If Osama bin Laden had been as smart as he thought he was, he would have used couriers who could not be followed and could not betray him carelessly or under torture. But, of course, the Arabs are *not* smart, as their fumbling, uncoordinated attempts to bring down the United States show. Even Las Vegas did little more than frighten Americans briefly, enrage them, and make them a harder target. You cannot change the course of empires with pinpricks.

Kimura's fingers worked at the fastenings of the small packet, which soon yielded a thumb drive. As he waited for his laptop to boot up—a laptop without connection to the Internet or any wireless device—he thought about his plan. Governments are so predictable. Individuals can be wily, but governments are ponderous. They rumble down well-worn tracks. That's why my plan will work—once I find the right man, the perfect boulder to initiate the landslide that will sweep away all obstacles to Nippon's greatness.

Eagerly, Kimura inserted the encrypted thumb drive and opened a Word file.

Chapter 3

Coeur d'Alene, Idaho

FAHIM SAW THE RACCOON CROSSING the road just in time. With a jerk of the wheel, he wrenched the F-150 toward the shoulder and was able to mash the beast with the right tire. Hearing the crunch, Fahim smiled. Distracted, he nearly missed the narrow gravel road to the double-wide he shared with LuAnn and her ten-year-old Charlie. LuAnn of the cow face and welcoming thighs and Charlie who was a damned nuisance.

LuAnn heard the truck and looked out, hoping Al wasn't in a bad mood. The slamming of the driver's door told her he was. Feeling the knot in her stomach, she hurried to the kitchen; he would be hungry and angry if he had to wait for dinner.

She was round, no doubt about it. A cruel person might have said she looked like a Teletubby. LuAnn believed her best feature was her hair, a rich chestnut that she wore long and kept shining by daily brushing. She was apple-cheeked and even without makeup she displayed a ruddy attractiveness.

Fahim stalked into the living room. "LuAnn, I want dinner." He dropped into a battered brown swivel chair facing the computer and swore because it was set too low. "Charlie! Dammit, I've told him not to leave the chair down when he's done with those stupid online games!"

At the computer Fahim's movements morphed from angry jerky to contented smooth, as if he had just begun playing a musical instrument he loved. His fingers flew across the keyboard. Soon he reached the Darknet, and then he was inside the site he sought, a bazaar of perversion and illegal offerings from false IDs to assassins for hire.

"LuAnn, get off your arse and fix my dinner!"

"Five minutes, it's bangers and mash," she said, hoping that the prospect of one of his odd British favorites would take the edge off.

"Not a minute longer, LuAnn!" Fahim's fingers slowed as he reached the section he sought. Now it was his eyes that darted, scanning the offerings rapidly, his right ring finger toggling down when his eyes had scoured each screen. As LuAnn delivered a can of Boddington's Pub Ale to his side, the welcome smell of cooking sausages reached his nostrils; his stomach growled.

Exactly five minutes later by the display clock, Fahim rose and stalked into the kitchen, feeling a moment of satisfaction that he had trained LuAnn to meet his needs. Firmness and self-control plus a little patience, it worked every time. Like the way he had taught her to play chess.

"Get our game down," he said through a mouthful of mashed potatoes.

LuAnn cringed and hoped Charlie would come home soon.

* * *

Qom, Islamic Republic of Iran

"Crazy Arab jihadis say crazy things every day," said the stocky man in a flowing white robe topped with a black turban. "Why worry about this Fahim al-Wasari, who calls himself 'Father of Martyrs'?"

General Adel Ghorbani, commander of Iran's Quds Force, met the Supreme Leader's eyes and said, "Because this one is not another crazy Arab jihadi. We believe he personally planned and led the Las Vegas operation."

The Supreme Leader stared out the window across the holy city.

Turning back to Ghorbani, he said, "You are sure of this?"

"Sure enough to be worried. You know the Americans haven't identified him, despite a massive investigation."

"So how did Quds Force identify him?"

"As you know, Leader, our nuclear weapon scientists collaborated with North Korea's nuclear bomb group. One of—"

The turbaned man interrupted: "At a ridiculous price! Some day we will even that score."

"Of course, Leader. But we do what we must for now. And doing what we must just yielded a bonus: Fahim al-Wasari is known to the North Koreans—he negotiated delivery of both weapons on behalf of al Qaida and received the technical training to transport and then detonate them."

"How do you know that, General?"

"Leader, one night at a party following dinner, a drunken North Korean scientist told one of our scientists about Fahim. He gave a detailed description of the man and said he seemed to be more British than Arab. When Quds learned this, it wasn't hard—"

"When Quds learned this, you say. It's been over two years since the North Koreans were forced to disband their nuclear bomb research group and accept the resettlement of all of its members in the United States. So that conversation is two years old. Why are you just learning of it now? Or have you known and not told me?"

"The scientist of ours who received this information was disobeying orders not to socialize with the North Koreans and was afraid to tell his superiors. As time passed and the Americans were unable to identify the bomber who had hurt them so badly, our scientist realized the information would be worth a fortune. Unfortunately for him, he was a better scientist than conspirator, and we caught him trying to establish his bona fides with the Americans."

Ghorbani paused, looking into the Supreme Leader's eyes for permission to resume his description. Seeing it, he said, "When Quds learned of the scientist's treachery—a few days ago—it wasn't hard to identify the man as al Qaida's master bomber. He's known to be a Palestinian, born and university educated in the UK. His ingenuity in bomb engineering is legendary, even among the Americans. This is all circumstantial, but it's compelling. And if I ask myself who al-Zawahiri would entrust with such a mission, surely his master bomber is that man. Fahim's last known location was Yemen. We've been using all our sources to discover his present whereabouts, but he's disappeared."

The Supreme Leader sipped tea, then rose and stood eye to eye with Ghorbani.

"It is never wise to assume one's adversary is an idiot. Since this Fahim is well known to the Americans from the harm he inflicted on them in Iraq, surely they are on his trail by now. They probably have him under surveillance, awaiting a propitious moment to arrest him, boosting Martin's reelection campaign."

"If we were in the place of the Americans, we certainly would be on to him by now. He probably never left the U.S. after Six-thirteen. But the Americans are distracted by many things. Their ideals get in the way of learning that a clever, Western-educated Arab among them has done great harm and is planning to do more."

"I grant the plausibility of what you say, Adel. But I come back to my first question: Why do we care what a crazy Arab claims or plans against the Great Satan? And if we do care, what we should be discussing is how to help him."

"We care because we know what will happen if there is another spectacular attack. The Americans will assign blame to an Islamic nation and do to it what they did to North Korea."

Ghorbani gathered his courage and locked eyes with the man who could dismiss him out of hand, then said, "In my judgment Iran would be the leading candidate for this role."

"Pah! The Americans wouldn't dare strike us! We are keeping the nuclear agreement with them—for now. And they know an attack on us would trigger the invasion of Israel."

"Kim thought his country was untouchable, too, Leader. Remember what this American president did to it and to him. And Israel? By striking the nuclear deal with us, freeing our frozen bank accounts, the Americans showed they are willing to sacrifice the Israelis."

The room, bathed in the warm glow of the afternoon sun, was silent as the Supreme Leader turned away and gazed across the Holy City of Qom. "And how would you propose to prevent the Americans doing what you fear?" he said, still facing the windows.

Ghorbani shifted position so that he could see the Leader's face.

"First we will put the Americans on this al-Wasari's scent through a contact in Pakistani intelligence who is spying for the U.S. We have given our contact a dossier on Fahim al-Wasari, and he will undoubtedly pass it to the Americans. Hopefully that will suffice to put an end to al-Wasari's plans. But if it does not, we will send Quds Force after him. We'll prevent him from carrying out another big attack."

"Why not instead work with him and together ensure that the trail leads to, say, China, or even better, to the cursed Saudis?"

"I don't think we have time, Leader. Rumors persist that something very big is soon to happen in the U.S. And from what we know of this abu Shaheed, as he calls himself, he is arrogant and unpredictable. And he is a Sunni. Unless the Americans get him, the only certain way to protect the Islamic Republic from the loss of a city, or worse, is to locate this man and kill him before he can carry out his plan."

The Supreme Leader returned to his desk and sat. Resting his elbow on the polished surface and propping his chin upon his palm, he sat motionless for several moments.

"Do it," he said. "Keep me informed."

Chapter 4

Boise, Idaho

Fahim nursed his coffee in the Denny's on Airport Way, dressed exactly as promised. He was four chairs from the right-hand end of the counter, as viewed from the restaurant's door and, by glancing at the security camera monitor near the cash register, could observe everyone who entered. When he saw a skinny bearded man wearing new Levi's and a scruffy green sweater, Fahim reached slowly into his right hip pocket, withdrawing his wallet. He saw relief in the newcomer's eyes and hoped that anyone else who noticed had pegged the look as the anticipation of a hungry man.

As Fahim moved to the cash register, a ten in hand, he made brief eye contact with the skinny one, nodding slightly. The inhabitant of the scruffy sweater moved alongside and then past Fahim to enter the men's room. Fahim left the restaurant and slid behind the wheel of a battered red F-150 pickup and waited, fingers busy at his cell phone to explain his delay to any observer who might be curious. Soon the man he had come for got into the passenger seat. Fahim greeted him in Arabic and clapped him on the shoulder as if he were a friend, then feigned a last swallow from a Styrofoam Denny's cup and tossed it out.

Three minutes later, as the F-150 accelerated along the ramp to Interstate 84, a Hispanic man walked toward a car parked near the slot Fahim had vacated and saw the cup. Pretending disgust at the piggishness of some folks, he picked it up and deposited it in the trash, after removing a wadded napkin on which Fahim had written a GPS position.

"This drive will take about seven hours," Fahim said, still in Arabic. "We'll use the time to practice your English."

"Okay," the man said, pleasing Fahim that he had not required prodding to switch languages. Fahim set the cruise control at seventy-five. As he expected, a car that had followed them from Denny's settled in behind at the same speed.

"What's your name?"

"Ali Hadrab."

"Are you an Arab?"

"Yes. I am Jordanian."

"Why are you here in Idaho?"

"I'm a student at Boise State."

Fahim walked the man through his limited English vocabulary and cover story for a few minutes, then waved his hand and said in Arabic, "You'll do."

Continuing in Arabic, Fahim said, "These are my rules. You must follow them exactly. You will stay with other shaheed in an isolated base where I am taking you now. You will wear a blindfold when we approach this place. There, all your needs will be met, and you will have the opportunity to pray and focus on your glorious martyrdom operation, which I will explain to you as the time nears. You are not to tell anyone, not even other shaheed, your true identity or background. Always remember that you have been chosen from many shaheed for the honor of striking directly at the head of the snake.

"Do you understand all that I have just said?"

"Yes. And I will strike a great blow, Insha'Allah."

With that Fahim went silent and settled in for the long drive to his safe house. After about thirty minutes, he saw the tailing car slide right, slow, and exit the interstate. He knew that meant the Mexicans had found the dead drop and extracted the remainder of the cash owed the Solano cartel for delivering the scruffy man. He also knew that if they had not, these men would have continued to follow them and, when the journey ended, shot both of them. Fahim respected the cartel's brutal efficiency.

The arrangement worked very well. Each shaheed was delivered to a different location. Fahim found his lengthy journeys in the truck tedious, but then many of the things he had done to strike the Americans required patience. He felt well compensated, anticipating the death, destruction, and disruption he would visit on America.

The pickup sped northwest through Oregon on a deliberately indirect route to his hideaway. Fahim would blindfold his passenger just south of the Washington border, a few miles before taking Interstate 82 northeast toward Spokane and on to Idaho's panhandle region.

Chapter 5

Two Weeks Later

Denver, Colorado

IT WAS THE WORST SOUND Carlos Baker had heard in eighteen years of teaching, maybe in his entire life. It was the sound he'd dreaded ever since Columbine, and now it was here in his high school.

Gunfire.

Carlos sat at his desk in a compact inner office off a large room with a service counter. "Administrative Offices" appeared in gilt-bordered white letters on a pane of frosted glass in the outer door that opened onto the hall.

Three shots came in rapid succession; Carlos thought maybe they sounded closer. He became aware of a keening wail and someone calling, "Oh God oh God oh God."

He rose from his chair and strode toward the door of his inner office, banging his right shin against a coffee table that he usually avoided without thought. Swinging the door open, he bumped into Leona Darcy, her arm outstretched for the knob. Befuddled, Carlos pulled the door to him, paused for a moment and opened it again, as if waking from a dream. She was still there but had backed off a few feet, a glazed look in her eyes. As he walked past Mrs. Darcy, he saw Frieda Campbell, crouched behind the counter wailing.

Better give them something to do.

"Mrs. Darcy, call nine-one-one and keep the line open. Mrs. Campbell, lock the door, then make a list of everyone reported absent. Have either of you seen Officer Pokowsky?"

Neither had seen Officer P, the friendly cop whose title was School Resource Officer.

I should get my pistol.

Baker darted into his office, elbow brushing the lettering on his door saying "Principal." He went behind his desk, pushing his chair against it, making room to squat before the safe set low in the wall.

His hand shook slightly as he reached for the dial. As his fingers touched it, his mind went blank.

OK. Relax. Don't try to recall the combo; just let muscle memory take you to the first number and the others will come.

Thirty-eight!

Thirty-eight, eight, seventeen.

Swinging the door open, he saw the matte black of a Beretta nine millimeter, butt toward him, slide retracted. He picked it up, remembering his training. A glance revealed both an empty bore and an absent magazine clip. He grabbed for the clip, fingers fumbling as he withdrew it from the safe. A moment later he had a loaded and locked firearm and was trying to remember the "on" position for the safety. He cursed his poor eyesight as he was unable to read the small markings.

Must be I left it on safe. I'm gonna leave it as I found it.

Baker returned to the front office, gun in hand. The women's expressions said they had forgotten about the pistol in his safe.

"Mrs. Darcy, do you have the police?"

A quick nod. He took the handset.

"This is Carlos Baker, principal. We need help, right now!"

"Officers have surrounded the building. SWAT is on the way."

"We're dying in here, kids and teachers. You can hear the shots. You've got to help us *now.*"

"Mr. Baker, this is Captain Swanson. I'm the watch captain. Follow your training. Stay locked down. Shelter in place. Officers will clear the building room by room."

"Nooooooooo!" The terrified voice coming from the hall was smothered in gunfire. Baker handed the phone to Leona Darcy.

You're here, he thought. *And you've got a gun.*

Baker sat suddenly atop Mrs. Darcy's desk, pushing papers and files to the floor with a swish. He fixed his eyes on the door as if it were a cobra. He couldn't shift his gaze. Sweat slicked his face and his breathing grew ragged. He felt his companions' gaze.

You took a one-day course two years ago. You've gone to the range, what, two, three times? Go out there with a pistol against what, and how many?

Baker stood and slid a chair to the right of the door. Seating himself, he put the pistol in his lap, gripping it in his right hand.

"If he opens the door, I'll shoot him. Go over behind the counter and lie down on the floor. That's the safest place."

Leona Darcy looked as if she was about to speak, but compressed her lips and disappeared behind the counter. She launched Twitter on her smart phone and began to type. With a scrabbling sound, Frieda Campbell, who was already on the floor, crawled behind the counter.

Baker sat rigidly. But with every shout and burst of fire he twitched. His shirt was soaked through. He heard a roaring in his ears. His eyes burned. The shots were closer.

He stood. Hearing his chair scrape, Mrs. Darcy stood and peeked over the counter. Baker started to move, then froze. They each heard unhurried footsteps approaching. Darcy tweeted frantically. Baker raised the pistol in a two-handed grip, planted himself in front of the closed door, squinted his eyes, and waited. A shadow appeared through the frosted glass.

A shotgun roared and the principal's midsection buckled, the force of impact driving his frame backward. Through the opening Leona Darcy saw a dark-eyed figure whose crown was swathed in checkered cloth. The shotgun roared again and Mrs. Darcy joined her principal. Frieda Campbell, who had a bad heart, literally died of fright a minute or two before the gunman found her and put a pistol shot into her head and another into her torso.

With a final glance the man in the black – and white-checkered keffyieh left the room, pumping the action of his shotgun and leaving behind a smell of gun smoke, blood, and urine.

* * *

Coronado, California

The young man who crossed Orange Avenue at Tenth Street and

walked toward a coffee shop known for its breakfasts was unremarkable in appearance or bearing, clad in dark shorts and a baggy San Diego Chargers jersey. Across Tenth Street from the coffee shop, another ordinary man, wearing a backpack, gazed into the window of a boutique but paid more attention to the reflection of the coffee shop's entrance than to the clothing.

The popular eatery was crowded as usual at seven a.m., with all its booths and most of the counter stools occupied. From a booth to the left of the entrance Chief Petty Officer Cary Franklin called the waitress's name in a pleasant baritone and asked for his check as he enjoyed the last of his scrambled eggs and chorizo. Franklin had a certain presence about him, a readiness for action that he wore effortlessly. Alert blue eyes in a tanned face that hinted at dangers surmounted in obscure places. Square, blunt-fingered hands wielding knife and fork. Although Chief Franklin wasn't in uniform, a curious diner might have deduced, from his bearing and that he was a regular he customer, that he was a SEAL.

Drawing what he knew would be one of his last breaths, the man in the Chargers shirt entered the crowded coffee shop. He pulled a hunting knife from beneath the shirt's loose folds, shouted "Allahu Akbar," and plunged it into the back of a woman at the counter. Spinning left, he slashed the man next to her across his shocked face. Continuing to the left, the assailant charged toward the far end of the U-shaped counter, slashing and stabbing as he dashed behind the stunned customers seated on stools and in front of those in booths.

Chief Franklin remained motionless until the knife wielder rushed past his booth. Then he rose, exploded across the space separating him from the terrorist's back, shot his left arm across the man's chest, pulled it into a crushing position against his throat, and grabbed the man's knife arm at the wrist. An instant later Franklin had broken that wrist and the knife was on the floor.

The window shopper who had been watching from across Tenth Street pushed through the front door, shouldering between fleeing patrons, and hustled toward Franklin. Halting five feet behind him, the second terrorist shot the chief twice between the shoulder blades. Freed from Franklin's choke hold, pain lancing from his broken wrist, the man just rescued sucked several deep breaths and, as best he could, helped his rescuer drag the chief's body to the sidewalk fronting the coffee shop.

Its siren dying in a low moan, a Coronado police car braked violently to a halt on Orange Avenue in front of the coffee shop. The bogus shopper suddenly had a pistol in his hand and used it to shoot the officer as he scrambled from the car.

The terrorist whose wrist was broken said in Arabic to his partner in martyrdom, “Is this guy a SEAL?”

“I think so. He seems to have gotten the better of *you* when everybody else was too scared to resist.”

The speaker plunged his hand into the backpack and pulled out a short-handled ax. Moments after he completed his gruesome task, two more police cars slammed to a halt at the scene, and both terrorists achieved the martyrdom they sought.

Chapter 6

Washington, DC

WITH THE TV RUNNING IN the background, Ray Morales read the second draft of the speech he was to give to the Western States Association of Police Chiefs and sighed. Although he relished every opportunity to speak to street cops, border patrol officers, and first responders, he hated talking to senior groups of local law officials. Each had a wish list, little of which they actually needed, in comparison to their need for patrol officers. But the gadgets were paid for by federal dollars while beat cops' salaries and benefits came with local price tags. He was expected to hand out some grant money at each of these gatherings and did, but he regretted it.

Ray sensed the changed tone of the network anchor's voice before he registered the content of his words. His TV monitor displayed a mob spilling from a New York subway exit, their panic blurred but visible through the smoke overtaking them from below.

The anchor said, "Twitter is reporting an explosion in a New York City subway. This is the feed from a traffic cam, and we are seeing the East Forty-second Street exit from the Seventh Avenue line."

As Morales watched, a firefighter appeared and began shouldering through the throng, looking like an astronaut in the Scott Air-Pak face mask.

His secure smart phone bleated.

"Morales."

"Watch officer, sir. At this point that traffic cam is the best eyes we've got, but FBI's on the way. So is the NYPD bomb squad. I'll—"

After interrupting himself in order to listen to someone, the watch officer blurted, "Sir, we just got a report of active shooters in a school in Denver!"

Morales returned his attention to CNN, saw the crawl scrolling " . . . shooter. Police are on the scene" below a slightly agitated anchor man, who was handing off to a helo-borne reporter above the school.

"Sir!" said the watch officer. "A bomb, maybe a pretty large one, has detonated at O'Hare terminal three."

The ten-foot display screen behind the anchor now showed three active incidents. The anchor had one hand to his earpiece and his expression said, "Slow down—this is too much, too fast." Gamely, the anchor picked up his pace, but his words became gabble. A fourth incident scene popped up on the screen behind him, displaying masked gunmen stalking shoppers in a mall. He stopped midsentence, his eyes vacant as he tried to absorb several voices in his earpiece, each pouring out information about a different incident.

Morales heard the double bleep of call waiting and saw "White House." He mashed the button, putting the watch officer on hold, and heard, "Hold for the president, sir." Ray knew Rick and Ella Martin were on a campaign swing, California today, he thought.

"Ray, what's going on?"

"Right now CNN knows as much as I do. That'll change soon, but at the moment I'm monitoring the situation and waiting for word from response teams. FEMA is on the move, and I'm sure FBI is rolling. I haven't heard from Justice, but I'm betting the Hostage Rescue Team is moving out for the mall incident. But for a while, sir, it's the first responders' ball game."

"Well, I can't tell the press that!"

Morales waited, frustrated that Martin seemed to believe the campaign rhetoric that a president was all-seeing, all-powerful, and could fix anything from potholes to the Arab-Israeli conflict. His own experience was that, in battle, you had to let the commander on the ground carry out his mission.

Besides, it rankled him that the lead agency for response to terrorism, the FBI, wasn't under his control. When Martin had asked him to leave Congress and take the job, Ray had argued for shifting the FBI from Justice to DHS but lost as Martin bought the civil libertarians' argument. Now he felt like saying, "Tell the press this is just the occasional price we pay for honoring our founders' insistence on keeping federal power diluted so our democracy will not be endangered."

Instead he said, "I'm sure Sam and Bart have something for you, sir. And you might remind the press that the effectiveness of those first responders they're watching has been greatly enhanced by training and funds from the federal government."

"This could hardly have come at a worse time! It could knock me down in the polls!"

Morales stifled his irritation at the president's political nature. He reminded himself that Martin had made an incredibly tough decision after Six-thirteen, one he feared would cost his soul. The president made it out of duty and contrary to the beliefs of a lifetime, taking on the label of murderer in some parts of the world and also in, so Ray thought, his own conscience. Of course the president's reaction was political! This could become the day that made Rick Martin a one-term president.

Ray heard voices in the background and was pretty sure one of them was Martin's campaign manager, Winston Hernandez.

"Win and Sam are here to work the statement. Keep me informed!"

The line dead, Morales picked up the holding line, wondering if the watch officer was still on. He wasn't, which pleased Ray. His watch officer in the National Counterterrorism Center had better things to do right now than sit on hold.

Glancing to the TV again, he saw a fourth incident on the screen behind the anchor: EMS and police were surrounding a figure sprawled on a bloody sidewalk. The crawler announced a man had been shot on the street in Coronado, California.

The anchor had wisely ceased attempts to comment on each incident, letting the news crawlers tell the tale while he framed the shocking events.

"We've had five apparent terror attacks, in widely separated locations across America: a New York City subway, a Denver school, Chicago-O'Hare—the nation's busiest airport, a Baltimore shopping mall, and the shooting and beheading of a Navy SEAL on the streets of a California city near the base where SEALs train."

The anchor pressed his left hand to his earpiece, then said, "Shit!"

The anchor grimaced at his breach of professional decorum before saying, "Another attack, this one an apparent truck or car bomb outside Washington DC's Union Station."

The screen behind him had morphed into a two-by-three grid, where the latest addition, in the lower right, showed the façade of Union Station blasted to rubble and people staggering or running from the scene as first responders moved in.

Morales's smart phone bleeped again.

"Ray, this is the vice president. Based on the authorities granted to me after Six-thirteen, I'm taking charge of the national response to these attacks until the president can return to Washington. I'm convening a meeting of the Homeland Security Council immediately."

For a moment Ray Morales was speechless at the effrontery of Vice President Bruce Griffith. The president—aboard Air Force One—was unharmed, informed, and able to direct the full resources of the government.

"Mr. Vice President, you are way out of your lane! The president is fully capable of performing his duties. Have you spoken with him about this matter?"

"I don't need to speak to him to know that someone needs to take charge at the seat of government, and because of my role after Six-thirteen, I'm the one best prepared to do that."

Warily, for Bruce Griffith was clever and ruthless and on a recorded line, Morales said, "With all due respect, Mr. Vice President, you should stand down. As you know, this administration has procedures in place to deal with this situation, procedures that supersede the temporary authorities the president gave you and later withdrew. I sympathize with your passion to protect Americans, but unless we all hear otherwise from the president, we need to follow those procedures."

"Ray, I'm surprised you don't see that the president needs to have a single point of contact in Washington now. He can't be calling every cabinet official who has a piece of this and telling them what to do!"

He does, and it's me, thought Morales.

But now was no time to have that fight—even though he would win it—so he said, "If the president wants *a cabinet officer* in overall charge, he'll say so. If you're so sure your plan is right, call him. I have to take a report from the Counterterrorism Center now. Goodbye, Mr. Vice President."

Shattered.

That was how Ray imagined the schoolchildren's parents and grandparents felt. He and Julie had married in their forties; he had no children but saw the faces of his nephew's kids, seven and nine. He imagined their bodies riddled with automatic weapons fire. He knew very well what an AK-47 did to human flesh. A long time ago in years, but not in emotions, he had seen and smelled it, had left his footprints in the gore of it. He had held the dying as they bled out, unable to save them because high-velocity bullets had shredded their bodies.

And today, the bodies belonged to kids. He imagined the pain rippling out through their families as the news traveled. *If that happened to Maria or Carl . . .* He looked at their picture on his desk. So eager, so confident, so trusting that the world was good. That people were good.

Without warning, his shoulders shook and his breath came in gasps, a tsunami of unexpected personal grief. Tears streaked his cheeks. Snuffling, Ray wiped a big hand across them, then fumbled in a desk drawer, found a tissue, and blew his nose twice.

It's him again. It's that same monster who got away after doing Las Vegas—I can feel it. This time we've got to get him. As head of Homeland Security, that's on me. I'm going to find that sorry bastard; I'm going to find him and make him pay. And I don't care what it costs me. Whatever it takes.

Chapter 7

Coeur d'Alene National Forest, Idaho

THE STUBBLE-FACED, WIRY MAN WATCHED the screen fervently, working to contain his elation and triumph so as to remain objective. Fahim al-Wasari, a.k.a. abu Shaheed, a.k.a. Al Hassan, lost that struggle and shot a fist triumphantly into the air. He sprang from his chair and began to pace the sparsely furnished room, never losing sight of CNN.

"Do you see? Do you *see*? Behold the glorious success of our martyrs that you will soon surpass!" A dozen men and two women, who sat to one side of the men, gazed hungrily at CNN.

They were gathered in a nondescript A-frame cabin in an unremarkable clearing, guarded by the dense white pines, spruce, and larch of Idaho's panhandle region. All were attired in casual clothing, mostly jeans and flannel shirts. But even dressed in that fashion, they would have stood out in nearby Coeur d'Alene because the woman wore the hijab, the head covering, and all were ethnic Arabs. There weren't many Arabs in northern Idaho. That's why they had arrived individually and would depart covertly, never leaving Fahim's compound until their missions began.

Suddenly, he *had* to tell them. He knew he should not; it was forbidden by the Council, but they would soon die as shaheed and would not leave this mountain hideout until their time had come. They deserved to know.

"Our comrades died with the shaheed's glory. The Americans are reeling! We have begun the second and final phase of their destruction. You are the ones who will bring them down. You will cut off the head of the snake!"

Whirling to point at the largest of the men, Fahim said, "But what was the first phase? What was the great blow that prepared the way for your acts of glory?"

The man's beetle brow knitted momentarily, and Fahim recoiled slightly at the man's simplicity. Then the burly fellow spoke: "It was the bombing of Las Vegas, praise be to Allah!"

"And what happened?"

"A glorious shaheed exploded a nuclear bomb in the heart of that devil's den."

"And who was that shaheed?"

"Allah the merciful, the great, the beneficent knows. I do not."

"*I* know! And I will tell you this great mystery because of your bravery."

Fahim looked around the room at a deliberate pace, holding the eyes of each man and woman for a moment. His eyes lingered a moment longer on the woman sitting nearest to the fireplace, caressing the ripe body that her Western clothes displayed for the first time in her life.

"It was I, abu Shaheed! Allah refused my martyrdom because he has other work prepared for me. But it was I who brought the bomb in a truck and set the timer in the heart of the Las Vegas Strip, the epicenter of unrighteous behaviors! You are now in the presence of the one who struck the greatest blow ever against the Great Satan!"

Fahim's gaze returned to the woman. Her eyes held the look he knew meant he could have her. But he also knew he must not. He must continue to make do with his infidel woman in Coeur d'Alene. The mental balance of a suicide bomber is delicate as the day of martyrdom approaches. She should have the peace that comes from knowing all her life is in order; surprises must be avoided, especially surprises that could create a will to live.

Fahim spoke fervently for a few minutes, then dismissed them to their bunkhouses—one male, one female, of course.

Settling in before an unending stream of bodies and wreckage on his satellite TV, Fahim nursed a scotch, held in a way that he could hide it if one of the martyrs should break the rule and enter unbidden. Well before his present forty-three years, Fahim had learned that Allah would forgive certain failings in those who had power and used that power for the cause. That was fortunate because he was so helpless before the devilish wiles of shameless women, first those of his native England and now these in

America. Until Sharia held sway, and women were properly covered and controlled, he would remain vulnerable, helpless before their rapacious desires. Fahim was thankful Allah had shown him how to compensate for this abject failing.

There are uber-hackers who could bring down the U.S. electric grid, he thought. That would plunge the country into darkness and economic and social chaos. I know how to reach them, and I have the money to hire one. But my purpose is to create shock and terror throughout America. That requires TV and radio and social media and telephones. All those would be gone if I took the grid down. Besides, while America going dark would create chaos, it wouldn't shed blood. Bloodshed for all to see and fear, not hacking, is the mark of a jihadi. And I am the greatest jihadi!

Fahim was a bomb maker. Not just *a* bomb maker. He was the best in the world.

He had become legendary during the American occupation of Iraq by devising ever more powerful and sophisticated IEDs. Fahim's British university degree was computer science with a minor in chemistry. It was a perfect education for a bomber, which he put to use with creative flair.

Getting Fahim had been the Holy Grail for American bomb squads and Special Forces. As EOD technicians studied the debris of thousands of explosions that tore through Iraq, they developed an exhaustive catalogue of Fahim's techniques. Unfortunately this didn't help them much because Fahim was endlessly inventive. Whenever EOD divined how to defeat one of his ingenious, deadly creations, Fahim came up with something new, and they started all over again.

There was actually an exhibit devoted to Fahim—who had been nicknamed "Einstein"—in the museum of the Joint Explosive Ordnance Disposal School at Eglin Air Force Base.

Chapter 8

Air Force One, en route from Las Vegas to Los Angeles

"So, I NEED TO GET back to Washington. But before or after my speech?" said the president.

The others deferred to Chief of Staff Bart Guarini, happy to let him handle a question flung as suddenly and as threateningly as a live grenade. Everyone remembered the blowback from Bush's attempt to combine governing with sympathy. Overflying Katrina-ravaged New Orleans as he rushed back to Washington was spun into a refusal to get his hands dirty, into "not getting it."

Guarini, second only to Ella in the intimacy and length of his political partnership with Rick Martin, was comfortable with the back and forth over the teleconference link that he knew the key campaign staff would witness. Bart understood that whether he had no clue or whether he was certain of the course of action, the way to answer the president's question was not to answer—it was to begin a conversation. With Rick you had to let him chew over the issue and believe he had made up his own mind.

Guarani said, "The case for giving the speech is that it shows resolve, shows calm, unswerving leadership. Assuming, of course, that Sam's writers can prepare the material in the next"—he glanced at his watch—"three hours."

"They can," said Samantha Yu, adding, "The president doesn't need much—he's got an instinct for this sort of thing."

Rick preened visibly, causing Ella to reflect that despite the maturing fires he'd been through—that *they* had been through—vanity was still strong in him. And with the exception of Bart and Ray, all of Rick's advisors found opportunities to stroke that vanity irresistible.

"Wait a minute," said Ella. "This is an incredibly dynamic situation. We have no idea what may happen in the next few hours, or while Rick's speaking. We don't know whether the Secret Service can secure the venue against a much higher threat in less than three hours. And what is this plane going to do until it's time to go to the speech? Circle LA? Sit on the runway at LAX surrounded by police and Strykers? How will either of those play with the forty-odd journalists sitting in back? Not well, I'm thinking!"

"Well, since we learned on Six-thirteen that Wilson"—with a rueful grin Rick nodded to a man standing against the cabin wall—"owns me, let's hear from him right away."

The head of the Secret Service presidential protective detail put on his war face, hyper-alert and expressionless, as he answered the president. "Mr. President, you shouldn't leave Air Force One until we get back to Andrews or to another military base. Any form of ground transportation for you and the first lady is out, and there's not time to set up secure helo transportation in LA. The speech venue is prepared because we always consider venues high-risk, but in this security environment there's no acceptable way to get you to and from."

Rick said, "Well, that's it, then. We're heading for Andrews."

They all knew that Rick Martin would have argued strenuously with Wilson before Six-thirteen. But after Six-thirteen, he accepted that in time of crisis any president becomes a totem whose continued safety is critical to national resolve. Rick hated that, but he now knew it was true.

The president's military aide called the flight deck. Colonel Roberts, who at the moment he got his instructions, was thinking gratefully that his family lived on Joint Base Andrews and had no need to leave its security, put the Boeing 747 in a sweeping turn toward the east and advanced the throttles.

* * *

Miami, Florida

The Republican presidential nominee felt a tightening in his throat. His eyes burned, then leaked tears. Governor Walter Rutherford's emotions were always close to the surface, and as he watched rescuers combing the debris of Union Station, he cried.

But Rutherford's emotions weren't deeply felt. They were part of his appearance at any given moment, like his hairstyle or the tie his valet selected for a specific event. So he had no difficulty dismissing the pathos that had brought on his tears and turning instead to campaign strategy.

"The attacks change everything," he told his campaign manager and his communications director. "That's obvious. What's less obvious is the best way forward now."

Communications Director Megan O'Malley kept her own council as her boss, Fred Bolton, responded to Rutherford's raised eyebrows: "For sure the Martin administration isn't going to be able to shut these guys down soon. That's clear from the scope of the attacks. This isn't just one nut with a grievance and the current issue of *Inspire.* Martin's going to be vulnerable on homeland security."

Bolton paused before continuing, "But that's not like being vulnerable on the economy. If it were, we'd just pound away at him. No, with this we've got to be careful. People rally around the president when they believe the country's under attack, so if we slam him, we could end up looking unpatriotic."

"So?" said Rutherford impatiently.

Bolton knew his client was completely uninterested in principle or process. He just wanted to know what he needed to do to benefit from a situation. Like most of the politicians on his client list, this one believed that winning an election was everything. And what won was riding the coattails of an issue. It didn't matter what the issue was, so long as it was one that touched a sizable group of citizens powerfully enough to attract their passion and their dollars.

"So for the moment we suspend campaigning, saying it's out of respect for the victims and their families and so as not to distract the Martin administration from the fundamental responsibility of government—protecting its citizens."

O'Malley knew better than to define campaign strategy because Bolton would brook no challenge to his domain. He was well known for leaving behind the bodies of those who foolishly attempted it. But now she had her opening.

"That's really something we can work with. Without seeming political we've put full responsibility for public safety on Martin—almost as an afterthought, a civics lesson—and we can hammer on that later, when the rally-round-the-flag sentiment fades and people absorb the way this impacts them personally."

"Get out a statement right now," said Bolton. "And tell the press that the governor will speak to them in about an hour."

O'Malley left them alone.

Chapter 9

Coeur d'Alene, Idaho

FAHIM, OR AL AS THEY knew him at Mother's, paused briefly in the vestibule. He then pushed his way through the inner doors into the dark interior, feeling over-amped bass notes vibrate through his soles. The bar had vaulted ceilings with exposed rafters, pillars, and ductwork—some architect's idea of warehouse chic. The walls were occupied mostly by flat screens soundlessly displaying ESPN and other sports networks. Here and there a deer peered glassy-eyed from the wall, sharing its habitat with NASCAR posters and Bud Light advertisements. Rafters and pillars were wrapped in strings of violet LED bulbs, and the large, tubular ventilation ducting was dull orange. Fahim thought of his little sister's room during her Goth stage.

Smiling as he passed the hostess, ignoring a sign bidding him wait to be seated just as she ignored him to check her email, Fahim sauntered inward. The barkeep, pulling a beer, nodded as he approached the much-abused mahogany slab that now, just after the start of happy hour, still offered elbow room and smelled of Pledge. Booths along the walls waited patiently for the later crowd. Fahim's gaze lingered appreciatively on a gaggle of young waitresses chatting near the kitchen. In the large stone fireplace at the far end of the room, a hurriedly laid fire struggled to become a welcoming blaze.

Without appearing to, Fahim scanned for unfamiliar faces, his caution as habitual and necessary as his breathing. Now confident that his surroundings were benign for the moment, he slid one cheek onto a stool and leaned an elbow on the bar. This posture allowed him to twist enough toward the door to observe arrivals without seeming to do so.

"Do you know that it's illegal to be off the grid in Maryland?" said a bearded man with a trace of military bearing that still survived the assault of his belly. He was a regular Fahim tried to avoid because he lectured endlessly. Fahim didn't know his name but thought of him as Mountain Man. At the moment his victim was the barkeep, who, like most in the trade, could converse without thought.

"So after I decide to go to wind and solar, I have a guy from the battery company come to my place to figure out what size storage bank I need. He tells me what I'm fixin' to do is illegal, says after a while the feds will come check me out and tell me I gotta hook up to the grid. Can you believe that? Talk about the nanny state!"

Mountain Man thrust out his hands, palms up, and continued: "What's the big deal? I mean, it's not like I'm hiding. I got my army retirement check coming to the address. Yes, I raise my own food and barter or pay cash for everything, but I earned my retirement and pay my taxes.

"So I decided to move. Read up on Idaho and decided they pretty much let you do what you want on your own property here. Bought a couple of acres near Hayden Lake. I got my A-frame, my solar panels and windmill, my garden and my livestock. Nobody cares. In fact lotta my neighbors think we oughtta do more about the nanny state than just ignore it, know what I mean?"

"If what you mean is what's going on now, I think that's going too far," said the barkeep.

Mountain Man smirked.

Sipping his beer, Fahim tuned out, in his own world of thought. The attacks are working, throwing American citizens and their government into panicked reaction. Overreaction, in fact.

Everyone of Arab appearance approaching any point of entry is pulled aside, and most are denied passage into America. This fuels Arab anger against America and damages U.S. relations with so-called allies like the Saudis and the Qataris. Of course I planned for this reaction by hiring the Mexicans to smuggle in the believers from Gaza and Yemen and Pakistan, eager to become martyrs. They stand out because their English is poor, and most are in the West for the first time, awkward with its customs and gawking at the women.

I've solved that problem, but I face another. The Mexicans are smuggling the Somalis I need to do this great thing, but I need someone to lead them who is at home in the pilothouse of a large ship. It's one thing to seize a big ship in the open sea. The Somalis know how to do that. But what my plan requires is much more complicated.

In fact lotta my neighbors think we oughtta do more about the nanny state than just ignore it, know what I mean? Mountain Man's words suddenly registered, several beats later, in Fahim's mind, captured by that part of his brain that remained ever attuned to what it might use.

Forcing his lips into a smile, Fahim turned to the speaker.

An hour and several beers later, he left Mother's, pleased that Allah had once again shown him the way.

"Who's the A-rab?"

The short, slit-eyed man who spoke had shoulder and arm development that strained his black tee shirt. The barkeep glanced at the man and slipped a wineglass into its slot in the rack overhead. "Not an Arab, not really . . . He's no more Arab than I'm Norwegian. My grandparents were Norwegian but not me. He's actually British. Name's Al."

"Uhmph! Well to me he's just another mud-race loser. He come here often?"

More often than you. And he tips a helluva lot better. Mud-race loser—that's Aryan talk. I don't want to mess with one of them.

"I don't keep track. I just pour the drinks and collect tabs."

He turned away to a shelf and began rearranging glassware. Wonder why he cares? Al's a good enough guy. No trouble. Keeps the bar lively cracking jokes and playing liar's dice; never welshes when he gets nailed with a round.

The barkeep turned to face his customers and was relieved that the muscular man was gone.

But there's something a little odd about Al, thought the barkeep. Everyone else in the place checks their messages every few minutes. I've never seen Al do that—he rarely pulls his phone out. In fact, it's a cheap burner, just a clamshell. And he always pays cash. So why would a guy with plenty of money not use plastic and earn points or have a smart phone?

A chime from his phone called his attention to Twitter:

> Armed bystander kills terrorist after one shot; victim in stable but critical condition.

Chapter 10

Ginza, Tokyo, Japan

The geisha attending each man filled his sake cup with liquor poured from graceful serving bottles, bowed deeply and departed, leaving a full bottle at each man's place. After the senior geisha slid the door closed, Isoroku Kimura looked around the low table and waited for the others to acknowledge his leadership by ceasing their conversations and looking to him.

The six men in the private dining room called themselves Divine Wind, a phrase that in Japanese, oddly, would be familiar to many Americans: kamikaze. Most of those would understand the word only in reference to the swarms of suicide aircraft that were the Empire's desperate effort to forestall invasion in the closing months of World War II.

But for this group of politicians and executives, none of whom entertained thoughts of becoming a suicide bomber, the symbolism went deep into Japan's history and national mythology. When thirteenth-century Mongols launched two massive invasions of Japan, each was stymied by a super-typhoon. The Japanese then believed the typhoons had been sent by the gods, the kami, to save Japan from foreign domination. They called the typhoons "kamikaze."

This group calling itself Kamikaze intended to save Japan from its present domination by the United States and future domination by China. They would do it by creating a super-typhoon of fear, distrust, and conflicting national interests that would reshape the contours of East Asia. Japan would regain its rightful leading position.

"Gentlemen," said Kimura, "this has been an excellent meal and a pleasant evening. Now to our business."

After placing a small flag on the table, displaying the blood-red rising sun of Imperial Japan, he said, "Goto-san, your report, please."

"I can report promising results from the search. We've located a North Korean defector living here who has a sister in the camps."

"How did you find this Korean, Goto-san?"

"Initially through social media, Endo-san. He made his feelings plain on Facebook and through Twitter."

"Many people say things they do not mean on Facebook, chatter about plans they will never undertake."

"True, Endo-san, so we have gone beyond social media. As you know, the Korean community in Japan is riddled with factions and agents—for the North, the South, for Japan, for China, for the CIA, sometimes for several at once. Considerable government resources are devoted to keeping an eye on the Koreans. One of my cell members is an officer in our internal security service. He put this Korean, whose name is Chung Ma-ho, under surveillance. Chung is obsessed with getting his sister out of the North. He has importuned every embassy official within his reach—Korean, Russian, Chinese, American—making a thorough nuisance of himself. He has haunted our Ministry of Foreign Affairs. He has even tried, clumsily, to reach out to the yakuza. Fortunately for him they think he's amusing."

"So has someone from Kamikaze established a relationship with him yet?"

"No, Shibata-san. But I believe the time is ripe to take that step."

The group fell silent. Although each of these men was protected by multiple, isolating layers in the Kamikaze organization, each felt the potential danger in recruiting a Korean to sacrifice himself. Each was attempting to gauge the degree of consensus before speaking.

"It is of course a risk," said Kimura, "but boldness is the mark of the samurai."

The silence that followed indicated consensus.

Kimura nodded to Goto, but it was Jiro Imai who spoke.

"Kimura-san, the terrorist attacks taking place in America—perhaps they affect our plan."

Kimura disliked Jiro Imai. He lacked politeness, delicacy. Not as bad as an American in pushing his ideas, but not our way.

"They do, Imai-san. They will increase Martin's hesitation in responding. We don't need the Arabs' help for success, but if the Kamikaze blows soon, Martin will become even more conflicted."

"And Kato-san?"

"Our prime minister will count the votes and go along. There are enough Kamikaze members and sympathizers in the Diet that he will have no choice, other than risking a vote of no confidence—which his coalition would lose."

"Goto-san," said Kimura, "do you have a plan for the next step with the Korean?"

"I have a few thoughts. I'm sure this group can improve upon them."

Kimura was pleased by Goto's implied rebuke of Imai.

"I thought perhaps one of our people could approach him, pretending to have been sent by the American CIA. It is well known among émigré Koreans that all the spy organizations are looking among them for recruits. Such an approach would not be especially suspicious to this Korean. He is, after all, a defector and must have already been questioned by CIA. Our representative could sound him out about undertaking an extremely dangerous mission, one that may well cost his life, in return for American-brokered freedom for his sister."

"A good beginning, perhaps," said Imai, "but how does it come to fruition? The Korean will no doubt insist on seeing his sister safely out before doing our bidding. How do we deal with that?" Imai did not wait for an answer.

"And since the CIA routinely fishes these schools of Koreans—and Chung's already known to them—they might genuinely reach out to him. If that happens, he will know something is wrong, seek clarification, and perhaps reveal our plans." Imai concluded, "This won't work."

Kimura's dislike of Imai's style flared again, but he suppressed it. First, the man led an important caucus in the Diet, and second, in this case, he had spotted a major flaw in Goto's plan, even if he did point it out in an unharmonious manner.

Kichirou Shimizu spoke for the first time: "You say this Chung approached the yakuza, right?"

"Yes, Shimizu-san," Goto said.

"Perhaps we should use our yakuza contacts to make the approach. Yakuza could say they require his services for their own purposes and offer to extract his sister in return. He will no doubt insist on evidence of her safe escape before doing yakuza's work. They can then agree to that sequence of events: first the sister, then the work, provided that he signifies his commitment in the yakuza's special way before they extract his sister. Chung's acceptance or refusal will give us a gauge of his commitment."

Kimura gazed into each man's eyes and knew that Shimizu's plan had prevailed. He looked at his watch. "It is late. We'll meet again when circumstances require."

The men rose and lined up along the left wall, facing the Imperial flag. Hard-eyed, raising their arms with each chorus, the men chanted *banzai* three times, their fealty drowned out by the nightclub's hubbub.

Resuming their seats, the men drank, told stories, and sang. After about an hour of noisy revelry, they began departing at irregular intervals. They appeared to be drunk—but they were not. By eleven the Divine Wind had vanished.

* * *

Washington, DC

Ray Morales hated being confined. Since the attacks began, he had been more confined than ever. One of the reasons he had chosen the Marine Corps is that Marines don't hunker down in trench networks and bunkers; they maneuver and shoot, advancing at every opportunity. Now he was confined to government buildings, armored vehicles, and phalanxes of security operatives. He didn't even have a home anymore: like other senior officials, he had moved his wife to an "undisclosed secure location," which she hated and he rarely had time to visit. The government had requisitioned Virginia's Greenbrier Resort, and he saw Julie there occasionally.

Swaying as the Suburban carrying him to a meeting with the FBI director took a hard left turn, Morales felt his smart phone vibrate, glanced at it and saw a Tweet:

Administration asks Congress to approve gun licensing law

with purchaser record. Enraged NRA calls this a "national gun registry."

How's that for a totally predictable reaction! thought Ray. But no way can we make Operation Sudden Touch work without being able to check that someone we've swept up with a weapon is allowed to carry it. Pete Boylston takes the cake!

The Suburban tipped forward as it descended the ramp to the Hoover Building's secure underground garage at 935 Pennsylvania Avenue, NW, in Washington.

Chapter 11

Wings House, Pensacola, Florida

Lieutenant Colonel Jeremy Thomas, USMC, parked the white government sedan registered to Naval Air Station Pensacola a block from his destination. "Jerry" Thomas, who was Ray Morales's executive assistant, was as lean as his boss was chunky. His face was narrow and his eyes hinted at his profession. They were a hunter's eyes, set in shallow sockets that offered slightly better than average peripheral vision and had about them a cold, questing quality. The crown of Thomas's head was balding and he was considering going for the shaven-head look. But not yet, so while he didn't affect a comb-over, he did let his hair get longish, for a Marine. But then, Thomas was a fighter pilot, not a grunt. He wore a lightweight tan suit and a grin as he carried out Morales's odd orders. He was grinning at being out of Washington and within the sound of aircraft engines, but not at this assignment, which was downright weird.

"Colonel Thomas," his boss had said, "a prudent military planner considers many contingencies, does he not? Even those that are low probability, if they are high impact."

"Yes, sir," said Thomas, his expression adding, *where are you going with this, boss*?

"Ever hear of 'enhanced interrogation techniques'?" said Morales.

"Yes, sir. Waterboarding, for instance. Bush used them; later presidents shut them down."

"What presidents shut down, Jerry, they can also resume. We're in a new ball game with these widespread, continuing bombings and shootings. I need to be prepared."

Morales had fixed Thomas with cold eyes. Thomas knew he was at a threshold. If he made an ambiguous but negative comment, Morales would reply in kind, the subject would change, and this conversation had never happened. Or he could walk across the threshold into a place where there were no rules. The land of whatever it takes. He knew that's where Ray Morales was already.

After a deep breath, Thomas said, "That's my job, sir. Keeping you prepared."

"Yes it is. Jerry, I want you to have a talk with Captain Red Clevenger. Know who he is?"

"No, sir."

"Former navy flyer. He's one of the last surviving POWs from Vietnam. Lives somewhere in Florida. Jenny will get you the scoop."

So here he was in northwest Florida. Shortly after giving his name to a bored receptionist with the leathery skin of years spent pursuing the perfect tan, Thomas had sat down with Captain Clevenger. He had assessed the old man seated before him: mostly unremarkable for an eighty-something, but with unusually clear eyes. While the rest of his face was the wreckage of old age, his eyes, and the lids and brows that framed them, had no age. Those eyes were gray, alert, and probably ice cold when the guy was pissed, thought Thomas, who was posing as a university researcher. After twenty minutes of questioning about topics intended to mask his real purpose, Thomas headed for the goal line.

"Just a few more questions, Captain Clevenger. I really appreciate your help on this project."

"Go ahead, son. I'm doin' just fine."

"Sir, other POWs tell me you were the bravest among them. That makes you the bravest of the brave. But at some point, surely, you would have broken. There must have been some form of torture that would have broken you. Can you tell me about that?"

"Son, that 'bravest of the brave' stuff is bullshit, and we both know it," said the old man. "No one can understand torture until he's been tortured.

Until that happens, you're a dilettante. That's not in the cards for you, and you should thank God for that. But since you're doing a study for DOD, to help prepare our folks to resist, you get more from me than you really deserve.

"What would have broken me and would break anyone I've ever known is mutilation, and seeing that your torturer enjoyed it. Really got off on it! And believing there were no limits for him; that he didn't have to keep you alive and presentable to placate his bosses. *That*, son, is the worst I can imagine and would break anyone pretty fast. I mean, imagine a guy cuts your finger off and you see a bulge in his pants! Or a woman slices off the tip of your nose and starts moaning like you're the greatest lover she ever had."

Yep, thought Thomas, that would do it for me! He scribbled furiously on his lined yellow pad.

"Thank you, Captain. I'm done, unless you have anything I should have asked but didn't." The old man shook his head.

Rising from the wicker chair, Thomas shook the old man's hand, spun on his heel and left the well-furnished, comfortable solarium of Wings House, an assisted living community themed for military aviators.

If he's an academic, I'm David Letterman, thought the old fighter pilot.

As Thomas was about to put his rental car in gear, his phone chirped. Glancing at the screen, Thomas read the Tweet:

NRA headquarters hit, heavily damaged by truck bomb.

Chapter 12

Tokyo, Japan

STANDING WITH A DOZEN ZOMBIE-LIKE commuters waiting to board a Tokyo Metro bus, Chung Ma-ho saw a blacked-out Toyopet limo glide silently to the curb near him, and both rear doors pop open. His forebrain idly said "banker" as he shuffled forward, determined not to lose his place in the queue. The man emerging from the far door, however, was huge, far bigger than any banker Chung had ever seen. "*Not* banker," said his forebrain.

The giant politely nodded his head, saying, "*Ohaio*, Chung-san. I have news of your sister. Please enter this car." Then a second, smaller man exited the near back door and stepped aside, motioning for Chung to enter the limo. Suddenly panicked, Chung took a half step back. His alarm and his difficulty speaking Japanese rendering him incoherent, he said, " . . . sister? My . . . how . . . who are you? How do you know this?"

The bus chose that moment to close its doors and accelerate away from the curb in an overwhelming roar of diesel noise and oily brown exhaust. The smaller man stepped close to Chung and said, "You approached *us*." With his right hand he removed his sunglasses, staring straight into Chung's eyes.

Chung noticed he was missing the pinkie finger from that hand. "Yakuza," moaned Chung's forebrain, as he silently entered the car. He controlled his panic by imagining his sister alive and free in Japan.

* * *

Twenty minutes later Chung was seated alone in a conference room high in a building in downtown Tokyo. He heard a latch click, and moments later someone entered, someone with a presence that filled the room. He was relatively dark-skinned for a Japanese and had a receding hairline. Chung rose as the man approached and found himself looking up at him, as he often did with Japanese, because his growth had been stunted by childhood malnutrition.

The man looked at Chung with hard, appraising eyes, then motioned for him to sit.

"I am Ota," the stranger said. "I understand your sister, Chung Eun, is in the camps. You have made many inquires seeking help to get her out of North Korea. What you have heard is that it's impossible. I say it is not, but there is a high price to pay. Do you wish to learn more?"

"Yes, yes, Ota-san, but I am not a rich man. I—"

He stopped in obedience to Ota's raised palm.

"For us, the price will be in American dollars. For you, the price will not be counted in money."

Chung's brow wrinkled and his eyes widened.

"Then what, if not money?"

"An extremely dangerous mission, one that may well cost your life."

"I see. You want me to return to the North, and you will give me dollars for bribes. I am willing to do it, but why should you give me the bribe money?"

"No, Chung-san, we do not require you to do that."

"Then what—"

Again the commanding raised palm.

"We have been asked to obtain a certain item. It is small and easily carried by a man. It is already in Japan. We know exactly where it is and that it's almost unguarded, unguarded by humans, that is."

"You mean it is guarded by divine spirits? I don't believe in what you call 'kami.' I'm not afraid of them."

Ota smiled. "You sound like our man."

He continued: "Let me tell you exactly what we require of you. The object is radioactive. Shielding will contain the radiation but make it so heavy and awkward to handle that we cannot use it, at least not as we remove it from its present location. This requires someone wearing a radiation protective suit to fetch it from its site, carry it several hundred yards in a lightly shielded bag, and deposit it in a heavily shielded container.

"That's all," said Ota, a smile flickering on his lips. "Perhaps thirty minutes' work. Easy. But not safe. The person who does this will likely receive a radiation dose sufficient to cause death by cancer within a few years. It may kill even sooner. That's what we require of you in return for your sister's rescue and new life in Japan."

Trade my life for Eun's? She kept me alive through that winter. She starved herself to feed me. She drew the police away from me, and I escaped. How can I do otherwise?

"I will do this for you, but first I must see Eun safe in Japan. Then I will do what you ask."

Ota's lips flickered again. "That is good. Your loyalty to your family does you credit. We will begin Eun's rescue very soon." He paused.

"Chung, I understand that you don't trust us. But we, too, have a trust problem. How can we trust that you will do your part once your sister is safely in Japan? Her rescue will be very expensive. We need to have confidence that you are making a total commitment."

"How can I give you that confidence?"

"Follow me."

The room to which Chung was taken appeared to be in the basement, judging from the elevator ride.

I must do this. It's for Eun!

The blade flashed down. His left pinkie skidded across the table, followed by a gout of blood.

Chapter 13

Philadelphia, Pennsylvania

"This is Carleton Fiske with an ABC exclusive interview with Governor Walter Rutherford, who moments ago announced he is resuming his campaign for the presidency." The camera pulled back from its tight opening shot on Fiske's face to include Rutherford.

"Governor Rutherford, you suspended your campaign immediately after the first attacks. Today you're re-launching it. Why did you suspend it, and why are you resuming now?"

Rutherford smiled and settled himself a bit more comfortably in his chair. "Carleton, I suspended it because in the first wave of attacks—for which the country was totally unprepared—I felt it was important that there be no distractions for the administration as they scrambled to catch up to reality.

"They've made some progress during the hiatus—probably all that can be made under this president—and it's time to resume speaking out for commonsense measures to protect Americans. Who knows? The Martin administration might even listen and adopt some of them.

"So that's one reason, Carleton. There's another: to show those behind these attacks, this attempt to bring America down, that we will not be cowed or constrained. We will carry on with our national elections despite them."

Fiske's body language signaled readiness to speak, but Rutherford ignored that, leaving an off-camera Fiske in the undignified pose of waiting with open mouth.

"And I'm confident the American people will elect a president who will be able to fulfill the most basic function of government: the protection of its citizens. This administration has failed to that and continues to fail."

Fiske wedged his way back in: "Well, Governor, that begs the question: What would a Rutherford administration do to meet that responsibility to protect our citizens?"

"Several obvious, commonsense steps could be taken immediately by any administration with the nerve to take them. First, demand that the nations of Europe do an effective job of keeping terrorists off flights originating there. Second, force the Gulf oil sheikhdoms to stop the flows of money from their citizens to terrorists. Oh, and stop permitting radical imams to poison their kids' minds in those madrasa schools. Third, unleash the power and courage of our citizens by permitting firearms to be carried anytime, anywhere by anyone over eighteen who isn't a felon or on a watch list.

"Those are things I would do immediately, by executive action. I'm sure that, working with Congress, we would soon conceive and authorize other effective protective measures."

"Governor, several of the measures you described require the cooperation of other nations. They aren't new ideas, but rather old ones that have proven impossible to implement. How would you accomplish them immediately, as you said?"

"Look, this isn't rocket science! All it takes is leadership and firmness. I would tell the Europeans that if they didn't make their screening effective, I'd cut off their . . . landing rights. As for the sheikhdoms, I would subsidize America's shale-oil industry and dump cheap product on the world market. When oil dropped below twenty dollars a barrel, they'd holler uncle."

"But subsidies would require congressional funding. How would you get it?"

"Congress will respond to strong leadership from the White House."

"Tell listeners more about your plan for arming people."

"That isn't rocket science, either. Look, America has more guns per capita than most countries. We need to put those weapons to use for more than hunting, or I should say for a different kind of hunting.

"Every time one of these radical Islamic terrorists starts shooting, he's in a race against the clock. How many innocent Americans can he kill for Allah before the cops arrive and shoot him dead?"

Rutherford paused, then said, "Which is what he wants. You're not going to capture these people; they won't allow that. So what I call the time to takedown is the name of the game. If we rely on the cops to do it, it takes probably ten minutes. I'm not knocking law enforcement; they can't be everywhere at once. But, if there are armed Americans among the intended victims or, say, right next door, time to takedown will be a lot shorter. And that will save lives, a lot of lives."

"But what you're proposing is against the law in most states. How would you deal with that?"

"I'm sure state legislators would be as anxious as anyone to reduce the carnage, to end the scenario of Americans being shot down like ducks in a shooting gallery. Look, I've been a governor. I know that in a pinch, when the citizens really, really want you to find a way, you can find a way.

"That's one aspect," he said, waggling his forefinger. "Another is that state and city prosecutors don't have to prosecute every crime that they find, and in fact they don't do that now. They have what's called prosecutorial discretion. Come on, some gal with a Glock drills a terrorist after his second shot, saves a lot of lives—you think any prosecutor would touch her for that? If you think so, you're way out of touch with the ordinary citizens of this country."

"You make it sound so simple," said Carleton Fiske.

"It *is* simple. It's very straightforward. You wanna kill Americans? Then you're gonna get a real quick trip to paradise, courtesy of an armed citizen nearby. It's sad—tragic really—that the current occupant of the White House doesn't have the courage to do what needs to be done."

Chapter 14

Washington, DC

SEATED AT THE FAR END of a recently polished cherry table in the Presidential Briefing Room, Rick Martin said, "How long has that thing been around? And why wasn't I informed?"

Ray Morales, FBI Director Brian Leek, and Director of National Intelligence Aaron Hendricks looked expectantly at Lieutenant General Pete Hsu, who ran the National Security Agency.

"Technically you were, Mr. President," said Hsu. "This surveillance program—it's called 'Argus'—is a line item in the defense budget you approved. But there are so many line items, and they are, admittedly, a bit deceptive."

Hsu hoped against hope for some backup from his boss, Hendricks, but got none.

"Mmmph! Well, let's see it."

The video screen showed the Second Street entrance to Union Station, a mass of rubble swarming with construction crews.

"As you see, this is Union Station today, Mr. President," said Hsu. "This"—the screen faded and returned—"is how it was at fourteen-ten hours one week before the attacks."

On the screen, cabs came and went, pedestrians ebbed and flowed, private cars dropped off and picked up. From near a row of large concrete planters that served as a discreet barrier to vehicles, a man approached the entrance. The man's image could be seen with startling clarity. This was no ordinary surveillance video. He looked Middle Eastern to the president, who like most Americans couldn't tell a Lebanese from a Palestinian from an Egyptian. There was nothing to distinguish this man from many of DC's Arab and Persian diplomats, cabbies, international bureaucrats, businessmen, and restaurant staff.

"Here he is again, three days later."

It was unmistakably the same man, dressed differently but easily recognizable. As the five men watched for several minutes, he strolled from the planters to the revolving door and back. After a pause he seemed intent on the traffic light. Judging by a glance at his wrist after each change, he appeared to be timing the light cycle.

"And, once again, about ten minutes before the explosion."

The man walked out of Union Station, his face head-on to the video camera, details of his clothing clearly visible, eyes darting, wearing an expression of anticipation. He picked up his pace and walked briskly down East Capitol Street. The shot cut to the same man, seen from a different angle, bent over to tie his shoelace. Before he had finished, the sound of a bomb exploded in the background. The man leapt to his feet and looked expectantly for perhaps fifteen seconds. He hailed a cab. In the next shot, taken from above, a cab passed under a bridge headed down Interstate 295 toward Anacostia. Then the screen went blank.

As Hsu expected, President Martin skipped the obvious tactical questions he must have had and went to the big picture.

"If you had him under such close surveillance, you must have suspected something pretty big was up. What did you know, and why wasn't security stepped up once it seemed Union Station was under surveillance?"

Brian Leek said, "Mr. President, we didn't have this man under surveillance. What we just saw was an ARGUS flashback."

Martin looked at Hsu.

"Mr. President," said Hsu. "ARGUS uses a combination of high-definition video surveillance of large areas plus massive storage capacity and data retrieval. When a site is put under surveillance with ARGUS, everything within a wide area is captured and may be played back with digital enhancement. ARGUS routinely recorded everything in northwest DC visible from drones and traffic cams, kept it on file, and played it back for us as if in real time. We could then search for now-suspicious activities and observe them as if we were on stakeout. Most of Washington is under

ARGUS surveillance. So are a number of other sensitive locations. In fact, we have video of this same individual prior to the attacks apparently casing the SEALs' basic training site near Coronado, California."

"This guy gets around," said the president. "Who is he?"

"We think there's a good chance he was in the bomb business in Iraq or neighboring countries," said Leek. "We have thousands of mug shots and biometrics on suspected terrorists, and he's probably among them. Unfortunately, about twenty-five percent of the images aren't of high enough quality for our software to analyze. CIA and FBI are running with some hits from the automated search. We're using human analysis to check the remaining twenty-five percent."

"Anything for me on the ones CIA and FBI are running?"

"One of them is Persian, Mr. President"

"You mean he's an *Iranian* operative?"

"We don't know if he's Hezbollah, sir, or a hired gun freelancing for cash and thrills."

"Make him your number-one priority. Rutherford's pushing me on Iran; I'm looking for something to hammer Tehran with, and that guy would do nicely."

Chapter 15

Coeur d'Alene, Idaho

"THERE HE IS. THE PRESIDENT of the Jewnited states." The speaker, clad in Levis and a faded green tee shirt, pointed to the muted TV screen behind the bar.

The man next to him at Mother's Saloon said, "At least we don't have to look at the monkey anymore."

The first signaled for the barkeep, holding up two fingers, and said. "That's when I really knew we'd been screwed, blued, and tattooed, Ken. When this nation founded by white Christians, with Christian principles in its Constitution, ended up with a black, Muslim president, who wasn't even born here."

"And now the Jews are back in charge, buying the election and pulling the strings on this clown Martin," said Ken.

"How did millions of hardworking, God-fearing American men let this happen?" said green shirt. "We built this country; we fought and died and bled for it; we—"

The speaker noticed Fahim apparently following the conversation from a stool to his right. He glared at Fahim, who toasted him with a bottle of Coors.

"What it's to you, raghead?" said green shirt, scowling.

Forcing a smile, Fahim said, "I'm not a raghead. I'm a Brit. But my family comes from Palestine; my people live in Palestine, where the Jews—the Israelis as they call themselves—have taken their land and jobs and freedom. But not their pride. We Palestinians hate the Jews, and we strike at the Jewish state often and fiercely. Judaism is a conspiracy to rule the world and will unless people take power into their own hands and destroy the Zionists and their supporters. So when I hear others who hate what the Jews have done to them and their brothers, it makes my day." He sipped his beer and set it down. "That's what it is to me."

"Well thank you for *sharing*, but I don't give a damn about you or your Palestinian brothers." The green shirt turned his attention to the barkeep, signaling for the tab.

His companion, Ken, whose shirt featured the same twin lightning flashes worn by Mountain Man, looked more closely at Fahim, eyes narrowed. "So, if you're a Brit, and you sure sound like one, why are you in Coeur d'Alene?"

"I came to the U.S. to study. Fell in love with an American and decided to stay. Did not fall in love with the Jew-dominated state of New York. Came out here because you're a long way from the big cities full of Jews."

"So you're a hoity-toity Brit whose daddy has enough money to send you over here for college, because we got the best in the world. You a Muslim? Carry your prayer rug around and kiss Allah's ass three or four times a day?"

"If I was a Muslim, would I be knocking back a cold one? No, I'm not a Muslim. I'm not anything. I'm on this earth to have the best time that I can, for as long as I can."

"So does daddy send your allowance regularly?"

"If he did, I'd just use it for beer money. I've got a job that pays me a boatload."

"Doin' what?"

"I blow things up."

"What do you mean you blow things up?"

"How do you think coal mines and rock quarries get dug? How do you think big office buildings get demoed? How do you think oil gets found? That's what I do. Between jobs I hunt and fish around here."

"You're bullshitting me."

"Try me. Got something you want blown up?"

"Yeah. Washfuckington, DC."

"No, I'm serious. Some tree stumps?" In a tone much lighter than he felt, Fahim said, "Look, here's my card."

Ken took it and read: Al Hassan, Demolitions.

"Go ahead, google that."

Grudgingly, Ken keyed his smart phone.

After a pause he said, "So you really are . . . You do this stuff all over the world, right?"

Fahim's roll of the dice had worked. The hacker hired through the Darknet had subverted Google's servers. This was only a casual glance, but a deep dive would produce hits on Al Hassan Demolitions going back five years. In England, where accents were defining, Fahim's wasn't helpful. It was decidedly middle-class. But in America it somehow gave reassurance to those suspicious of his Arab features and had an exotic attraction for some women. He skillfully used both effects.

"Yeah. Actually a lot more blasting outside the U.S. because of fewer regulations, you know? Plus, the oil companies do a lot of it, usually in real shit holes where they're looking for oil."

The man held out his hand. "I'm Reverend Ken Wescott, Church of the Tabernacle of the Righteous," he said. "Anybody who hates Jews is a friend of mine."

"Al."

"The Zionist conspiracy is powerful," said Wescott. "They crush people who get in their way. So people like you and me—and Fred here—should stick together. There's a group of us—a growing group—that gets together from time to time. Gonna give you a call next time we plan something; you oughtta come."

"Ring me up; if I'm in town, I'll try to come."

Chapter 16

Indianapolis, Indiana

SHE WATCHED HIS CHEST, RISING and falling regularly under the sheet. Her mind did not accept that this would soon cease. His face is peaceful, completely normal, she thought, while realizing, but not wanting to, that if she had leaned left to her son's other profile, she would see the damage done by bits of metal propelled by about fifteen pounds of Semtex.

Somewhere, out there . . . he's gone, I know, but . . . his blood circulates, carries oxygen to his body, keeps his skin pink, his eyes clear. The life I gave him is still there.

The neurologist's voice was kind, but he was direct: "A bolt—they usually wrap the suicide vests in metal fragments, nails, nuts and bolts, whatever they have—penetrated his skull. Only the most basic, primitive functions of his brain remain. He sees nothing. He feels nothing. He tastes nothing. He does not have any cognitive capacity. He never will again. As long as we keep him on the ventilator, his heart and lungs will function; he will be alive in the primitive sense that his other organs function, his tissues live. But your son is gone, ma'am."

Danny, she thought, looking at her son's face. She reached out and stroked his hair.

You started moving so early. I didn't feel your brothers and sister nearly as soon as I felt you. And you had that direct, impish way about you. At three, scooting away, with your hands protecting your bottom after some transgression I hadn't noticed yet. On your birthday, standing on the porch and announcing to your playmates, "Things are different now—I'm five."

The doctor had been equally direct that he wanted her agreement to the transplantation of her son's healthy twelve-year-old organs and tissues.

With a sad familiarity on his face, the doctor said, "I can't begin to know what pain this is for you. But I do know what the transplant surgeons can do with Danny's organs and tissues. They can save the lives of other kids whose hearts, livers, lungs, kidneys . . . are shutting down or have been torn apart by a bomb or an accident. His bones and tendons can enable other kids to run and play. His eyes can restore healthy vision to someone who has lost it."

She agreed.

And so it was. Later today she would kiss him and hug him one last time, and the nurse would take him to the operating room, where they would turn off the ventilator, remove the tube from his throat, the tube that now protruded obscenely from his gaping mouth like some horrible worm violating his body. And reverently take that familiar body apart.

Like the waters of a half-dozen springs that rushed through a canyon and onward, her pain, her happy memories, her life itself fused into a single, swelling desire: Get the people who did this and the ones who will kill other Dannys tomorrow and next week and next month, if they aren't stopped.

I don't care what it takes!

She was not alone. Rage and determination were building across America, a rage not known since the Second World War. It was going to cause many injustices. But it was the end of the beginning.

* * *

Washington, DC

Ray looked at his insistently vibrating private cell phone. Whoever was calling had blocked caller ID. He took the call.

"Morales."

"Ray, this is Naved Singh. It seems that our paths cross once again."

Morales tensed. "Hello, Naved."

"Tell your embassy in my country the contents of an envelope, addressed to your defense attaché and handed to the Marine sentry about ten minutes ago, are for your immediate attention."

The call icon on Morales's phone disappeared.

Morales exhaled and thought about a night when death had come for him but turned away at the last moment. He looked at the ceiling—seeing Iraq's desert—and thought, for you, Naved, I'll do that.

Ten minutes later Morales was on the secure phone to the U.S. Embassy in Islamabad, Pakistan. "Thank you, Colonel Fellowes. Yes, it's a little strange, but this is need to know, and you don't. Wait two hours and then make any required reports up your chain."

Morales keyed his private cell phone with the eleven numbers that Colonel Fellowes had given and waited, the ring chirping in his ear. After five chirps someone answered, saying without preamble, "The bin Laden raid. You gave your word to bring me and my family out if my enemies got close. The time has come for you to honor that pledge."

"I will keep my word to Naved Singh. But first, let's establish your identity. Tell me something no one but Naved Singh would know."

Singh laughed. "When I introduced myself, you experienced loss of control of a certain bodily function."

That was Singh, for sure. *What happened was I pissed my pants. That's sure as hell not something I have ever told anybody.*

Morales would never forget that encounter. During Operation Desert Storm—dazed, alone, and lost after his helo crashed in a sandstorm whistling across far western Iraq—Morales had been attacked from behind. He felt an overpowering strength yanking his head backward and the cold sting of a knife against his throat. He also felt a feral, merciless presence, as if he had been attacked by an animal. It was that presence that did it, touching the primal fear that earliest humans had felt in the grip of a carnivore. His bladder voided.

But the slash that would have opened his throat didn't come. Although the night was too black to see it, Singh, who was leading a patrol of soldiers from the Pakistani Army unit in Desert Storm, had felt the body armor Morales wore. He knew ordinary Iraqi soldiers did not have armor, meaning that he was about to open the throat of a senior Iraqi officer, or someone not an Iraqi at all. Deciding to find out, he had spoken to the man in his grip. That decision saved Morales.

"OK, you're genuine. Do you have a plan?"

"One week from today my family and I will be in a location suitable for pickup by helo."

Morales wrote down the grid coordinates Singh gave him, then said, "This is gonna be a tough sell, Naved. After Abbottabad, your air force will be all over our aircraft if they detect it. It'll be shot on sight. You can't bring many people along, and they'll have to bring only what they carry in a single bag."

"We will be four altogether, with no more than thirty-five kilos of baggage each."

"It's also gonna be tough for me to get this mission tasked. I'm going to have to convince SECDEF and the president."

"I can help you there, Ray. I know how much you want the man who led the Las Vegas operation. The same man is directing the attacks in your country now. I'll be carrying a thumb drive with an Iranian dossier on him. Get us out, and you'll have photos, biometrics, DNA, and other interesting tidbits."

"That should do it, Naved."

Singh broke the connection.

Morales sat back in his chair, fingers drumming the desk. Then he keyed a secure number that rang on the desk of the secretary of defense.

Chapter 17

Chicago, Illinois

HER HANDS SHOOK SLIGHTLY AS she tapped the microphone. After hearing a pop over the loudspeaker, she took her text in both hands and began to speak to the half-dozen reporters covering the first press conference of the Guardians.

"I am Alison Greene. My twelve-year-old, Danny, was killed by a suicide bomber. With me are Sandra Pinkerton, whose seven-year-old was gunned down by the animals who slaughtered his entire first-grade class; Kaneesha Sprague, whose daughter and granddaughter were shot as they waited for the school bus; and Mary Kane, whose husband and three daughters were among those murdered by a terrorist while grocery shopping. All our loved ones, and hundreds more, were murdered by people who shouted the name of Allah as they killed."

Her voice growing stronger, Alison Greene continued, "We are here because we have had enough of the Martin administration's bungled attempts to protect the citizens of this country. We speak for hundreds of other mothers who have suffered loss and injury since the unwarranted and cowardly attacks began.

"As you can see, we are armed. We're armed because we—and our sisters around America—are going after these animals ourselves. From now on, armed members of the Guardians will be patrolling near schools, along school bus routes, in malls—everywhere that innocent Americans make tempting targets for the cowards who killed our children and husbands.

"From this day forward Americans are no longer the hunted. We are the hunters, and terrorists are our prey. We will not observe their civil rights. We will not attempt to capture them. We will shoot them!

"We say to the Martin administration: lead, follow, or get out of our way."

Alison Greene stepped out from behind the podium. In practiced unison the four women drew pistols, inserted ammunition clips, and racked their weapons' slides. They holstered their loaded weapons and assumed the ready position, wearing expressions that said, "Go ahead. Make my day."

The journalists were thrilled. Video of that fifteen-second load-and-lock routine would go viral. It would be on every evening newscast, would pull viewers to the stand-ups they would do with these women. Some would present them as warriors; others would portray them as gun nuts. Both spins would find avid consumers. It was the sort of day that reporters lived for.

* * *

Columbus, Ohio

President Rick Martin, thirty minutes before another campaign dinner and speech, hit mute and looked at Samantha Yu and Win Hernandez. Silence hung. Martin's eyebrows shot up as he waited. Bart Guarini's visage on the videoconference link was unreadable, while Ray Morales, on the same link, appeared guarded.

Hernandez broke the silence, as Guarini knew he would. "Mr. President, obviously, we have to respond. Probably we should send Ray and maybe Brian to the talk shows, give some interviews . . . explain that what we are doing, although less obvious than what we just saw, is keeping Americans safe."

"Well, if I do that," said Morales, "I should explain how groups like the Guardians make it harder for law enforcement and the army to respond to attacks."

"No. We don't want to take on the Guardians, or any of the other vigilante groups, directly," said Yu. "That image of women protecting children is too emotional and logical to go against. Rutherford would spin our objections into bureaucracy versus action. Late-night TV would mock us; there'd be new skits every show."

"Be that as it may in the world of spin," said Morales, "in the real world it's a huge problem for police to rush to an incident and find half a dozen people banging away at each other. The terrorists aren't wearing black hats. They're not all Arabic in appearance . . . that Anglo punk who shot up a church last week, for instance. We've already had a couple of instances of vigilantes shooting at each other and the police taking *them* down while the terrorist shooters slipped away."

"In a presidential election, imaging and message are just as real as bullets," said Yu with a glare at Morales's image.

"Mr. President, both Sam and Ray are right," said Guarini. "It's not a choice between one and the other. We've—"

"I get that, Bart," said Martin. "We've got to support, or at least appear to support, the vigilante groups *and* get some control of them. But how—any thoughts, Ray?"

"The police need to be able to identify the 'good shooters' and talk to them as the situation develops. Brian and I can put together a group to work out details."

"Fine," said Yu. "But we need a response to these ladies in time for tonight's news." Hernandez nodded.

Morales clamped his lips in a thin line, a mute statement that he would have no part of that.

Guarini's phone bleeped moments after the meeting.

"Yes, Mr. President?"

"Bart, what do you think of Ray? This campaign is going to get really ugly now. Rutherford's going to blast us over every attack. Win's people will counter-spin, but we also need someone outside the campaign staff to punch back, hard. You saw Ray—he's not going to be that person. Is he still right for DHS?"

"Mr. President, let's not confuse punching back at Rutherford with actually leading our fight against the terrorists. Do you know anyone better than Ray for *that job*?"

"No, but if we don't get a second term, someone less qualified than Ray will have *his job*. A Rutherford administration will make Ray's replacement their first cabinet appointment."

Knowing his boss, Guarini kept silent.

"But, what the hell. I'm not going to be known to history as someone who panicked and dumped the one guy who could get these bastards. No, Ray stays but . . ."

"How about Ella, Mr. President?"

"What are you smokin', Bart? The president's wife is hardly 'outside the campaign'!"

"She's outside *this* campaign, Mr. President. The Secret Service has her in a security cocoon. Except for the convention, there's no video of her by your side on the stump. She's not on the speakers' circuit. She's not doing the talk shows.

"And her personal history gives her a real platform to speak about countering terrorism. Her father was murdered by narco-terrorists . . . and she's a mom, like those Guardians. If the Rutherford campaign tried to discredit Graciella Dominguez Martin on this topic, they'd lose, big time." He paused.

"Just kick it around with her, Mr. President. See what Win thinks; Sam, too."

"Bart, I think this is one of your occasional wacky ideas. But I'll speak with her."

Chapter 18

Washington, DC

Ray Morales poured his umpteenth coffee of the day, rose from his desk, and began to pace. That call didn't go well, Ray, he thought to himself. The president needed your support, and you didn't offer it. I'll bet Win and Sam are chattering about that right now. Well, I didn't become a politician when I took this job, and I won't act like one.

Ray's mind returned to his personal war with "the bomber," as he thought of the person whose identity he would learn soon—if Singh had the information he claimed and it was accurate. I feel pretty confident about the first part of that, he thought, but not about the second. Right now the bomber is a black hole; his effects are visible but he isn't. And Singh's information may not be the silver bullet I hope it is. We know from forensics that our bomb maker learned his trade in Iraq or Afghanistan. But that's it. Unless we catch a talkative martyr before he goes to paradise, I'll never get this guy.

And that's what we've gotta do. I'm betting we'll get our hands on one of the shooters. Amateurs like the Guardians will just blaze away if they encounter a terrorist, but every street cop, FBI agent, Marine, and soldier knows we need to take one alive. Eventually, we will. And then we use what Jerry Thomas learned from Captain Clevenger. But it has to happen fast, before the DOJ gets involved. We'll have at most a day to interrogate before that animal gets lawyered up and locked in a nice, safe cell complete with prayer rug. So I'd better start setting that up.

Vic Carpenter, director of the Federal Bureau of Prisons, saw "Morales" on his cell phone screen and punched the button.

"Hi, Skipper! What, you need a get-out-of-jail card? I knew you were in the shit with Congress, but didn't know they'd nailed you."

"You always were a wiseass, Staff Sergeant Carpenter!" His voice changed. "But actually what I need from you is a teeny bit like that."

Carpenter went on guard. He knew his old platoon commander was famous as the camel with his nose in the tent.

Morales continued, "You have a prisoner in the Golden, Colorado, Supermax. Name of Ruby Karpinski. A serial killer—life without parole." He paused for a beat. "I need unsupervised access to her, and I may need to move her to a black site. I need the access starting right now, and I don't know whether or when I'll need to take custody and put her deep under—"

"Whoa, sir! First I gotta know what's this about!"

"Vic, you know what my job is. *That's* what it's about. I can't tell you more than that. I haven't told anyone even as much as I've just trusted you with."

"Then I gotta say what I said when Second Lieutenant Morales told me to bring that helo into an unsat LZ. 'Bullshit, sir. This is wrong!'"

Morales sighed. "Vic, this really, no shit, could become my last shot to save thousands of lives. Look, I know I'm asking something really hard. You think on it and call me back in a couple of days, OK? And this stays between us!"

"OK, Skipper."

Carpenter rocked back in his chair and stared at his "I Love Me" wall. His eyes found the photo of him shaking hands with General Ray Morales, chairman of the Joint Chiefs of Staff, the two of them grinning like maniacs. With a grunt he rocked to the floor, swiveled to face his computer, and opened Ruby Karpinski's Prisons Bureau file. When he closed it ten minutes later, he had a faraway look.

Shit! he thought, that woman is Hannibal Lecter come to life. Most of her file was devoted to psychiatry. Stripped of its clinical language, it said that Ruby loved to inflict pain and had done so to at least nine victims over a twenty-year period. And her finale was always the same.

The tumblers in Carpenter's mind fell into place. More than anyone else I've ever known, Ray Morales is motivated by duty. It's just that damn simple. If you want to know which way he'll jump, just figure out where he sees his duty. Look what's goin' on around America: suicide bombers in malls, guys with automatic weapons hosin' down schools; it's insane! And we don't have a handle on it yet. And it's *his* duty to find that handle.

Carpenter keyed his phone.

"Morales."

"Are you sure about this, Skipper?"

Ray Morales, seated behind Andy as his Suburban headed for a meeting of the Homeland Security Council, said, "Yes."

"Just let me know when you want her. Semper Fi, sir."

"You're still a good man, Sergeant Carpenter. Semper Fi."

Ray stared out the window as familiar Washington sights passed by, but didn't see them. I wish I were as sure as I pretended to Carpenter, he thought. I'm OK with putting myself on the line to get the bomber. But Thomas is involved and now Carpenter. And inevitably there will be others, others who, like the two of them, are acting out of patriotism, personal loyalty, and the conviction that General Morales knows what he's doing. If this goes south, how do I protect them?

Chapter 19

Washington, DC

"Mr. President, we've got to get out in front on this," said Vice President Griffith.

The other nine members of the Homeland Security Council, who were gathered in the Situation Room, listened more closely, particularly Ray Morales. Each of them knew the political-speak code: "get out in front" means "take drastic action."

"Our Achilles' heel is the speed with which these massacres occur. Terrorists start shooting and in what, two, three minutes? The bodies are piled up. Assault rifles are very efficient. We've never been able to take down a shooter in less than about ten minutes; in most cases it's about twenty.

"But yesterday," Griffith continued, "at Skylark Mall there was an armed man in the crowd, and he drilled the bad guy moments after he started firing. It was the smallest number of casualties we've had from an attack like that. You know where I'm going with this, Mr. President, and so does Rutherford, you can bet on it."

"But there's more to the story, Mr. Vice President," said Morales. "There were five killed and wounded yesterday. The terrorist's weapon was only fired three times. So, at most, three of the five casualties were hit by the terrorist. The others came from the bystander's weapon."

"Ray, so what?" said the vice president. "My point is, even granting what you say, this was a victory for the good guys. The press narrative is 'they probably would have been shot anyway if the Good Samaritan hadn't acted. Unfortunate, but unavoidable and better than letting the terrorist bang away until the cops arrived.'"

Folding his arms across his chest, Griffith said, "I rest my case."

"Rest your case for what, Mr. Vice President?" said Bart Guarini.

"Why, for 'good guys with guns,' of course. We need to reach out to legally armed individuals and organize them in some way to be sheepdogs."

"Sheepdogs? Sheepdogs won't accidentally harm the sheep," said Morales. "Do you know how far a nine-millimeter round carries? A dog can tell a wolf from a sheep. A bullet can't. It rips into the first thing it encounters, whether it's a terrorist or a kindergartner. And when our guys arrive, how do they tell a terrorist from a Good Samaritan? If, say, four people are banging away, which one or ones do our guys take down? This idea makes a bad situation worse."

"With respect, Ray, I think you're getting down into tactical details where none of us in this room belong," said Griffith. "I have confidence that law enforcement can deal with the issues that crop up. The more that cops and sheepdogs work together, the better both will get at it.

"At the strategic level," Griffith raised his right hand high, "up here, where we should focus our attention, this is a force multiplier. It turns what has been a problem, the easy availability of guns and the desire of Americans to own them, into an asset. And also at the strategic level, the fundamental duty of government is to protect its citizens, as Walter Rutherford reminds us daily, and to this point we have been unsuccessful at it."

Martin stiffened and said, "Bruce, all my political life I've fought to reduce the availability of guns in our society. Doing this would be turning my back on that. It would amount to getting in bed with the NRA."

Glaring at Griffith, Martin continued, "And once this genie is out of the bottle—the idea that it's up to each American to protect himself or herself with a gun—we'd never get it back in. We'll be permanently worse off after we defeat the terrorists. They will have forced us as a society to change in a fundamental way. People will be shooting each other over traffic incidents!"

Leaning forward, shoulders hunched, Bruce Griffith said, "Mr. President, this is precisely what I'm here for. I'm here to say things no one else on your team will say. I'm your junkyard dog. You need to get over your history and your feelings, Mr. President. If getting in bed with the NRA is the best way to protect Americans, you have to do it!

"And here's something else, Mr. President, something no one can honestly deny: if you don't do this, Walter Rutherford will. He and the NRA don't need our permission to do this. If we dither and let them act first, we'll eventually be dragged into supporting their program in some way."

Words tumbling out, Griffith went for the close. "You have the opportunity—if you act immediately, if you go on TV today—to force Rutherford to follow *you*. And this will be a game changer. It will throw the terrorists off stride. It will save American lives. It will buck up morale all over the country. Americans aren't good with waiting and hoping nothing bad happens. They want to take action!"

Martin rose, waved the others back down, and turned his back on the table. He gazed at the wall, dominated by the Great Seal of the President of the United States, for a long time. Then he sat.

"All right. Let's do as Bruce suggests. Bruce and Ray, I want an initial plan in two hours. Bart, I'll announce this tonight."

Morales glanced at Griffith, saw the hint of a smile, and wanted to strangle him.

* * *

"And there you have it," said the ABC White House correspondent. "In a stunning reversal of policy and certainly of personal belief, the president a few moments ago announced a partnership with the NRA. They will organize ordinary citizens into a sort of ad hoc police force to help cope with the terror attacks that have turned malls, schools, and city streets into war zones." The correspondent then addressed the anchor: "I thought the body language was fascinating, didn't you, Bob?"

"Yes, Carlton, fascinating is the word. The president looking as repelled as a home owner carrying away a dead mouse from his doorstep and Pete Boylston, head of the NRA, looking like the proud cat that had put it there. And then Attorney General Ed McDonnell and the head of Homeland Security flanking them: the attorney general looking embarrassed and Ray Morales stone-faced. I'd say there's some disarray in the Martin administration right now."

"Yes, Bob, and probably in the Martin campaign, too.

"We return you now to our regular programming."

* * *

About seven p.m., the president rose from his desk in the Oval Office and slouched to one of the doors that kept him in splendid isolation. Swinging it open, he said, "I'm heading upstairs, Bart."

"I know that announcement was hard, Mr. President. I couldn't believe the way Boylston used it to say, 'I told you so.'"

"Today will stay with me as one of the worst moments of my presidency, of my life actually. Not as hard as signing the nuclear strike order that killed the city of Sinpo, but almost.

"You know what those two events have in common, Bart? They're situations where the facts on the ground and my duty to Americans left me no choice but to violate my conscience. That's the part of this job that I didn't expect; that probably no president expects or, if they do, believe themselves clever enough to find a way around it."

Martin grimaced. "But—you can't. In this job, there's no way around it. Eventually, every president comes face to face with this dilemma. That's when you—and the country—find out if you're the right person to sit at that desk. Well, good night, Bart."

"'night, Mr. President. And you *are.*"

Leaving the chief of staff's door open, Rick Martin glided across the iconic carpet, with its eagle clutching the arrows of war and the olive branch of peace. Reaching the remaining door, he opened it and said, "I'm done here, Dottie. Let's each of us blow this joint."

The president's personal secretary, Dottie Branson, whose black hair framed a squarish face, nodded.

"Here's tonight's bag, Mr. President. Entirely routine, so don't stay up all hours to finish it. On top of the pile are talking points for your nine o'clock call with the Belchers to thank them for organizing last week's fund-raiser."

President Martin hefted the bag, exaggerating its weight, and said, "You're a slave driver, Dottie. Thanks for cutting me some slack tonight."

"Well, I figure you've earned it, Mr. President. That announcement with Pete Boylston must have been really tough!"

Martin glanced at the floor, and his features settled briefly into resignation. Then he looked at her, squared his shoulders, grinned, and held his nose.

"Sometimes, you're the windshield, sometimes you're the bug, Dottie." He then turned and told Dottie good night.

"Good night, Mr. President."

Martin strolled the south portico as he always did, taking his time so that he would have a few minutes of contemplation before greeting Ella in the family quarters. The evening air was cool, so he shoved his left hand into a suit pocket. He was aware of the loom of familiar shapes beyond the pool of light bathing the walkway. Usually he used this time to clear his mind of the mental debris of another nonstop day, but tonight he could not.

You need to get over your history and your feelings, Mr. President. If getting in bed with the NRA is the best way to protect Americans, you have to do it!

Bruce *is* right. I had to reverse my policy, I had to stand in the Rose Garden with that preening blowhard and let him have his star turn.

But how will I feel about this day ten years from now? Will I then know that the terrorists were already on the ropes, running out of steam, about to slink away? And that today, unnecessarily, I empowered the ugliest side of human nature, our readiness to kill each other?

As the president entered the family quarters of the White House, Ella said, "Rick, when did you decide you needed to abandon your principles to beat Rutherford? Why didn't you tell me this morning at breakfast you were thinking about this NRA alliance?"

Yanking his tie loose with jerky movements, Rick saw his wife stalking toward him from across the room, lips compressed, eyes hard.

"Ella, I . . . didn't know this morning what I know now. Bruce Griffith—"

"Rick, you know how much I hate Pete Boylston and the garbage he and his organization dump into the gun debate. How could you do this without telling me! Were you just planning on letting me find out watching the six o'clock news?"

Rick saw that she was fighting tears and reached his arms toward her for a hug. She batted them away.

"You think you can fix this with a hug? God, Rick, what have you become? What am I to you, just another doubter to be managed?"

"Ella, of course not!"

"Then what's going on here? Why did you cut me out of the loop on something you *know* is so important to me?"

The president's expression changed from shock to anger.

"Look, Ella, I'm fighting for our reelection. Yours and mine. You don't want to be forced out, to have to abandon our plans for our second term, any more than I do.

"We're in trouble. We've got to get off the defensive, both in protecting Americans and in this campaign. Although I hate the source and the motivation for the idea of encouraging people to go around armed, the truth is, in these circumstances, it will save lives. The shooters are usually into their second magazine by the time the police or the army arrive. That's five to ten dead mothers, kids, fathers. What Bruce did in that meeting was force me to face the truth, a truth I didn't want to face."

"You bastard!"

Ella rushed into her study and slammed the door.

Chapter 20

Coeur d'Alene National Forest, Idaho

IT WAS NINE A.M. IN the forest compound when Fahim climbed three steps to the porch of the male shaheed's bunkhouse. He stamped his feet loudly as he always did, to heighten the drama of his arrival with a mission for one of the bored, eager martyrs within.

"Ali Hadrab," said Fahim. "Today you begin your march to eternal glory. Before this week ends, you will be in paradise."

Fahim waited impatiently on the threshold as the thin bearded young man said farewell to the other shaheed. Moments later Ali Hadrab followed Fahim across the compound to the A-frame. The hungry eyes of every other shaheed followed them until they disappeared inside.

"Ali, are you ready to give your life to hasten the arrival of the caliphate?"

"I am, Sheikh."

"Then learn your mission. You will destroy a crowded food court in the largest shopping mall in America. You will do this at mealtime, and the explosion that carries you to paradise will kill dozens of Americans and further terrify the American people.

"Come, we will make your martyrdom video, and then I will launch you like a deadly missile into the heart of the Great Satan."

Fahim gestured to a small room to his left: "Prepare yourself."

Hadrab entered and dressed in black military combat garb and tied a colorful scarf around his head. Then he put on a suicide vest, its webbed pockets bulging ominously, and picked up an AK-47. Both were props; Fahim was far too cautious to allow shaheed to be armed here, even briefly. Hadrab stepped in front of a backdrop showing the collapse of the second of the Twin Towers and, at a nod from Fahim, who wielded a GoPro, began speaking.

Fifteen minutes later, Hadrab was dressed in Levis, flannel shirt, and battered New Balance athletic shoes, walking alongside Fahim to the red F-150. Once in the truck's cab, Fahim handed Hadrab an envelope. "These are your instructions. They are brief because you will be delivered to your target when the time is right. You have only to enter the mall and detonate your vest. You have about half an hour to memorize them as I drive you to meet the ones who will take you to your target."

Hadrab tore open the envelope and concentrated on its contents as the pickup rattled and bounced over the gravel road toward the highway.

"Here they are," said Fahim, shortly after taking a dirt road leading east from State Highway 3. Ali Hadrab looked up from the instructions and saw an ambulance parked in the thick grass alongside the rutted road. It was headed in the direction of the highway. Fahim halted the truck and put the transmission in park.

Turning to Hadrab, he said, "These are not people of the Umma, but you can trust them because they know I will pay them very well when you have reached your target—and not before. They have done this for several other shaheed already. The ruse they employ is completely effective against the roadblocks that the Americans call 'Operation Sudden Touch.'

"The nurse in this ambulance will inject you with drugs that will painlessly put you into deep sleep. You will be in the state of a critically ill person who must be transported for treatment at a specialist hospital. This is not a sham; you will be unconscious and breathing with the help of a machine. Any medic who examines you will agree with the diagnosis on the medical chart made up for you. You will pass easily through any inspections that occur during your journey. When you reach the safe house where you will make final preparations, the nurse will give you drugs that return you to normal."

Fahim locked him in his gaze: "Are you ready?"

"Yes, Sheikh."

"Then be on your way toward eternal glory, in the name of Allah, most merciful and most compassionate."

Hadrab smiled. "It is as Allah has pleased."

As Ali opened the door, Fahim said, "The instructions, Hadrab. Give them to me."

Hadrab handed the envelope to Fahim. They made eye contact for a moment, then Hadrab was gone. Fahim wanted to envy him, but he didn't. Life was too much fun; he would enjoy it until Allah took him.

A heavyset woman with gray hair motioned Hadrab up the two steps leading into the ambulance. An attractive brunette and a bearded man were already inside. All wore scrubs and medical gloves.

"Please take off your clothes and put this on," said the older woman.

When Hadrab had complied, the man said, "Lie down on the gurney, and we'll get started."

Guided more by the man's hand motion than understanding his words, Hadrab slid onto the bright yellow gurney in the center of the ambulance. A large light fixture was directly above his face, and he was glad it wasn't on.

Fahim said this wouldn't hurt, thought Hadrab. I hope he was telling the truth. But, even if it does hurt, I must bear it.

The three medics, who were a team as skilled at complex, rapid action as any NASCAR pit crew, went to work. The younger woman stuck the leads to a heart monitor on his chest. The older woman slipped a blood-pressure cuff onto his left arm, then placed the pincer of a blood-oxygen meter on the index finger of his left hand. The man bent over Hadrab's right wrist. Hadrab felt a burning sensation as he inserted an IV needle into a vein. He taped it in place and glanced at the bag containing the powerful anesthetic propofol hanging nearby, being sure its stopcock was closed. Hadrab panicked momentarily as the younger woman paced a clear plastic mask over his mouth and nose, but relaxed when he realized he was breathing easily. Nothing else happened for five very long minutes.

Is this all? thought Hadrab. Fahim said I'd be unconscious. Did they make a mistake?

The gray-haired woman looked at her watch, then at the other two medics. "OK, thirty seconds," she said. The man reached for the stopcock on the propofol.

"Now," she said.

"Starting propofol," said the man, opening the stopcock. Five minutes later, Hadrab was deeply unconscious, his breathing done by a ventilator inflating his lungs through a white plastic tube protruding from his mouth.

"You guys done yet? We need to roll."

The three looked through the open door at the rear of the ambulance, outside toward a paunchy man with a bored expression, wearing a paramedic shoulder patch.

The older woman looked first at the respiratory therapist and then at the other nurse. After nods from each, she said, "Yep. Let's get this show on the road."

The younger nurse and the respiratory therapist climbed down from the ambulance. The gray-haired nurse settled herself into the rear-facing, high-backed chair on the driver's side of the ambulance and fastened the seat belt. The paunchy man closed the rear door, climbed into the seat beside the driver, and the ambulance started ponderously along the dirt road toward the highway.

* * *

Yasukuni Shrine, Tokyo, Japan

The Pilgrim stood before the wall of photos. As was his custom, he opened his mind and heart to the heroes' voices. Each was true to its owner, so each spoke in a different tone and often a different accent. Sometimes a voice came through from centuries past in a dialect he could barely understand.

But however it was conveyed, the message was the same: *Japan must become great again. You must end the shame we feel at Nippon's weakness. Give us rest. Do not let our heroism be in vain.*

He moved to a display case near the door of the museum and began to read the final letter of a young soldier to his parents:

Dear Mother and Father,

This young body of mine obeys the Imperial Army. From the start I have resolved to die. The great cause of dying for His Majesty is my sign that shines clear and bright for the Divine Imperial Land.

The Pilgrim sensed an arrival to his left. Without turning his head, he recognized the reflection of the man he awaited. The Pilgrim strolled through the door. Soon the man was at his side, matching his strides.

"Sensei-sama, the heroes' voices were strong today."

"Yes, Kimura-san. I trust you have something to report that will please the kami."

"We have our man. He is brave and committed to his role in Divine Wind."

"How do you know that, Kimura-san?"

"He willingly sacrificed a finger to the yakuza in order to demonstrate his sincerity in the yakuza way."

The Pilgrim emitted a deep guttural.

"What does this Korean know?"

"He committed himself to a false plan, a plan that would cost his life, in return for the rescue of his sister from a camp in the North. Naturally, he will not do his part until he has seen her established in Japan."

"Why are you confident that when the Korean learns his real mission, he will carry it out?"

"His sister will not only be in Japan, she will be under our—or I should say yakuza—control. He has personal experience with their use of knives. In truth, his bargain is unchanged: his life for his sister's."

The Pilgrim nodded and increased his pace.

"They won't treat him gently, Kimura-san. Will he stand up under their interrogation?"

"Sensei-sama, we will prepare him thoroughly. He bore the yakuza trial with strength and courage."

"Hah!" grunted the Pilgrim, stepping away with an acceleration that ended their walk so abruptly that Kimura found himself bowing to his leader's back.

Chapter 21

Interstate Highway 70

THE BLUE-AND-WHITE TRANSPORT AMBULANCE ROLLED eastward across Indiana, driven by a trim man of Latino appearance who handled the ten-ton vehicle, custom built on an International Harvester chassis by Braun Industries, with the precision of a professional.

"Whaddya think, man?" said the paramedic through a mouthful of candy bar. The pudgy man's slovenliness—he carpeted the floor on his side of the cab with crumbs and wrappers from constant snacking—had irritated the driver since leaving Idaho. "I mean, this is my first trip, but I'd sure like to score more of these rides at double-time. How about you, Antonio?"

The driver, whose real name wasn't Antonio, grunted a response the fat guy seated next to him didn't understand and kept his eyes on the interstate and its surroundings. Hearing a faint but familiar sound, he shifted his gaze skyward. After a moment he said, "You know what to do, Paul—how to handle it if we're stopped?"

"You give us the paperwork, then Trish and I steer them through it. Easy."

Actually, thought Paul, I'm wondering about this deal I made. I don't know who the guy in the back is, or why he's being moved in a fake patient transfer. If he's just some wetback with the cash to buy special treatment on his run north, fine. But what if he's somebody really dirty? I could find myself in deep shit if we get found out and he's some major bad guy. That new law—the Protect Americans Act—gives the cops authority to jail anybody they think is a terrorist for up to year—just lock 'em up, no questions asked. Double pay or not, maybe I shouldn't have taken this run.

And Antonio—or whatever his name really is—seems like a very tough customer. I wouldn't be surprised if he's carrying. Hell, everybody's carrying these days; half the bar fights end up in shoot-outs. If things go to shit and Antonio tries to shoot his way out of a roadblock, this ambulance will look like Swiss cheese—or get incinerated by a Hellfire from one of those army helos. That wouldn't be the first time that's happened.

An army captain aboard a Blackhawk helicopter loitering above keyed his microphone and said, "Echo two-six, this is Echo two-six Actual. Drop the hammer."

The driver of an Indiana state police cruiser with the number fifty-five on its roof released the emergency brake and dropped the 3.6-liter V-6 engine into gear. Checking his mirror, the trooper accelerated, turned on his red-and-blue flashers, and shouldered the car into the traffic stream headed east on Interstate 70. Nearby, seven other police cruisers pushed into the passing traffic. Lights flashing, they gradually slowed; within two minutes the eight police vehicles blocked travel in both directions on all lanes of the highway, capturing several dozen vehicles like fish in a seine.

The ambulance driver looked at the paramedic in the right seat, said, "Here we go," and switched on his lights and siren. Drivers ahead of the ambulance, which bore the logo of AAA Medical Transportation Service, were already irritated at the delay they knew was inevitable. Antonio's short, harsh bursts of the ambulance klaxon made them even grumpier. He expertly threaded the boxy vehicle through what had recently become a parking lot. As the ambulance approached the police cruisers, now parked across the traffic lanes, three soldiers trotted toward it from a nearby soybean field, where four Blackhawk helicopters had just landed.

Halting near one of the white-and-blue cruisers, Antonio twisted right to reach a backpack stowed behind his seat. Hauling it out, he removed a stack of fat envelopes, selecting one marked "Indiana." Antonio opened it and read a patient transfer order, then handed the documents to Paul.

"Remember, Paul, our destination is Concordia General, right here." He pointed to a dot on the vehicle's map display. Paul nodded and studied the papers. Then he moved to the rear of the ambulance and opened the doors.

A dark-haired man with a scar above his left eyebrow lay on his back atop the stretcher. Padded straps across his chest, waist, and thighs secured him against rolling off. A white plastic tube, about the diameter of a quarter, extended from his mouth and was attached to a ventilator that hissed as it assisted his breathing. Saliva flecked with blood had dried on his chin and on the medical tape holding the white tube securely in position.

As the soldiers approached, a rifleman trotted to the driver side of the ambulance and said to Antonio, "Stay seated and keep your hands where I can see them." Another rifleman halted about ten yards from the rear of the ambulance. The third soldier, carrying a bag marked by a red cross, drew near the portly paramedic waiting beside the open doors. Paul noticed that the armed soldier shifted position as the army medic approached, always keeping both him and the nurse, Trish, in view.

"OK, tell me about your patient," said the medic, looking at Trish. The tape on his uniform declared his name was Carson.

"Twenty-two-year-old male OD'd on opioids. In a coma. We're transporting him to Concordia General, about another hundred miles."

"Here's the transfer package and his chart," said Paul.

I hope this medic's not real curious, thought Trish. But what could he find to bust us? The guy really is comatose, thanks to the propofol drip. The lab results are fake, but this medic has no way to check them. Nothin' to worry about.

Shit! What about the transfer order? Suppose he calls Concordia and they've never heard of this guy Deukmajian?

Carson looked at the man's chart for about a minute, reading the doctor's orders, test results, and recent vital signs. They added up to a very ill person, identified in the record as Frank Deukmajian.

Next Carson climbed into the ambulance, crouching slightly to avoid the large overhead light fixture. He glanced at Ali Hadrab, now in a drug-induced coma. Looking at the hospital identification bracelet on the man's left wrist, Carson verified that the name there matched the chart.

Observing the patient's unfocused, unblinking eyes, the medic fished a penlight from his bag and probed them with its beam. He got no reaction. Scanning the ambulance's monitor screen, the medic observed the patient's blood pressure was one hundred over ninety-four and his oxygen level was eighty-five percent. Pressing the patient's wrist, the medic felt a weak, rapid pulse.

"Dude's pretty much a vegetable," said Paul.

"Looks that way," said Carson.

The paramedic went on: "I think his family just wants to get him home before they pull the plug."

Carson hopped to the ground.

"Duval!" he said to another soldier carrying a wireless tablet PC. "Scan 'em."

Under the gaze of the two riflemen, Duval scanned the faces and index finger pads of the ambulance crew, the bits and bytes he collected flashing over the ether for comparison to a biometric database that was continuously updated.

About thirty seconds after his last scan, Duval said, "No hits."

"OK, you're good to go," said the rifleman covering the driver.

Three minutes later the ambulance was rolling eastward again, continuing the so-far unbroken string of deceptions through which shaheed reached their assigned targets.

Behind them a platoon of soldiers from Northern Command began processing their catch. Anyone who didn't have one of the newly issued national identity cards was handcuffed and held for investigation. Anyone with a firearm was disarmed, and those without permits were cuffed and taken to the holding area. Soldiers with explosive-sniffing dogs circulated among the trapped vehicles. Children cried, drivers swore, appointments were missed, frozen foods thawed in grocery bags. This was a scene repeated dozens of times each day on highways and roads throughout America as law enforcement and the military struggled to prevent bombings and shootings by means of the stop-and-search program called Sudden Touch.

Chapter 22

Near Coeur d'Alene, Idaho

SMILING, FAHIM SCROLLED THROUGH CHARLIE'S Twitter account. They all fear me, he thought. Americans don't yet know my name, but they know the fear and bloodshed I bring them. When the time comes, when I reveal myself, I'll be known forever as the greatest jihadi!

Fahim glanced at the computer's clock. The time propelled him to his feet. He slid back from the computer, hurried to the refrigerator, hustled to the double-wide's largest room, dropped onto a battered leather sofa, and punched the television remote.

Damn, I missed the beginning of the debate, he thought. But that was probably just the introduction and ground rules. And, anyway, the part I want to see won't happen for another ten minutes.

He popped the tab on his Boddington's Pub Ale and saw a tight shot of Walter Rutherford at a podium.

"The first duty of any administration is to protect America and Americans. This president seems to think he's protecting Americans from one another rather than protecting us from Islamic terrorists. He appears to believe he can protect Americans by turning the nation into a gun-free zone, which, magically, terrorists and other dangerous thugs will observe.

"It's obvious from what's going on—like that brave American in St. Paul who was legally armed—that in this crisis what America needs is more guns, not less.

"Look, it's like those paddles to jump-start hearts. You don't need medical training to save a life with one of those babies, and lots of lives are saved because they're everywhere Americans gather—malls, airports, stadiums.

"With saving lives from terrorists, it's the same: minutes count, even seconds. Americans have heard me say this many times: time to takedown is critical, and the shortest time to takedown is a good guy—or gal—with a gun who is right there in that mall or classroom with the shooter. You don't have to be an FBI marksman; you just have to be there and carrying."

"I can see you want to respond, Mr. President," said the moderator, Carleton Fiske.

"I certainly do, Carleton. Why do you suppose it is that virtually every law enforcement group—chiefs of police, leaders of state police forces, the FBI—is leery of Governor Rutherford's encouragement to every American eighteen or over to carry a weapon as they go about their lives?

"Well," said Martin, drawing out the word, "the incident that the governor just referred to shows us why. There were five killed or wounded in the attack at Skylark Mall. The terrorist only fired three times before he was shot by a bystander. So at most, three of the five casualties were shot by the terrorist. At least two were shot by the so-called good guy with a gun.

"And I'm sure we all recall that the armed bystander—whose bravery I acknowledge—was nearly shot by arriving police. He was standing over the terrorist—who wasn't known as such by the police—with a drawn pistol.

"Look, our experience shows that encouraging armed citizens to be some sort of vigilante corps is not the best solution. Not only does it result, as we saw at Skylark, in bystanders becoming the victims of other bystanders; it makes the job of police and security forces harder.

"Let's revisit the governor's example. But this time you'll hear the whole story. What he didn't mention—like in so many of his pronouncements—was the risk. If you use an AED—that's the device he was referring to—on someone who doesn't need to be shocked, whose heart is OK, you can harm them, seriously. That's why the devices won't deliver a shock until their software has read the patient's heartbeats.

"If large numbers of Americans walk around armed, common fits of anger—whether road rage, or quarrelling neighbors, or people who've had a drink or two—will result in shootings. Plain old common sense will tell you this. In terms of loss of American lives, the governor's solution would be like giving an AED shock to someone who didn't need it. Do that and you've just made the situation worse.

"A lot more bullets will be flying around and hitting people who aren't terrorists or 'thugs'—by the way, what's a thug? Someone Governor Rutherford happens to dislike?"

"You've just confirmed it!" said Rutherford. "You're so out of touch with ordinary Americans, you can't even imagine who or what a thug is."

Rutherford's eyes gleamed. "Since you don't know, I'll tell you who the thugs are: the rapists and murderers that Mexico shoves across our border. The gangs who terrorize neighborhoods in many of our cities, the folks who expect to use our social services but won't learn English and don't pay taxes. The people who worship a murderous god who requires that they kill those who don't follow him. I could go on but we've only got half an hour."

"And move on we must," said Fiske.

The camera cut to Susan Stratford of PBS.

"Mr. President, Governor Rutherford has repeatedly urged that what he calls 'the Gulf oil sheikhdoms' be 'forced'—again his words—to cut off the flow of donations their citizens make to Islamist organizations in the name of religion. You've responded that this is a goal of your policy, but one which can't be achieved quickly. Governor Rutherford asserts that it can be achieved soon by using our shale oil as a weapon. Why do you reject that approach?"

Fahim, whose attention had wandered when the candidates had become mired in AED metaphors, listened again. Money from those donations was crucial to his jihad.

"Susan, those Gulf states are among our strongest Arab partners in opposition to terrorism and to Iranian attempts to dominate the region. They provide valuable intelligence. They flew with America and other coalition partners against ISIL.

"They know this funding is a problem, but they have to walk a fine line. Charity is an important duty of every Muslim. They can't cut off all donations, both the truly charitable and the questionable alike. That would play into the propaganda of the terrorists, thus helping their recruitment. When information implicating a charity or foundation in funding terrorist organizations comes to them, they investigate thoroughly. And they do, indeed, bar contributions to organizations shown to be fronting for terrorists.

"But that's not all that's wrong with Governor Rutherford's 'solution.' If we destabilize the price of oil, force it down below its true economic value, we hurt ourselves and all our allies, not just the Gulf states—which are, remember, our allies, too. If Governor Rutherford would take off his blinders, he could see that. Let me give some examples: The fledgling Republic of Scotland depends heavily on petroleum revenues from the North Sea fields. A crash in petroleum would accelerate deflation of Russia's economy. It wouldn't be good for European stability if Russia reached desperate straits. Mexico and Canada derive significant income from their petroleum. Venezuela, which has finally emerged from years of left-wing dictatorship, depends on oil revenues.

"The price of petroleum products affects many other prices in the world economy. That's why our own stock markets are sensitive to the rise and fall in the price of oil. Typically, when oil price tanks, our stock market is hurt badly.

"And then there's the small problem of how to structure Rutherford's subsidy of our shale oil so that it doesn't result in massive windfall profits for big oil. And the little matter of how the federal government would pay for this very expensive scheme. Perhaps Governor Rutherford has tax increases in mind?"

To Martin's right his opponent said, "No such thing. That's a lie!"

Ignoring him, Martin rolled on. "In sum, Susan, Governor Rutherford's plan to use shale oil as a weapon is dangerously naïve. It would force our allies to do things that will ultimately increase the number of jihadis we face. It's a perfect storm of unintended consequences."

"I'm sure Governor Rutherford has a response."

"You bet I do!"

Fahim noticed the time and smiled.

Any minute now, he thought.

* * *

St. Louis, Missouri

The first of Fahim's shaheed blew herself up at the northwest corner of the debate's outer security perimeter. About five minutes later, as more police and EMS vehicles arrived and first responders began to render aid, the second of Fahim's shaheed began a suicidal attack on them, throwing a pipe bomb and charging the police and EMTs while shooting his pistol. Nearly simultaneously, a third shaheed emerged from a car on the top floor of a four-story garage and commenced firing an AR-15 into police and soldiers manning the outer perimeter's southern boundary.

Both the press panel and the debaters' Secret Service details learned of the attacks through their earpieces. The second and third attacks set Wilson's assessment of the situation to flashing red. He ran for the president, shouting into his microphone as he dashed across the distance separating them. As the quickest of the panelists interrupted Governor Rutherford's spirited defense of his shale oil plan, Secret Service agents erupted from stage left and right, engulfed their respective charges, and swept them away to pre-designated secure rooms.

Rutherford was still expostulating when he disappeared under Secret Service bodies like a quarterback being sacked.

Fahim laughed so hard he choked on his beer.

Chapter 23

Washington, DC

"Ray, they're handling me! It's like I'm some nutty, important senator who has to be humored but kept out of the loop."

A nonplussed Ray Morales identified the voice and smiled. First Lady Graciella Dominguez Martin was full of energy, and he imagined that her Secret Service detail took a lot of grief because she was confined to "secure locations."

"Who is, Ella?"

"The president and his campaign minions! I hardly hear from Rick these days. He's so busy winning reelection he barely has time for anything else—especially for me. I'm an afterthought, if that!"

"Ella you were a big part of getting him elected in the first place—you know that!"

"I was, but you'd never know it now. Since the Secret Service won't let us travel or appear together on the campaign—except for the convention—I never hear from Rick, except the occasional pat-on-the-head email or—and this is rare—phone call when one of his staffers reminds him about wifey."

"Hah! Wifey—that's pretty funny, Ella. Nobody would ever call you wifey."

"You know what I mean! Look, you know that if it hadn't been for us—*both* of us—Rick wouldn't have been able to handle Six-thirteen. He's too cerebral. Sometimes what it takes is fire in the belly. We have it. I still don't think Rick does. Now on top of that, he has a tendency to postpone hard decisions by studying all sides; plus he's got the campaign to occupy him.

"We're drifting, Ray. The Martin administration is responding to the terrorists with nutty ideas like enabling the NRA's good guys with guns vigilante program. And I'm out of the loop—I can't help Rick because we're never together. Griffith talked him into getting into bed with the damn NRA, and I learned about it on Twitter!"

Morales's first reaction was to formulate an angry retort. *He* had a large slice of responsibility for stopping the attacks that came nearly every week. But he stopped himself. Ella had a unique perspective on these attacks. She had seen this play out before in her native Mexico. That gave her strong opinions about why that government had failed to control its homegrown terrorists in the cartels.

"Drifting? What would you do that's not being done, Ella?"

"Ray, I'm so out of the loop I can't answer that. You well know that Rick took Winston Hernandez's advice and moved the fight out of the White House. Win wanted to insulate his candidate from the inevitable screw-ups and hindsight experts. That battle is being run from where you sit and from where Brian Leek sits in the Hoover Building. There's no Presidential Daily Intelligence Briefing over here—Rick gets briefed on the campaign trail. I can't sit in anymore, or read his copy."

Morales decided not to respond. He knew what would be coming if he did.

"Ray, do you hate being cooped up as much as I do?"

"Yes, I do, Ella. I haven't been on such a short leash since I was a midshipman. But we both know it's necessary. The terrorists would love to nail any prominent American. We've just got to accept that and not make the security guys' work any harder than it is already. The president has told you that, I'm sure."

"Look, I'm going out of my mind. You're the only true friend I've got who's inside the security bubble and not on the campaign trail. Can we have lunch sometime, or maybe dinner? If I can't talk to a real person soon, they'll have to put me in a straitjacket!"

Morales assumed a thoughtful expression.

Julie wouldn't like it, he knew. She'd be a little jealous at the thought of me having an evening alone with my college sweetheart. And Julie's also feeling bored and neglected. In fact, she *is* neglected. And *I'm* busy every waking moment; meals just show up at my elbow while I work my inbox or teleconference or take another briefing. And besides, if I give her any opportunity, Ella will pump me for information to try to get into the loop herself.

"Oh, Ray, it's more than that. It's about Rick again. Please—we need to meet."

That got Morales's attention. And he knew the topic she referred to was not one for the phone.

"OK. Ask the head of your protective detail to coordinate with mine and work something out. Ella, I should get on a videoconference now. I expect we'll get together pretty soon. Hang in there!"

As he waved his executive assistant through the door, Ray Morales was uncomfortable.

Chapter 24

Near Killarney Lake, Idaho

FAHIM'S BATTERED RED F-150 ROUNDED the bend in the dirt road, giving view to a clearing containing a two-story building with a sharply sloped roof. The road led to an open area of dark soil speckled with struggling grass, intended for parking by the look of the trucks and cars there. Fahim's hyper-vigilance had immediately noted the armed man in the parking area and another on the second-story deck of the house. He didn't react visibly but continued slowly toward the parked vehicles.

A bearded blue-shirted man in the parking area motioned him to halt and strode to the truck. His belly, bifurcated by a dark blue necktie, bulged over his belt buckle, and a pistol rode at his hip. Fahim recognized him as Fred, who had been with Ken Wescott at Mother's.

"Identify yourself and state your business."

Fred was behaving as if he had never seen "Al" before, so Fahim played along.

"I'm Al Hassan, invited by Ken Wescott."

"You here for the meeting?"

"I'm here for whatever Ken invited me to. He didn't call it a meeting."

"Step out of the truck."

Fahim killed the engine, removed the keys, and slid out to stand beside his truck, moving unhurriedly and keeping his empty hands in view.

"You carrying?"

"No."

"You better not be. Come here so I can pat you down."

Sighing at the man's incompetence as a sentry, Fahim positioned himself before Fred and allowed him to wand and then pat him down. He observed two points in the process where he could have taken Fred down but defied his urge to bury his right fist in Fred's belly and watch him gasp and flop like a fresh-caught fish.

"OK, you're clean. Park and go on in. Ken will be starting pretty soon."

Fahim managed to look interested during the next hour as Wescott harangued the group of twenty-five or so men. Occasionally he heard movement and female voices through the open kitchen door nearby. Once, a heavyset woman with lightning flashes tattooed on her neck appeared there and observed Westcott's rant for a few moments. She nodded solemnly when Wescott said, "They're using the media to distort the truth about us!" then withdrew into the kitchen again.

After his talk Wescott called on others, who presented brief reports on projects the group had under way. Finally, he invited all to enjoy a meal together, prepared and served by the "auxiliary," whose kitchen activities Fahim had heard.

Fahim joined the shuffle through a buffet, exchanging introductions with several muscular, shaven-headed men near him, while feeling their caution and suspicion toward a newcomer. As he was scanning for a seat, a fit-looking man confronted him and said, "I'm Bobby Garst. Welcome to the club . . . the Guys' Book Club. That's what we call ourselves, a nice harmless-sounding name, you know?"

Crew-cut and of medium height, Garst wore a black tee shirt displaying a rectangular logo lettered above with "Aryan" and below with "Nations." Garst's confident bearing, shrewd eyes, and trim moustache signaled to Fahim that this one wasn't a loudmouthed clown.

"Ken'd like you to sit with him and some of us old-timers. Right over there."

"Al, glad you could make it," said Ken as they arrived at one of the simple pine picnic-style tables in the room.

"This came at a good time for me—I'm between trips—and what you said at Mother's . . . well, I wanted to know more."

"Let me introduce you around. Bobby Garst here is a little like you, because his work takes him all over to hell and gone; then he comes here to hunt, fish, and screw until his money's low. He works cargo ships."

Al nodded at Garst, a thought beginning to swim up from his subconscious.

"This next guy is Jake Pierce," said Ray, thrusting an index finger at a tall, goateed man with "Remember Waco" inked in bloody letters on his right biceps.

"He drives logging trucks."

Ken pointed. "Next to him, with a pile of food on his plate, almost as big as his belly, is Sam Wecht. He sells Fords in Coeur d'Alene."

"Hey, I'm an F-150 man myself," said Fahim to the only man besides Wescott wearing a tie.

"Hope you don't mind talking while you eat, Al," said Wescott.

"No problem." While the mashed potatoes were a favorite of his, Fahim had no liking for the fried chicken on his plate and was glad he would have an excuse to leave most of it untouched.

"So, Al, tell the others what you told me at Mother's. I know they're hot to know what a damn raghead's doing here."

"I'm not an Arab, I'm a Brit."

Fahim repeated his cover story while Ken observed and listened keenly. Fahim observed Ken and the others just as keenly. After Ken said he had checked Al's story and vouched for it, most of the suspicion in the eyes surrounding Al dimmed, although it remained in Garst's.

I'll need to be careful with Garst, thought Fahim.

"I've been thinking since we met at Mother's, Al. About what you said about hitting back hard at the Jews. I think it's time we stepped up and did that. And you're the one to help us. We've decided to blow up a synagogue, one of the ones over in Spokane." He paused. "But there's a problem, Al. You could be FBI setting us up."

"I could be, but I'm not."

"Can you prove that?"

"Can you prove I *am* FBI?"

Wescott shrugged. "So we have a standoff."

"Maybe not. If I were FBI, I'd be wearing a wire now, right?"

"Maybe, maybe not."

"So strip-search me, right now. If you find a wire or anything else suspicious, you've got me dead to rights."

"Nice choice of words, raghead," said Pierce. "Because if we find something, dead is what you'll be."

Wescott jerked his thumb toward a stairway, and Pierce led Fahim in that direction, trailed by Garst.

Every eye in the room followed them.

Wescott sat with his hands folded on the table for a minute, then pulled a KA-BAR and began to clean his fingernails. Wecht lumbered off to refill his plate. They sat in silence for a few minutes after Wecht's return.

"You think he's FBI, Ken?"

Wescott inspected his fingernails and returned the knife to its sheath, then said, "If I did, I'd kill him myself. If he's *not* clean now, he's got to be the dumbest agent who ever lived. Right now I don't know, and Jake and Bobby aren't going to find anything up there. But like they say, no guts, no glory. If he's what he claims to be, a British explosives expert who hates Jews like we do, he's perfect."

In the cadence of a politician making a stump speech, Wescott rolled onward. "We've gotta get off our asses and *do* something to stop the Jews from taking over this country! You know it's the Jews who are trying to take our guns, don't you? In fact, it was the Jews that bombed NRA headquarters; you can take that to the bank. Doesn't it make you a little ashamed that the only guys blowing up Jews are ragheads? I mean, damn mud-race losers—and their women, for Christ's sake—are the only ones killing Jews. That has to change! When the time is right for holy war to eliminate the mud races and Jews, they'll have the combat experience and skills, and we won't. We'll whip their asses anyway, but we can do it quicker and with fewer casualties if we get into the fight and get experience before we face 'em."

Wescott saw Wecht's eyes cut to the stairs. The three were descending. Fahim, in the middle, looked unconcerned despite the fury building within. But Fahim was used to holding himself in check.

"He's clean—today," said Garst.

"OK, Al. Here's the deal," said Wescott. "You get a chance to prove yourself to us. Within two weeks I want to see a smoking pile of bloodstained rubble where one of those synagogues in Spokane used to be. Do that and we'll work together on something really important."

Wescott held out his hand. "Deal?"

"Deal!"

The red F-150 bumped its way along a fire road back to State Highway 3 east of Killarney Lake. Pretty good, thought Fahim. Amusing that Ken assumed I'd be eager to work with them "on something really important."

He snorted. They're clowns, playing at a game that takes far more courage and imagination than any of them possess.

Bombing one of the synagogues will be a piece of cake. It's a bit worrisome, causing an incident so near my base. But the Americans don't know I'm in their country; I'm just a shadow in their nightmares about Iraq. They'll never connect me to this bombing. And when I've done for the synagogue, when I've made my bones with the Guys' Book Club, I'll be able to get them to take the next step, a step in my plan, not theirs.

The time for that plan is coming soon. By arming themselves, the Americans have not only limited the damage my shaheed can inflict before martyrdom; they now see themselves as hunters, not victims. Many of them are eager for the next shaheed to appear so they can use the guns they carry everywhere. They're unfazed that the martyrs' deaths are usually accompanied by casualties from mistaken or wild shots.

But I knew that martyrdom operations couldn't last, and I'm prepared.

At that moment his subconscious thoughts about Bobby Garst surfaced. As they bobbed in his consciousness, he saw that Garst was the solution to his problem with the Somali operation.

Chapter 25

Mall of America, Bloomington, Minnesota

HADRAB BEHAVED EXACTLY AS HE had been instructed: stroll to a spot near the entrance, linger, and slide into a random cluster of shoppers entering the huge complex.

I must not fail. I must get inside to do this. For that I must appear relaxed.

Unclenching his fists, Hadrab glanced at his watch. This bit of tradecraft also allowed him to overtly scan shoppers approaching the entrance, as if he were waiting for someone running late.

There! A group of teenagers that would pass between him and the security guard. And several wore jackets. He was grateful that a cold snap created conditions in which his own jacket concealing the explosive vest was unremarkable. Matching their pace, he crowded through the entrance among them, being careful not to make eye contact.

Find a restaurant or a food court. He had studied the Mall of America and quickly oriented himself. Hands in pockets, Hadrab strolled toward one of his landmarks, a store called Forever 21.

Soon I will be forever twenty-one.

That this store identified with his own age should be just steps from the site of martyrdom seemed a good omen. Hadrab increased his pace.

Focus, focus, focus, said one voice in his head. If you don't focus, you will be discovered and will die in failure. But another voice, which he couldn't silence, urged him to savor his last few minutes of earthly life. Yes, there will be paradise and its rewards, but you are coming to the end of the only existence you have known. Surely you can spare a few moments to reflect on your life.

It was Hadrab's good fortune, but also at this moment his curse: life had not ground away his humanity. Yes, he had experienced violence and brutality in jihad, but as a child he had received love and care and encouragement.

Rounding the corner, he saw his goal. The food court was busy with lunch customers in lines and seated with their meals.

The first voice whispered: Those near you will die as you will in the blink of an eye. Those farther away will suffer major injuries and some will die. You have the power of a god now—you determine if that child eating at McDonald's will die or live today. Or whether the arguing couple over there will die angry with each other.

Hadrab started toward Starbucks then caught the eye of a woman entering with twin boys about the age of his cousin.

No, not them.

He stopped, started toward McDonald's, then stopped again. Hadrab was sweating now and looking around the food court with quick, jerky head movements and darting eyes.

I know the fatwah says it is my duty to kill infidels whenever and wherever I can. But will Allah really *forgive my killing children?*

The woman in Starbucks with her twins pointed toward Hadrab. People near her looked in his direction. Hadrab's right hand flew toward the button in his pocket. Simultaneously, he felt an impact that buckled his knees and caused his sweaty fingers to slide from the button.

No!

Wind driven from his lungs by a second impact, Hadrab struggled against the grip of desperate hands to reach the detonator. He felt his legs pinioned by someone very heavy. A spike of pain stabbed his nose as an adrenalin-jacked bystander performed a knee drop on his head, smashing his face to the cold tile.

Failure!

Screams, angry voices shouting in his ear, hands tearing at his clothing.

Allah! Forgive me!

Hadrab felt his arms being drawn behind his back. Twisting his head from side to side, he learned that he was the captive of two men and a woman. An infidel police officer arrived, and soon he felt the pinch of handcuffs around his wrists.

Hadrab began to sob, whether from shame or relief he did not know.

* * *

Edina, Minnesota

Taking a deep breath, Ray Morales looked at the camera's eye and began his descent into hell. It was about two in the morning.

"My name is Raymond Morales, and I am the secretary of homeland security. What will be recorded next is the interrogation of a terrorist who was captured approximately eighteen hours ago, wearing a suicide vest, attempting to attack shoppers at the Mall of America in Bloomington, Minnesota. I believe he has knowledge that will allow security forces to thwart other attacks in the near future. He can lead us to the leader of the group that has claimed twenty-three terrorist attacks that have killed five hundred and thirty-one civilians and fifteen uniformed officers.

"I am solely responsible for this interrogation. I'm accountable."

Morales's eyes swept across the small surgical suite inside the office of a vacationing plastic surgeon. He entered an adjoining room and introduced himself to a man there in scrubs. As they watched the camera feed from the surgical suite, a slight, brown-haired woman entered. She was clad in an orange jumpsuit, and they could hear her humming as she approached an operating table near which were arrayed surgical instruments.

"You know what those instruments are for?" said the man in scrubs.

"Nope. I just know she asked for them specifically."

"Well, they're both used in grafting. The larger instrument is a Brown dermatome. It allows a surgeon to remove long strips of skin. The smaller is called Silver's knife and it's useful for removing skin in smaller sections."

Morales swallowed hard, said nothing.

All right, Ray, one last gut check, he thought. Anybody who deliberately kills women and children is an animal. He should be hunted and killed like one. I'm the guy responsible for protecting our homeland. It's my duty to find and stop this master bomber. Every day it takes me to do that, he kills more people. Duty isn't an option; it's my sworn obligation. I knew when I became a Marine that sometimes I'd have to face things I didn't want to face, do things I didn't want to do. And I've done them when duty demanded it. As it does now.

Ten minutes later, Morales entered the surgical suite supporting a man wearing boxer shorts and a tee shirt. The man's unsteady steps and unfocused eyes suggested he was drugged. The woman in orange watched raptly as Morales freed the man's legs from shackles and his hands from zip ties, then strapped him to the table at his chest, hips, ankles, and wrists.

"Remember our agreement, Ruby. You start when I tell you and stop when I tell you."

Eyes bright, Ruby moistened her lips and said, "Yes, of course. May I keep the strips? I do so love to have them."

Forcing his gorge down, Morales said, "Yes, provided you do exactly as I tell you."

The slight woman nodded her head vigorously.

Returning to the anteroom, Morales said to the man in scrubs, "How long until he's out of the fog, Doctor?"

"Probably five minutes."

"Why did you agree to do this?"

The doctor in scrubs shot Morales a challenging glance. "Why are *you* doing it?"

"Because it's my duty. This is the only so-called shaheed we've captured. I'm sure this bastard knows something that will lead us to their nest, so I have a duty to get it out of him."

The doctor nodded. "I'm a plastic and reconstructive surgeon. I've been trying to repair people torn apart by explosives and scrap metal and ball bearings and nails and seven-point-six-two-millimeter bullets. Some of them just preschoolers. I've had to tell mothers their kids are brain-dead and ask for permission to use their organs and tissues to try to save others. I wouldn't raise my motive to the level of duty. With me it's just that this has to end, has to! Plus, out of med school I was a navy doc assigned to the base at Pendleton. I know people who know you and say I can trust you. You said what this guy knows could end it. So here I am."

"You're willing to patch him up afterwards—right?"

"That's my job, and I'm damned good at it."

The men's eyes caught movement on the camera monitor. The pinioned man was turning his head and struggling against his bonds.

Over a hastily installed intercom, Morales's voice filled the surgical suite. "Mohammed, I'm glad you're waking up. I'm going to give you a few minutes to get acquainted with the woman there, and then I'll have questions for you."

Ali Hadrab spat. He eyed the woman standing nearby, who began to speak in a soft voice: "It's so good to be able to do my work again. Do you know the muscles of the human thigh? They are some of the most beautiful in our bodies. It's such an amazing, intricate world, you know, the world of our bodies. Most people, except for doctors and nurses, never see that world, never appreciate the interplay of muscle and tendon and bone and artery. But you will. I'm going to give you that gift."

Moving alongside the prisoner's left thigh, Ruby began to stroke it gently, humming softly. Occasionally she kneaded and prodded. With a grease pencil she made several marks at points along the thigh.

"There, I have it planned now. I'll use the Brown dermatome to cut long strips here," she touched his thigh, "and here. Then I'll use Silver's knife on the smaller sections. You'll have a beautiful view of your muscles and tendons. I hope it will be as sublime for you as for me."

Ruby held the dermatome in her left hand and inserted a blade with her right. The prisoner turned his head to keep her in view, his face contracting into a squint. Morales saw that, whatever the limits to his English, Hadrab understood his own helplessness, saw the blade in her hand, and sensed her growing arousal.

"Since you deserve a clear view of your muscles and I want the strips for my collection, I'll be making deep cuts. I really don't need a dermatome for these, but I can work faster with the dermatome."

Next door, the surgeon said to Morales, "She can't inflict life-threatening injuries on him with those instruments. Oh, she could remove so much skin that he died of blood loss and infection, but that would take days. Whichever she chooses, he will hurt like hell and bleed a lot. In his place, I'd be terrified."

Ruby lowered her face to Hadrab's right thigh, her lips brushing it. Hadrab heard her moan. He began to buck and writhe against the restraints, his head sweeping left and right in swift, jerky movements.

"You feel it too, don't you, my sweet. It's so exciting, so satisfying to be able to do this for you."

Grasping the dermatome's six-inch handle, she pressed the roller and blade firmly to his thigh and began to draw it toward his kneecap. A strip of bloody skin curled from the instrument while the site from which it was peeled became a lengthening path of exposed muscle and welling blood.

Hadrab's scream was louder than Morales had imagined was possible. He jerked and bucked, muscles bulging, head arcing side to side. Morales hurled himself through the connecting door, and Ruby, startled from her sexual reveries, dropped the instrument. Her face puckered in disappointment.

"That's all for now, Ruby."

With a shriek she launched herself at Morales, swinging the dermatome but missing and knocking a tray to the floor. Morales caught her tiny frame easily, spun her around, and pinioned her arms.

"*No*, Ruby! Maybe later but not now."

Sobbing, she sank to the floor.

Breathing heavily, Morales locked eyes with the prisoner, holding his gaze as he bent over him. The man's eyes popped; his breath came in gasps; he moaned and cursed and babbled in Arabic.

"OK, Doc, take over. When you get him stabilized and have his pain reduced, I'll bring an interpreter, and we'll have a chat with Mr. Jihadi." Brushing past the doctor at the door, Morales strode from the room.

He hoped to reach the bathroom before vomiting, but he didn't make it.

Forty-five minutes later Morales strode into the recovery room, his nose detecting the odor of his vomit, some of which had hit his trousers and shoes. He found "Mohammed" on the gurney, now daubed with his blood, panting with the pain of his thigh and knew he must be weakened by the fear of a hellish unknown that was now his life.

"How's his state of mind, Doc? How loopy did the pain meds make him?"

"I didn't give him much, just enough that his mind isn't consumed with riding out the pain. You can see that for yourself. He's lucid, or as lucid as I can imagine someone willing to mow down civilians by blasting himself to kingdom come."

"OK. You better leave the room now. Send in the 'terp who's waiting next door and stay there until I call you."

As he waited, Morales gazed down at the terrorist. He stared back at

Morales fiercely, but Morales knew the fierceness was a thin veneer hiding shock, horror, and confusion. He had seen that look on the face of young Marines after battle, men whose reserves of courage had been consumed. Courage would return, but in the moment their composure would shatter at the next loud sound.

With the interpreter standing behind "Mohammed," Morales began to speak.

"Her name is Ruby and she's a serial killer. I borrowed her from a facility for the criminally insane. She murdered nine people that we know of, maybe more. She gets off on inflicting pain, as you have just experienced. You will spend more time with her unless you answer all my questions truthfully."

As the translation was completed, Hadrab's expression changed from pained to terrified. Since the 'terp was behind him, the terrorist had nothing to distract him from Morales's hard gaze. It was as if he and Morales and Ruby, recalled with terror, were the only people in the universe. He inhabited a small space in the company of a man who was clearly merciless and a woman who was clearly a sadist. He had no hope of escape, except by an excruciating death or shameful compliance. After about fifteen seconds' silence, Morales said, "All right, back to Ruby."

Before Morales reached the door, the man's resolve crumbled.

"My name is Ali Hadrab, and I am from Jordan, from Amman."

Morales wheeled, looming.

"Who is your father, and where does he live?"

"My father is Kapur, and he lived in Amman until his death five years ago."

"Where did he live when he died? The address."

Hadrab stuttered it.

"Why are you in the United States?"

"I am a student at Boise State University."

"All right, Hadrab, that's enough for now. I'm going to give this information to my people. If they confirm it, we resume our conversation. If they tell me your words were lies, I'll decide you are a useless fool and let Ruby have you until she is finished. There will be no second chance."

Morales left, guessing Hadrab had used his last reserve of courage to stick with his cover identity and was now frozen with fear and loathing.

As Morales's car eased out of the darkened shopping mall his phone rang.

"Morales."

"He broke, sir. Gave us his true name. He's babbling about his infiltration route, where he met his U.S. controller; he's spilling his guts."

"OK, Jerry. Give him a full going-over, and let's see what we can do with what he says."

Chapter 26

Washington, DC

"RAY, I'M SO SORRY! BUT I'm feeling miserable and coughing and wheezing, and I'd throw up if I ate. It makes no sense for me to come to Camp David with you and Ella."

"Julie, I'll cancel with Ella and have the detail overnight me at the Greenbrier."

"I'm about to take an antihistamine and go to bed. You know how the Secret Service hates to have you at the Greenbrier. Don't use one of your silver bullets to come out here and watch me sleep—between coughing fits, that is. You go on. Give Ella my best. We'll all get together another time."

"Well, OK. I may cancel anyway, Julie. I'm scheduled to testify on the Hill tomorrow at ten and that means a rush in the morning if I'm at Camp David."

"Ella will be disappointed if you do that. You know she's going stir-crazy. But do what you need to do, Ray. What *I* need to do now is take this pill and get in bed."

"OK, bye. I love you!"

" . . . love you back, Ray!"

Ray leaned back in his desk chair and frowned. Shit! he thought. Women are complicated. I know Julie is uncomfortable with me having an evening alone with Ella, but she won't say it. And Ella's going to lay a guilt trip on me if I cancel. If Julie had asked me to cancel, I would. But she didn't. She assumed I'd go. What the hell, I'll go. I'm not going to be ruled by something Julie is unwilling to say.

An electronic chirp drew Ray's eyes to the Tweet on his phone:

Car bomber at Sudden Touch checkpoint kills 15, injures 23.

* * *

Camp David, Maryland

Hard as we try, we can never completely tune them out, thought Ella, as her attention was caught by the movement of the Secret Service agent in the corridor responding to his earpiece.

"Ma'am, Mrs. Morales won't be coming tonight. We just heard from the head of her detail that the move has been canceled."

"Oh, I'm sorry to hear that, Mark. Do you know how it came to be canceled?"

"No, ma'am. They just told us it was off. You want me to check?"

"No, that's all right."

Ella, who had reached Camp David in a chilly drizzle an hour ago, pulled a chair close to the fire and opened her book. But she didn't read it.

Wonder why? Well, Ray will let me know.

Once again I'm reaching out to Ray.

He's the one person I could think of to turn to when Rick was frozen, couldn't make a decision, and America was coming apart from fear of another nuke. I knew in my soul that Ray might be able to help him when his advisors and I couldn't. When I called him that day, it was the first time we'd been in touch for at least five years.

Why Ray? I . . . Subconsciously, I must have extrapolated from what I knew of him and felt for him thirty years ago. Maybe it was because he has made life-and-death decisions; his orders have gotten people killed; he has killed people himself. Because I knew that was the key to unlocking Rick: showing him a way to live with his signature on that nuclear attack order.

Ella's cell phone buzzed; she saw that it was Rick. *Someone must have reminded him to call wifey.*

"Hello, Rick."

"*Querida*, I've got a few minutes before the Chicago fund-raiser, so I thought I'd use them by giving you a call."

Rick's such a jerk these days! He knows I'm pissed, yet he thinks slinging a little romantic Spanish at me is a good opener. And then his next words are all about him.

Ella remained silent. She could hear voices in the background, one of them Win Hernandez.

"So how are you, Ella?"

"I'm hanging in there, Rick. When are you coming home?"

"If by *home* you mean the White House, next Wednesday. Just for a couple of days, though. Our numbers are soft in the Midwest, and Win insists that I do more to fire up my base. And you know the donors demand a lot of face time."

Ella grimaced. "And then there's that little thing going on with terrorists that should get at least some of your time, Rick!"

"Of course, Ella."

She visualized him rolling his eyes, while looking at Win hovering nearby, as he had with her many times while stroking a contributor with his voice. She knew—and knew that Rick knew—that exchange was about more than terrorism. It was about the state of their relationship.

"I know we disagree on this, Ella, but I'm not gonna let these attacks dominate the campaign narrative! I will *not* stay in Washington chairing NSC meetings to show I'm in command, personally dreaming up masterstrokes against al Qaida or whoever these bastards are. There's certainly no reason to do that when I've got Ray Morales at DHS. I've told him to do what he thinks best and never mind how that might play in the campaign. *My* job these days is to get reelected so that Ray and I have another four years to make America and the world safer. Jimmy Carter let the Iranian hostage crisis dominate his reelection campaign and his own attention, and that's why he lost in nineteen eighty! I'm not going to set Walter Rutherford up to play Reagan to my Carter."

Rick paused, and in that space Ella felt the sting of being left out of Rick's thinking about a second term.

In a wistful tone Rick said, "Ella, please. I don't want to spend the little time we have arguing."

Neither do I, she thought. He's not really a jerk; he's just dead tired and showing the effects of being surrounded by sycophants. She moved to safe ground.

"Rick, do you realize that this may just be the year Gio wins twenty?"

"Well, he's on a roll, and if Harper and Murphy stay healthy, the Nats could go all the way. I could be throwing out the first ball in the Series at Nats Park. Wouldn't that be a kick? Oh, Win's waving at me; gotta go, sweetie. Take care of yourself!"

"Remember, you're the biggest target, Rick. Don't buck Wilson. I love you!"

"Love you too."

With a sigh Ella slipped on a Camp David windbreaker and left Aspen Lodge. She was glad the drizzle had stopped, allowing her to enjoy strolling Camp David's paths, which granted at least the illusion of privacy. The Secret Service presence, while no less constant, was less visible here.

Ray should arrive pretty soon, she thought.

Rick and Ray. I've known them both for over thirty years.

I met Ray first, at Princeton after a track meet with the Naval Academy. I was swept up in his masculinity, his intensity. When he wanted something, he went after it all-out, and he wanted *me*. That was exciting for a young woman raised in a Mexican Catholic culture and later at Princeton, surrounded more by intellectual guys than by physical guys.

Ray was both. He was very physical, a hammer-throw and shot-put star on Navy's track team. He had decided to become a Marine even before he entered Annapolis. And yet . . . his grades were good. He said he kept them up because there were only a limited number of slots to go into the Marine Corps, and they went by class standing. But behind that . . . he had a quick and curious mind. He studied the bio-kinetics of his sport.

He believed knowledge gave him an edge. And that was one thing Ray always wanted—an edge. He was the most competitive person I had ever met, maybe still is, despite the crabs-in-a-bucket competitiveness of politics and politicians.

Ray was my first lover. He made love like he did everything else—in a hurry. There, too, he studied and learned foreplay, but it just as a step toward his goal. At the time I didn't know any better; thought that's just the way guys are.

But later I met Rick, at Columbia . . . If Ray's first impression was masculinity, Rick's was charm. And he had this way of making me feel that I was the only other person in the universe. Later, I learned he could make *anyone* feel like that. It was a talent he had, like being handy with tools or great at playing cards, and when he used it, that didn't mean you truly had his attention or interest. But I need to be fair to Rick. I've known him as friend, lover, and partner for twenty-six years, seeing more deeply into him as we moved through life. Not like Ray, who was a comet flashing across the sky and off to another solar system.

Anyway, I can't make an apples-to-apples comparison.

Rick is by far the finest person in politics. He doesn't have a mean streak. He's not completely self-absorbed. He relishes praise but doesn't thirst for it; still he *is* self-absorbed. I suspect that if he could be honest about it, he'd agree that he's his own favorite person. Certainly he's more self-centered than ever during *this* campaign. It's a familiar pattern.

Rick's a deep, dispassionate, rational thinker. I guess that's another point of contrast. He wants to worry an issue until he's come up with the optimal solution. Ray believes that best is the enemy of good enough; he wants to find a good-enough solution and move on. Rick's the tennis player who hits long rallies from deep in the court, and Ray is the one who charges the net.

Before Six-thirteen I would have said I trusted Ray more than Rick, even though I'd had little time with him since college. But I learned in those awful months that Rick has real courage. Before, I never thought of him as my protector. My partner, yes, but not my protector, not someone who would sacrifice himself for me.

But after Six-thirteen Rick sacrificed himself, in a real sense, to save the country. He killed about sixty thousand North Koreans, pretty much in cold blood. It took him a long time to decide to do that; at first he tried to run from it, but at the last moment he accepted his duty. Ordering that nuclear strike was a moral crucifixion for him. He's called a monster and a murderer by many.

And his pain hasn't ended. He's subject to second-guessing by people who had no idea what to do at the time, who just hunkered down to see if someone would lead, would rescue America. Because he never in his wildest dreams contemplated taking human life, Rick had to work his way around to doing that. It had never occurred to him that leadership sometimes requires self-sacrifice.

Ray would have made the same decision much sooner and would have put the burden in his soul's rucksack, along with all the other deadly orders he's given. As he told Rick, you have to do your duty, but that doesn't give you a moral pass. You carry your deeds on your soul and will have to give an accounting to God.

I'd trust Ray in all circumstances and trust Rick in most, but not all. So that means, I guess, I trust Ray more than Rick.

But here's something else: Rick is kind. I'm not sure about Ray. He'd be kind if he felt a duty to be kind, but I don't think kindness is instinctive with Ray. It is with Rick.

Wait . . . Ray is like my father. Papa was fierce. He felt that duty demanded all you had to give, even your life. Duty cost my father his life. After Las Vegas and the close call in Baltimore, I knew that Rick had to accept his duty to sign that order even if it killed him, in the sense of destroying his soul.

Ray and Julie married in their forties, when Ray was clearly marked for big things and she was a top rainmaker at Booz Allen. No kids. Relationship seems rock solid. Ray's true to himself; he showed that by resigning as CJCS in the Rogers administration, on a matter of conscience. He seemed to have no need to speak out after he was free to do so. I'll bet he refused big-bucks offers to become a consultant to one of the networks or write a tell-all book.

Ray returned home, and Texas's governor appointed him to the House after a Republican congressman died. He has political skills of a sort; he must because he won in his own right at the next election. Kept a low profile as congressman. Being smart as well as tough, Ray quickly intimidated the few left-wingers who tried to take him on. When Rick asked him to take DHS, it didn't take much convincing. He appealed to Ray's sense of duty.

Ella glanced skyward as an unusual sound, neither airplane nor helicopter, announced Ray's arrival.

Chapter 27

Camp David, Maryland

STRIDING AWAY FROM THE MARINE V-22 Osprey tilt-rotor aircraft, Ray felt awkward. This doesn't seem as natural as it did right after I hung up with Julie, he thought. I wonder if Ella feels awkward. But why should she? We were done twenty-five years ago. I'm over-thinking this. She just wants to speak with somebody as an equal, not as a political wife, and I fill the bill. But why do I feel this twinge at knowing my time of arrival and departure from Aspen will be recorded in Secret Service logs? And in the minds of the agents, never mind that they are sworn to secrecy. That I'll feel a little guilty, as if I deceived Julie?

Feeling his phone's vibration, Morales fished it out; Twitter reported the bombing of a synagogue in Spokane, Washington. The attacks were so frequent these days they no longer triggered a call from the president. Ray realized unhappily that it would have felt awkward to speak to Rick from Camp David, another indication that this meeting was wrong.

Mounting the steps of the presidential "cabin," Aspen Lodge, Ray Morales dismissed his uneasiness, nodding to the Secret Service agent posted on the porch.

As she opened the door, Ella smiled and said, "Ray, thanks for making this happen. The agents told me Julie's trip was canceled. Thanks for coming yourself anyway."

Ella beckoned him toward her spot by the fire. As he crossed the room, he thought of her not as the first lady, but as a woman, a woman of mature beauty, intelligence that he respected, and whom he had once known intimately.

"Julie's got some nasty bug, maybe the stomach flu. She sends her best and said she'd be both lousy company and a Typhoid Mary."

"I'm so sorry."

Ella smiled. "I remember your appetite, Ray, and how you always wanted to eat early. I asked for dinner as soon as you arrived. I thought trays by the fire would be nice."

"Fine by me, Ella. And I still like to eat earlier than most folks in DC."

Responding to her gesture, Ray moved to a sideboard topped with beer, wine, and hors d'oeuvres.

"That's something else you remembered: my Miller. And I see you still like this sweet white."

Ella watched him fixing their drinks. What a contrast he is to Rick, burly with a broad, oval face that Hollywood would cast as that of an aging boxer, while Rick is slender, has a streamlined look and a nearly unlined face. Ella realized she was thinking of Ray as a person and not as a piece of the Washington power puzzle.

As Ray returned with drinks, their eyes met and held, longer than either had intended. It was Ray who looked away.

Turning to the fireplace, he said, "Ella, your staff needs a course in fire building." He busied himself with fireplace tools and wood for longer than necessary, then sat to her right. When he looked at her again, he had masked his feelings.

"Ella, on the phone a few days ago you were pretty upset." He raised his eyebrows.

"Ray, how do you think, *really think*, this is going?"

"About as well as could be realistically expected. Americans were caught by surprise. Their first reaction was almost hysteria. Social media and journalism screamed 'the sky is falling.' But, actually, people were already accustomed to schools and theaters being shot up by madmen. They came out of their funks. Now, they're pissed. They're carrying weapons, and quite a few of those with weapons are looking for a chance to use them. Often they use them on the wrong people."

"That's one of the things that worries me, Ray. Rick thinks I'm wrong to think of my birth country's experience as a template. But I saw violence spiral out of control there, with guns everywhere and groups using them to settle all kinds of scores. The carnage wasn't only from drug cartels. Once people lose confidence in the government's ability to protect them, it's nearly impossible to get them to give up their guns and their vendettas. I think—"

Ella's words stopped at a knock. She rose and walked toward the door. "Yes, please come in. We're ready for some of that great Camp David country cookin'."

After the navy steward had delivered a crock pot of Yankee pot roast, the two served themselves and sat by the fire. Ray had refilled her glass with Riesling and poured himself a Pinot Noir. As the daylight faded, the fire filled the room with warmth and intimacy, pushing away both the dusk and the world.

As Ray ate heartily, Ella gazed in silence at the fire, which cracked and sparked against the screen. A faint smell of wood smoke mingled with the dinner's aroma.

Ray resumed his seat after serving himself another helping and said, "So, Ella, you were saying . . ."

"I think Rick's on the wrong track. He's obsessed with 'not playing Carter to Rutherford's Reagan,' and he's not as engaged in getting these terrorists as he is in his reelection campaign. That's not only morally wrong; it's bad politics. But he just brushes me off and recites the latest poll numbers and talks about firing up his base."

"You know, don't you, Ella, that he gave me a green light to do whatever I think best to nail these people? Not to come to him for permission, use Bart as a sounding board if I want, but in the end use my own judgment."

"You know he's using you, right? Setting up deniability for himself if what you have to do goes over the line with his base."

"Possibly, but I'm not so sure, Ella. Our base wants safety for themselves and their families as much as Rutherford's does. As this continues to get worse—and it will for a while—Rick's base will be a lot less concerned with principle and a lot more with personal safety. You may not be giving him credit, Ella. Yes, leaving the dirty work to me gives him some deniability, but it also means that security decisions are not being made by someone whose attention is focused on reelection politics."

"Did you hear yourself just now, Ray? You said 'our' base. You're starting to think like us politicians."

"Don't read anything into that, Ella, except that I serve the president. In that sense his base is also my base."

Ella shrugged, then stood and held out her hand. "Let's walk, Ray. This is one of the few places we can be outside as long as we want." Automatically, Morales took her offered hand; he felt a tingle as they walked the few steps to a closet before dropping their shared clasp. Ella put on a windbreaker.

As they strolled the camp's neat, narrow pathways side by side, hands occasionally brushing, Ella guided them to a section without illumination.

"This is the best place in camp to see the stars, Ray. I grew up in LA and went to college in Princeton and New York City. I never really saw the stars until we began using what the press calls the Aberdeen White House. The view to the east, across the river mouth, over the Chesapeake, was dark. I was amazed at what that let me see in the sky."

They had stopped walking, and Ella fumbled with the collar of her hooded windbreaker. Ray reached his left hand out to help, and their hands touched at her neck. He smelled her hair mixed with the oddly familiar fragrance of the lotion she still used. Leaning in, he followed those scents toward her face, then pulled back.

"It's OK, Ray. I feel it too. We were a long time ago, but the feelings are still there. Things were a lot simpler then."

"Let's go back in."

Ella looked at him for a long moment. "OK," she said.

Wordlessly, they walked to the main path and on to Aspen. Mind spinning, Ray was careful not to brush against her as they navigated the narrow path, as if he had nearly touched a third rail and became hyper-alert not to repeat that dangerous experience.

Dinner had been cleared, and the fire, freshly fueled, enfolded them in its glowing arms, painting the room in gold and flickering shadows. As Ray helped Ella take off her windbreaker, she turned toward him and tilted her head. He leaned toward her; she didn't pull away. Their lips touched lightly, then hungrily. A part of Ray watched in amazement as he kissed her, but that was a tiny part. Most of him was in hot pursuit, and as Ella returned his kiss, the watching Ray vanished entirely.

A voice in Ray's head said, "No, this is not only wrong, it's stupid." But a louder voice said, "the world's upside down, there's nothing wrong with this now."

They melted together. After a moment, Ella pushed Ray away, whispering, "Secret Service." She took his hand and led him to a bedroom.

* * *

Ray Morales felt the Osprey bounce slightly as its oleos flexed in the last seconds before breaking with the ground, then the familiar tilt and pressure into his seat as the bird headed for Washington. His mind whirled nearly as rapidly as the big blades he saw through the window.

Last night after he and Ella had made hurried, needy love in Aspen cabin, he had felt overwhelmed, shocked at his own urgency and weakness. Dressing, Ella had said, "That was good, Ray. In fact, it was great. It's been a long time for me . . . probably for you, too. But it happened only because our lives are so wrenched out of joint now.

"We each have far too much going for us outside of this old relationship. I'm the wife of a president, who's struggling for reelection. The mother of two children with him. You know how much you love Julie and would never want to hurt her. And you're the most valuable member of Rick's cabinet. No, we were good together, and it was what we both needed in the moment. But we can't do this.

"Ray, don't look so stricken. We have a long relationship. This is not some hook-up. We both saw this coming, we both wanted it, and we both know it will never go anywhere. We each needed this now, and let's be grateful we were able to give to each other."

"Ella this is my fault. I never should have—"

"Ray, shut up! There is no fault here." Ella's smile took the sting out of her words. "This happened, it was good, and it's not going to happen again. Rick and Julie won't be hurt because neither will ever know."

But *I* will know, he thought, as the Osprey sped him to Washington. Arms crossed and head bowed, he plunged into a spiral of self-recrimination.

What have I done? In a single week I've broken my marriage vows and *become a torturer. What have I become? How do I get my life back?*

Chapter 28

Washington, DC

SENATOR ARLENE GUSTAFSON OF MINNESOTA rode the Capitol subway car, about the size of a golf cart, toward the Dirksen Senate Office Building. She sat alone, something unusual for this outgoing, veteran political figure.

I do love this life, she thought. Most people don't make a difference, but I do. And the Senate is such an important institution—the world's greatest deliberative body.

That thought passed through Arlene's consciousness without a trace of cynicism or even a hint of tongue in cheek.

Martin's campaign is stumbling a bit. Walter Rutherford's not the sharpest tool in the box, but he has a great campaign manager, who has brought on a strong staff. The word is that Win Hernandez is pushing Martin to dump Bruce Griffith; that Bruce's positions on guns and civil liberties are too right of center for important contributors. That's a plus for us—however it turns out—because it distracts Martin's focus from Rutherford.

And I'm going to create another distraction, but not because I care about Rutherford. I'm going to do it for you, Matt. Morales let you go down the drain when he could have stopped it. Yes, I made a mistake, but not one you deserved to die for.

The car came to a smooth stop, and she made her way to ground level, smiling and nodding to colleagues and to the occasional journalist who had been allowed into this sanctum of superior human beings. Everything about the Dirksen Senate Office Building and the other Capitol office buildings was designed to reinforce the self-esteem of senators, few of whom needed that particular reinforcement. Still, it was comforting to be treated deferentially.

Gustafson, ranking minority member of the Homeland Security and Governmental Affairs Committee, entered DS 342 through the members' entrance, coming out on the raised dais that visually established their superior status. She didn't join the group of senators chatting with Ray Morales in the open area between the witness table and the dais but rather seated herself immediately to the chairman's right.

She scanned her briefing notes and smiled.

Today I'm going to get you, you smug, macho Marine bastard! I've waited a long time for this.

"So, Senator, I wish it were otherwise, but we don't have enough people, actionable intelligence, or tactical assets to protect every city, town, village, and sporting event in the United States one hundred percent of the time," said Morales, reaching for a water glass on the green-covered table before him. He was well into his second hour of testimony.

Gustafson straightened her shoulders, stuck out her chin, and said, "Secretary Morales, I don't think you get it! You sit here in Washington, or in some 'undisclosed secure location,' protected by armed guards. Your family is protected twenty-four seven. Whenever you travel you're accompanied by heavy firepower."

Journalists, photographers, and videographers alerted, hoping this was going to become a Big Moment.

"You're safe, and the people in my district aren't safe. And you don't care about them. You don't have any sense of what they're going through, just trying to live their ordinary daily lives. It's very easy for you to say 'we can't protect everybody.' I'm hearing 'I've got mine, sorry about you and yours.'"

Gustafson picked up her pace, dialed up her voice, and added a dash of outrage to her manner. "You've got no idea how it feels to be under constant threat of attack, to know that any minute a car bomb or a suicider might blow you apart; or maybe worse, just blow off a leg and leave you a cripple. Not to even mention how my constituents fear for their kids, fear of holding a wounded child and seeing the light flicker out in her eyes!

"Mr. Secretary, that last answer of yours was totally unacceptable! I want you to retract that unfeeling brush-off of the men, women, and children in my district." Gustafson's index finger snapped out like a switchblade. "I want you to apologize to them—and I demand that you do it right now!"

Despite the rapt silence of senators, staff, and spectators, Ray Morales heard a roaring in his ears. He felt his neck flush, his muscles tense. His eyes became slits of rage.

She's just baiting me, and we both know why. I'm not walkin' into her ambush!

Then Ray heard a voice, a voice choking on the blood pouring from his radio operator's mouth, as more gushed from his nose and trickled from his ears. *Skipper, it's all right. You did the best you could. Nobody lives forever and today's just my day.* Morales was back in the Iraqi town of Zubayr on a very bad afternoon in 1991. The mortars came out of nowhere. He and his Marines could only pray and scatter like ants being beaten with a stick.

With a posture at variance with his words, Morales said, "Senator Gustafson, I respectfully disagree. Unlike you, Senator, I know exactly what it's like to wait and wonder whether you'll hear the next blast or won't because it killed you. Unlike you, Senator, I know what it's like to hold a dying kid in my arms and understand that I can't save him and he knows I can't. Unlike you, Senator, I understand that when you refuse to give people that you send to battle the resources they need, more of them die getting the job done.

"I can only assume you don't know these things or have these feelings, Senator, because of your voting record. You voted to cut the proposed appropriation for Homeland Security by twenty-five percent." Morales used his meaty fingers as a tote board. "You voted against a bill that would have given me the authority to shift resources to the places that I believe to be in greatest danger. By your thinking, the cities most under threat should get no more than those less at risk."

Morales placed both palms flat on the green baize, flanking the microphone into which he leaned. Lights bathed his face, and cameramen pushed and shoved for the angles they wanted.

"Yes you, Senator, who have never dodged a real bullet. You, Senator, who are just trying to settle an old score, as we both know, have absolutely no standing to accuse me of 'not getting it'—Morales's big hands mimed quotation marks—not getting the dangers and the costs of this nation's battle against terrorists seeking to bring us down! So, no, I will not retract my earlier statement. It's true and accurate. You can go—"

With a huge effort, Morales throttled his outrage before finishing the sentence. The room had grown pin-drop silent. That silence continued for a few moments, then became Babel.

The first senator to move was the committee chairman. Red-faced, he gaveled furiously, calling for order without effect. Realizing it was hopeless, he declared the hearing in recess until two p.m. and fled. His colleagues, glancing warily at Morales and ticking off their own votes on homeland security, shuffled rapidly off the platform and through the door.

Senator Gustafson, red-faced and shaking with rage, shouted in her legislative assistant's ear, "You tell Marty he'd better get that guy. I want everything he's ever done since kindergarten. Every gum wrapper he dropped. Every time he jaywalked. I want Marty to talk to every Marine who ever got near that pig, talk to every girl he ever jilted, every guy he ever beat out for the football team. I want every bit of dirt on Morales. And tell him if he can't find it, he'd better look for a new client!"

Chapter 29

Washington, DC

"SENATOR, MAY I OFFER YOU a ride? Those black clouds are going to let loose any minute."

Senator Arlene Gustafson startled at the words coming from the open rear window of a black Suburban. The car had drawn alongside her quietly as she walked along E Street SE toward her Capitol Hill row house. Recognizing Ray Morales, she shifted from apprehension to anger.

"What are you doing, Morales? Stalking a U.S. senator? No, I'm not getting in that thing. Why are you cruising E Street?"

"Senator, I just thought we should talk privately. Neither of us much enjoyed that hearing today or accomplished anything for our country. Let's find some common ground."

"If there is any common ground, it's where I'm standing. If you want to talk, get out of your chariot and tell your security goons to back off."

Morales yanked his door handle and erupted from the Suburban, making eye contact with his driver, who nodded curtly. As the bodyguard's door opened, Morales waved him off and turned his back to the vehicle, which pulled away.

"Senator, you baited me, and I fell for it. I know better than to take on a senator in a hearing room, especially one full of press, but I did. What I said to you was true, but I shouldn't have said it. I apologize.

"But that's not all I came to say this afternoon. Your son was a good Marine and a good person. But when he outed himself very publicly while the implementation of repeal was pending, he made a huge mistake. It's a mistake I've seen other young Marines make on other issues. They get all fired up and forget that the military—hell, even the air force and especially the Corps—is unforgiving of direct defiance of authority.

"Had he just waited a year, he could not only have declared himself; he could have taken his partner to the Marine Corps Birthday Ball! But he didn't. And so the system ground him up and spat him out."

"You could have stopped it, you bastard!"

"I was chairman of the Joint Chiefs of Staff. You would have been the first to hold hearings if the chairman of the JCS had intervened in a Marine Corps investigation on any other subject. It would have been grossly improper. You know that!

"But, Senator, I wouldn't have intervened even if it hadn't been. Your son deliberately exposed himself to discharge by violating Don't Ask/Don't Tell on the NBC Nightly News. He was lured into doing that by people who didn't care about him and who wanted to turn the heat up on the Pentagon. They wanted to make things so hot for SECDEF, he would order an immediate change in policy rather than an orderly transition."

"You have his blood on your hands!"

"I do have blood on my hands—and on my soul—but not your son's. Matt committed suicide, and we both know that the despair that drove him to that was the result of his realization that his partner and so-called friends had used and discarded him like a wad of Kleenex. I'm genuinely sorry for his fate and your loss, but I am not responsible, not even close to responsible!"

Gustafson's face twisted as if tears were coming. But then she gave Morales a dry-eyed look of pure hate.

"You sanctimonious bastard! You think you're morally superior to politicians like me because you bailed out on President Rogers and called it a matter of conscience. You and the other brass hats made her believe we'd turned the corner in Iraq. She gave the order to bring the troops home, and then, when it turned out you hadn't actually pacified the place and she had to send them back again, you claimed she wouldn't listen to military advice and resigned your commission.

"You're every bit as big a hypocrite as anyone on the Hill. You fit right in. Maybe that's why the governor of Texas appointed you to fill Lamar's seat when he died. And then you supposedly held President Martin's hand through the North Korean crisis. Which positioned you to leverage what you knew he wanted hushed up into the cabinet position you wanted.

"You blind, rigid son of a bitch, you are responsible because *I* hold you responsible! And I'm going to bring you down. Count on it. Now get back in your armored vehicle with your knuckle-dragging guards and get off my street and out of my neighborhood."

Gustafson darted up three stairs to her door, fumbled with her key, then was through, slamming it behind her.

One of the watchers spoke into her wrist, bringing the Suburban to the curb beside Morales, who gazed at the door for a long moment, then slid into the car.

I am *a hypocrite, but not for the reason she thinks. Only Ella and I know. But for how long? And what happens if it comes out?*

* * *

The Greenbrier, White Sulphur Springs, West Virginia

Julie Morales watched her husband wolf down the last of his room-service dinner as she toyed with hers. His words had tumbled out around bites, painting an ugly picture. The man she loved enough to give up a high-dollar, high-prestige consulting role at Booz Allen eighteen years ago could be bullheaded. She knew that for sure. But he rarely made a misstep that was outright stupid. Today he had. Should she wear her wife hat or her consultant hat now? She decided on consultant.

"Ray, you've told me what happened and why you behaved as you did. That's water under the bridge. Now tell me how you're going to repair the damage."

"Dammit, Julie, I'm not. If the president can find anyone to take this job, he's welcome to it! There's so much real work to be done, and none of it is on Capitol Hill. We've got to find a way to integrate and control these armed neighborhood-watch groups that are springing up and frequently shooting the wrong people. We've got to get a handle on roadside bombs. We've got, absolutely got, to protect our schools!"

Pointing at the coffee table across the room, Ray said, "How about that

Newsday cover, the one showing the bodies coming out of Red Rock High with 'Will your school be next?' splashed across it?"

Julie waited a beat and said, "Ray, letting the injustice of Gustafson's attacks get to you is only going to make her happier and you less able to do your duty. And as long as you hold the office, you owe that duty. If you're going to stay this pissed off, you should resign now."

As she knew it would, her reminder of his duty squelched her husband's high dudgeon.

A grimace. A sigh. "Shit! OK, back to earth. What should I do, counselor?"

"Reach back into your Catholic soul and perform an act of contrition. Only instead of a hundred Hail Marys, you apologize publicly to Gustafson. You announce that you've asked for an appointment to see her and apologize. You go to her office, accompanied by how-the-hell-ever-many media hyenas will wait to gnaw your carcass after she throws it out her door.

"You can cut the legs from this story. If you do a full mea culpa before she and the White House and the campaign force you into it inch by inch, this becomes a one-week story. If you don't, it will get you mauled for a month, left swinging in the wind, and finally you'll learn from the *Washington Post* that you've offered your resignation and the president has accepted. That's the way these things work and you know it."

"Yeah, that's pretty much what Bart said. And probably what Win Hernandez would have said if I'd taken his call. He's such a slimeball! Stands for nothing except saying the shrewd thing. I can't believe the president chose him over Bart to run the campaign."

"You just don't like political consultants, Ray. Actually it was a good move by an incumbent who's willing to admit to himself that governing will be a distant second to campaigning for a year. Plus, Bart knows how the president thinks—in fact I believe *he* does some of the president's best thinking—and has none of Martin's reluctance to act."

"He certainly has stood back from these terror attacks. Eric, Ed, Bart, and I are pretty much on our own. Defense, Justice, the undeclared acting president, and Homeland Security. I'm not complaining. We get more done, more rapidly this way, but it's sure not what the guys who wrote the Constitution had in mind."

"You don't know what they had in mind. This isn't constitutional law 101 and that doesn't matter a tenth as much as making the country safe again." Julie broke the tangent: "So, let's return to your situation, however unfair and unpleasant it may be. Are you going to go out there and let Gustafson step on your neck for the cameras so we can put this behind us?"

Ray grinned. This woman, who was the best thing that ever happened to him, had his back when he was right, but put it to him when he was wrong. In the fifteen years since he had put on his first star, very few others had done that.

"Yes, ma'am."

Ray stepped close and took her hands, looking her in the eyes.

"Thank you, Julie."

"It's just one of the many services I provide." She gave an exaggerated wink.

As they walked toward their suite's bedroom, Ray had to confront his betrayal.

Julie was gentle about his impotence; they'd had episodes since his early fifties; as always, she joked kindly about it, this time pointing out that a Marine general could make big bucks endorsing Viagra.

But today was different.

Chapter 30

Pakistan and Florida

IN DARKNESS AT THIRTY-TWO THOUSAND feet above Pakistan, the MC-130J Combat Talon aircraft rolled out of its final turn and leveled for the run-in. By great good fortune, the drop zone was beneath Air Traffic Service route Alfa four-six-six through Pakistani airspace, enabling the Special Operations–configured Hercules transport aircraft to masquerade as a civilian plane en route to India. A sixteen-man platoon and its commander from SEAL Team Three moved to the cargo ramp, now extended and sloping slightly downward into the roaring, freezing void. Although the aircraft had the traditional parachutists' signal light that changed from red to green to mark jump time at twenty-two hundred hours, each man heard and reacted to the SEAL jumpmaster's commands on the platoon tactical radio net: "Go!"

After shuffling to the end of the ramp, nine SEALs vanished into the night. The men had shuffled because, in addition to main and reserve chutes, oxygen, warm coveralls, weapons, ammunition, and helmets stuffed with communications and navigation modules, each had a sixty-to-seventy-pound jump bag containing his ground combat equipment and more ammunition. Five seconds later the second squad of eight entered the night sky. The aircraft was invisible and inaudible to those on the ground, and the SEALs' jump position was fifteen miles east of their landing site.

As he slowed and dropped below the aircraft, the mission commander, Lieutenant Mitch Trossen, stabilized himself, counted to ten, and—guiding on position lights—steered to a safe distance from others. He deployed his parachute and concentrated on inspecting the canopy and lines to determine that he had a safe, controllable chute. Satisfied, he scanned the blackness for his platoon.

Trossen counted eight green lights below and ahead of him and steered to follow the nearest. The lowest SEAL in the stack led the others by means of his GPS display, and they descended silently, gliding beneath their parachutes to cover the fifteen-mile offset from their landing zone. Craning his neck, Trossen looked above and behind for the lights of the second squad. His canopy obstructed his view, but he was able to count six lights following him down.

Feeling the high-altitude cold, Trossen thought about the mission as he guided on the closest green light. An awful lot depends on the guy we're picking up, whether he comes in clean or not. If he's attracted surveillance, we'll be in the shit for sure. If we have to be extracted hot, there's a damn good chance the Pak air force will nail us before we get to Afghanistan. Well, the hard stuff is what we do; if this were easy, they'd have sent Delta. He grinned beneath his face mask.

Forty-three minutes later, with all accounted for, both squads moved out from the landing zone, which was two miles from where they were to meet their quarry in four hours' time. At a word from Trossen, the commo SEAL reported to the Tactical Operations Center at Bagram Air Base in Afghanistan that they were moving toward the objective. Over a landscape lit only by the sliver of a setting moon, the team moved quietly across the high valley, seeing through their night-vision goggles the broken ground before them and rugged ridges to their left and right.

A half mile from the objective area, the men halted. Trossen moved swiftly from man to man, looking at each with the unspoken question: are you ready? After receiving a thumbs-up from each, Trossen extended his right arm vertically and pumped it twice. Trotting quietly, the SEALs took up their positions.

Three and a half hours later and ten thousand miles away, Ray Morales—feeling pleasantly like his former self, General Ray Morales, USMC—sat to the right of General "Rifle" Remington, who led the U.S. Central Command and was responsible for operations in Pakistan and several other hotspots.

The two men were in the front row of Remington's briefing theater at MacDill Air Force Base, where an army major was speaking to the small group assembled to observe an operation that was about to reach its climax.

"General Remington, Mr. Secretary, as Operation Persistent Justice is conducted, the Blue Force Tracker system will display the positions of the Special Operations team and all support resources, such as aircraft, on the screen. These will be in real time and will be displayed on this map of the op area. In the pop-up to your left"—he pressed a hand controller and it appeared—"you will receive periodic summary information from the TOC at Bagram. The 'crawl' at the bottom of the screen"—he pressed again and the words Persistent Justice began moving right to left—"will provide any national level intelligence indicators, such as NSA intercepts, that may have a bearing on the operation. The screen on the far left is video from the Reaper that's been on station for ten hours. Do you have any questions, sirs?"

"None, as long as you hang around to push buttons for us when we need it," said General Remington.

"Oh, yes, sir. And as you can see, you have a sivitz open with all command reps and with General Polk in Kabul."

And so it begins, thought Morales. Just like I told Singh, this was a really hard sell. And Singh was ever so right not to rely solely on a years-old pledge to protect him and his family. As it went down, honoring that commitment counted far less than the dossier Singh claims to be bringing. Damn! I hope he's not stringing me along.

"The operators have been set up for several hours now," said the major. "They've verified the area is clean, set over-watch on the road from the town of Sadda, and established a defensive ambush. The asset and his family are to drive from Sadda to this point on the road, exit the car, and walk eastward, led by the asset."

Realizing his fists were clenched, Morales deliberately relaxed them and steepled his fingers on the polished table. *Suppose he's not there? Suppose it's a trap?* Ray felt a sudden stab in his stomach. He didn't actually have an ulcer, but whenever he was helplessly awaiting the outcome of something crucial, his tension always went straight to that spot and lodged there like a dull knife blade.

"Major, why don't you tell us what we're seeing, give Secretary Morales a commentary as we go so he understands the full picture."

Morales bridled at the jibe but wasn't surprised. He and Remington had never gotten along.

"Yes, sir. If you notice off to your left, across the border over into Afghanistan, are four aircraft. And this square"—he used a light pen to point to the object—"is the objective area."

"Major, what's the mission of the four aircraft orbiting there, in eastern Afghanistan?" said Morales.

"Sir, two are F/A-18s for CAP if the Pak air force launches interceptors; two are MH-60s: one for the exfiltration, the other with backup operators. The exfil bird will commence for the pickup area so as to arrive at zero four hundred hours."

As zero two thirty approached, Lieutenant Trossen and tense observers in Afghanistan, Washington DC, Nevada, and Florida saw an automobile appear on the UAV video feed. Soon it crested a rise and came into their sight. Moments later it turned off its headlights and continued at a crawl along the faintly moonlit road, closely and invisibly observed by SEALs.

The vehicle halted, and four people emerged; each was immediately centered in a shooter's sights. As they walked single file away from the road, they entered the kill zone of the SEAL ambush. Trossen waited as SEALs scanned each through infrared optics, looking for telltale silhouettes against the heat of their bodies that would reveal wires or explosive vests. Voices spoke softly in Trossen's earpiece.

"Eagle one. Mine's clean."

"Eagle two. Clean."

"Eagle three. Clean."

"Eagle four. Clean."

"Take them," said Trossen.

Six SEALs materialized from the darkness, swiftly taking control of the four, forcing each to kneel and zip-tying their wrists. A child's wail was cut off by a firm command in Punjabi.

Petty Officer First Class Keaholu captured Singh, who wore the field uniform of the Pakistan Army with the insignia of a regimental sergeant major. After Singh answered the whispered password correctly, Keaholu said, "asset secured," on the tactical net, and Trossen trotted over. As he moved, he heard on the platoon tactical radio net that their video downlink from the Reaper had been lost.

"Nice of you to drop in," said Singh. "There's a flash drive in my left breast pocket for my friend General Morales."

"I'll deliver it," said Trossen, who took it and made a circling motion over his head. Over the platoon radio, Trossen said, "Coors." Immediately the commo SEAL transmitted, "Shadowdancer, this is Sunrise. I pass Coors," to the TOC in Kabul.

At MacDill, the pop-up opened. "Singh and family secured. Package received." Tension in the room dropped a notch but only briefly, because the crawl announced "Pak radio chatter re: aircraft orbiting over Afghanistan."

General Remington thumbed the button on his sivitz microphone and said, "NSA—got any more on that?"

A balding man in a brown suit and repp tie appeared in a window that opened within the main videoconference screen. "Sir, we've heard Northern Air Command discussing four unidentified aircraft with Pakistan Air Defense Command. They say the aircraft are just across the Afghan border. They're intermittent contacts, but they've persisted long enough that the Paks are beginning to believe they're valid and wonder what they might be up to. Northern command speculates that at least one is a helo."

"OK, NSA," said General Remington.

Morales looked at Remington, who shrugged and said, "Now the cheese gets binding."

Chapter 31

Pakistan and Florida

"VEHICLE INBOUND," THE SEAL OVER-WATCHING the road from Sadda announced on the platoon tactical net. "It's about two klicks out, moving slowly."

The SEALs of first squad returned to their ambush site and eased into firing positions. "Nothing unless they make us," said Trossen over the tactical net.

The crest of the hill glowed, and then the bright dots of headlights appeared, their beams sweeping downward after the vehicle crested and puttered down the sloping road. Moments after the beams revealed the auto abandoned by the Singhs, the second vehicle, a pickup, halted.

The truck's driver emerged and hurried to the car. Through night-vision goggles the SEALs could see that the driver's two companions were armed and covering his advance. Shooters peered at each of the three through night optics, putting each man a trigger pull from death.

The driver looked into the car, leaving its front and rear doors on the driver's side open. He opened the trunk, peered in, and then waved his companions forward. As they walked, they chattered, their words audible but incomprehensible to the SEALs.

Trossen leaned toward Regimental Sergeant Major Singh, who whispered, "I left the keys in our car. They want to take it but are afraid it's booby-trapped."

After much shouting and arm waving, two of the three men returned to the truck and backed it up until it was hidden by the hill's crest. The third, who had remained by Singh's car, opened the hood and leaned in.

"If it was booby-trapped, he'd be dead," whispered Singh. "What an idiot!" Trossen nodded but held a finger to his lips, and Singh subsided.

Silence also reigned in the briefing theater at MacDill, where video from the MQ-9 Reaper filled the screen uninterruptedly. On it Morales saw the man close the car's hood, then seat himself at the wheel. Moments later, the car's headlights came on. The pickup emerged from the reverse slope of the hill, drew alongside the car, and halted. There appeared to be a discussion across the gap between the vehicles. The passenger-side pickup door swung, and a man got out and began to walk away from the truck. Morales estimated from a Blue Force Tracker symbol that a SEAL was in the man's path. This is going south in a hurry, he thought.

Abruptly, the man halted.

Trossen and Singh saw a man emerge from the pickup but lost sight of him as he walked away, their vision blocked by the truck. Trossen didn't know the exact locations of the men in first platoon, but he realized the man might stumble across one. In that event the wanderer would die before he could raise an alarm, but Trossen knew his disappearance would soon spook the other two.

Trossen made his decision: if they were discovered, he would send the squad around him to take the Singhs to the landing site, while the second squad dealt with the three locals. He considered remaining with that squad but dismissed the thought—they didn't need him to handle those guys, and the mission was getting Singh out. He'd stick with Singh.

When the man reappeared, unaware that relieving his bladder had been a near-death experience, Trossen relaxed slightly but remained focused on the two vehicles like a pointer on quail. He heard the truck's door slam and watched it pull ahead of the car and head down the road, followed closely by the car.

Minutes later the crawl across the screen in Florida announced, "Pak air defense control elevated readiness." The man at NSA popped up again.

"General Remington, the two Mirage fighters on alert at Peshawar have been moved from thirty minutes to fifteen minutes."

General Remington said, "Buster, what do you think?" to General Polk in Kabul.

"It's time to get out of Dodge," said Polk. "They've got the people and the package in hand. I'm sending in the extraction bird now."

The commo SEAL spoke to Trossen: "Boss, you're wanted on C2."

Trossen pushed a button clipped to his web gear and said, "Sunrise-six is on," and heard: "Sunrise, this is Shadowdancer. Due to possible air activity we're going to extract early. Blackbird is on the way. Is your present location green?"

Trossen considered a moment, then said, "That's negative, Shadowdancer. Those guys in the truck are probably close enough to hear Blackbird and come back. My link is still down, so I have no eyes on them."

"Sunrise-six, we have eyes on them. If they turn back, we'll discourage them with the Reaper. If you're secure there now, we're good to go."

"Nobody here but us, Shadowdancer."

"Roger that. Blackbird will be there in two five. Shadowdancer, out."

Trossen keyed the platoon net. "Eagles, change of plan. Kabul is worried about the air situation. We'll extract here. Set up now."

As the platoon took up positions, Trossen turned to Singh, who said, "I heard you. We'll wait here for the bird; I'm glad my children won't have to make that hike. Can you free our hands now?"

Twenty-eight minutes later an MH-60M helicopter, flat black and without lights, touched down, its rotor wash throwing dust and debris. The SEALs hustled their charges aboard. Trossen counted his men, took a final look around the area, and climbed in. The MH-60M lifted and vanished into the blackness.

Three hours later an armed courier took off from Bagram Air Base with a dispatch case chained to his waist.

Chapter 32

The Pentagon

"Mr Secretary, the courier is here."

A ruggedly built man with anger behind basset-hound eyes in a pockmarked face looked up. He finished a marginal note with print as precise as a draftsman's, closed a folder, and gestured to his personal secretary in the door of the E-ring office.

"Tell Carpenter."

SECDEF grinned at the man who appeared next.

"Come on in. You've had a quick trip."

A stocky man in cammies with a Beretta on his thigh moved across the cavernous room to the stand-up desk occupied by Eric Easterly, whose face bore vitiligo's inexorable spots like cream in coffee. As he approached, Easterly saw the SEAL trident on his left breast, discreetly black on this uniform, and black collar devices denoting a chief petty officer.

The SEALS never change, he thought, never miss an opportunity to kiss the pope's ring. The SEAL commander in Kabul knew enough about what the team was bringing out to bet it would be couriered to me and made sure a SEAL was ready to go. It's boom time now for the teams, all the goodies and down-range time you could want. But their leaders know it won't last; the wheel will turn, and they'll be scuffling for nickels like it was when I wore the trident. Staying visible to the powerful is how they survive lean years.

The chief saluted and began unlocking the security chain from a brown dispatch case. In a moment he handed the case to Easterly.

"Which team, Chief?"

"Three, sir."

"Who's your skipper?"

"Liam Reddy, sir"

"My God, I *am* old. I served with his father in Team Two. You remind him that he's got a lot to live up to, OK?" The chief nodded vigorously, and Easterly waved him toward the door: "Now off with you to my mess, and tell 'em I said give you the coldest beer and the biggest steak in Washington."

"Hooya, sir!" Grinning, the chief vanished.

Easterly looked over the shoulder of Rear Admiral Carpenter, head of the Defense Intelligence Agency, who was scrolling through the thumb drive he had inserted in a sanitized laptop with a clean hard drive. "So what do you make of this package?"

"Well, sir, it's a start. We had nothing before; now we have a photo, a DNA sample—can't be sure either's genuine—a three-page document in Farsi—"

"That's a piss-poor picture we got from Morales's Pak buddy!" interrupted Easterly. "Our guy, this Fahim al-Wasari, is turned away from the camera. We've only got a left profile and a bit more to go on."

"That's right, sir, but we can still do quite a lot with it. I'm no expert, but I think our analysts have enough to construct a pretty accurate face-on look at him."

"Have your guys do a quick and dirty—two hours—then be back here with a translator and a biometric analyst. Keep this in-house. Nothing yet to CIA or His Highness, the DNI! *We're* taking this to the White House."

Three hours later Easterly and Carpenter were sitting in the Situation Room with Bart Guarini, Brian Leek, and Ray Morales. Admiral Carpenter was walking them through the material turned over by Singh.

"Since we have no chain of custody on the DNA sample, we can't rely on it. We've now got a photo of this guy—not great but good enough to ID him as the guy on the ARGUS video—and this document in Farsi is purportedly a Quds Force dossier on al-Wasari. If true, it tells us a lot about the man, including that he's the one who ran Six-thirteen. But—"

"I gotta say, Ray, this Sergeant Major Singh did a bait and switch on us," said Easterly. "If I'd known his file on this guy al-Wasari was as thin as it is, I'd have thought a lot harder about risking a team and the mother of all diplomatic incidents to extract him and his family."

Morales tried to stifle his irritation at Easterly. It wasn't the message—which made sense—but the messenger. Although the two shared the bond of military service, they had become rivals in the Washington power game. Morales was frustrated because Brian Leek's FBI had the lead on domestic counterterror ops and yet wasn't under his direction. Easterly was at a further remove from domestic action and even more frustrated. He seemed always ready to take a shot at Morales or Leek. Morales shot back: "He's the man who gave us bin Laden's location. How could you of all people discount that! We owe him."

"And we paid him," said Easterly, slapping the tabletop. "Singh got the twenty-five mil reward for fingering bin Laden, paid to his Swiss account."

"And the dossier that Singh brought out tells us this is the guy who led Six-thirteen. We've never had that before."

"That's *if* the dossier is genuine and *if* the Iranian information is correct. It could be disinformation."

"What would you have done in his place, Eric? The same damn thing, I'll bet!"

"What I would have done doesn't matter. What matters is he played you and you played us."

"Stop wasting my time, you two!" said Guarini, who spoke for the president and they all knew it. "So what have we got here?"

"If I may?" said Rear Admiral Carpenter. At Guarani's nod, the analyst flashed a slide on the screen above the far end of the table at which they sat. Carpenter gave a short tutorial on biometric identification—ostentatiously, Morales thought—then said, "We've got at least three points of reference in this picture, and one of them is quite clear: his ear. That matches the ARGUS video. We can do a thorough database search."

"We don't need a database search," said Morales. "We need something we can feed to ARGUS and other security scans so if he's caught by a camera anywhere in North America, we identify him immediately. We need a photo or drawing of his appearance that we can give to every FBI agent, every street cop. We want anybody who looks even a little like al-Wasari pulled in for questioning. This is the guy who did Las Vegas and has been thumbing his nose at us for nearly three years. We need to do everything we can to bag him."

"Maybe not."

The four stared at Brian Leek.

"Make that kind of a fuss, and he'll know it real quick and go to ground. Right now he's probably careful about his tradecraft, but as a matter of routine. He doesn't have any reason to think we have a clue who he is and what he looks like. Put his picture on FBI dot gov, put him on our Ten Most Wanted List, and he'll become hyper-cautious.

"The dossier Singh handed us has more than an imperfect photo," continued Leek. "It tells us this guy's a huge ego. That he's a braggart. Right now he knows he's kicking our ass and we don't have a lead. A big ego who feels on top of his game is prone to mistakes. Let's give him the chance to make it his last."

"Yeah, but remember our job is to stop the attacks," said Morales. "If we spook al-Wasari and he goes to ground, he won't be able to be active in directing these attacks. If the attacks drop off, we've saved lives, even if he is still on the loose."

"Look, why not do this," said Guarini, "Have his photo cranked into the ARGUS system. Do a look-back and see if he's been caught by the system, but not flagged as a person of interest. That may tell us quite a bit."

Guarini looked at Carpenter. "How many priority one triple-A individuals in ARGUS?"

"Ten, sir."

"OK, if we put him at that level, we cause the stir we want to avoid. How about priority one double A?"

"A hundred or so."

"And, Admiral, what effect does that difference between double A and triple A make?"

"Some but not a great deal. It might delay us a few hours in reacting to a security cam hit."

"Which means we forfeit the chance to grab him on the spot, or to evacuate the area in case he's planting a bomb," said Morales. "I'd call that a big difference."

Guarini spoke, in a tone signifying that 'the president and I have decided': "We keep this quiet for now. Put him in ARGUS as double A. Bring it back to me if necessary."

Guarini was pushing his chair back from the table when Brian Leek caught his eye. He motioned Leek to walk with him.

"So there's a big question about the dossier we didn't talk about: Do we believe al-Wasari is the guy who did Las Vegas?"

Guarini shrugged. "You're the FBI, Brian, you tell me."

"Everything in the dossier is circumstantial. If this guy was Mafia and I was trying to prove he did a hit, this wouldn't do it for me in federal court."

"Well, then, get busy and use what we do have to develop leads, build a case, all the stuff you guys do."

"Bart, you need to give this some thought and probably your boss does too. Right now Las Vegas is history, all neatly tied up and filed. A terrorist used a North Korean nuke to blow it up. Despite Kim's protestations of innocence, we nuked Sinpo in retaliation. And his leading general, told by the Chinese he could have the job if he gave up nukes, assassinated Kim and took over his palaces, women, and Swiss accounts. Neat, symmetrical, and *done.*"

Leek stopped, halting them both.

He continued: "If we put al-Wasari on trial in a U.S. court, it's open again. We don't know where his testimony would lead."

Leek put his hand on Guarani's elbow.

"Do we want that? When we locate this guy—and we will—I'm going to need some very specific presidential instructions. I suggest you think about them now."

Chapter 33

Washington, DC

THE PRESIDENT, FLANKED BY BART Guarini, said, "Bruce, I'm concerned that you're getting too far right of me. Extraordinary times do call for extraordinary measures—sometimes—but using drone strikes in the U.S., possibly killing our own citizens, is too much for the party and the public to swallow. We've already reinstituted nationwide stop-and-search ops by the army, Operation Sudden Touch, and that's not going down well among some important groups of voters. They didn't like it during the North Korean crisis, either—thank God that wasn't an election year! Turning Predators loose on folks who may only be stopped to change a tire is just too much. And I find it morally repellant besides."

"Yes, Mr. President, I have no doubt that you do," replied the vice president in an even tone. "We don't entirely share the same values, you and I. I think that the greater good—and the oath of office we each took—demands that we be willing to accept, and even cause, collateral damage in order to save the republic. After all, that's what Lincoln, Wilson, and FDR did, and history hasn't treated them so badly!"

A reddish flush spreading up his neck, Martin slapped his palm on the desk and said, "Collateral damage. What a sterile term for blowing apart the wrong people! For leaving a trail of orphans and widows across this country. I can't take that lightly, Bruce, even though you seem to."

Although they remained in his lap, Griffith's hands became fists. He locked eyes with Martin. "Mr. President, please! There's already a trail of widows and orphans, as you put it. It's a trail left by al Qaida or whoever is masterminding this barrage of terrorist attacks from coast to coast. The most basic duty of a government is to protect its citizens. We're failing in that duty now, and Walter Rutherford is pounding away on us.

"Look, Mr. President, I know that Win is telling you to dump me, and I'm pretty sure all that's keeping you from nodding your head in assent is a concern that I'd challenge you at the convention, or maybe even go third party and screw your chances the way Perot screwed Bush. And I might.

"But the best thing for you, for me, and for the country is that we stay on the ticket together. What I say and do gives you cover on the right. And remaining on the ticket and getting a second term is my best chance to become president. I want that. I want it a lot. Enough to bite my tongue when that's best for the ticket. Enough to be the campaign's frequently scolded attack dog. Enough to publicly support half measures even though I feel we need a full-court press. What do you say, Mr. President?"

Displaying his uncanny sense of what Rick Martin wanted, Bart Guarini replied for him.

"Mr. Vice President, I fear you're jumping to conclusions when you say that Win is advising the president to drop you. But I can tell you that several of the campaign's biggest contributors are urging me and urging Win to convince him to change the ticket. We can't just ignore them."

"Bart, excuse me, but I want to hear from the president."

Guarini scowled.

"Bruce," said Martin, "your views are a problem, even if you don't express them publicly. They're well known, so just having you on the ticket is concerning to some campaign contributors. And I haven't forgotten your attempt to undermine me during the Korean crisis. You try that again and you *will* be out!"

Griffith's eyes flashed. "Mr. President, then and now I am not disloyal, nor will I ever be! But you've surrounded yourself with people who think like you do."

"Ray Morales thinks like I do?"

"Well, no, but he's the only one besides me on the Homeland Security Council who accepts that you can't make an omelet without breaking eggs. But even he, Mr. President, doesn't challenge your thinking like I do. He's still got that military obedience thing of yessir, yessir, three bags full."

"You're wrong about that, Bruce."

The president rose, forcing Griffith and Guarini to do the same. He moved briskly to Griffith's side.

"Bruce, look: I do actually value your opinion. And I never would have gotten the country through the Korean thing if I hadn't had a capable vice president; what you did overseeing relief and internal security was invaluable to the country and to me. I owe you for that.

"Plus, I agree with you that it would be bad for the country right now if we dropped you and caused an already bitterly contested election to become a three-way contest. Whoever wins this election—and it's going to be me—needs to have a clear mandate in order to lead us through this even worse crisis. So you're staying on the ticket unless you do something that leaves me no choice."

Martin extended his hand to the vice president.

"Deal?"

"Deal, Mr. President."

As he left the oval office, Bart wondered if Martin's distaste for personal confrontation and his instinctive resistance to closure were his Achilles' heel.

* * *

Thurmont, Maryland

He didn't really know why he had taken the picture. The act was, like many things that caused problems in his life, impulsive. There was something about the way they were standing, he thought. And I just had the idea to shoot with my phone. I hope nobody saw me.

Couple of years ago when I answered the ad in the Thurmont paper, I was really excited that the job was to fill in on short notice at Camp David. All those forms. The polygraph test. Then the interview with Secret Service. And I actually got the job! Nothing special like that had ever happened to me before. Then after that, nothing. Oh, I got called in a couple of times, but not like I had hoped. Just like always.

Well, maybe yesterday was the payoff. The regular maintenance guys come from Washington. One called in sick and I got to replace him.

Jimmy Roper pulled into the lot of Fitzgerald's Shamrock, a one-story cream-colored building with green trim. There were only three other cars. He slouched into the Blarney Lounge, waving to the barkeep, who slid a mug of Harp his way. Jimmy sat on a green-cushioned bar chair, his face a pale green in the shamrock-colored lighting. He glanced at Twitter:

> Law enforcement facing hard choices confronting explosion of illegal arms sales and widespread unlicensed carry.

Well, what did they expect? he thought. He pushed his phone back and forth across the bar top, fingers flicking while his mind churned.

OK, Jimmy me boy, now what? You're stuck in shit jobs in this crap town. Janitor at Catoctin High. Clerking at Sheetz. Whatever else can you do to earn a few bucks? Walmart would be a step up for you.

He heard footsteps and halfway turned. Randy Barnes came in with Sabrina hanging all over him. Randy was set: a U.S. Postal Service job. He winked at Jimmy, and the wink said, "and I'm sleeping with her tonight. Eat your heart out."

Jimmy picked up his phone—another piece of junk he had to make do with—and punched up the picture. It wasn't sharp—the light was low—but anyone would be able to recognize Ella Martin. He didn't know the big guy who was leaning toward her, his nose almost brushing her hair, but it wasn't the president. They were outdoors in the darkest area of Camp David. He had watched them lean together, separate, speak briefly, and then walk side by side toward Aspen cabin, the one the president used.

As he thought over what he had seen, Jimmy realized that when they headed back toward Aspen, their bodies moved differently, especially the guy's. They seemed less relaxed. Maybe it was an argument he had seen. Or . . . maybe she had told him to back off. Maybe he had tried to get something going with her, and she said no . . . or maybe it was "no, not out here."

His mind drifted to the Orioles game, and he glanced at the television above the bar. A woman was being interviewed, speaking soundlessly but showing her anger. He glanced at his watch; sports usually came about now, in the middle of the broadcast. He kept watching, waiting for the ball score. The woman vanished, but she was replaced by a man sitting at a table with microphones and a sign "The Honorable Ray Morales, Secretary of Homeland Security."

That's the guy in my picture! Now Jimmy paid attention to the closed captioning. He learned in the thirty seconds before the sports report that this woman was a senator and that she was really pissed at Morales for something he had said to her in some hearing in DC several days ago.

The Orioles had beaten the Rays, two to zip, but Jimmy didn't linger over that thought as he usually would.

This might be something I can work with.

Chapter 34

Pusan, Republic of Korea

DEEP IN THE GIGANTIC HULL, Chung Ma-ho wormed his way through another lightening hole, an oval cutout in one of the massive steel hull ribs. The hull of this containership was just under one thousand feet long. With the engine room near the stern, over eight hundred feet of cable, each thicker than Chung's wrist, had to be run forward to power the ship's bow thrusters. Hauling cables through the hull was a grueling, claustrophobic, smelly job given to laborers like Chung, whose small size made him especially well-suited for this work.

The blare of a klaxon signaled an early end to the shift. Chung began to work his way into the huge, open hull area where tracks to lock containers in place would later be installed. His palms were sweating.

Just act normal, he thought. Everything they told you to do has worked so far. This will work, too.

Cautiously, Chung climbed eighty feet up the temporary ladder to the vessel's deck. Soon he was one of a throng heading for the cafeteria.

OK, this is a good time.

Chung halted abruptly, earning a curse from the man behind, who caromed off his shoulder and swept by on his way to a special meal. Chung turned around and, dodging hungry workers, headed back to the ship.

"Chung, what are you doing?" said a supervisor who passed near enough to read the name-tape on his coveralls.

"I forgot my tool bag."

"Well, next time don't be careless, Chung. Maybe missing this meal will teach you to pay attention."

Chung dawdled slightly, and soon the wave of workers had swept past. He sidled over to a shoulder-high stack of steel plating, each sheet about ten by twenty feet.

There, right where it's supposed to be.

Fumbling slightly because of the straps on his safety harness, Chung secreted two flexible tubes, each about two feet long, by means of Velcro fasteners inside his coveralls.

This feels a little awkward as I walk. There're bulges if you look, but it should be OK.

Chung started down the ladder toward his objective deep in the hull. He saw a figure below in a light blue jumpsuit worn by Maersk line employees monitoring construction.

We're going to pass each other! What if he's suspicious?

Sweat beaded Chung's forehead as he moved steadily downward while the Maersk employee climbed toward him. Reaching the single remaining platform between them, Chung halted and stepped clear of the ladder, forcing a pleasant expression. The blue-clad man chugged past him with a smile and a clap on the shoulder. Chung controlled the panic he felt when one of his hidden burdens slipped slightly. He slid his right hand into a pocket and steadied the tube.

Drawing a shaky breath, Chung continued down. Nearing the place he had been working, Chung stopped. He turned his head left, right, up, down. He was alone.

Removing the tubes of Semtex from his coveralls, Chung stripped the protective covering from adhesive strips and fastened the tubes to the hull, hidden beneath the web of a girder. He set the timers, primary and backup, and got to his feet.

Good. It's invisible unless you're on your belly.

Soon, security men and bomb dogs will sweep the hull, but the smells from welding and paint and piss from workers too lazy to climb out will negate the dogs. Just as they told me, this project is behind, and we have worked up until two hours before he arrives. Security men won't have time for a complete search, especially down here, where the man will never set foot.

* * *

The first explosion, deep in the hull, wasn't as loud as Chung expected, but it was enough to alarm the crowd in the cafeteria listening to President Gwon speak. Chung waited, crouching behind a stack of wooden pallets near the shipyard entrance, for the sound that would call him to action. When he heard the second explosion, the one that turned President Gwon's retreating car into a twisted, burning nightmare, Chung scrambled from his hideout.

It worked—just as the yakuza told me. The explosion from my bomb drew attention to the hull under construction and caused the security service to pull their president back to his car and rush him away from this place. Straight into the bomb planted just outside the shipyard gate.

Chung jogged toward the gate, taking care to follow a path visible to security cameras. In his haste he seemed to trip, going to his right knee and rolling onto his back. Feigning disorientation, Chung gave the cameras a clear view of his face. As he scuffled to his feet, he dropped a cell phone. Regaining his bearings, he loped out the gate, turning away from the smoking wreck of Gwon's limousine.

* * *

Qom, Islamic Republic of Iran

Adel Ghorbani strolled beside the older man, hiding his impatience. The Supreme Leader could not be hurried.

"So, Adel, what brings you to visit me this beautiful day?"

"It's time for a move against Fahim al-Wasari."

The Supreme Leader's eyebrows shot up, so Adel followed promptly with a reason: "We believe he has an operation under way to seize an American ship and use it to destroy a major U.S. port."

"Destroy? How?"

"Not with a nuclear bomb. Not after the U.S. nuclear destruction of Sinpo in retaliation for Kim's part in the Las Vegas bombing. No nuclear weapon state, not even Pakistan, will have anything to do now with anyone seeking a bomb. They guard each of their own nukes zealously. The old USSR bombs sold by Russian arms merchants have been recovered or destroyed. It's no longer possible to buy or steal a nuclear bomb."

Ghorbani paused, hoping the Supreme Leader wouldn't argue this point. To Ghorbani's relief, the Supreme Leader resumed the narrative: "So he packs the ship with explosives, enters a harbor like New York's, and blows it up?"

"That's possible, Leader, although to create a really huge explosion is technically challenging. There is a better option for him."

The Supreme Leader was silent, so Ghorbani continued: "Al Wasari has a giant ego. We think he will try something that has never been done before and would probably produce greater panic than any other."

A turn of the turbaned head told Ghorbani he now had the Leader's full attention.

"Leader, after what the Americans call the shale revolution, they have quickly become the world's largest exporter of liquid natural gas, called LNG. Huge ships purpose-built to carry it are constantly moving through American coastal waters, en route to and from the export terminals. The terminals are considered hazardous, and there are only a handful of them. It is probable that al-Wasari intends to seize a ship and explode its cargo while the ship is moored at a terminal.

"Such an attack would have great value," continued Ghorbani. "It would be visually spectacular, as spectacular as the towers' collapse, and beyond that it would halt the entire American LNG export trade. Martin would have no choice but to cease operations at every LNG terminal. That would not only deal a blow to the U.S. economy; the loss of supply would seriously hurt the Europeans."

"And coming during the campaign," added the Supreme Ayatollah, "it would surely hurt Martin's chances for reelection."

"Indeed it would, Leader. I see you understand why it is believed al-Wasari will do this."

"I understand that this is *your* hypothesis. What evidence do you offer me?"

"We've heard that Latin American drug cartels are smuggling Somalis into the U.S., and one of the most successful pirate bands has entirely disappeared. The so-called pirate coast of Somalia is full of rumors that they were offered a huge payday for taking on a job far away."

"That's it? The only piece of evidence you present me is the disappearance of a Somali pirate band. All else may be just the wind whispering. I expect that you came here with a proposal as well as this story?"

"Leader, we should insert Quds Force groups into the Great Satan, positioning them near LNG terminals. As we continue to gather information, we may be able to identify al-Wasari's target and disrupt his plan. Because we don't know his timing, we must put the teams in now."

They continued walking, in silence. As they strolled, Ghorbani noticed that his palms were damp. And no wonder, he thought. If this doesn't go right, it will be on my head. He didn't dare weave his web of rumor and deduction farther today, even though he secretly believed that he knew Fahim's target: the one LNG terminal located alongside a nuclear power plant.

The Leader spoke: "I will think on this. You will have my answer soon."

Chapter 35

Tampa, Florida

RICK MARTIN WORKED THE ROPE line, smiling, pointing, shaking hands, signing.

Not like it used to be, he thought. I'm wearing body armor; all of these folks have security clearances. Last time around, the rope line was spontaneous, fun, a break from the choreographed campaign rituals.

Not any more.

Wilson, at his elbow, leaned in.

"Mr. President, you have an urgent call from Mr. Dorn."

Martin, far more sure of himself than he had been on that fateful June thirteenth, nodded and shook a few more hands before leaving, waving to the crowd and shouting his appreciation.

* * *

Seated in an armored chair in an armored helicopter, Martin picked up the handset, feeling the bird lift as he did so. Making eye contact across the cabin with Win Hernandez, he spoke: "Hello, John. What's up?"

"Mr. President, the president of South Korea has been assassinated."

Hernandez saw Martin's quizzical expression harden.

"The North?"

"We don't know, but the DPRK has to be the first suspect for South Koreans."

"What's going on militarily?"

"Our commander in Korea, General Tedford, has put his forces on high alert, recalled everyone to their bases, and requested that the transportation command prepare to start flowing forces assigned by the contingency operations plan. We have no major units other than Tedford's in the Korean AOR, but the pacific commander, Admiral Swafford, has put air and ground units on Guam on twenty-four-hour standby, ready to move to South Korea. She's ordered the USS Reagan carrier battle group to leave Hong Kong immediately and position itself within strike range of the DMZ."

"I won't remember half of that, but I gather the appropriate military wheels are in motion." Martin added, "Where's Eric?"

"Secretary Easterly is over the Atlantic, returning from the NATO defense ministers conference."

"And Mac?"

"Actually, sir, he's in Beijing—the military staff talks."

"I like that. I'm sure interested in China's military posture—how they may respond when we trigger reinforcement of our guys in Korea. What's the likely ROK reaction?"

"I'd prefer not to speak for Secretary Battista, sir."

"What—you two feuding again? I'll talk with Anne before I decide anything, but right now my head is stuffed with names of mayors and precinct chairmen here in Florida. I need a general grounding. Speak to me."

"President Gwon's limo was blown up as he left a shipyard near Pusan," replied Dorn. "He was pulled out alive but died en route to a hospital. They haven't announced it yet, but my counterpart told our ambassador that Gwon's dead. They're probably waiting until they've got Prime Minister Kang to the Blue House, or more likely the command bunker, before announcing."

"How do you think they'll play it?" said the president. "And what do we know about Gwon's successor—what's his name again?"

"Kang Nam-gi, sir. I don't know much. Our book says he's a former air force general. I don't know if he was forced on Gwon by their military or if Gwon wanted him to help *control* the military."

"So now we've got a former fighter jock running South Korea on the edge of a shooting war. That's not encouraging. When can you gin up an NSC, John?"

"Shooting for thirty minutes, Mr. President, but that may be without General MacAdoo. He's got to get all the way across Beijing to a secure site at our embassy."

Martin heard the chopper's rotor sound change and felt it descending to the airport ramp near Air Force One. "That it for now, John?" he said.

"One more matter, sir. We probably should think about Pandora."

"What's that, John?

"I'll refresh your memory on it later, Mr. President. I know you need to move on."

Martin put down the handset and looked at his campaign manager. "You got the gist of that, Win?"

"Somebody killed President Gwon, and the North Koreans are the first suspects. This could ratchet up real quick to a North-South military confrontation, with our troops in it."

"What about campaigning?"

"To be just as cynical as I'm expected to be, this could give us a boost. There's now a part that only the president of the United States can play."

"Should we play it that way?"

"Depends. For now I'll cancel the rest of today so you can attend to this shocking, potentially catastrophic, international crisis."

"You're probably going to have to cancel my campaign schedule for more than just today, Win. I really need to dive into this one. It could turn into war, maybe nuclear war, if some hothead misjudges the situation. Better crank up the surrogates because I've got a hunch I'm going to be doing some international traveling."

A smile on the president's face told Hernandez how he felt about that. The campaign manager frowned, nodded, and followed Martin from the helo to begin the thankless job of turning Martin's campaign on a dime.

I want to speak to Ming, thought Martin, now aboard the presidential Boeing 747. It's the middle of the night there, but I'm pretty sure that China's president has gotten a wake-up call about this. Anne and John would both say it's too soon, but we can't contain this thing alone. The sooner I get some idea of his reaction, the better. Just the fact that he takes—or doesn't take—my call will tell me something.

Damn! I'm glad to be doing my real job again, not kissing babies.

"Set up a call to President Ming."

Martin took a deep breath and put on a headset through which he would hear a simultaneous translation of the words of China's president, Ming Liu.

We managed to get on the same page about Kim and his nukes three years ago. I think we came out of that with mutual respect. Here's hoping . . .

* * *

Beijing, People's Republic of China

Ming Liu, president of the People's Republic of China, lit a cigarette.

Korea again! he thought. Back when it was merely rhetoric to do so, the Americans called the DMZ "the most dangerous spot on earth." Now that may be exactly what it is. Martin's under enormous pressure because of the terrorist campaign in America. And, he's running for reelection against an opponent who shouts that the answers to America's distress lie in being tougher. If this turns out to have been done by Young San-ho—and it just might—we could have war.

And Martin, for all his insistence that "standing tall" is not the only way to protect America, nonetheless repaid Kim's role in the destruction of Las Vegas by detonating three nuclear missiles in the North Korean city of Sinpo, forcing me to arrange Kim's removal.

Did we truly find all Kim's nuclear bombs? I really had no choice but to take Young's word because at the time the only way to save North Korea was to declare that we had removed them, as well as the engineers and equipment that made them.

But if the North is implicated in this assassination and still has a nuke or two . . .

I'd better speak with Young. He will of course lie to me, as Kim did before him, but I want him to hear directly from me that, at least for now, China does not want war in Korea.

The secure phone line on his desk started ringing. Ming Liu smiled and crushed his cigarette into an ashtray. He picked up the receiver and put it to his ear.

"Yes, put him through."

* * *

Aboard Air Force One

Martin's translator said, "President Ming's coming on now, sir."

"Hello, Rick. I can of course guess why you've called. China had nothing to do with Gwon's killing, and I am aware of no evidence that North Korea did, either. I hope you are not going to accuse Young San-ho."

"I'm not accusing anyone, Ming. I'll go where the facts lead. Right now the only facts are that Gwon's dead and South Korea's leaders are trying to cope. Some will see this as a prelude to an invasion by the North. Young will probably grow alarmed at the South's military posture, even if it's purely for internal security. Neither of us wants a North-South confrontation. Let's each urge restraint."

"Restraint? Your navy is rounding up sailors ashore in Hong Kong so that your carrier can get out to sea. I know where it will go. You call that restraint?"

"Ming, I call it a precaution."

"I don't think Young San-ho will see it that way, Rick."

"I'm relying on you to help him understand that if his country's hands are clean on this, neither the United States nor South Korea will threaten him."

"Rick, it seems to me that America is once again relying on China to save it from the results of your foolish policy of alliance with South Korea."

"Just as China relies on the United States to keep the Strait of Hormuz open to the oil tankers that China needs despite your acquiescence to Iran's dangerous behavior in the region!"

Rick's remark met with silence.

"Ming, this conversation is only a first step in a long, dangerous process that will, we hope, achieve our common goal of peace on the Korean peninsula. Now let's both turn to calming the situation. We should talk again soon."

Rick kept his tone even but firm: "Goodbye, Ming."

Chapter 36

Arlington, Virginia

JERRY THOMAS WAS SHAKEN. I'VE seen worse wounds, he thought, but never anything like the way that woman went about it. Captain Clevenger was so right: just being in the room with someone who loves to inflict pain, who gets off on that, gave me the shakes—imagine being under her control, being completely helpless in her hands. No wonder this guy broke.

But what did he give us? The guy who he knows as abu Shaheed picked him up at the Boise, Idaho, airport. Abu Shaheed told him the trip would take about seven hours; he didn't time it, but he thinks that's about right. This Shaheed guy, his handler I guess, checked out his English and his cover story, told him the rules, then pretty much shut up for the rest of the ride. Our guy was blindfolded for the last part of the trip, for about an hour, he guesses.

Oh, and when they reached the safe house, he asked our guy what time he had and then told him to set his watch back one hour. He gave a little lecture on the importance of timing in the coming operation and said if he needed a better watch, he'd give him one. America is a big country, he said, and one martyrdom operation had been ineffective because the martyr had failed to set his watch correctly.

Thomas speed-dialed his phone. "Thin crust, marinara, extra cheese, Italian sausage, mushrooms . . . oh, and some of those sweet cherry peppers."

"What's that? Yeah, I'll take a balsamic drizzle.

"Twenty minutes? OK."

So what do we have so far? Assuming that the handler drove about sixty, which I would do if it were me, this safe house is somewhere within about a four hundred mile drive from the Boise airport. Just for argument, call it three hundred and fifty miles as the crow flies. So we've got the location narrowed down from the entire country, but it's still a hell of a big area to comb. As for the safe house, it's actually a sort of compound containing several structures and it's in the woods. He said the trees were big, the biggest he'd ever seen. There are two bunkhouses—one male, one female—and an A-frame cabin where the handler lives and briefs the martyrs on ops. There are two more structures, sound like sheds really, and the martyrs are strictly forbidden from entering either of those. There are lots of rules—this abu Shaheed seems to run a tight ship—but no clues about location in them.

On the day our guy shipped out for his op, there were three men and two women in the compound awaiting their own ops. No one is told anything about their op until the day they leave. The drill is that the martyr is called to the A-frame, briefed, and leaves immediately.

We also have a description of the handler, but that's unremarkable: short, black hair, beard, wiry, maybe five eight or five nine, black eyes. The guy's an Arab and looks like one. Lots of Arabic-looking men in America—although probably not so many in that part of the country. So, maybe his appearance is more useful than I thought at first. He comes and goes from the compound, sometimes staying away for a couple of days.

When the knock came, Thomas stopped gazing at a map he had pulled up from the tablet connected to his big screen; he'd been zooming in and out within a three-hundred-fifty-mile radius from Boise airport. Opening his door, he saw a woman he recognized.

"Hi, Sue. Thanks for getting this here fast," he said, handing her a five-dollar tip.

"Thanks, Mr. Thomas. Enjoy your pizza."

Thomas carried his pizza back to the coffee table between the couch and the big screen. You need to get a life, Jerry, he thought. The only people outside your job that know your name are Pizza Hut drivers, your ex-wife, and the lawyers who handled your divorce. That's pitiful! Popping a Coors

Light that wasn't very cold yet, he attacked the pizza, using knife and fork so he wouldn't smear his equipment with sticky fingers.

The circumference he'd drawn included parts of Nevada, California, Oregon, Washington, Montana, and nearly all of Idaho. We can eliminate most of Nevada, he thought. Except for a small area, the part within this circle is definitely not forested. That leaves Idaho, northeastern California, eastern Oregon or Washington, maybe western Montana. He cut another bite of pizza and stared at the map. What's that squiggly blue line running mostly north-south but zigzagging east or west in places? He clicked to increase the area displayed, revealing more of the line running from top to bottom of his screen. Mountain Time. Pacific Time. That's the demarcation line—and Boise is in Mountain but northern Idaho, the panhandle, is in Pacific. One hour behind. So is northeastern California and eastern Oregon and Washington.

Yes! So if our guy had to set his watch back one hour when he reached the compound, the compound is in the Idaho panhandle or eastern Washington or northeastern California. We eliminate Montana, most of Oregon, Nevada, and most of Idaho. And, at least according to Google, eastern Washington is not forested.

I think the compound is in the Idaho panhandle or northeastern California!

He left the rest of the pizza in the box and rinsed his plate at the sink.

What the heck, Thomas thought, I couldn't sleep anyway.

He headed for the office.

Chapter 37

Washington, DC

When Ray arrived about seven, sweaty from his usual run, Jerry Thomas greeted him and fell in alongside as he headed for his private bathroom to shower and shave.

"Can't this wait, Jerry?"

"No, sir, and where you're headed is a good place to talk."

Morales's eyebrows shot up. He was about to respond with a quip, but Thomas's expression stopped him. He grunted and waved Thomas along.

Once in the bathroom Thomas closed the door and turned on the shower. Morales's expression told him this had better be good.

"It's about what we learned from the would-be martyr."

Morales sat on the toilet seat and went to work on his shoes and socks. "What's your bottom line, Jerry?"

"I've narrowed down the cell's safe house—compound, actually—to parts of four western states. I think if we put resources on that probability area, we'll find it. But getting resources while staying mum about our source is going to be tough."

Morales, now barefoot, nodded, then said, "That's why I have you, Jerry. Anybody work with you on that analysis?"

"No, sir. Actually, I worked it out last night at home, then came in and used one of our workstations to double-check and refine my hypothesis."

"Hypothesis? That's a mighty big word for a Marine, Jerry. You referring to your wild-assed guess?"

"It's more than a WAG, sir. Let me walk you through it."

Five minutes later, Morales had digested the key points without dissenting.

"So what's in each of those areas, Jerry? I'll bet on industrial-scale marijuana production. Seems to me what goes on will help us sort out a priority for looking at each region."

"Not really. It's all about the same: logging, hiking, hunting, and fishing and, yes, pot and meth. All of the probability area is sparsely populated. Northeastern California is isolated, and a lot of it is designated national forest. Shasta-Trinity is huge and has some heavily wooded areas. Eastern Oregon is similar—a lot more open space than cities or towns and several national forests. Wallowa-Whitman is certainly a possibility.

"Southeastern Washington doesn't have many heavily wooded regions, but north of Spokane is a big mother of a national forest, Colville. And to the east, in the Idaho panhandle, you've got nothing much but lakes and trees. One national forest after another. Plus a large Indian reservation. Coeur d'Alene is pretty good-sized, but most else is just a wide spot in the road. And there aren't many roads."

"Jerry, we need eyes overhead and boots on the ground. What assets could we commit quietly?"

"Yes, sir, that's the problem exactly. Keeping this quiet, not raising questions about our source. We've got our dozen DHS-model Predators, but they don't have video gear sensitive enough to identify individuals from clandestine patrol altitudes. They've got dumbed-down optics to reduce concerns about domestic spying and civil liberties. Still, they could be a big help in narrowing down the initial probability area by spotting structures that might be the safe house compound. But how do we pull them away from current ops on our southwest border without causing questions?"

Morales waved a big paw dismissively.

Thomas pushed on. "As for boots on the ground: The U.S. Forest Service has authority over a big chunk of the probability area. They're on the ground already. But they're not looking for this compound. Maybe if we ask them to look for meth labs . . . but they're already doing that, at least on paper.

"Here's an idea—maybe screwy," Thomas continued, "but should one of our drones spot what appears to be the compound and should a forest fire happen to start at that location, it would flush the terrorists and bring firefighters and forest service into the area."

Morales's expression killed that idea. He was now stripped to his running shorts.

"Jerry, think about it for a couple of days and get back to me with some real options, not fantasies."

Thomas looked angry, then controlled his expression.

"Yes, sir. How about options that require outside resources, like FBI or army?"

"No. I can't go to Brian Leek for help without telling him why I think it's worth pulling his guys away from what he has them doing."

"You sure you couldn't, sir? I mean, you two have a good relationship."

"Yeah, he'd humor me with a few agents, but unless he knew why, he wouldn't go beyond that. And if I tell him we got a tip from a high-value detainee, next thing we know his intel guy is calling my intel guy for the details. Which, obviously, nobody but you and me can have. Shit!"

"What about going to the Pentagon—Secretary Easterly?"

"Same problem. He'd smell a rat real quick if I asked for what we need and just said to him, 'trust me, Eric.' Yeah, he used to do black ops when he was a SEAL, but that was almost as long ago as when I was a company commander. He's not just a lot older; he's got a lot more to lose. He's already out there on the bleeding edge because of Sudden Touch. When one of his choppers put a Hellfire into an eighteen-wheeler that ran a roadblock last week . . . see what I mean?"

"Yes, sir. So it'll be up to us alone to put the information from our detainee to use."

"That's how it seems to me, Jerry. But I'd love to be proven wrong."

Damn, that shower felt good, thought Morales, working a thick towel across his shoulders and back. It's getting so my run and shower are the high point of my day. Most days they're the only things I actually complete; everything else is juggling crises, kicking cans down the road.

A soft chime drew his attention to his phone.

Police responding to theater shootings kill woman said to be Good Sam protecting audience.

Don't whine, Morales. Your troubles aren't anything compared to what cops face.

He thought of the media file in his personal safe. And one of those balls I'm juggling is the guy I turned Ruby loose on. The way he screamed! Why did I do that? It seems stupid now because we didn't get anything immediately useful, nothing that let us block an attack and save lives.

And now what do I do with this guy? He's fine; leg healing nicely. But if he's interrogated, or if he's in contact with other prisoners or with guards, he'll tell what happened. If I were the guy I'm hunting, I'd have him shot and buried in the woods.

But I'm not. I'm bad enough; I'm a torturer, but I won't do *that.*

I could send him to Gitmo and then just deny his story. There've been plenty of unfounded allegations from that bunch of bad boys. His word against mine. And the doc says that scarring on his leg looks similar to scarring from a motorcycle accident. But anything he claims will be investigated, and it will drag out because no military judge will want to be the one who shut it down.

So I can't put him into the detainee system, and I won't kill him. Morales, you really screwed yourself this time!

Wait a minute. So long as he's alive there's no way to stop him talking. Suppose he talks and nobody listens? No one puts the matter into the justice system. But how could that happen? The guards, the press . . .

Suppose I just turn him loose in Yemen? Once over there he's just another jihadi with a story. And no evidence. And hardly any access to the press; they don't go poking around Yemen. It's not as if I were turning loose somebody like KSM—one more would-be suicide bomber in Yemen wouldn't make any difference.

Morales felt a lot better when he stepped out of the shower.

Until he looked in the mirror.

I've solved my problem, but I can't save my soul.

Chapter 38

Osan Air Base, Republic of Korea

RICK MARTIN TROTTED DOWN THE stairs from Air Force One into the twilight, waving at the distant cameras. He clasped Kang Nam-gi's hand.

"President Kang, I appreciate your agreeing to this meeting on short notice. I congratulate you and the citizens of the Republic of Korea on the steadiness and calm determination you are showing."

"President Martin, we in South Korea appreciate this showing of American support. We know that you will fight beside us if this cowardly murder was an attack by North Korea."

The two had reached their limos and would have parted to their respective vehicles, but Martin put his hand on Kang's forearm. "Mr. President, we are with you, but even if this does prove to be an act by North Korea, war may not be the best course."

"Then, Mr. President, we have much to discuss when we reach the command bunker."

Eyebrows arched, Martin said, "I expected to meet at Blue House."

"The security situation has changed. Blue House may not be safe."

Kang turned away abruptly to his limo, leaving Martin alongside the front fender of his own vehicle. Scowling, Martin seated himself for the journey.

"We've just been diddled!" said Martin to Anne Battista, seated to his right. "Holding this meeting in the command bunker is really bad symbolism. But we've got no choice at this point." He added, "I think we just learned a lot about the Kang administration."

* * *

As soon as Martin and his aides had seated themselves in the command bunker, the chairman of the ROK JCS gave a detailed briefing on the disposition of South and North Korean forces. He declared the South's forces were on highest alert and ready to respond to any provocation.

Leaning toward his guest, Kang said in English, "Mr. President, let's dispense with translators and aides. Your Korean is inadequate, but my English will suffice. Let us talk man to man."

Martin thought briefly of his last such conversation with a Korean head of state—Kim, shortly after Six-thirteen—that had turned into a disastrous shouting match. I don't like the idea of having any serious conversation with Kang without note takers, but he'll think I'm weak if I don't agree.

"All right, President Kang."

After their retinues had withdrawn, Kang said, "Know this: if North Korea is responsible for the murder of President Gwon, there *will* be war."

"President Kang, the United States will stand by its obligations to the Republic of Korea. But if your country initiates war, we have no obligation to join you in aggression."

"The murder of our president by North Korea cannot be treated as a mere crime. It is an act of aggression by the North, following a history of hostile activities that you well know."

"President Kang, we both saw the military dispositions. You are even more aware than I am that Seoul is so near the DMZ that it would be devastated in the first week of a war, even a war that you won decisively. I would think you would seek every reasonable path to avoid war, which is all I am asking you to do."

Kang looked at the digital map of the peninsula, bristling with symbols denoting military units and facilities. He grimaced, then turned and locked eyes with Martin.

"President Gwon was a good man. Almost three years ago you forced him to fall into line with your blockade of the North. That ruined his standing with our people. Then you nearly caused a war here, a war we weren't prepared for.

"I don't trust you, President Martin. We have taken steps since then. Today, we *are* ready for war. Our people will never stand for the dishonor of accepting this act by Young San-ho. Never!"

Holding Kang's stare, Martin said, "Well, let's be thankful we aren't at that point now. As we speak, so far as I know, the killer or killers have not been identified. It's crucial to have a thorough and impartial investigation, and I'm confident that you are doing that now. But while the investigation is conducted, it is essential to keep military activities on both sides of the DMZ tamped down."

Breaking eye contact and pointing to the map, Martin said, "If you rush troops to the border, then Young will do the same."

"Mr. President, my people expect their government to defend them. I cannot act as if nothing has changed!"

"Would it help if we returned American units to the area north of Seoul where they were stationed until a few years ago?"

"Yes, Mr. President, it would—at least for the moment."

"Then let's instruct our defense chiefs to work on that."

Martin rose and extended his hand.

"Thank you for speaking frankly. When I reach Beijing in a few hours, I can say to Ming with confidence that the ROK will not react against the DPRK in the heat of the moment and that your country and mine will stand together in our determination to hold the perpetrator accountable. Because of our conversation, I can urge that he use China's influence to reassure Young San-ho and insist that he make no military provocation."

Kang took the outstretched hand: "Goodbye, Mr. President."

Chapter 39

Pyongyang, Democratic People's Republic of Korea

INTERIOR MINISTER BAN HAN-BIN PAUSED in his departure from the Venerated Leader's office. This had been a fearful half hour for him, as it would be for any minister with bad news for Field Marshal Young San-ho, and he had saved his sliver of good news for this moment.

"Venerated Leader, we have another buyout offer. One of the yakuza families wants to purchase prisoner Chung Ma-eun, now in Camp Ten. They offer fifty thousand dollars."

"Why do they want this miserable woman?"

"The usual reason, Venerated Leader. A wealthy relative living in Japan is willing to buy her."

"In that case, fifty isn't enough. Tell them it's one hundred."

"Yes, Venerated Leader."

Ban Han-bin scuttled through the door into the unsympathetic view of Young San-ho's secretary.

Field Marshal Young San-ho lit another Marlboro, and his axe-blade face grew even sharper as he squinted through the smoke.

Ming Liu, he thought, is such an arrogant bastard, like all Chinese, believing it's his birthright to disrespect Korea and Koreans. He thinks we killed Gwon, and for now I'm happy to let him think that. Of course he didn't say so, but I could tell. And he wanted my assurance that we wouldn't make what he called "provocative" military moves. After getting his agreement to ship an extra fifty thousand tons of heavy fuel oil, I said what he wanted to hear.

He's more afraid of what the Americans might do than I am. If need be, I can get out quickly. And I have enough in foreign accounts—soon to be joined by the yakuza contribution—to live safely and well. Ming would be left with millions of starving, leaderless Koreans surging over his borders like stormy seas crashing over a breakwater.

Besides, since we didn't kill Gwon, there can be no solid evidence that we did. And anyway, the Americans will never allow themselves to be pulled into another Korean war, especially not now, so they will restrain the fools in Seoul.

This year Ming has an especially big reason for avoiding war on our peninsula. His reelection to head the Chinese Communist Party is coming up and is far from certain. Maybe I can tip the scales against him. Bring down Ming Liu; now *that* would be a pleasure!

Maybe the anxious snakes in the South will do something I can use. Suppose the South were to reinforce the DMZ because of Gwon's killing? American troops would probably return to bases north of Seoul. If I attacked in response to that threat, the American troops between the DMZ and Seoul would be in it. The Japanese would be paralyzed by fear of my ballistic missiles, and the Russians would be happy to watch China and America clash. I could cry for Chinese help, and Ming would turn a deaf ear because war with America would be a financial disaster for China. But failing to answer my call for help would be a great loss of face for China, and perhaps Ming's enemies could use that to defeat him at the CCP congress.

I will think on this!

* * *

As the U.S. Air Force VC-20 climbed through ten thousand feet, leaving Seoul and a very prickly meeting behind, Secretary of Defense Eric Easterly unbuckled and moved to a small table set for one. Against the chill of the cabin's overactive air conditioning he wore a faded olive field jacket with a name tag bearing the SEAL insignia and "LT Eric Easterly, USNR" in battered gold letters. As soon as he was seated, a staff sergeant served dinner and poured a glass of California merlot for him.

Easterly savored a sip of wine and popped a Ritz cracker topped with Vermont cheddar into his mouth.

Well, that really sucked, he thought. Defense Minister Nam and Admiral Su worked me over like a tag team of wrestlers. They're shocked, worried, and a little defensive that this assassination could happen in Pusan but see big leverage in it for the ROK. They believe they hold the key to peace—or war—in Korea right now. 'Course, Field Marshal Young probably thinks *he* holds it. Here we are, America and China, hoping this won't lead to war while our respective Korean allies growl and snap like junkyard dogs, ready to go at it. And I'm supposed to produce a juicy hunk of steak to satisfy ours and get him quieted down.

Ten thousand U.S. troops! I'll be damned if I'll give Nam that many soldiers' lives as skin in the game!

He took a second sip of merlot, pecked at a salad, and then attacked his porterhouse and baked potato with gusto. The handset next to his former seat emitted an irritating double buzz. Easterly ignored it.

Soon the staff sergeant reappeared.

"Mr. Secretary, General MacAdoo says it's urgent."

"Shit! OK."

He moved to the chair beside the handset.

"Mac, how are you so damn good at interrupting my meals? You got the crew on my plane trained to let you know when I sit down for a bite?"

"Sorry, sir," said General Jay (Mac) MacAdoo, chairman of the Joint Chiefs of Staff. "I really hate to do it, knowing the wonderful time you've had with Nam and Su today. But hey—I was sitting in a room with half the generals in the PLA when they heard about Gwon's assassination. They got the news first, so here I am sitting across the table from these guys, watching as they pass a note down the line and glare at me.

"When he saw me read the note my aide passed me, General Ma announced a recess and hustled me off to a side room. He was really worried. I don't believe the Chinese had a finger in this pie. If the North *did* do it, they blindsided the Chinese military.

"After Young San-ho shot Kim to take over and Ming sent the PLA into Pyongyang to stabilize things, General Ma was the operational commander. He dealt with Young then and told me today he thinks the man's dangerously overconfident—a real loose cannon."

"Thanks, Mac. You're really making my day."

"But what Ma really wanted to say was this: do not return American troops to their former positions north of Seoul. Young is crazy enough to kill a bunch of them, thinking that will surely draw China and America into confrontation in Korea."

"Well, Mac, that makes three of us who don't want to do what the ROK is asking us to do in exchange for treating the assassination as a crime rather than an act of war."

"Sir, I went a little off the reservation with Ma."

"What? How?"

"I brought up Pandora. Ma didn't jump at it, but he didn't reject it either."

"You're not off the reservation, Mac. You just seized an opportunity to implement one of the president's ideas. Let's put it that way when we tell him. And we're not gonna mention this to anyone else."

"Yes, sir. Glad to hear that. Now about the ROK. How bad is it?"

"Their minister of defense demands that ten thousand U.S. troops dig in north of Seoul on an east-west line across the country."

"And you told him no way, right, sir?"

"The president didn't give me that authority. I've got to bring the deal to him."

"That makes me real nervous, sir."

"Me, too, Mac. I'm stopping at CINCPAC on the way back to DC and telling Admiral Swafford to stand by for heavy seas."

PART TWO

One month later

Chapter 40

Frederick, Maryland

Marty Sanders pulled his battered blue Toyota Camry into the half-empty parking lot. Well, this sure ain't The Palm, he thought, as he walked toward the tired-looking Olive Garden restaurant. But the important thing is nobody here will know me.

He entered and approached the hostess stand. "I need a quiet spot. Guy'll be joining me soon—he'll ask for Marty."

The hostess led him to a satisfactory location, and Sanders sat looking toward the door. He texted Jimmy Roper, who had cold-called him claiming to have important information about Ray Martin for Senator Gustafson: "I'm the bald guy in the corner to your far left as you enter. Ask the hostess for Marty."

As he watched the pudgy man in jeans and a tee shirt follow the hostess, Sanders thought, yep, he fits the loser profile like so many of the folks I have to deal with. Let's get this over with so I can beat rush-hour traffic on the Baltimore beltway.

After the waitress had taken their orders—coffee for him, Harp for the loser—Sanders said, "OK, you asked for this meeting. Show me why it was worth my time to drive to Frederick-by-God, Maryland."

"I work at Camp David. Not every day but once in a while to fill in when one of the regular maintenance guys is out. You know what goes on there, right? Meetings the president wants to keep private, hush-hush stuff."

Sanders nodded, impatient at this "briefing," but he let Jimmy talk.

"Camp David's a pretty big place, you know? Lots of work to keep it nice. Sometimes I see the president or his wife walkin' around or playin' tennis while I'm cuttin' grass or rakin' leaves. They just sort of ignore us workers, like we were invisible, like they can somehow block us out of their sight, even though we're standin' there. It's kinda weird until you get used to it."

"So is this about something you saw?"

"Something I saw and got a picture of. Right here on my phone."

"You know you could get arrested for taking a picture in Camp David without permission."

"I could? I knew I could get fired, but I didn't know it was against the law."

"You could get fired and prosecuted. But don't worry. You came to the right person. I have the clearances and the contacts to deal with it. If they come after you, I've got your back."

Projecting a practiced trustworthiness, Marty continued: "Now, what've you got?"

"One night when I was workin' outside after dark, I saw the first lady walkin' along the path with a guy. I didn't know who he was, except I did know it wasn't the president. There was just somethin' odd about it, about the *feelin'* in the air. Sorta sneaky somehow. So I took this picture. Here, look for yourself."

Sanders took the small, outdated phone, the kind cell companies unload as free upgrades, and looked at the screen. A glance triggered the rush that always came when he had information that was going to put money in his pocket.

"I don't see anything much here. Two people with their heads together, like they were looking at something. What do *you* think this is, Jimmy?"

"Well . . . I don't know for sure. Maybe it's not so much just seein' it. But bein' there was . . . well maybe there was some hanky-panky going on, you know? I found out that guy is Ray Morales. I remember readin' that him and her had a thing goin' during college. Maybe they started up again."

"How long did you watch them, Jimmy?"

"Oh, maybe five minutes. I saw them stroll by, acting real familiar and comfortable."

"Were they holding hands? Did they have arms around each other?"

"No."

"Either before or after you took this picture, did they kiss or nuzzle or anything like that?"

"No. But right after, they suddenly stepped back from each other. She said something I couldn't hear; then they walked back the way they came. But it was different. It wasn't familiar and comfortable. They were stiff. They didn't look at each other."

"So spell it out for me, Jimmy: What do you think you photographed?"

"I think he was comin' on to her, and she shut him down. But she may have just told him to wait till they got back inside the cabin. Ten minutes later they might have been getting' it on."

"That's quite an imagination you've got, Jimmy. You have what my mom used to call a dirty mind. They could just as likely be looking at a picture of her kids. Look, you meant no harm when you took that picture. Maybe the most significant thing about it is that it could be used as evidence you broke federal law. Let's just drop this. You're safe with me. I've got your back."

Jimmy Roper snatched the phone out of Sanders's hand. "How about you pay me for this phone? I took a big risk, and I deserve something for it."

"Jimmy, Jimmy! I *will* pay you for it. I'll give you enough for a high-end replacement, any model you want, and you have my protection against the feds if it comes out that you took a picture in a restricted area. You know, with all this terrorism going on, something at Camp David gets the FBI's full attention, not to mention the Secret Service. You could really get hammered for this innocent mistake."

Jimmy's expression said he was wavering but not convinced.

"Look, Jimmy, I'm a busy, important guy, and I've come all the way out here to listen to your pitch. Truth is, you may have something here, or you may have nothing. It'll take a hell of a lot of investigation to find which it is. Investigation I know how to do and you don't. I'll give you a thousand cash. Final offer."

Scowling, Jimmy nodded and handed his phone to Sanders, who emailed the photo to himself. Moments later he saw it on his phone and deleted it from Jimmy's.

Chapter 41

Southwest Texas

I SHOULDN'T BE IN THE UNITED States again, thought Adel Ghorbani. The CIA has my four years at the University of Southern Illinois under their microscope. They have photos of me. My biometric markers are in every database. Probably they have my DNA. I'd become the subject of a manhunt within a day of walking the streets in any major Western city, much less here in America.

But . . . but if this operation doesn't go as I have promised, I'm through as leader of Quds Force.

Faintly, Ghorbani heard a Spanish-language radio station the driver had tuned in hours ago. He glanced at the others in the hot, foul-smelling truck: each dark-skinned, dark-eyed, and bearded like himself. But they weren't like him. They weren't Persians but Mexicans, soldiers of the Solano cartel, and they were taking him to meet the rest of the Quds team, each of whom had arrived in this unpleasant manner. And were this eighteen-wheeler to be pulled over for inspection, they would flee in all directions. Their seemingly mindless panic would distract attention from him while his escort hustled him purposefully to a trail car driven by another cartel member.

The driver downshifted. Ghorbani tensed, but when his companions were unconcerned, he relaxed.

"Now we turn you over to the next group," said his escort. It was clear from his tone that he could care less about Ghorbani now that his responsibility was ended. Ghorbani wasn't surprised; the cartel's soldiers had long ago sloughed off their humanity. This was strictly business, and the cartel's leader was happy to be taking money from both Fahim and his nemesis. At first he didn't know Ghorbani was intent on killing his other customer. But he was as alert for synergies as any other CEO, and, eventually, he discovered this one and found a way to profit.

* * *

The interior of the ambulance was brightly lit, assaulting eyes that had been in semi-darkness for half a day. Inside Ghorbani encountered two women in scrubs, one of whom wore a white coat over hers. With them was a man wearing blue trousers and a white shirt with a paramedic shoulder patch. Off to the side stood another man in blue trousers and white shirt.

"I'm Doctor Gupta," said the white coat, "and this is Nurse Sandra. That paramedic is Paul. He and Sandra will travel with you. We're going to put you under, and then I'll be on my way. Lie on the stretcher, please."

"What do you mean, 'put me under'?"

"We're going to give you an anesthetic that will make you unconscious. That's how they'll get you through the roadblocks and searches."

"I don't want to do that. I don't want to be unconscious."

Paul and the doctor cut their eyes to the second man, who shook his head.

"Look, mister. I don't know who you are and I don't want to know," said Doctor Gupta. "But clearly you're someone the government wants to arrest; otherwise why travel this way? This ambulance *will be* stopped, probably more than once. If you're unconscious and Sandra says you're critical, the soldiers will rush. They won't do all the checks they usually do. They'll run the ambulance through quickly, and you'll be on your way."

"No! I didn't know this before. It wasn't part of our arrangement."

Glancing again at the second man, Gupta squared her shoulders and stepped closer to Ghorbani.

"Look, mister, the only way you do this is unconscious and intubated," she said. "You'll be identified if you're conscious. And you won't get away—they shoot people who run. This isn't the same country it was before."

"What is this 'intubate'?" said Ghorbani.

Gupta sighed and rolled her eyes. "After you're unconscious we put a breathing tube in your mouth. We tape it in place. Also, we bandage your skull. That makes you unrecognizable to the biometric scanners the soldiers and cops use."

Ghorbani briefly considered his complete vulnerability, then pushed the thought aside and accepted what the doctor—if that's what she was—told him. He had already lost control; this was just another step in the gauntlet of his supreme helplessness. He had decided to take this risk in order to reach his goal undetected by Operation Sudden Touch or any other of the extraordinary surveillance measures the Americans had unleashed.

"Sandra's going to run an IV line in your arm. We're going to put you on a normal saline drip and give you a light sedative. You'll be much more comfortable in here than you were in that truck."

Ghorbani hesitated, then nodded. Sandra probed his right wrist with clammy – gloved fingers, then inserted the needle painlessly. She hung a bag of clear liquid on the fixture attached to the stretcher. After inserting a second IV into his left wrist, she inserted a syringe's needle into the IV's port and gradually injected one hundred eighty milligrams of propofol into Ghorbani's bloodstream. Soon, his mind stopped racing for the first time since the Leader had given him the go-ahead for this operation. "He's out," said Sandra, seated on Ghorbani's left side near his waist.

Fifteen minutes later Sandra sat in the back of the ambulance with Ghorbani, his features concealed by a breathing tube, tape, and bandages. Paul sat next to the driver, a hard-looking Latino, who had not spoken during the stop. The blue-and-white transport ambulance slipped into eastbound traffic on Interstate 10 at the speed limit, without lights or siren. Sandra checked her Twitter account.

> Heroic woman tackles would-be suicide bomber short of goal, dies in blast.

* * *

Coeur d'Alene, Idaho

"So you really blew up a synagogue!" said Bobby Garst in a low voice. "I thought you were just talking big at the meeting. But you did it. You're the real deal, Al."

"Yes, I am," said Fahim, the man Garst knew as Al Hassan. "And so are you." He glanced around the parking lot at Mother's where he had intercepted his quarry, pleased that Garst had arrived before the happy-hour crowd destroyed the opportunity for a discreet conversation. "I'm glad we ran into each other. Let me buy you a beer and tell you why."

Seated in a quiet corner, both men gazed admiringly at the waitress's tight-jeaned bottom as she left them. "Cheers!" Fahim clinked his glass with Garst's.

"I'm a pretty good judge of people," Fahim continued. "Most of the guys in the book club are posers, big talk but no action. You and Ken aren't. We can help each other. You needed someone who knows explosives and has the balls to use them to kill Jews. I came through for you. But blowing up that synagogue was just a beginning. I have something much bigger going down soon, something that will show that America's Zionist-occupied government can't find its arse with both hands. Interested?"

"Why should I be interested? We got too many of you Arabs in this country, never shoulda let you in. And the ZOG sucks but doesn't bother me much here in Idaho."

Fahim smiled through his rage. "First of all, the government. How about what the government did to Aryan Nation? You and Ken were members, right? Went to national meetings, recruited brave men proud to wear the colors, stocked up on weapons and ammo to be ready for racial holy war, when the white race would purify America and the world. Remember those days?" Garst nodded and took a swallow of beer.

"And what happened to Aryan Nation, Bobby? Where are the national conventions, the parades, the thousands of proud men? You know what happened, Bobby. The Jews, the ZOG, took 'em down. Passed laws that made standing up for the white race a 'hate crime.' Took the chapters to court on phony charges, arranged for the cases to be heard by Jewish judges, who handed down verdicts that allowed the feds to seize Aryan property and bank accounts. Come on, Bobby, you're too smart to really believe this overreaching, liberal, Jew-infested government doesn't matter here in Idaho."

Garst's eyes flashed but he said nothing.

"As for working with an Arab," continued Fahim, "Hitler did it; why shouldn't you? Here, look at this!" He stroked his smart phone and handed it to Garst. Jaw dropping, Garst gazed at a picture of a beaming Adolf

Hitler shaking hands with a man in Arab robes while smiling Nazi officials looked on.

"Bobby, that's a 1941 photo taken in Berlin of the visiting Grand Mufti of Jerusalem, the leader of all my people in those days before the Jews stole our country, Palestine. You know the saying, Bobby: 'The enemy of my enemy is my friend.' Hitler dedicated his life to preserving the purity of the Aryan race. The Grand Mufti was no Aryan, but Hitler welcomed his support against their common enemies, the Jews and the British government that supported them. Come on, man—we don't have to like each other. I don't want to marry your sister, I want to drive the Jews out of Palestine, my people's land! And I'm able to pay well for help doing that."

Garst smiled. "I might be interested," he said.

Fahim clapped him on the back and signaled for another round. "Here's the thing, Bobby. Any idiot with enough explosives can blow up a building. But to do what I do, drop them straight down without breaking a single window across the street, you've got to know a structure's weak points and put your explosives there. Same with the ZOG. You and I can break the ZOG's hold over the people of America. I know where to put the explosives."

"What's it worth to you?" said Garst.

Although this conversation was going as planned, Fahim pretended to consider. Then he said, "With the ZOG out of the picture, my people can drive the Jews out of their land . . . Seventy-five thousand and a passport that'll let you disappear with your cash."

"Make it a hundred, half up front, and I'm in."

"Done."

Chapter 42

Denver, Colorado

Rick Martin wolfed down a sandwich and scanned a summary of the private polls and focus groups that Win Hernandez, seated across from him, had commissioned last week. He had twenty minutes before his next campaign event.

Looking grimly at his campaign manager, Martin said, "Looks like I'm really getting hammered."

Before Win could answer, the president's secure phone rang.

"Mr. President, you have a call from President Kang," said John Dorn.

"Any ideas, John?"

"He didn't drop any hints, sir."

"Is he using Korean or English today?"

"English, sir."

"Well then, at least I don't have to wear those damn ear buds!

"Put him through."

A moment later Rick heard, "President Martin, good evening."

"Good morning, President Kang."

"President Martin, our suspicions have been confirmed. President Gwon was assassinated by the North, on order of Young San-ho. It is time to act, Mr. President."

"That's grave news. What are the facts that lead you to conclude the North is responsible?"

"We arrested one of the North Korean assassins, and he has confessed. There can be no doubt."

"Please instruct your officials to provide full details of the interrogation and confession to our attorney general and permit our FBI to interview this suspect."

"Surely you don't doubt me! This assassin, Chung Ma-ho, has confessed."

"President Kang, I agree that it's time to act. You should announce full details about this man and publish your conclusions. Even better, put him on TV with his confession."

"That's not enough. We must respond with force. We must not show weakness or confusion. And America must stand with us."

"We do stand with you, but we must give North Korea an opportunity to respond to the man's confession. This guy—Chung? Chung claims to be North Korean, but is he? He says he was part of an assassination team, but was he, really? Suppose he was acting on his own, either because he's crazy or because he wants your country and mine to go to war with the DPRK? Are there not groups in your country that believe war is the only way to unite Korea?"

"Why are you asking such questions, President Martin? The man has confessed! I ask you again: Do you doubt my word?"

"Mr. President, this isn't about trust between you and me. You well know how our Constitution divides power. Congress will ask such questions. The American people will ask such questions.

"We're struggling now to defeat terrorists in our own country, enemies who are killing Americans in their schools, stores, and churches. Our army is heavily engaged in this fight. You want ten thousand of those soldiers returned to Korea. Many Americans will say they are needed more along our borders."

"Then the Republic of Korea will act without you! And we will denounce your cowardly failure to honor our alliance."

"Strong words, Mr. President. I will be equally direct. If you attack North Korea, or provoke them into attacking, without our forces Seoul will be rubble in forty-eight hours. Forty-eight hours! And tens of thousands of your citizens killed. Are you willing to have that on your conscience?"

"If that happens, it will be on Young San-ho's. His attack has left us no choice."

"The world won't see it that way, Mr. President. If you attack without building the case against the North, you'll make it very hard for me to help you. You may leave me no choice but a token effort, enough to observe our treaty but not enough to protect Seoul or spare your country from a repeat of the devastation of the previous Korean War."

"I can see that we are on our own. Our treaty and our years of alliance mean nothing to you, President Martin. The Republic of Korea will respond to this attack by the North."

Kang broke the connection.

"Was that as bad as your half of it sounded, Mr. President?"

"Pretty bad, Win. He believes Chung's confession is reason enough to go to war. I want to know a whole lot more, starting with whether the guy was tortured until he gave the answer the interrogators wanted."

"I didn't get the part about Seoul. Why is it a goner, Mr. President?"

"I had a talk about that with Mac. The North Koreans are big in artillery, and the northern outskirts of Seoul are in range from artillery on their side of the DMZ. And that's not all. The North Koreans have burrowed tunnels under the DMZ. ROKs are always looking for them and blow them up when they find them. But the tunnels are deep and hard to detect, even with ground-penetrating radar. Some of them are huge, large enough to move artillery through. So within a few hours after a war started, heavy artillery would be south of the DMZ and hammering Seoul. Their air force would bomb it; their missiles would hit it."

"And Kang knows that and would attack anyway?"

"Well, he certainly knows it. Would he attack anyway? Or is he blustering? We'll find out pretty soon."

Chapter 43

Washington, DC

THE WATER WAS JUST THE right temperature as Arlene Gustafson slid into it. Arms on the rim of the deep claw-foot tub, she slowly tilted back her head until it touched the tub, closed her eyes, and let the warmth envelop her.

The naked young man, whose presence she sensed before opening her eyes, gestured toward the tub.

"No, Ralphie. I've had enough fun for now. Be on your way. Remember to lock the door. And be sure and have your report on the F-35 on my desk by eight tomorrow."

Desire *is* powerful, she thought. Humans *do* take stupid chances for lust. Here I am making it with a twenty-something from my own staff, even after seeing all the trouble it caused Clinton.

Taking a sip of wine, she turned her thoughts to Marty's triumphant claim.

That photograph and his hunch are believable.

But what's he got, really? A photo taken illegally of a pair of college lovers thirty years later, apparently alone together, leaning toward each other. They could have been looking at pictures of her kids or something equally wholesome. And Rick Martin could have been standing just out of the frame. It was supposedly snapped at Camp David, but nothing in it reveals location. And of course, it could be Photo-shopped—although Marty says the geeks have declared it hasn't been altered.

If you want to believe they were alone, sharing a stolen, intimate moment on their way to bed, this picture gives you a hook to hang it on. But only if you *want* to believe.

Or maybe if it confirms your fears because you've dreaded this for years.

Gustafson began to wash with a large loofah, enjoying its roughness. *I should have had Ralphie scrub my back before I sent him away.*

After washing away the last of Ralphie, Gustafson stood, rinsed with the wand, and blotted herself just enough that she didn't drip as she walked to her sauna. She entered and clambered to the top bench where the heat was greatest. Her towel protecting her buttocks from the heated wooden bench, she leaned back gradually, easing her shoulders into contact with the wooden wall. Carefully placing her hands on the outspread towel, Gustafson let the heat bake her.

For those who want to believe . . .

If you want to believe it captured a sleazy moment, the picture and accompanying narrative would be convincing. It would headline the tabloids both here and in Europe. But it was explainable as a conversation between friends and easily spun as a serious breach of security by a disgruntled employee—who would probably be identified, since this guy Marty met is a nebbish—and the romance angle wouldn't have legs. Most likely, the story line would soon become an examination of security at Camp David.

And I couldn't do anything with it in my committee. Oh, maybe hold hearings from a security viewpoint, but all that would produce is video of the Secret Service director taking his lumps. There's no value to me in that.

On the other hand . . .

Gustafson lifted the ladle from a bucket of water at her feet and poured on the rocks in front of her. The water sizzled and vanished; immediately the air wrapping her felt hotter. The droplets on her skin she'd carried into the sauna were now replaced with a sheen of sweat.

On the other hand, publicity isn't the only use that this picture can be put to. Sometimes the tale not told is the most powerful of all, because the players are trapped in "what if?" In the real world a juicy scandal could be upstaged by a war or a typhoon or a pandemic. In the "what if?" world, those at risk have no relief, no distraction from their minds making doomsday scenarios. Sometimes they can be manipulated into paying far too high a price to suppress something.

Rick Martin must know of the college romance. Does he wonder if

Ella is attracted to Morales once again? Does he fear that she compares him to Ray and finds him wanting? Would this picture seem authentic to him because it confirms his fears? If I went to him with the picture and the story, would he feel embarrassed? Threatened?

Or would he laugh at me?

In some ways this picture is a hand grenade with the pin pulled. Marty—being the slimy bastard that he is—will certainly do something with it to line his pockets unless I throw it first. And the nebbish probably sent himself the file before he met Marty, so who knows where it might turn up? "Forget it" isn't an option. And Marty's already tried to get a bonus out of me for this; no way is this solid enough for that. So what if he's pissed off at me; he'll get over it.

Marty . . . he's one of the best opposition research guys around. And he of course has no scruples or loyalty. Does he know about Ralphie? How much could he hurt me if he did? It's not like we're screwing in the office—although there was that one time in the supply closet after we got turned on joking about the docs on *Grey's Anatomy*. He dared me and . . . that was really stupid!

She was beginning to feel dizzy from the heat.

Gustafson stepped carefully down from her perch on the upper bench, out the door, and into the shower stall. She turned on the cold full force and gasped as the stream hit between her shoulder blades. Her body involuntarily hunched from the shock of the one-hundred-twenty-five-degree difference in temperature. After perhaps fifteen seconds under the stream, she shut it off and stepped out of the stall.

Am I going in again? She pulled a Coors Light from the small refrigerator nearby and guzzled, the icy brew joining the coolness of her shocked skin, reducing her core temperature.

Yep! Another ten minutes.

Back on her perch, Gustafson let her mind free.

So, who do I go to with this? Not the press—I've settled that; not a good payoff for me. The president? But that means first convincing Guarini and maybe others. I lose some control once I tell Bart.

How about Morales? But what can I demand of him? Not money; that would land me in jail. What I'd like, what I'd give anything for, is to rewind and force him to intervene and keep Matt from being tossed out of the

Marines. If Morales had intervened, Matt would be alive. But he didn't—the bastard—and I can't change that.

The Marines were everything to Matt; he was in his dress blues when I found him. Because of his less-than-honorable discharge, I couldn't even bury him in a VA cemetery, much less in section sixty of Arlington with his buddies from Afghanistan.

Maybe that's it!

The LTH isn't an absolute bar to burial in a VA cemetery. There's an adjudication process that I lost because the Corps was so furious at Matt. Morales wouldn't help me then. But now . . .

This isn't solid enough to really put the White House over a barrel. I probably wouldn't get past Bart and Sam, and they'd find some way to punish me for trying. But if I go to Morales . . . and if this is the real thing, he'll want to suppress it. And if it's not, if he laughs at me, I'll just keep looking.

* * *

Marty Sanders looked at the video camera on the table in his man cave. That low-light capability was a good investment, he thought, the senator's current boy toy is clearly recognizable as he leaves her place.

That low-light capability was a good investment, he thought, the senator's current boy toy is clearly recognizable as he leaves her place. She thinks she can screw me over that photo of Morales and his old flame. We'll see about that!

Chapter 44

Coeur d'Alene, Idaho

LuAnn came quietly from their bedroom, knowing better than to disturb Al at the computer. The living room was dark except for the glow of the screen that silhouetted him. She could see that his hand was moving rhythmically at his crotch. She heard his ragged breathing and shuddered, knowing he would soon take her, violently.

All the men in LuAnn's life had been sexually abusive. She took that as a given in her relationship with Al and was thankful that he didn't humiliate her in front of Charlie, as other live-ins had done. She was also thankful that he treated her decently in public and didn't steal the money she earned cleaning houses and waitressing. In fact, Al seemed to have plenty of money and was relatively free with it. She didn't worry about paying the double-wide's gas and electric bill, even in winter. He took her out to dinner occasionally and didn't object when she ordered pizza delivered as a treat for Charlie. By LuAnn's standards this was a pretty good relationship. But still . . .

Al's taste for child porn gave her the creeps. She had long ago gotten used to her men poring over *Hustler* and *Maverick* and other porn magazines, but this went way too far, was too kinky. And LuAnn had been raped by her "father"—her mother's current boyfriend—when she was thirteen. She couldn't stand the sights and sounds of Al's online perversion and usually shut herself in another room when he was at it.

But tonight, well after midnight, she had groggily left bed in search of a glass of water from the kitchen and was witness to the depravity before she realized it. Over Al's shoulder LuAnn saw a pubescent girl, wearing a terrified expression and nothing else, standing near a rumpled bed. The camera cut to the source of her terror, a naked man staring hungrily at her from the doorway. The girl screamed. LuAnn snapped.

"Al, why do you watch that awful stuff?"

The man she knew as Al whirled to face her. From his expression LuAnn knew she was in for a beating. Al hadn't beaten her before, but others had; she knew the look.

"None of your damn business, you fat bitch!"

The first blow was a roundhouse that only stung her ear as it nearly missed but the next hurt like a knife in her left kidney. She shrieked and dropped to the floor, experience taking over as she tucked her elbows protectively to her ribs, jammed her chin into her chest, and protected her temples with her hands. Al's first kick landed on her buttocks, drawing another shriek; the second, aimed for her right ear, was cushioned by her hand but stunned her.

Charlie came out of his room behind Al and went for him like a missile. Al staggered slightly at the unexpected collision, then whirled and threw Charlie to the floor. Al drew back his foot then stopped dead, breathing heavily. He looked at LuAnn, then at her son, then back to LuAnn, as if he had heard a powerful command to cease his violence and was now under the control of the force behind that command. LuAnn and Charlie warily met his gaze and LuAnn moved between her son and their attacker.

His voice shaky, Fahim said, "LuAnn, I'm sorry. I don't know what came over me . . . I don't want to hurt you or Charlie. Look, I'm going to leave now, give us all some space. I'll be back tomorrow and I promise not to ever hurt you again. I'll make it up to you and Charlie. We'll go shopping . . . get the nicest dress you want, LuAnn. And Charlie—we'll get that PlayStation six for you."

LuAnn's expression revealed her surprise and disbelief. Charlie's face showed fear and confusion. Fahim grabbed his jacket, yanked open the front door, then halted on the threshold. Turning, he said, "LuAnn, Charlie. I really am sorry." Then he disappeared into the darkness. Neither LuAnn nor Charlie moved until they heard the F-150 flinging gravel as it sped away.

Charlie was drawing shuddering breathes and his face showed how hard he was trying not to cry. LuAnn wrapped him in her arms. "Don't worry, Charlie. I won't let him hurt you. We're leaving soon, going to your Aunt Margaret's in Great Falls. Al can't follow us; he doesn't know I have a sister."

This was a situation all too familiar to LuAnn. In fact, it was how most of her relationships with men had ended. She hated to leave the doublewide, it had been one of the best homes she'd had and, until tonight, Al had been pretty good to her and Charlie. And Charlie was happy and getting B's in school; now he'd be forced to leave friends and familiar teachers.

But she had learned that, when things go south like they had, no use staying around. All the well-intended help offered to "abused spouses," the counseling, the social workers, the restraining orders wouldn't protect them. She had learned that offering a second chance to an abuser only led to more beatings. All the concern and encouragement of support groups faded, and she was left vulnerable to the rage of her ex. These guys had long memories, hard fists, and a way of finding her; the social workers had only a big caseload and a million forms to complete. No contest.

LuAnn kissed her son, tousled his hair, took his hand, and gently pulled him toward his bedroom. "Come on, Charlie. I'll sleep in your room tonight. He won't hurt us again."

As LuAnn sat at Charlie's bedside holding his hand, she made her plans. She'd need a couple of days to make arrangements, then they'd leave—*with* that nice dress for her and the PlayStation for Charlie. She wasn't dumb enough to file a police complaint that could force her to confront Fahim but she knew another way to flag him to law enforcement.

* * *

An hour later in the A-frame of his forest hideout, Fahim sipped his second whiskey and assessed his situation through the psychopathic lens that shaped his life. Damn that woman for interfering! What I choose to watch is none of her affair. She deserved the lesson I was giving her when Charlie showed up. I should have given them both a beating they wouldn't forget but if I had they'd need a doctor and I don't want the questions that would bring.

Well, she's passive and has no self-confidence so she won't go to the cops. After I take her and Charlie on a shopping spree and shower them with apologies, she'll settle down. Her bruises will heal and once they do, she'll have nothing to support her story. I'm in control and this is a minor setback that I can manage.

Chapter 45

Washington, DC

GUNNER GLANCED RIGHT, STIFFENED, AND accelerated, reaching the end of his leash in four bounds, about six bounds short of the squirrel. Surprised, Ray nearly lost his footing on the wet turf and swore at their bulldog. Unrepentant, the animal continued to leap against the leash, whining. Like many a good Marine, thought Morales, sometimes Gunner's commitment exceeds his wisdom.

The animal was especially glad to see Morales this evening because his life, like so many lives in America, had changed abruptly after the attacks began. Because Ray and Julie Morales could no longer live safely in their Chevy Chase neighborhood, Gunner was now a boarder at Royal Pedigree Pet Care near Rock Creek Park. Since Ray was in Washington more often than Julie, he had become Gunner's primary visitor and walker. That's why he was one of the few people in Rock Creek Park this drizzly evening.

"You'd better be careful, Secretary Morales, or that dog will put you on your ass."

Ray's head snapped left, revealing the speaker, Arlene Gustafson. His jaw dropped.

"Don't chew out your goons. I didn't sneak past them; they were alerted that I was coming because I tracked you down through the Counterterrorism Center duty officer."

"So now who's the stalker, Senator?"

"Me, I guess. Look, I've been thinking about what happened in the hearing and later near my house. I took a cheap shot at you, and then you—very unwisely—took one at me. In that sense we're even."

With a shift in tone, Gustafson continued: "But only in that sense. I'll never forget Matt; what you could have done but wouldn't."

"Senator, my conscience is clear. Your son was a grown man and a good Marine. He knew serious consequences would follow if he went on TV. If a Marine, any Marine, thumbs his nose at the Corps on national TV, he's going to get hammered. What he didn't know was that his partner and quote-unquote friends would abandon him when he was no longer useful to their agenda. And you—"

"Step over here, Ray. I have a picture to show you."

Tugging the now thoroughly bored dog, Morales moved left until he was standing at Gustafson's elbow. Her fingertips brushed the screen of her smart phone, and Ray was staring at himself leaning close to Ella at Camp David. It was a moment he immediately remembered. He knew the picture was authentic. Alarms clanged. Panic scuttled toward him, and he barely kept it from hopping up to sit on his shoulder.

"How . . . who . . . where did you get this?"

Gustafson said nothing, keeping her eyes locked on him, a lioness watching with slitted eyes as a Cape buffalo grazed closer.

Morales reddened and his neck bulged.

"What is this shit? What are you trying to pull?"

"This 'shit' is you and Ella about to jump into bed like old times. If Julie and Rick Martin see it, this shit is something that can ruin your marriage and get you canned"

The world that Ray sensed seemed to slow to a crawl; Gunner's tail wagged with dreamy slowness. His mind, by contrast, went into hyperdrive, bouncing from guilt to anger to remorse to defiance.

"This is nothing, nothing like that. Try to make it that, and you'll be censured by the Senate; I guarantee it. This is as phony as Joe McCarthy's crap was, and you'll end up as he did if you try to use it to hurt Julie or the Martins. You're beneath contempt, Senator!"

But his eyes spoke differently.

This photo is genuine, and my shot was on target, thought Gustafson. Matt, we're going to beat this guy! He's going to pay.

"Well, Secretary Morales, I can see that this conversation has been quite a shock. I'm going to give you the opportunity to digest our encounter. I want you to think through the implications of this proof of your dalliance with the first lady. And also to think creatively about what you might do, even at this late date, to make the small amends possible for the way you brushed Matt's life aside. Feel free to call me when you've got an idea—or two."

She smiled at the nearest goon, patted Morales on the shoulder, and walked away, head high.

For a moment Morales didn't move. Then he yanked Gunner to his feet and marched off in the direction he happened to be facing, seeing little around him but much within himself.

This can't be happening to me. First Hadrab, then Ella, now this. What the hell is going on with my life? How am I going to fix this? And this monster Fahim is kicking our ass.

Approaching a stand of trees, Morales realized he was behaving erratically. He halted, and Gunner obliged him by spraying several unfortunate young silver maples. Morales hoped this would keep his security detail from thinking their man had gone around the bend.

Get hold of yourself! That picture doesn't prove that Ella and I got it on. All it shows is that we were together. And Julie and the Secret Service and the Camp David staff and my staff know that, and it's all aboveboard. And probably the president knows it, too. So there's nothing to it.

Who was the son of a bitch who took that picture? How did it get to Gustafson? Who else has she talked to about it? And who else has it?

Surveying his surroundings, Morales saw the Nature Center several hundred yards to his left. That's where his Suburban was. He headed for it, Gunner resisting unsuccessfully in his lust to spray more trees.

What now, Morales? Should I let Ella know about this, maybe develop a strategy together? What if Julie finds out—maybe from Gustafson—before I tell her? How about the president? I'll bet his main concern will be to bury this so it doesn't take him off message, as Win likes to say.

Shit, shit, shit! Why didn't I keep my trousers zipped?

Morales shoved the unwilling Gunner into the Suburban, slid in, and slammed the door. Andy, riding shotgun, half-turned but saw Morales's expression and quickly swiveled front. No quip about dog walking passed his lips.

Chapter 46

Near Yangdok, Democratic People's Republic of Korea

FIELD MARSHAL YOUNG SAN-HO SWAYED as his armored limo took the sinuous mountain road at high speed. His thoughts mirrored the road.

The fools to the south present this Chung person as a member of one of our Special Action teams, captured after assassinating Gwon. I know that's another of their lies.

But is it? It's a lie of course that he's one of ours. But *whose* lie is it? Is it Kang's or is it Chung's?

If Kang is the liar, he's probably behind the assassination. If that's it, why now? Kang must know his lie can lead to war. Why would he feel ready for war? Does the South have a new weapon that will protect Seoul, ensure victory? A nuclear weapon perhaps? But they couldn't acquire one secretly; I would have heard rumors.

I don't believe Kang is the liar. He's among those deceived by the liar.

Chung is the liar. But why?

Perhaps he's simply crazy. After all, he was in Camp Ten, and many people go crazy in there. But Kang's interrogation team would figure out that he's crazy . . . and if they're using him to prove their accusation, even knowing he's crazy, then he's simply a pawn. And that conclusion leads back to this whole thing being Kang's plot to justify attacking me. But I still doubt that because I don't see his motive for so risky a course.

Young's thoughts leaped from the theoretical to the practical. He lifted the handset and instructed his driver: "House of the Golden Orbs."

Having selected which of his palaces and courtesans he wanted tonight, something he never announced in advance, North Korea's Venerated Leader continued musing.

So why would this Chung Ma-ho sacrifice himself by pretending to be the assassin? He must realize that his fate will be either execution or life in prison, a life made particularly painful by other prisoners because of his crime. Why would he give up his life for a lie?

Perhaps he's a true believer in some cause that would benefit from another Korean war. What cause might inspire such sacrifice? Who would benefit from war here?

I might, if I could keep it under control. If war brought China and America into confrontation and if Ming were shown lacking in resolve, his rivals in the CCP would have a serious charge to bring against him. But just as that might bring Ming down, it might harm me. How could I control the crisis?

From her perch in Japan, Chung's sister has claimed he's innocent. She's appeared on television several times insisting her brother doesn't have it in him to be a killer, that he just wants to have his life back after the camps. I don't believe that. I know that under the right circumstances every human has the capacity to kill.

And then there's the timing of her own release from Camp Ten. The yakuza bought her only a few months before Gwon's assassination. Perhaps the wealthy relative who hired the yakuza didn't do it for family reasons. Perhaps there is no wealthy relative but instead some group that stands to benefit from increased tensions or war.

I can't interrogate Chung Ma-ho, but I can probably learn a lot through that sister! He's not within reach, but she is. I have many agents in Japan. I'll put her under surveillance, and she may lead me to her real benefactor.

No! That's a half measure. I'll have her brought to me. Knowing who actually wanted her release might lead somewhere useful, but it might not. And surveillance might frighten her into going to the Japanese authorities.

But if I have her, I create leverage with whoever wanted her out. I don't need to find them; they'll have to come to me. And when her brother learns I've got her, he'll be desperate to get her out. That might be revealing.

Chapter 47

Coeur d'Alene, Idaho

Two days after his explosion of temper Fahim pulled his F-150 into the parking area in front of the double-wide. Frowning because LuAnn hadn't brought the empty trash cans back from the end of the road where the pickup crew had dropped them, he stalked toward the door. The absence of her old green Dodge meant his irritation would simmer for a while. He was surprised to find the front door unlocked—another dereliction by LuAnn. Damn that woman, he thought as he entered. I bought her that dress, Charlie got his PlayStation, and now *this.* Does she think she can ignore me because I apologized for swatting her?

Fahim used the toilet, then seated himself at his computer, which was billed to LuAnn's identity for its Internet account. A few purposeful keystrokes brought up a screen that told him it hadn't been used since his last session. That's odd, he thought, usually Charlie is on this for hours every day. LuAnn and Charlie are gone, probably since I left this morning. That's abnormal for a Saturday.

Suppressing his irritation and wariness about LuAnn, Fahim brought up the porn site that had upset her. Using a porn chat room as my communication channel to Zawahiri and the few others I need is amusing. The faithful are offended by such ungodliness, but I am the greatest jihadi, so they must accept my decisions in this and all other matters.

Fahim smiled, then keyed in several salacious paragraphs that would be understood to mean he needed a cash replenishment. Soon a courier from the Solano cartel would be on the way.

I don't like using couriers. It was a courier who unwittingly betrayed the Sheikh. But in their clumsy way, among all the stupid measures they've taken since Nine-eleven, the Americans have made it impossible to transfer more than small sums without providing far more information than I will give any bank. But since cash is my most important resource, the enabler of all else, I have to have it. And the only way to get it is by courier.

Hearing tires on gravel, Fahim shot a glance through the window, anticipating the roasting he would give LuAnn. But instead of her battered Dodge he saw a dark colored Ford with several occupants. Fahim never invited anyone here and he discouraged Lu Ann from doing so. The unexpected arrival melded with his surprise at LuAnn's unusual absence, jolting him into action. He triggered his crash program on the computer and bolted into the kitchen, grabbing the TV remote as he scooted. By the time someone knocked, he appeared to be absorbed in a British football match washed down with Boddington's Pub Ale.

Upon opening the door with one hand, clutching his can of ale in the other, Fahim saw two uniforms and a suit.

"We're looking for LuAnn Petersen," said a female cop. Her high voice and tiny physique made Fahim want to laugh, but her eyes told him he'd better not. He wondered what her boobs would look like if not squashed by her bulletproof vest.

"LuAnn's not here right now. Why are you looking for her?"

"May we come in?" she said.

Coppers everywhere are the same, thought Fahim. They need to establish dominance. He waved them in with his drink-laden hand.

She entered, followed by the others, and said, "Who are you, sir?"

"Her fiancée."

"And your name is?"

Fahim swigged from the can, then said, "Al Hassan," pleased at the irritation this triggered in the diminutive officer.

"May I see some ID?"

Fahim switched the ale from his right hand to his left. Then he fished out his wallet, not missing the way the male cop's right hand moved close to his pistol when he reached for his hip pocket. With teasing eyes he handed over his Montana driving license. It was a very expensive and very good forgery. The lady cop looked it over, glancing from the photo to his face and said, "So you live here."

"I'm her fiancée, like I said. We've been together quite a while." He took another drink of ale and smiled at her.

"Put that down, please," she said. Fahim considered refusing but decided he'd shown enough contempt for the moment. He smiled, "of course," and ignoring the end table near the door, he walked away, deposited his can on the dinette table, and returned to the three cops.

She handed the license to her partner, who handed it to the suit, who hauled out a smart phone and scanned it.

If LuAnn went to the police . . . but she wouldn't do that, Fahim thought; she's too passive. But still . . . when this is over, LuAnn is a loose end I will tie up.

"Officer, I want to know why you're looking for LuAnn. Has she been hurt? Has Charlie been hurt? You've got me worried."

"They're OK as far as we know," said the suit. "That's not why we're here. Is there a computer in the trailer, Mr. Hassan?"

"Yes."

"May we take a look at it?"

Sure, because I'm a lot smarter than you are, and you won't see anything.

"I guess so. Why?"

The suit stepped closer and said, "Mr. Hassan, I'm from the Idaho Task Force on Internet Crimes Against Children. We have reason to believe this computer is being used for illegal purposes."

LuAnn! thought Fahim. He said, "Well, it's not. At least not by me. Actually, the damn thing just crashed. I was checking email when it flashed a blue screen and went dark."

"Let's take a look."

"Sure. Hey, maybe you can fix it for me." Fahim's tone neared mockery but didn't cross the line.

Twenty minutes later Fahim was alone again, staring at the computer that had provided nothing but frustration to his unexpected visitors. He drummed the fingers of his right hand on his thigh, then rose abruptly and strode to the kitchen, where he scooped up the ale can and drained it in two swallows.

This place is blown, he thought, removing another Boddington's from the refrigerator. Obviously they have the means to use IP addresses to get user account information. I thought that wasn't permitted, but now it must be. My compound is sterile: No Internet at all. I never turn on a cell phone there. No landline phone. It's entirely off the grid except for the satellite TV account and the electrical account, both of which are in LuAnn's name and billing address.

Now LuAnn has ratted on me. I'm not worried about those internet crime idiots, but she's given them an excuse to put her and this trailer under a microscope. They'll find accounts in her name that she can't explain. Then someone more dangerous than porn coppers may get interested in those accounts.

Well, this couldn't last; I knew that and planned for it. They'll never figure out the connection to Garst and the Somalis in time. And that's not even the best of it.

Chapter 48

Washington, DC

MARTY SANDERS WAS CELEBRATING WITH dinner at The Palm. Maureen, his "date" seated across from him, was his most frequent request, and he was looking forward to the rest of the evening in his Capitol Hill apartment.

"Honey, enjoy your crème brûlée while I go out and have a cigar. I know you hate 'em, but this dinner just demands a Havana finish."

"Sure, Marty," said Maureen, pulling her phone from her bag. Soon she was lost in dessert and her reading assignment for Constitutional Law 202.

Sanders nearly skipped through the restaurant crowded with Washington's power elite. The really fine thing about this, he thought, is that the information I have gives leverage over not one but two people, neither of whom I like at all, *and* it's worth a bundle. Reaching Nineteenth Street, he pulled out his cigar case, triggering the doorman to hustle toward him with a cigar cutter and a lighter that looked like a blowtorch. Sanders and the doorman lingered over their cigar ritual, one pleased with the prospect of a tip, the other with the prospect of the phone call he was about to make.

"Hello, Senator, it's Marty."

Arlene Gustafson rolled her eyes. As if I don't know this number, she thought. "Hang on a second." She put her hand over the phone and whispered.

"Ralphie," she said to the naked young man massaging her back, "beat it for a minute, will you?" As he left the bedroom, Gustafson said, "OK, but keep it short. I've got company."

Sanders reminded himself that one of these days he'd find a way to use her boy toy against her, then said, "Senator, I've got something huge on Morales. And it's really a twofer because it implicates Martin. Trust me, you can hold hearings that will dominate the news cycle for weeks."

Gustafson felt a little flutter in her stomach. "OK, Marty, you've got my attention. What've you got?"

"Senator, unfortunately you disappointed me greatly when I brought you the picture of Morales and Ella. That was definitely worth a bonus, but you stiffed me. What I've got will kneecap Morales and put the Martin campaign on its heels. Rutherford will owe you big-time, and this just may put him over the top in the election. You could write your own ticket, Senator."

Silence. Gustafson knew where his slimy mind was headed.

"You still with me, Senator?"

"So, Marty, for all I know you could be drunk or looking to settle a score with me or both. It's possible we could work something out—if this is really as big as you say—but you gotta give me something to work with."

Pacing the sidewalk near The Palm, Sanders smiled. "Morales has broken several federal laws, big-time. And he's done it in his official capacity as a cabinet officer and head of DHS. This isn't adultery, Senator; this is a federal crime. I got a witness whose testimony will send Morales to jail. Think how that will play in the campaign!"

"Sounds like one of those cases that depend one hundred percent on a single witness. Back when I was an ADA, I saw a few of those that didn't work out because the witness wasn't credible or got scared—or got shot."

"Nothing's risk-free, Senator. I'll bet at least a couple of those cases were slam dunks and big career boosters for you. This is another one. No guts, no glory, Arlene."

"What do you want, Marty?"

"It's worth a hundred K."

Gustafson laughed, a nasty barking in his ear. "Marty, I'm a senator, not the friggin' CIA!"

"Well, speaking of third parties, I know several who would give me that hundred K without blinking—like the Rutherford campaign, or Martin.

I'm givin' you first right of refusal, Arlene. And, by the way, I know about your campaign slush fund. You've got the money."

That was a shot in the dark, but Marty figured every senator had one. And he was right.

"OK, Marty, here's what I'll do: I'll deposit the hundred K in an escrow account. You get it after I've had the witness in front of me and am satisfied with his story."

"Senator, my guy isn't in the country right now. It's going to cost me cash and favors to bring him to DC. I can't do that and have you decide later you don't want to pay the balance owed. So, let's do it this way: Set up the escrow account, and I'll set up a Facetime. If you like what you get—and you will—give me twenty-five K, and I'll bring him here for face-to-face. When he walks in your door, I get another twenty-five. When you're doing backflips over him, I get the last fifty. Send me the escrow account paperwork, and I'll set up your chat in twenty-four hours."

Marty relished his power of negotiation: "Trust me, Senator, you'll love this!"

"I *don't* trust you, Marty, but that works for me."

Gustafson hung up and called for Ralphie. Lying there, she tingled with more than his ministrations.

Chapter 49

Boise, Idaho

"SO, WHAT BRINGS YOU HERE, mister?" said the apple-cheeked blonde, shortly after Jerry Thomas climbed into her Chevy Impala at Boise International Airport.

"Want to see some of Idaho; maybe do some fishing," said Thomas to the woman who had responded to his hail on Uber.

"You a pilot?"

"Yep," said Thomas. Clad in faded jeans, a checked shirt, and light windbreaker, he wanted to be just friendly enough to leave no flag in her memory but not be drawn into conversation about his plans. He pulled out his phone, saying, "'Scuse me. My boss doesn't know the meaning of 'vacation'."

As Thomas pretended to read email, his mind churned. When I spoke to this fixed base operator, Bill, about what I needed, he didn't seem all that pleased at the prospect of a three – or four-day rental. Wonder why? He's going to get a good chunk of change for the use of his plane.

I figure it'll take me three days to check out the areas I'm interested in. Looks like decent flying weather, except a little dicey tomorrow with that frontal boundary over the Sierras. Today I'll scout the Modoc National Forest and then the Shasta-Trinity. Overnight at Weed airport. Tomorrow I'll work up to the north and west to check the Wallowa-Whitman and the Colville; then Thursday I'll finish up with the Coeur d'Alene region and be back to Boise that night.

"Here we are. Bill's Flying Service," said his driver. Thomas paid her using his phone, adding a five-dollar tip. Wishing her a good day, he hoisted his black roll-aboard and a forest green backpack from the Impala and marched toward a small building attached to a hangar. Someone had scrawled "wash me" on the grimy window next to the door. Above it was a faded sign with lettering that had been vandalized to read "Bill's F ing Service." A thin smile flashed across Thomas's face. That's just the sort of crap *I* used to pull as a kid, he thought. I hope Bill takes better care of his aircraft than he does of this building. Thomas opened the door and was hit by the smell of cigar smoke.

"You got a lotta F/A-18 time but not much inna one eighty-two," said the man, sitting at a battered desk behind the counter, who had introduced himself as Bill. Wrinkles crossed his weather-beaten face like airway routes on a Jepson chart. A holstered automatic rode at his left hip.

"I've been in the business forty years. Some of the military fighter jocks who've wanted to rent from me thought they could fly anything with wings, never mind they're newbies in a light plane. Don't have the giddiyup to blast out of trouble; power curve inna one eighty-two's trickier than in a jet fighter. No radar altimeter. No HUD. Carrier guys slam the aircraft onto the runway—beats the hell out of the main mounts. Shit like that."

"Not me. I'm carrier-qualified, but most of my flying time is out of air stations. I'll be gentle with your aircraft. You'll see on our check ride."

Bill handed Thomas's logbook back and thumbed toward the door.

Thomas accompanied Bill across the concrete toward a Cessna 182 with dull white paint and faded red trim. As they walked, Thomas said, "Doesn't the TSA or the FAA get upset at your walking around armed?"

"Probably some bureaucrat somewhere would be pissed, but the country is full of Islamic assholes shooting up schools and malls and whatnot. And this is Idaho."

They reached the Cessna, and Thomas began to examine it. He didn't like the oily smudge on the engine cowling, so he popped the cover and peered inside, poking and prodding the innards. He found one of the hose clamps was shiny new, obviously recently installed. He ran his fingers over it; when they came away dry, he grunted and said, "Let's have the log."

"You'll see it passed the test hop fine just yesterday. I keep good records."

Thomas read the entry, tugged again at the hose clamp, and said, "It'll do." He did a preflight walk-around of the plane, pulled the chocks, and climbed into the left seat. Bill planted himself in the right seat, observing Thomas with a critical eye.

After retrieving a battered card from the pocket in the door to his left, Thomas perched it on his thigh and began to read the start-up checklist. He worked his way through the steps carefully, pausing now and then to locate an item. After his forefinger flicked the master power switch, he saw and heard the aircraft come alive, gyros whining, dials lighting. After turning on the anti-collision lights, he asked Bill to verify their operation. Working slowly but confidently, the Marine flier prepared the aircraft for engine start.

The check ride turned out to be uneventful, mostly. Thomas had demonstrated he could control the aircraft during slow flight, turns, level flight, and touch-and-go landings in a brisk crosswind. He did have to abort one landing when a coyote scampered toward the runway, his alertness and caution earning Bill's approval.

"OK, you know what you're doin," said Bill. "I'm satisfied if you are."

"Yep," said Thomas and brought the aircraft down once more, earning Bill's further approval by greasing the landing.

Bill motioned Thomas to a rickety chair next to his cigarette-scarred desk and went to work on the rental agreement.

After filling in the blanks of the contract, Bill looked up and said, "Three days, huh—that'll be $140 per flight hour plus whatever it takes to top off when you bring her back."

"That's fine," said Thomas, taking the pen Bill proffered and signing.

As he handed Thomas his copy of the contract, Bill said, "Headed anywhere in particular?"

Thomas smiled and shoved the Cessna's key into his jeans. "Just want to clear work out of my head and get back up in the air."

Thomas topped off the fuel tank, fetched his bag and backpack, and heaved them into the cabin behind the right seat. Settling into the left seat, he twisted to the right and pulled stabilized binoculars and a camera from the pack, placing them on the right seat. He put a sectional map, folded to display the area, on top of them. A moment later he turned to the pack again, burrowing until he touched his Beretta M9. He started to remove it, then stopped, leaving it inside atop a jumble of clothing.

* * *

Climbing out of Boise, the aircraft felt stable, if slow, since Thomas had flown the F/A-18 for fifteen years. He felt a jolt of excitement at the kickoff of his plan.

This really is a little wacky; I'm one aircraft, with only my own eyeballs and a big-ass area to recce. But this is the only idea I've had that Morales will go for, so here I am. I've studied satellite photos and have specific locations to check. If I find this guy's compound, it'll be luck, but I've been lucky all my life. And besides, I wanted to get out of DC and into the cockpit. At the worst, I've gotten away for a week and had some stick-and-rudder time.

The first possible site on his list was in California's Modoc National Forest, about three hundred miles southwest. After what seemed like forever compared to his fighter, Thomas reached his cruise altitude of ten thousand five hundred feet above sea level and set the propeller to 2300 rpm and the mixture at best power. He scanned the cockpit instruments and focused on the aircraft's sound and feel, senses alert for untoward noise or vibration. Deciding it was performing normally, he relaxed. With an unusual east wind pushing, he figured he'd make about one hundred sixty miles per hour ground speed, which meant he'd be over his first objective in an hour and forty minutes.

Both mountains and cloud built up as the Cessna approached the Modoc Forest. Thomas reached the clearing he sought. Passing five thousand feet above it, he saw three structures. *The terrorist camp had five. But maybe lower and from a side angle I'll see others in the trees.*

Caution, he thought. I don't want to attract attention—or a bullet from some angry recluse or pot farmer. He descended and put the Cessna into a port turn, adjusting it until he circled two thousand feet above the clearing. He set the autopilot and began to scan with binoculars. The aircraft bumped and bobbed in rough air, making his field of view erratic. After about five minutes he decided to take a closer look at a larger structure beneath the surrounding trees—was that an A-frame?

Thomas flew a thousand-foot pass from south to north that gave him the offset he needed to peer under the trees. He nearly failed to see the structure in the shadows, and his hurried glance was insufficient. *This is where I really need another set of eyes; I'm gonna need another, lower pass.*

On his second run, five hundred feet above the clearing, he picked up the building much earlier in his pass and was reaching for binoculars when someone appeared below and to his left with a rifle.

Oh, shit!

Thomas kicked in left rudder, skidding the Cessna off its previous flight path, then added power and clawed for altitude. After fifteen seconds the altimeter had barely moved. *You idiot! This isn't a Hornet. You're hanging here like a grape, an easy target.* He slammed the throttle and mixture controls into the stops and pushed the nose down to gain air speed and distance from the armed stranger. Its engine screaming and wing tips vibrating, the Cessna fled the clearing about fifty feet above several towering spruce trees. Once out of sight of the armed man, Thomas climbed to a more comfortable altitude and circled.

OK, what have we got here? I don't think that guy took a shot at me, but he brought out that rifle for a reason. I could make another pass . . . So what does it mean that he showed himself and in a threatening way?

Probably it means he's not our guy. A cool customer like this al-Wasari wouldn't panic and is too shrewd to come out waving a rifle like that. He'd hunker down until I left and be extra alert but would assume the overflight was an anomaly, unless it happened again. So the guy I just flushed is a survivalist or a druggie. I'll cross this one off.

After refueling at Alturas airport, Thomas, grateful for the bathroom break and a short, brisk walk, began searching nearby Shasta-Trinity National Forest. Four fruitless hours later he turned the aircraft to final approach course into Weed airport, his spirits lifted briefly by a spectacular view of Mount Shasta. Shoulders stiff and eyes aching, Thomas wasn't as lighthearted as he had been climbing out of Boise that morning.

As he left the office after arranging fuel, he called a taxi and, to his pleasure, was picked up in less than ten minutes.

Now for Jacuzzi jets on my back and shoulders, a steak, a few drinks, and lights out!

Chapter 50

Washington, DC

RAY MORALES LOOKED AT THE phone on his desk as if it were a pistol he was about to put to his temple. Several days of thought ranging from panic to cool calculation had delivered him to this point. That picture changed everything, destroying Ella's idea for handling the aftermath of our neediness and weakness by never speaking of it.

Even if I could satisfy that blackmailing bitch Gustafson, others—people I can't approach or control—have that picture. That slimeball she uses to dig her dirt. Whoever took it at Camp David. Maybe an intermediary between the photographer and the slimeball—Marty Sanders, that's his name.

This picture *will* get out. I've probably got only a couple of days to tell Julie. And Ella, too, so she can prepare for it.

He picked up the phone.

Two hours later Ray Morales sat miserably in a speeding Suburban taking him to The Greenbrier. Julie sounded so happy when I told her I could get away tonight, he thought. That makes it even worse.

Is there *any way* I can avoid this? Really, is this just about *me*, about getting it off my chest?

No. That damned picture forces me to tell her now.

I'm going to cause my best friend such pain. Just hit her out of the blue. And then her anger and contempt, both of which I deserve. We saw infidelity around us among Washington's power people and believed—we both believed—we would never . . .

How do I begin? She'll know as soon as I walk in that something is really wrong. I'll only make it worse if I fudge and then circle back to it later. I'm going to dive in as soon as she asks me what's wrong. But what about Julie's feelings—will it be harder for her if I do that? I don't know . . . but I don't see any other way. Of all the things I've done in my life that was the stupidest. And most selfish.

Was it? said a mocking voice within his skull. *What about torturing that guy?*

Morales' mind careened off down that path, rehearsing all the reasons he had for using Ruby, until he stopped it. But he was barely able to put that memory back in its box.

Moments later he noticed the car slowing and knew his reckoning was near. He felt numb.

Sitting in the living room of their suite, Julie heard the door open. Her heart lifted as she hurried the few steps to the foyer. Ray came in and at the sight of his face her excitement turned to apprehension. They embraced and she felt the tension in his neck and shoulders.

"What is it, Ray? Something's tying you in knots."

Morales opened his mouth to speak but paused, a jumper unable to leap from his ledge. Then the words that changed everything tumbled out: "I've done something terrible. I slept with Ella that night at Camp David—I'm so sorry, Julie!"

Julie froze and felt the bottom drop out of her stomach. Unmoving except for her crumpling face, she said, "Do you love her?"

"No, *no* . . . I don't love her; I love *you*. It was weak. It was crazy. I . . . I'm so ashamed." Ray's voice cracked.

Facing Julie, he took her hands. Her eyes flashed and she pulled back as if he were a rotting corpse. She stepped away, feeling a little dizzy, fighting for composure. Where does this go? she thought. How does it end? How do I *want* it to end? Can I still love Ray? Does this mean I'm no longer desirable to him?

Ray stood silently, hearing Frank Sinatra from a set of small, blue speakers flanking the couch.

"Did she seduce you?"

"No, not in the sense of luring me to Camp David with that in mind. But . . ."

Ray looked at the cocoa-colored carpet, then continued.

"She arranged dinner alone in front of the fireplace . . . Led us on a walk to look at the stars . . . I guess I'd say she didn't warn me off when my temperature went up."

Arching her neck, Julie said, "Did you enjoy it? Was it like old times?"

Ray gulped, then said, "I . . . I . . . for a moment. It was more like falling into a river and being swept away. Unexpected, quick, like that. And no, it wasn't like old times!"

"Why should I believe you? You two have a history!"

Ray flushed, threw back his shoulders and said, in what Julie thought of as his Marine voice, "It was not like old times."

Julie turned her back and approached the fireplace. Feeling vulnerable and afraid, she stared into the flames. I was a consultant for eighteen years, she thought, a damn good one! Like my dad told me, "Never let them see you sweat." I'm good at handling surprises and thinking on my feet. So although part of me wants to run off and curl up in a ball and dissolve, I will not do that.

If this was *a one-night stand . . . and if Ray is genuinely regretful and committed to us . . . I think I still love him . . . we have so much good history.*

She turned to Ray and said, "What did you talk about afterwards?"

He slumped but held her gaze and said softly: "I told her it was my fault . . . I apologized. She told me not to apologize; that it was what we both needed in the moment. She said something about just being glad we could be there for each other." He paused and said, "And that it would never happen again and no one else would ever know."

"Well, the second part of her prediction is already wrong! Why should I believe the first?"

Julie's eyes widened and she stepped toward Ray, arms folded across her chest. "So she hasn't told the president?"

"I don't know. We haven't had any contact since then. But I don't think she's told anyone."

Julie's eyes bored into his and her head tilted quizzically. "So why are you telling *me?"*

Ray felt her question drive a spike into his belly. He dropped into an arm chair upholstered in green leather and glanced down for a moment. Then looked up, squared his shoulders and said, "Because . . . Arlene Gustafson got her hands on a picture that she may use to accuse us of having an affair."

Julie threw up her hands. "*What?* You mean this wasn't a one-night stand?" Her voice was almost a shriek.

Ray leaned back, pressed his fingers to his temples and drew them down his face. He looked up at Julie and said, "It was only once. And this picture just shows us with our heads close while we were walking outside at Camp David. It's not sleazy unless you want to believe it is, want to wrap it in lies and serve it to the media."

"Or the president. Do you have it?"

"No. She showed it to me on her phone."

"What does she want?"

"She said she wants me to get Matt buried in Arlington."

Face as hard as marble, Julie said, "Well then, for God's sake, *do it!*"

She squatted to Ray's eye level and her gaze sifted through the layers of his existence until they reached his soul.

"What does all this mean for our marriage, Ray?"

"That's up to you; I'm the one who was unfaithful. I'll do whatever you want—separation, divorce, whatever you want."

Julie stiffened. "No, Ray, I want to hear what this *means* to you."

"Julie . . ."

Ray looked down, then met her eyes. "It means I've hurt you, betrayed you. It means I'm not who I thought I was or who *you* thought I was, who you thought you married . . . It means I'm ashamed of myself, so ashamed of myself!

"I never failed in my duty, not in fifty-eight years. But now I have. That night at Camp David I broke my marriage vows to you and to God."

Scowling, eyes blazing, she said, "This had better be about more than your duty, Ray!"

Her husband looked stricken.

Julie's expression softened slightly. "Do you want our marriage to make it, Ray?"

"Yes, Julie, please forgive me. I don't deserve your forgiveness, but I love you and I want to stay married to you. Nothing like this will ever happen again.

"Please?"

She rose and gazed down at him, measuring him with her eyes.

"Ray, I may be able to forgive you, but I don't think I'll ever again trust you completely. The appearance of our marriage remains and will remain; I don't want a separation or divorce—at least not now. But the heart of our marriage, the soul of our marriage? You've ripped out a huge piece. Can we repair the damage? I don't know whether we can, but I'm willing for us to try. My question is, are you?"

Ray looked up hopefully. "Yes!"

Julie's eyes flashed. "But it has to be more to you than frickin' *duty*! It has to be about love.

"Is it?"

Ray met her gaze. "Yes . . . I love you and need you. That sounds so pat, but I don't have any better words right now."

Julie nodded and put her hands on her hips. *I understand this man. I can read him like a book. This wasn't some carefully planned tryst he had set up. For as long as I've known him—twenty years—he's set boundaries of fidelity and morality around his behavior—and maybe his thoughts, too—and has never before crossed them. He walked into this, stupidly for sure, but without premeditation. I have some sympathy for that. But he failed to take control and walk away, which he had plenty of opportunity to do. That's unforgivable! Except . . .*

"What happened at Camp David wasn't entirely your fault, Ray. I knew when I backed out that an evening alone with Ella was a risk, but I wouldn't tell you, didn't say it. I should have.

"If I had said I didn't want you to go without me, would you have cancelled?"

Ray met her eyes and said, "Yes, I would have cancelled.

"But none of this is on you, Julie."

"I say some of it is. You're not the first man to think with his penis. I could have prevented the circumstance where you did that. I shouldn't have had to. But you're human, Ray. I knew, but didn't want to face it.

"This is done, for the moment. We'll talk more and figure out how to handle this, but right now I've had enough. Come over here and hug me—but that's all."

Ray wrapped her in his arms. His throat ached and his eyes stung with tears.

Hours later, exasperated by swirling thoughts that kept her awake, Julie sat up. Slowly, she swung her legs out from beneath the covers, relieved that Ray was asleep, or wise enough to pretend. She moved quietly into the living room, lit the gas fireplace, and stared into the flames.

Ray betrayed me, she thought. And Ella. Especially Ella! But I'm also angry at myself . . . I didn't face the obvious possibility of what might happen at Camp David, of them alone. Dammit, I failed myself by not telling Ray I was concerned.

As for Ella . . . I'm *very* angry with her! First, leaving aside the sex, she's been selfishly pursuing this good, overworked man for companionship that is the responsibility of her husband. All of us are lonely and at least a little frightened; she should just suck it up, like me. Second, she knows Ray well enough to understand he's not the kind of person who can just shrug off infidelity, as she apparently can. She seduced him knowing full well it would eat away at him afterwards. "Hey, it was great, but we're not doing this again and we're not telling anybody," works for her but not for Ray, and she knew that!

I'm going to watch and wait. I want to get in Ella's face and let her have both barrels but where would that lead? She's pretty volatile and she misses being part of the policy action. I don't want her deciding *not* to let this go, to instead fill the void in her life with a campaign to win Ray. Maybe I'll let her know that I know about them but nothing more than that. No shouting, no hysterics.

And Gustafson . . . Ray doesn't know what to do—and that's frightening. Maybe he needs to get off his high horse and intervene in the system to give her what she wants, propriety be damned! But the problem is, the photo's digital. Who knows where else it is besides Gustafson's phone? It's going to come out, I know it!

Julie gazed into the flames, her mind whirling.

Wait a minute! Ray said *the picture* was the reason he was telling me. *Not* that our relationship couldn't be based on deception. *Not* that keeping this secret was tearing him up. Apparently, he was *fine* with their secret, just like Ella.

Julie crossed her arms deeply, hands pulling inward on her shoulders, as if holding herself together. She didn't know which was greater, her hope that they could survive this or her disappointment and anger towards Ray.

Chapter 51

Tokyo, Japan

GO KI-NAM HATED THIS ASSIGNMENT. He always hated rush jobs, and this was the worst ever.

As the elevator rose, Go fumed. Seize this woman, Chung Ma-eun, in the city and take her to the coast for pickup by a fishing boat. It has to be done immediately. The boss said, "Here's her address—get her." No time for surveillance. No time for a backup plan. No time to set up a snatch when she's out shopping.

Go exited the elevator on the twenty-third floor, glancing left and right. Nothing but tired carpeting, smudged beige walls, and brownish doors. He spotted apartment 2342 across the hall to his left and 2341 to his right. Turning right, he willed himself to walk confidently to 2341. He took a deep breath and knocked.

A frail woman in a green dress appeared. Looking over her shoulder, Go saw a sitting room, apparently empty. Relief washed over him.

"Yes?" she said in Japanese.

"Chung Ma-eun," he said in Korean. "I have come from your brother, Chung Ma-ho, with a message for you."

Chung's eyes widened, but she said nothing. He saw the muscles in her right forearm tighten as she took a firmer grip on the door. He slid his right foot across the threshold and prayed that he could keep her calm enough to gain entry.

"He is anxious to speak to you. I can take you to him in Seoul."

"Come in," Chung said, the wariness in her eyes belying her invitation.

As the door closed, Go had a flicker of optimism. I'm inside without a fuss, he thought. Maybe she'll come quietly.

"Who are you? How can you take me to my brother?"

"I'm KCIA."

Go offered his forged credentials. Chung took them and held them close, squinting with eyes damaged by years of malnutrition. After a moment she returned them.

"How is my brother?"

"He's being treated correctly. But things are not pleasant for him, as I'm sure you understand. After all, he has confessed to killing our president."

"So why would your government permit me to visit him in prison?"

"You've said his confession is false, that Chung Ma-ho didn't have any part in the assassination. We want to talk with you, to learn more about why you make this claim and what evidence you can offer.

"We've shown your brother newspapers and videos of your statements. He says you're just trying to protect him because you're his older sister. He insists he was one of the assassins. Look, we want to get the truth. We think you can help us do that. So come with me now to talk to him."

Chung looked away. Go saw her hands, resting on her thighs, pinching the fabric of her dress. Go followed her gaze to a picture and waited as her eyes lingered there.

She turned back to him and said, "My brother didn't do this. I'll come with you."

Go wanted to grab her arm and hustle her away but instead said, "Pack a few things. You won't need much; it's just for a few days."

Ten minutes later he was opening the door when Chung stopped them, saying, "I almost forgot. I need to leave a note for Sasaki-san."

"Who's that?"

"A friend of my brother who visits every day, usually about this time. He's helping me adjust to Japan."

Go's shoulders tensed and glanced toward the elevator.

"Well be quick about it!"

Chung Ma-eun's face told him he'd blundered.

"I'm sorry; it's just that we have a flight to catch."

As Chung scribbled—in Korean, he noticed—Go realized he'd need to send someone back for the note—and maybe to take care of the friend.

And what if he steps off the elevator as we enter? I'll have to kill him, and this operation will be in the news within hours. The boss will blame me. If I'm lucky, I'll end up in a Japanese prison; if not I'll be sent back to Pyongyang for interrogation and end up in one of the camps.

"Chung, would Sasaki-san want you to come with me to Seoul?"

She was silent for a long moment.

"No . . . probably not."

"But you want to do this, don't you?"

"Yes."

"Then leave a note that says you've gone shopping or something that won't concern him."

Chung wadded up the note, tossed it in the wastebasket, and dashed off a second note.

When she had finished, Go said, "We mustn't run into Sakai-san as we leave. Let's take the stairs up a floor and take the elevator from there." Chung nodded and moved across the threshold, prodded by Go's hand at her back.

* * *

Washington, DC

Vice President Bruce Griffith was angry. When he was that way, he knew he had to be careful of his tongue. That was especially important for this meeting. He was seeing this damn Gustafson woman to soothe her, not to insult her.

"Senator Gustafson is here, Mr. Vice President."

Forcing a smile, Griffith stalked to the door of his office in the vice presidential residence, on the grounds of the Naval Observatory. In a society where every nuance was analyzed, setting was important. He selected this place to signal she was important, but not top-tier. She read his meaning and so each began the meeting in a sour mood.

"Senator, nice to see you," said the vice president, offering his hand with a forced smile on his pockmarked face, the result of severe teenage acne.

"Thank you for seeing me on short notice, Mr. Vice President," said Gustafson, briefly raising the corners of her mouth, a blood-red slash of lips across impossibly perfect teeth.

Motioning toward a pair of chintz armchairs near the fireplace, Griffith said, "Some refreshment?"

Gustafson merely shook her blond head. Griffith nodded to his Secret Service agent, who withdrew and closed the door.

"Well—"

"You can skip the preliminaries, Mr. Vice President." She folded her arms and glared.

Griffith scowled, then shook his head and grinned.

"OK, Arlene, no bull. Look, we know Morales was insufferable at the hearing, and the president slapped him down, hard. And then he made him do *American Morning* and grovel a bit on camera. And I know Morales sought you out and apologized in person the evening after the hearings. Then he did it publicly, in your office. I think you've had your pound of flesh; you've shown the world that nobody screws with a U.S. senator. So why are you still on the warpath?"

"Because he not only lied about me, he accused me of using the hearing to settle a personal score. It makes no difference that he was right about that. By bringing it up he caused me and my family great pain; his words sent the press scurrying to dig up the details of my son's death and rehash them on front pages and on television. He hasn't paid enough for that, not nearly enough!"

"Arlene, I'm sorry. But we're in a tough business, you and I. Like the man said, 'politics ain't beanbag.' Every once in a while we have to suck it up and move on if we want to stay in the game. This is one of those times."

"No, it's not." Her pointing index finger a missile launcher, Gustafson said, "*Morales . . . must . . . pay.*"

Griffith leaned back, as if her words had struck his chest. "Damn, Arlene! I thought you were Scandinavian, but you must have a lot of Sicilian in you."

Gustafson's face told Griffith his attempt to lighten them up had failed.

"Morales is dirty, Mr. Vice President. He's gone rogue, done something that's a ticking time bomb for the Martin administration. I can reveal that at a hearing, or the White House can do it. I'm positive that when you know the facts, you'll want to break the story from sixteen hundred Pennsylvania."

Gustafson had the satisfaction of seeing Griffith's mouth drop open. His gaze dropped to the Aubusson-replica carpet.

"So . . . what's next?" said Griffith, looking at her as if she were a bear trap he had narrowly avoided.

"What's next is my meeting with the president. In the Oval Office."

"*Arlene* . . . I don't know enough about this to arrange a meeting. You're going to have to walk me and Bart through this. You just don't get to walk in and surprise a president—especially *this* one."

"Bruce, I'll tell you just this much: it's about treatment of detainees. If you guys have any sense at all, you'll set up the meeting. If you don't . . ."

Chapter 52

The Pentagon

MAJOR GENERAL CASEY HERSCHAK, MILITARY assistant to the secretary of defense, stood silently at the threshold of his boss's office waiting for him to look up. The secretary of defense hated paperwork and would ignore documents as long as possible, then force himself to tackle them nonstop, as if he were gulping down castor oil, knowing that if he stopped, he wouldn't finish the dose.

"What!" said Eric Easterly, eyes jets of flame rivaling a shaped charge.

"Sir, there's a SEAL officer on secure from Yemen. He wants to speak with you; wouldn't say more than that he has urgent information, for you only. He's Commander Liam Reddy, and he claims you and his father served together in Team Two. That's why I decided to interrupt you."

Herschak saw Easterly's anger subside to irritation.

"OK, Casey. I did serve with his old man. I'll take it, but if he's abusing my respect for his dad, you're gonna cut him orders to the dark side of the moon!"

After Herschak withdrew, closing the door as he left, Easterly rammed his personal NSA crypto card into its slot in the STE console on his desk, pushed speakerphone, and said, "Commander Reddy, this had better be good."

Seven thousand two hundred miles away, a slender freckle-faced man in desert camo trousers and a sand-colored tee shirt took a deep breath. "I'm afraid good's not the word for this, sir. Thought hard about how to handle it and decided to go direct to you. I know how irregular this is but—"

"Get on with it, Reddy!"

"Sir, I need to know what to do with a local who claims Secretary Morales tortured him at a black site in the states and had him dumped in Yemen."

"All right, Commander. You've got my attention. What are the facts?"

"One. Some Blackwater Security guys—former SEALs—came to me yesterday with an Arab named Ali Hadrab. Guy had walked up to their compound with the torture story.

"Fact two. Hadrab has a long, wide scar on his left thigh; looks like a burn, but he said it was from some sort of skinning knife used by a crazy woman Morales had turned loose on him. His story is he was captured trying to bomb Mall of America, brought to some sort of medical facility, strapped to a stretcher, and sliced up by this woman. Afterwards, Morales came in and questioned him. Said he'd bring the woman back again if Hadrab didn't spill the beans. Hadrab said this woman got off on skinning him and he couldn't face her again, so he talked.

"Three. Hadrab says once he talked, he was given medical care until he healed, then blindfolded and flown to Yemen, helicoptered to the Rub al Khali desert—that's back of beyond—and dropped off with a backpack of food and some water. Last thing his guard said to him was, 'If you ever speak of this, we'll find you and kill you.'

"Fact four. I spent six hours sweating him, and he stuck to his story."

"Five. So far as I can tell, only me and the Blackwater guys have heard Hadrab's story. I've invited them to stay in our compound for a few days and keep their mouths shut. I hear they were pretty good SEALs, and I trust them to keep quiet for at least a little while. That's all so far, sir."

"OK, Commander. You did right in coming direct to me. This is way above your pay grade. Keep everybody there and keep 'em quiet. I'll get back to you soonest."

Spearing the hook button on his STE, Easterly exhaled, the sound of a tired man looking at a wall he must find the strength to climb.

What the hell am I gonna do with *this*? he thought. Do I go to Morales? Do I go to the AG or straight to the president?

Sitting on this is not an option.

Chapter 53

Coeur d'Alene National Forest, Idaho

For the past two nights Jerry Thomas had gone to bed frustrated. He had pushed the battered Cessna around the sky for a total of twenty-three flight hours, without anything he could call success. And he was down to the last few areas he had selected from satellite photos, all in the Idaho panhandle near Coeur d'Alene. His left butt cheek had found those two broken seat springs on day one and started griping at him during takeoff this morning. And he was really sick of staring at trees. *Coffee; that'll help*. He leaned over for his thermos.

Fahim heard the plane well before he saw it. I hear airplanes occasionally, he thought, but this one is different. It sounds like a small one, and it's nearby. Fahim rose from his computer, where he had been studying photographs and diagrams of Washington, DC's Nationals Park, and passed cautiously through the door of the compound's A-frame.

The A-frame was in a clearing surrounded by mature larch, spruce, and saplings struggling to find sunlight beneath them. Fahim glanced up and saw only tree-ringed sky. He scooted across the clearing into the concealment of a spruce and looked again, but saw nothing alarming. To his left, at the edge of the clearing, his gaze swept across the male and female accommodations for his shaheed, and farther away under the trees, the shed he used for making bombs.

The buzzing from his right grew louder, and Fahim looked in that direction. A dull-white single-engine aircraft swept over the clearing.

How high is he? thought Fahim. Not so high, not the altitude of a pilot randomly overflying during a journey. There's a meadow not far away, maybe a mile. That plane looks small enough to land there. Is that why he's low? Maybe dropping off some hunters. Or picking them up. If not something like that, then what's he doing around here? Maybe police searching for meth labs.

As the aircraft's sound warned that it was returning, Fahim's brain boiled with possibilities. Could the authorities have some inkling I have a hideout in this area? Could that plane be searching for me? If I take to my truck, will I hit a roadblock before I even reach the highway?

Fahim's eyes were drawn to a flicker of movement at the clearing's edge. His two remaining shaheed were walking into the open, heads craned, looking for the aircraft they had heard.

He shouted furiously to them but too late; the airplane rasped over the clearing. If those aboard had any interest at all in what was passing beneath them, they saw the two men. Fahim yelled and cursed at the pair, but instead of running back into the trees, they froze.

Jerry Thomas was *very* interested in the scene below and, upon seeing two people, he yanked the Cessna into a turn banked so steeply he nearly stalled the aircraft. As the Cessna came around, he looked over the port wing that pointed nearly straight down and saw a third person running toward the first two.

OK, so three guys in the open, and I certainly got their attention, thought Thomas. But what does that amount to? Nothing. There was a building in that clearing; I think maybe it was an A-frame.

You *think*, Colonel Thomas? He imagined the sarcasm in Morales's voice at his using that word. I've gotta make another pass, even if these are the guys we want and that spooks them. At the worst I'll have forced them to abandon their safe location, and that will probably scramble some of their plans.

At the worst, Jerry? Not quite. The worst is if a guy puts an RPG into this plane. If these are the bad guys, they just might have one.

Screw it! In for a penny, in for a pound. I'm goin' back. I've gotta confirm the A-frame and check for the three other buildings that Hadrab described.

Having chased the shocked pair back into the trees, Fahim crouched between saplings, watching and listening. Heart pounding, he heard the aircraft return, this time passing behind him, offset from the clearing. Then it made a fourth pass, now flying over the clearing. As the aircraft crossed Fahim's field of view, an object trailing an orange streamer dropped from it, landing about thirty yards from him.

Fahim remained hidden, trying to make sense of the fly-by while waiting until he was confident the airplane had left. Why was he here, and why did he turn back for another look when he saw those idiots in the clearing? Is he FBI? Is a SWAT team closing in right now?

The sky above the clearing remained blue and empty. The aircraft's urgent buzz mellowed to a drone that seemed to come from off to the east and was growing fainter. Fahim jogged to the orange streamer, discovering that it marked a small canvas pouch. He extracted a sheet of paper on which was the picture of a dog and a note: "I'm trying to find my Bluetick Hound, Ranger, lost while hunting near here. If sighted, call 208-994-1924. Reward."

Maybe, maybe not, thought Fahim. He hustled to the A-frame. Seated at his security console, he was relieved when surveillance cameras showed nothing threatening.

He returned to the clearing and launched a quad copter bearing a video camera. Once above the trees the little aircraft, which had cost $399 at Walmart, rotated quickly through three hundred sixty degrees in response to his movements of the joystick. Seeing nothing alarming, Fahim commanded another, slower panorama and once again saw nothing but birds, trees, sky, and hints of the gravel road between the compound and the highway.

After landing the quad copter, Fahim took stock of his situation. Don't lose your head. Even if this place has been discovered by the authorities, you've got time. You saw in Iraq how much trouble the Americans had passing information from their drones to their assault troops. They got better, learned to react more quickly, but this isn't Iraq, and the authorities in Coeur d'Alene are just local coppers.

Once I leave this compound, I'm on the run. I can't take the shaheed. I'll have to abandon my weapons, explosives, and suitcases of cash because I'm certain to be caught in a highway sweep—Sudden Touch, they call it—at some point. Here, I've got all that plus communications and independence. Once I run, I'll be dependent on those pathetic Aryans and the cartel.

No, I'm not going to run because of that plane. But I am going to put a few surprises along the road in here. And I'm going to have a surprise ready if it comes back.

* * *

Jerry Thomas, en route to Boise at eleven thousand feet, tried to coax every bit of speed from the Cessna.

I'm pretty sure that's the terrorist compound, he thought. It has the buildings Hadrab described. And the way those guys reacted! It looked like one was trying to chase the others under cover before I got overhead. Something about my arrival upset the applecart; that's for sure. There are certainly enough indicators to justify checking it out again, from the ground.

Chapter 54

Crisfield, Virginia

"You're sure they've decided to hold the wedding there, in Idaho?"

Adel Ghorbani considered what he heard from the caller, then said, "I don't completely trust our sister's judgment, but I think it's definite since they've rented a compound for the guests."

Another pause, then, "Well, I have complicated plans to make in order to attend, so I'm depending on you to be right, brother. I know she's hard to pin down, and I appreciate your efforts . . . Talk to you later."

Ghorbani, who liked to keep telephone codes simple, shoved the phone into a pocket, continued a block along Main Street in bright sunlight, and then strode through the door of the Captain's Galley. He saw recognition in the waitress's eyes, and the tactical part of his mind decided he wouldn't come here again.

Once seated, Ghorbani hauled out the knock-off smart phone he had purchased with cash at Seven-Eleven and began to manipulate it. In fact he paid no attention to the images, for the activity was merely tradecraft; he was doing what almost all Americans do when waiting. Ignoring what his hands were doing, Ghorbani wrestled with the problem.

Our reaction force is on the bay today, keeping an eye on an LNG ship. The American requirement that all large ships in the bay transmit their identity, cargo, destination, and movements gives us the means to be ready when an LNG carrier passes Hampton Roads, heading for the terminal at Calvert Cliffs.

Our operation is going smoothly, but nothing has happened on the bay. Did al-Wasari also conclude that Calvert Cliffs offers his best target area, or is he going to strike somewhere else while we sit here beside the Chesapeake?

And even if I am right, even if he attempts to seize the ship we are shadowing this very moment, where will he himself be? Will he be with the attack force or somewhere more secure? He's arrogant; we know enough of him to know that. His arrogance may drive him to see for himself. But we also know he's clever; the Americans weren't able to get him in Iraq, even though he was their top target in the final years. Now they have our dossier and, if they believe it, know he's the one who carried out what they call Six-thirteen. They should be working frantically trying to locate him.

The waitress arrived with his bowl of vegetarian bean soup with rice and scallions. He deliberately kept his head down and eyes on his smart phone.

"Can I get you anything else?"

"No, thank you. I'm not very hungry."

Al Wasari's still out there, somewhere, planning and directing his terror campaign, the one that will lead America to destroy Iran.

Unless I stop him.

But first I must find him.

We paid the Solano cartel a great deal of money for a talk with the courier. Then we paid *him*. If money can buy truth, we know the truth: al-Wasari has a compound in the forest near Coeur d'Alene in the state of Idaho.

If.

And if this compound is indeed his base, is he there?

Ghorbani rubbed his eyes then steepled his fingers across his mouth, gazing into the distance.

The waitress, who had indeed recognized him as a repeat customer, observed from across the restaurant. On slow days she played a game with herself, listening to conversations and studying body language, then making up stories to fit what she saw. She would remember this man because not only was he good-looking; he looked foreign, Middle Eastern, and the clientele didn't often offer her an opportunity to imagine foreign adventures as she played her game.

She saw him motion and ambled over.

"Check, please."

I should go to Idaho. This operation will run just as well without me; Sahel is a good fighter with a cool head—if they try to destroy an LNG ship, he will prevent it. This compound may be our best opportunity, and I must find out.

I will go.

* * *

Camp David, Maryland

"Bart, one more time: Are you *sure* about having this meeting?" said President Rick Martin, standing by the fireplace in Aspen cabin. He put his plastic water bottle on the mantle and waited for his chief of staff to answer.

"Yes, I am, Mr. President. Arlene Gustafson hates Ray's guts—and doesn't like us much, either—but she's been in the Senate a long time and never been one to cry wolf. She says Ray's gone rogue. If that's true, we have to manage it very carefully. We need to hear her out, in person."

"What could it be, Bart? Ray's honest and honorable—one of the few people in Washington who are."

"Let's find out," said Guarini. At Martin's nod, he told the Secret Service agent on the porch to fetch the senator from the cabin where she had been kept waiting just long enough to show they didn't fear her.

After the door closed behind the agent, Gustafson wasted no time. "Mr. President, this is going to be your Watergate unless you, not Congress, address the problem I'm about to describe."

Gustafson saw she had their attention. "Ray Morales took the would-be bomber who was captured in Mall of America and tortured him. The bomber's name is Ali Hadrab, and my associates have him sequestered awaiting the opportunity to describe his horrific treatment. I can provide that opportunity on the Hill, or I can turn him over to the White House. I—"

"Wait a minute, Arlene! Have you talked to this terrorist? Have you met him? Where is he?" said Guarini.

"His location is my secret, Bart," said Gustafson, her gaze challenging them. "I'm not giving you anything for free. You want him, you play ball."

Guarini's hands formed fists at his side. "Listen, Arlene–"

"Arlene. Bart." said the president, "Let's not get excited here."

Martin continued: "Arlene, this man is a wanted terrorist. You are obligated by your oath of office as a senator to turn him over to the FBI or to the police. I'm sure you'll do that." The president's voice could be a Stradivarius, and now it was. Gustafson's fight or flight reaction waned.

"Mr. President, I will do that when appropriate. He won't escape justice. But the issue I came to discuss is whether the American people will learn about Hadrab and hear his story from Senate hearings or from sixteen hundred Pennsylvania Avenue."

The president frowned. "We're not political allies, Arlene. Why would you want this discussion? Why not just hold hearings?"

"Because I want a couple of guarantees from you, Mr. President. I want Morales's resignation and prosecution. And I want my son, Matt, buried in Arlington where he wanted to be and where he deserves to be."

"Arlene," said Guarini. "You can't come in here and bargain with the president on a matter of national security!"

"Well, that's what I'm doing, Bart. Take a few days to decide. But don't wait long; I'm feeling restless. And don't put me under surveillance. If you do, I'll call out Morales and announce my hearings."

She turned. "Good day, Mr. President."

Gustafson stalked across Aspen's living room and out the front door.

The president, red-faced, dropped into a rocking chair facing his chief of staff. "What do you say to that, Bart?"

"She's a piece of work! We need to reach our own conclusion about Ray, quickly. I'll have a heart-to-heart with him ASAP, and we'll talk again. She's a snake, and he's a stand-up guy. This could be nothing more than a smear."

"I want to be there."

"No, Mr. President, that's too risky. We don't know what he'll say, what could be revealed. We need to preserve deniability for the campaign."

"OK. But that's just for now."

I can't let Rutherford win; he'd destroy everything we've built in our relations with China and arm everyone in America. Back when it came to the crunch on North Korea, I froze. Ray got me moving again. I owe him so much! Our country owes him so much.

The Secret Service would take a bullet for me. Do I have the guts to take one for Ray?

Chapter 55

Yellow Sea, Latitude Thirty-seven Degrees North

KIM DAE-WU SQUATTED, THEN ROSE, grasping the periscope handles as the greasy tube glided upward from its well, rivulets of condensed, humid air and seawater from leaky packing glands running down its length. Like every sub skipper, the North Korean hated this moment. No matter how carefully the sonar crew had listened and plotted the tracks of nearby vessels, there was always the chance they had missed one. The 'scope might be rising dead ahead of an onrushing bow or into the hull of a fishing boat drifting overhead. If something like that happened, Kim and his crew could die in the next few minutes.

Now! Kim halted the periscope's rise and spun it, and himself, in a circle. He glimpsed a haze-gray ship and, after completing his rapid scan, positioned the 'scope to examine it. Did its lookouts see him? Later they would, but for the moment he wanted fiercely to remain undetected.

"Down 'scope!" said Kim. "Incheon-class frigate bearing zero five zero. Angle on the bow forty degrees."

"Captain, that correlates with track three. That ship is making turns for about ten knots."

"Set up for an attack on track three. Two torpedoes, tubes one and two," said the skipper of the ancient Romeo-class diesel submarine.

A few feet to the skipper's left, the sub's executive officer glanced up from his analog calculator and said, "Recommend course zero three zero to attack, Captain."

"Conn, make your course zero three zero," said Kim. The eight men crammed into the submarine's control room fell silent, breathing humid air laced with the odors of diesel fuel, sweaty bodies, and kimchee. Through the sub's hull they heard the thrumming of the frigate's screws and the pinging of its sonar.

"Up periscope!" said Kim. Hissing, the tube rose. Kim snapped the handles into position and pressed his right eye to the rubber-cupped eyepiece. He felt his hands slippery with sweat.

"Bearing, mark! Range, mark!" said Kim. "Zero four five," replied the exec. "Range two six zero zero," he added. "Down 'scope!" ordered Kim.

Now came the worst part of his orders. This had been a perfect attack approach, giving the skipper a surge of pride in his crew. The hours of drill had paid off. And now he was going to smash that perfection, deliberately, like a potter completing a beautiful bowl and then throwing it against a stone wall.

"Make your depth twelve meters," said Kim.

The executive officer's face twisted as his certainty the captain had misspoken fought his Confucian reluctance to challenge authority. After five long seconds, he said, "Captain, we'll broach at that depth."

Kim glared at the man and said, "Carry out your orders."

The executive officer's shoulders slumped, and the diving officer immediately said, "Make your depth twelve meters."

The planesmen obeyed, and the sub glided upward, rocking as it entered the influence of waves above.

"Up 'scope!" said Kim. Only he knew that the fury in his tone was directed not at his exec, but at his orders.

The sub's conning tower broke the surface and continued upward until some six feet of it was above the two-foot waves coursing along the sunny surface of the Yellow Sea. Through the periscope, Kim observed the South Korean frigate. He waited for the sign that they had been seen.

There! Kim followed the frigate's bow swinging to port until, eventually, it became a knife-edge rushing at him.

"Dive! Make your depth forty meters."

The sub's deck tilted down. Kim looked at the men in the control room with an expression that dared anyone to speak other than as necessary to conn the sub. The beating of the frigate's screws grew threateningly as it raced toward the spot where the conning tower had slipped beneath the waves. Everyone listened for another sound, the one they feared would announce the nearness of death: the splash of depth charges hastily dropped by the frigate's surprised crew.

The warship thundered past them, sounding as if it were a few dozen meters to starboard of the sub. They heard nothing else. Frightened eyes met across the control room.

"Course one three zero; make turns for ten knots," said Kim. His words and tone, exactly as the men had heard them hundreds of times in drills, put the attack team back into practiced action.

After six minutes on course, Kim ordered a full-rudder turn, leaving a patch of disturbed water that would appear on the frigate's sonar. Twenty minutes later, hearing the frigate on the bearing of his hard turn, Kim ordered another full-rudder turn and, when on the new course, directed the sub to periscope depth.

"Up 'scope," said Kim. "Bearing, mark! Range, mark! Angle on the bow twenty." "Bearing three five zero, range three four five zero," intoned the exec.

As the periscope glided down, Kim said, "Make ready tubes one and two."

After two more observations, Kim was satisfied with the attack team's solution. "Fire one!" The sub shuddered as compressed air launched nearly two tons of torpedo. The executive officer started one of the stopwatches he held and said, "Run time sixty-three seconds."

"Fire two!" The exec punched the stem of the second stopwatch.

Two torpedoes, each with two hundred fifty kilograms of explosive, raced toward the frigate.

"Both fish running normally," said a voice from the sonar cubicle.

"Up periscope," said Kim.

As the periscope broke the surface, Kim spun around and, seeing only the frigate, settled on it. A geyser of seawater erupted, climbing above the warship's starboard side and descending in a cloud that hid its starboard quarter. As the spray cleared, Kim saw that the blast had broken the frigate in two. Ten seconds later the second torpedo raced through the debris without detonating.

Kim stepped back from the periscope and motioned the exec to take a look. Cautiously, the officer sidled into position and pressed his eye to the rubber. After watching the frigate's bow disappear, the exec turned to the skipper with a smile.

Kim's right hand flashed across the short space between them, striking the exec's left cheek with a meaty smack.

"If you ever question one of my orders again, I'll shoot you on the spot!" he hissed.

Chapter 56

Washington, DC

Ma Xin was right, thought General MacAdoo, as members of the National Security Council made their way to seats around the large table where the secure videoconference would soon begin. But he didn't go far enough . . . Young San-ho isn't just overconfident; he's crazy.

As the screens morphed from static to video, MacAdoo saw his colleagues appear, as satellites did their work: Ambassador Ralph Kornheiser speaking from the consulate in Pusan, Ambassador Barton Caulfield in Beijing, UN Ambassador Oscar Neumann in New York, General George Tedford from his command vehicle in Korea, and Admiral Kelly Swafford from her headquarters in Hawaii.

"OK, John—everyone on now?" said President Martin.

"Yes, sir. Let's—"

Martin cut him off. "General Tedford, what's the military situation?"

"Sir, about six hours ago DPRK forces attacked all along the DMZ. The main axis of their attack is toward Seoul. The ROK Third Corps has fallen back to their prepared positions and is holding. Seoul—"

"What are your forces doing, General?

"As you know, sir, we have two infantry brigades north of Seoul—about forty-five hundred troops—and light scout forces deployed roughly east-west across the peninsula. The brigades have linked up with the ROKs as planned. Right now they're in light contact with DPRK infantry but under heavy fire from their artillery. We're going after the artillery with rockets and air—"

"Casualties?"

"At the moment, probably in the hundreds, sir. It's a fluid situation; after we've killed their artillery, I'll have a better idea on casualties."

"Mmmmph! So, are we going to lose Seoul?"

"That's not inevitable, sir, but it's too soon to tell. So much depends on North Korean intentions and on how the ROKs decide to play it. Will Kang tell the Third Corps to hold at all costs? Unfortunately, my liaison officer at Third Corps headquarters is pretty much being kept in the dark."

"Aaron! Is there any sign, any sign at all, the Chinese are in this?"

"No, Mr. President. Chinese military dispositions have changed very little since the assassination."

"DIA reports indications that the PLA aircraft carrier is putting to sea," said Easterly.

Scowling at the defense secretary's intrusion on his turf, Hendricks said, "That's pretty predictable, but at the moment DIA's alone in that judgment."

"The Russians?"

"No changes, Mr. President. The Russians haven't had much in East Asia since their interventions began in the Middle East."

"What do we know about how this began? Who shot first?" said Martin. "General Tedford, what can you tell us?"

"All our positions were hit simultaneously with artillery. ROKs somewhere might have fired first, but even so, the barrage we got in response was preplanned. At around the same time, an ROK Navy ship tracking an unidentified submarine was torpedoed and sunk. This wasn't a local skirmish that got out of hand on the northern side."

"Anne, remind me what we are obligated to do by our defense treaty with the ROKs," said the president.

Anne Battista glanced at her notes and quoted, "Each party recognizes that an armed attack in the Pacific area on either of the parties would be dangerous to its own peace and safety and that each party would act to meet the common danger in accordance with its constitutional processes."

"What action does that require, Anne?"

"It requires that we do *something* in response to this attack, Mr. President. *What* we do is up to you and Congress."

Anne Battista continued, "I'd say it's in our national interest to do something big. Not only because we've got skin in the game with our troops; but because if we don't go big, the Japanese will have no confidence in our alliance with them. In that case they would either align themselves with the Chinese, or build their own nukes, or both. And Prime Minister Kato is already angry because he wasn't included in your trip to Korea and China."

Martin frowned. "Yeah. That was a mistake; you should have pushed harder, Anne."

Battista didn't respond to the rebuke so Martin continued: "The ROKs have a large, well-trained military with up-to-date equipment, do they not?"

"They do, Mr. President," said Easterly. "We aren't facing the same situation we did in nineteen fifty. The ROKs aren't going to get pushed south to Pusan again anytime soon."

John Dorn cleared his throat and said, "Mr. President, I recommend we go into compartmented session now." Martin nodded. Looking at the staff members seated along the wall, Dorn said, "Thank you, ladies and gentlemen. This will be a principals-only session."

Once the video link was broken and only Martin, Easterly, MacAdoo, Hendricks, Griffith, and Battista remained, Dorn said, "Mr. President, I think we'd better consider initiating Pandora."

Easterly, MacAdoo, and Hendricks nodded. Battista and Griffith looked puzzled.

Martin said, "Anne and Bruce, it's time for you to read in on this. Mac, walk us through Pandora."

"Yes, sir. 'Pandora' is the code word for arrangements about military cooperation between China and the U.S. in the event of war between the Koreas, or any catastrophic event there involving large military forces. It has two objectives: to prevent military conflict between us and to keep North Korean nukes—if any remain—from being used or stolen."

"What do you mean, 'if any remain'?" said Griffith. "Ming told us the PLA had seized those nukes when they went in to ensure Young San-ho succeeded Kim. The president took him at his word and announced it as a done deal. You're saying they're not so sure?"

General MacAdoo shot a glance at the president.

"Bruce, General Ma spoke with Mac during one of our regular military-to-military staff talks," said Martin. "He said North Korea is so secretive and so riddled with hidden military sites that he wasn't certain the PLA found all the nukes in the short time they had. Remember, they were in and out in two weeks." Martin turned to Mac. "Tell 'em what went down, Mac."

"Ma said he was speaking with Ming's knowledge but not necessarily his approval. If word of these arrangements got out, China would deny their existence. I have to emphasize that we don't really have an operational agreement. What Ma offered, and I agreed, was to consult during a crisis and develop whatever specific procedure the situation called for."

"Mr. President," said the secretary of state, "Have you and Ming spoken about Pandora?"

"No, Anne, we haven't. Ma made it clear that Ming would never acknowledge even this minimal agreement to cooperate with us in operations involving North Korea."

Martin looked at his national security advisor. "John, this is your agenda item. What do you recommend?"

"I recommend that Mac be authorized to start discussions with Ma immediately to come up with procedures to avoid hostile acts between our forces on the peninsula."

Easterly grimaced and said, "What role should Chen and I play in this? I should be in the loop!"

Holding up a hand toward Easterly, Martin said, "Eric, Mac will ask Ma about a role for defense ministers. But it's Ma's call. If he wants to keep it among guys wearing uniforms, I want to respect that. We owe him for coming to Mac. And you'll be involved. You won't be in the room, but you'll be in the discussion, right, Mac?"

"Of course, sir. I value the secretary's counsel."

Martin glanced at the local clock, one of four on the wall, and said, "John, are we done for now?"

"Yes, sir."

"Good, because it's time for my call with Win. Thank you all."

* * *

Beijing, People's Republic of China

"President Ming, Young San-ho's forces aren't going to push the southern forces into Pusan again," said General Ma. "They'll take a heavy toll attacking Seoul in the next few days, but the ROK air force and the U.S. carrier and land-based air will soon own the skies and begin punishing the North's army badly. Young San-ho has made an incredible misjudgment."

"Has he?" said Ming. "That depends on his objective. If it's to defeat the combined forces of South Korea and America, he's blundered. But if his objective is less than that, or will be achieved off the battlefield rather than on it . . ."

"But he's unleashed forces he can't control," said Ma. "If the Americans have finally had enough of the DPRK and decide to destroy Young and his ruling circle, it'll be over for him."

"Unless."

"Unless what, sir?"

"Unless we stand with them. Perhaps his objective is to trap China and push us into war with America."

"He would gamble everything on that? His military forces would be destroyed anyway, and then he would have no means to stay in power."

"Unless he has some means to bring about a cease-fire when it suits him. Do you suppose he hid a nuclear weapon from us two years ago?"

Chapter 57

Washington, DC

"SO SHE CAME TO YOU and the president?" said Ray Morales softly as he and Bart Guarini huddled in a secluded corner of the Members' Library of the Army and Navy Club at Seventeenth and I Street NW.

"Yes, Ray—and we have to know if what she said is true. Did you torture this terrorist?"

"It's not that simple, Bart. It's more than a yes or no, at least to me. Let me help you understand the situation. How many people has this guy, the guy who did Las Vegas, killed, Bart?"

"I dunno for sure. About sixty thousand in Las Vegas on Six-thirteen and about another seven hundred fifty since the current attacks began."

"He killed fifty-nine thousand, two hundred and three in Vegas, and—as of yesterday—he's killed another eight hundred and ten. And there's no sign he's done. And there's no guarantee he doesn't have another nuke. We don't know how many Kim sold him."

Morales continued: "These two terror campaigns aren't separate acts, by a bunch of self-radicalized, isolated people. They're a coordinated whole, directed and controlled by one guy. Get that guy, the attacks stop."

"Yeah, I get that. But *you* can't break the law. Laws, even when we don't like their results, are one of the main things that separate us from the bad guys. If they force us, or trick us, into ignoring our laws, they win."

"Bart, you're arguing introductory civics while American families are being maimed and murdered! Look, during my confirmation hearings, I pledged to do everything in my power to keep Americans protected from terrorism. Those weren't just words to me. I wasn't saying that just to be confirmed. You politicians will forgive yourselves any retreat and break any promise in order to get elected or reelected. You call politics 'the art of the possible,' and if something seems impossible, you don't feel obligated even to try it.

"I come from a different tradition, Bart. That tradition is summed up in two words: Semper Fidelis. It's my duty to get this guy. Duty doesn't get me a pass from the law, or from Saint Peter. I know that. But I will *not* say 'too hard' to my duty!"

"Ray, I—"

"Let me finish!" Morales hissed. "This guy, this *monster*, has been kicking our ass. We know his name, have his DNA and his photo, but we don't have *him*. And he keeps sending out killers eager to murder our people—the people it's my duty to protect. And yours and the president's, by the way!

"So, Bart, when we got a break and captured one of those animals, someone who must have come from Fahim al-Wasari's hideout, I wasn't gonna let him spit in my face and keep his secrets because of our law. They're using our laws to defeat us! I won't say, 'too hard,' and let him do that. So, you ask, did I torture that guy? That guy the cops caught right before he could push a button and slaughter a food court full of people?"

Morales leaned in to Guarini. "Yes, Bart. Yes! And I'd do it again. Fahim is pure evil. Can he be defeated by good alone? Maybe. Eventually. But I can't just accept the carnage that will continue until 'eventually' arrives."

Bart Guarini was of two minds. What he had just heard confirmed his worst political fears. Morales had not only broken the law; he wasn't going to hide it. And, with a moment's thought, Guarini was pretty sure there were others involved; that there was a conspiracy to torture this detainee and get rid of him and other loose ends. This was Watergate on a world stage.

But he agreed with Morales: this had to be done. To say that security forces working within the law would eventually get Fahim ignored the fact that every day Fahim was at large was a day he could launch attacks to kill the very people the American government existed to protect. And Rutherford laid each death at the White House door. Martin's poll numbers were sinking while Rutherford's rose.

He wondered what Morales had learned from Ali Hadrab. Did he now have information on Fahim's whereabouts?

"Ray, for now I'm putting aside the consequences for your actions. There *will* be consequences. The president can't accept that your duty extended to breaking the law. But tell me: Did Hadrab give him up? Do you know Fahim's hideout?"

"He gave us enough to figure out a probability area. That's all I'm saying; I don't want to pull you or the president into my mess. Bart, look, I need some time, a week or so, to follow up on what Hadrab told us. Tell the president that after I've done that, I want him to handle this in whatever way is best. Walter Rutherford is a blowhard and a fool; he mustn't win because of this."

"We don't control this, Ray. Arlene Gustafson does—at least disclosure. The president and I will do our best, but move fast! If this gets out and Fahim is still at large, I'm afraid you're going to end up in jail. The president won't be able to protect you."

Chapter 58

Chesapeake Bay, Virginia

"LET'S COME LEFT TO THREE two zero," said the pilot. The enormous ship, as large as the nuclear aircraft carrier *Carl Vinson*, swung slowly until it was aligned with the red and green winking lights on buoys delineating the deep-water channel.

Captain Tim Cook loved his work. He had been a shipping pilot for fifteen years and reveled in his craft. It required encyclopedic knowledge of the long waterway and the delicate application of enormous power to control huge ships, like the 123,000-ton Liquid Natural Gas tanker *Exxon Energy* he guided this night.

Satisfied with the vessel's course, Cook walked to the rear of the large, spotless ship's bridge to refill his coffee cup.

Neither he nor the three bridge watch standers heard or felt the muffled thunk of grapnels gaining purchase on the deck railing aft on the starboard side.

The ship's Coast Guard escort didn't notice either, but for a different reason: they were dead, except for one very frightened third class petty officer. That young man would be forced at knifepoint to make the scheduled position reports to Coast Guard Sector Headquarters.

Jogging along the deck, then up a series of interior stairs, Bobby Garst and three Somali pirates reached the bridge. Like the tentacles of a sea monster, other Somalis surged smoothly into the crew's berthing area, the dining area, and the engine room control station deep within the vessel, until the small crew was entirely in their grip.

Cook heard the door open, saw a figure outside on the wing of the bridge make an underhand toss. His world became the blind chaos of a stun grenade's actinic flash and eardrum-stabbing boom. Dazed, Cook felt hands pulling him to his feet and the pressure of a hard, blunt object against the back of his head.

Undisturbed, the *Exxon Energy* forged on. The bulb at her bow parted the waters efficiently for the nine hundred foot hull behind, an immense bulk atop which sat three huge spheres. The autopilot maintained course down the channel despite chaos on her bridge.

"I'm in command now. Got that?" said a voice behind the pilot, an American voice with a southern slowness but cold ferocity.

"Okay," mumbled Cook, correctly identifying the object poking his scalp as a gun.

The man gripping Cook's collar released it and moved in front of him, keeping a distance Cook knew would be traveled far faster by a bullet than he could move, even if he wanted to, which he didn't.

"And just to make sure you obey . . ." Cook's captor motioned to a Somali, who shoved the ship's master toward Cook, prodding him with the muzzle of an assault rifle. Another pirate stepped up to the master, grabbed his left hand, and slashed it with his knife. The master yelled as blood welled from the web of skin between thumb and forefinger that the pirate had just slit.

Garst said, "I have an all-ocean, all-tonnage master's ticket of my own and I have *you,* pilot. I don't need this guy. If you fail to obey my orders or try anything at all funny, I'll let my man here cut off his fingers one by one and then move to other body parts. My Somali friends love to do that shit."

Eyes as black as the balaclava covering the captor's face burned into the pilot's. "Understand, pilot?"

Cook nodded, his mind reeling.

Bobby Garst didn't have a master's license, but as an experienced third officer he had watch-keeping skills sufficient to fool the terrified pilot for the time needed.

Cook swallowed, croaked, "Yes, I understand."

The *Exxon Energy* proceeded on schedule, on track, northward toward its destination.

Chapter 59

The Pentagon

"SO TELL ME AGAIN WHY I shouldn't pull the plug on the F-35 program. It's been over budget and behind schedule for years. Supposedly, we're at IOC, but that's a fudge. The only squadron that has 'em can't get 'em off the ground but three times out of five because the flight system computer goes belly up whenever ambient temperature goes over eighty-five."

The program manager, an Air Force two-star who had flown as a Thunderbird and later a test pilot looked down at his hands, which were in front of him at belt level, clasped around a remote control. His decision made, he selected PowerPoint slide seventeen and looked at Easterly, who was at the stand-up desk in his E-ring office.

The secretary of defense saw a graph with three scales and four colored lines swooping across it. He knew the answer to his question, and it wasn't in this graph. The program lurched along because several powerful members of Congress wanted jobs for their constituents. And because a president in a tight reelection race didn't want the embarrassment of announcing an expensive failure. He let the general drone, feigning an occasional note on the pad before him, but his mind wrestled with quite a different issue.

Come on, Eric, he thought. You can't chew on this much longer. Reddy can't keep sitting on that Arab and the security contractors; this is a grenade thrown into the outhouse. Very soon it's gonna blow shit far and wide. Is there time to heave it back before it explodes? Do I want to try?

Damn right I do!

"General, I'm sorry, but we're out of time. Your briefing has been very helpful so far, and I look forward to your return tomorrow to finish."

Easterly stood and shook the rattled general's hand, motioning vigorously to his military assistant, General Herschak. As soon as Herschak had ushered out the briefer and his assistants, Easterly grabbed his phone and punched the direct line to Ray Morales. Fifteen minutes later he hopped into the rear seat of an armored Suburban idling before the basement doors of his private elevator.

"Ray, I've got a SEAL commander in Yemen holding a local named Ali Hadrab."

Ray Morales, sitting in his secure conference room across a bare wooden table from the secretary of defense, remained impassive. I've been expecting it to get out, he thought, but not this way. Gustafson supposedly has Hadrab, not some SEAL. Is she blowing smoke? Is she trying to sell something she doesn't have, or have yet?

"How did that happen?"

"A couple of security contractors ran into Hadrab in the deep boonies. He had a story he was anxious to tell. After they heard it, they decided to deliver him to their former comrades in the teams."

"And? What was his story?"

"Ray, he claims that after his arrest you and another guy took him to a black site near Minneapolis and you personally interrogated him under torture."

The two locked eyes, telescopes probing deep space, each seeking the other's soul.

"Did you do that, Ray?"

"*Yes*. I was sure he had information that would lead us to Fahim, the ringmaster of this bloody circus; we get him, the organized attacks will stop."

"Did you get what you needed, Ray?"

"Most of it. His base is somewhere within about a four-hundred-mile radius of Boise, Idaho. The area is being searched as we speak. Eric, I need you to keep Hadrab out of play. Fahim doesn't know we have a line on his safe house. If he finds out, he'll vanish. He'll kill a lot more Americans if he gets away."

"Ray, you're asking me to join you in a conspiracy to cover up your violations of federal law." Easterly gestured his unspoken question: why?

Morales pinched the bridge of his nose for a few seconds, then said, "I'm not asking you to cover up. I'll answer for what I've done, to the courts and to God. But I need a few days. That's all I'm asking, Eric. A few days to nail this animal."

Easterly thought of the blood-spattered schoolrooms, of the shopping malls now pockmarked by bullets and bomb fragments, of the ordinary men and women who refused to be cowed by Fahim's messengers of jihad. More would die if Morales's secret got out now.

And he thought of Fahim. And wanted him dead.

He held out his hand and Morales grasped it.

"OK, Ray. But I can only keep the lid on a couple more days. What can I do to help get Fahim?"

"Eric, this has to be very quiet, small footprint. I can do it in-house. Besides, neither of us wants your fingerprints on this op. This conversation never took place."

"Right, it didn't. Good hunting."

Chapter 60

Washington, DC

"SIR, I BELIEVE I'VE JUST found al-Wasari's compound," said Jerry Thomas from Boise. "I don't have a positive ID, but circumstantial evidence is pretty compelling. We need to get our people in there to check it out."

"Wait one, Jerry." Ray Morales rose from his cluttered desk, crumbs from his pizza dinner tumbling from his lap and closed the door to his office in Washington.

Back at his desk, Morales switched to speakerphone and said, "And who are 'our people,' Jerry?"

"Well . . ."

"Never mind that for now. Tell me what you've got."

"I'll start with the geography. The location fits what Hadrab said about driving time, and the clearing with five buildings fits his description of the hideout—and it's the only clearing I found with five buildings. What I observed today in four passes overhead and some recce of the Coeur d'Alene area also fits, as does the presence of three people who were not glad to see me."

"I'm unconvinced, Jerry." Morales waved a blunt-fingered hand dismissively. "There could be many reasons they weren't glad to see you. Cooking meth comes to mind."

"Came to my mind, too, sir. But cooking meth produces so much toxic shit—about six pounds of the really nasty to one of the meth—that the vegetation around meth cookers usually gets killed off. The druggies are usually too lazy to hump the stuff very far; they just dump it nearby. But this place wasn't blighted."

Morales now looked less skeptical.

"Also," said Thomas, "when cooking meth out in the boonies, you need to bring in precursor chemicals regularly and move your product out. I saw a gravel road; the only vehicle-passable way in or out. It was pretty overgrown, clearly wasn't getting a lot of use. That doesn't fit with a meth-cooking operation deep in the woods."

"Jerry, maybe you saw three religious nuts who were out there waiting for the signal to drink their Kool-Aid."

Thomas's voice rasped. "Yessir, there will always be 'maybes' until we get boots on the ground in there, but this is worth a serious recce."

He's right, thought Morales. Time's running out—Gustafson, somehow, found Hadrab and knows the truth. Bart and Eric can't keep that bottled up much longer, and when it comes out, I'm done at DHS and probably looking at indictment.

"Which brings me back to my earlier question, Jerry—whose boots are going on the ground?"

"How about mine, sir?"

Morales grimaced as his mind raced. He's right again. But because we can't reveal our source after what I did to break him, there's nobody I can bring inside to back Jerry up. Well, who's already inside? Jerry, me, the doc, and Andy, who was my security detail that night. Well, hell, what about me and Andy? I was a pretty good tactical Marine, and Andy was Marine Recon. But who are you kidding, Morales? This isn't about company-level tactics; it's special ops stuff, and you were never *that* good. Dammit, I want this guy! I've set myself up to get fired and probably jailed by what I did to get this far. I've made a mess of my marriage. So now I'm gonna give it up, just wait for the jail cell and the divorce papers? *No way!*

"I can't send you in there alone, Jerry. But it's got to be done—so I'm going with you, me and Andy."

"Sounds good to me, sir. When do we go?"

"Soon as I can arrange to disappear for a couple of days."

* * *

Chesapeake Bay, Virginia

Boatswain's Mate Third Greg Aldridge was scared to death. It had happened so fast . . . the darkened boat drifting in the blackness ahead of the tanker . . . going alongside to investigate and remove it from the ship's path . . . the chug of silenced weapons, men swarming aboard their patrol boat.

Now the three Somalis who had killed his shipmates and left their bodies in an obscene pile belowdecks took turns observing him with raptor eyes as they scanned the bay. By some unspoken protocol, one of them always watched him as they shifted their lookout duties among themselves wordlessly.

"Coast Guard four-five-one-one-two, Coast Guard four-five-one-one-two, this is Coast Guard Sector Maryland NCR, over."

The one with a bulbous nose moved quickly, ripping the duct tape from Aldridge's mouth and grabbing the radio microphone. He held it near the young sailor's mouth.

"Answer normally. Whatever they say, wait for my orders before responding. Cooperate and you live; if not, I will slit your throat with *this*."

With one hand brandishing a fighting knife, he thumbed the transmit button on the mike with the other and looked into Aldridge's eyes. Aldridge was looking at the face of Death and he knew it.

"Coast Guard Sector Maryland NCR, this is Coast Guard four-five-one-one-two, over."

"One-one-two, Sector. Request your ops and position, over."

"Is that routine?" hissed Big Nose.

"Yes. I tell them we are normal and give our position."

"Do it," said Big Nose. He keyed the mike and held it near Aldridge's mouth.

Heart pounding, Aldridge said, "Sector, ops normal, position thirty-seven twenty-two point six north, zero seven six forty-five point four east, over."

In the Coast Guard Sector Operations Center near Baltimore, the watch officer's eyebrows shot up, and his gaze locked with that of the radio operator.

"Was that . . ."

She nodded. "Sounded like it to me."

"Ask for a repeat."

"Coast Guard four-five-six-four-zero, this is Coast Guard Sector Maryland NCR. You were stepped on. Say again, over."

With a flick of his wrist, Big Nose prodded Aldridge's neck at the carotid artery.

Eyes flashing, Big Nose said, "What got her attention? I should kill you just for that!"

Inanely, Aldridge apologized and said, "What they mean is another station transmitted at the same time I did and cut me out. Happens a lot. Sector is hearing radio comms from boats all up and down the bay. They're asking me to repeat."

"OK, but remember." Big Nose twitched the knife's point into Aldridge's skin.

Fighting to hold his voice steady, Aldridge spoke into the mike held in front of him. "Sector, I say again, ops normal, position thirty-seven twenty-two point six north, zero seven six forty-five point four east, over."

In Baltimore the watch officer and the radio operator looked at each other, Aldridge's words hanging in the air.

"What do you think?"

"Definitely the duress code."

"Yep. He called his position *east* longitude twice. That wasn't a mistake"

Sweat popped on the watch officer's forehead as he hit speed dial.

The radio operator said into her microphone, "Coast Guard four-five-one-one-two, this is Sector Maryland NCR, copy all. Sector out."

Big Nose glared at Aldridge, who said, "That's it. I made our position report, and Sector got it clearly the second time."

"Now what?"

"Nothing until they check on us again."

Big Nose clipped the mike into its bracket.

"Remember," he said, slashing the air very close to Aldridge's throat.

* * *

Supreme Command Bunker, Democratic People's Republic of Korea

Young San-ho, field marshal and Venerated Leader, sat on a balcony overlooking a room-size map of the Korean peninsula, tended by uniformed men and women as worker bees tend their queen. They pushed colored markers around with poles. Red markers—Young's forces—clustered near Seoul faced blue American markers and black ones representing ROK forces. Arrayed near the field marshal were bulky TV monitors showing his own government channel plus American, South Korean, Chinese, and Japanese programming. A flock of translators hovered anxiously nearby.

"What is Martin saying?" said Young to a slender, nervous man wearing a headphone and listening to CNN video of President Martin speaking to a mob of reporters.

"Venerated Leader, he is saying that forces of the Democratic People's Republic of Korea made an unprovoked attack on the capital of South Korea."

The man shuddered as he realized he had just spoken in direct contradiction of Young San-ho's broadcast to his slave-citizens.

The worm, thought Young. I could shoot him where he stands and he knows it. Smoothly, he pulled a pistol from its holster on his polished leather belt. The translator flinched and Young laughed.

"It's fine. I know you are only repeating the pirate Martin's lies because it is your duty." After a pause he said, "Continue."

"The pirate Martin says the initial advance has been halted by courageous South Korean and American soldiers. He says that if the North Koreans hoped to take Seoul and force a surrender, they have failed. Their forces have been halted by the fierce defense, and soon American and South Korean air power will destroy them and their supply lines. He says the North Koreans will soon see their own capital city leveled by allied air power."

"Enough!" said Young San-ho, palm raised toward the quivering translator.

The time is right, he thought. I'll go on television and ask Ming for China's support against American air power marauding our skies and threatening Chinese territory. When Ming refuses, he'll be discredited and perhaps brought down by his rivals.

And I'll put the woman on television, and she will undermine her brother's will to tell his false story. When he recants, the southerners will be forced to admit they caused war over a lie. When I suggest a cease-fire and mutual withdrawal of forces, they'll have no choice but to accept.

Chapter 61

Boise, Idaho

"Citizens are arming up, and I'm not losing any sleep over it."

Jerry Thomas stopped pacing the baggage area of Boise International and turned to the television mounted overhead. He saw the face and shoulders of a man with a few strands of gray hair combed over his freckled pate. The camera zoomed out, and Thomas saw that the speaker wore a police uniform with the eagles of a chief on the collars. "The citizens of this city have seen the pain and suffering terrorists are causing around the country, and we're not going to let it happen here. I say to anyone considering terrorist acts, if you try them, you'd better hope we cops get you rather than our friends and neighbors."

Thomas glanced around the room. At least half the people I see are carrying, he thought. I don't blame them. Guns are literally everywhere now. I had to visit three gun shops yesterday to find the weapons and ammo we need for our little expedition. Dealers can't restock fast enough.

With those weapons and ammo, plus three guys and some camping gear, and a full tank, we're gonna take off a little over max gross. A little iffy, but OK; it'll burn down in flight. But I'll have to land in that meadow about a mile from Fahim's clearing. I've never tried a backcountry landing like that; I'll have to estimate the wind and hope the long grass I saw there isn't hiding a gully or a fallen tree.

Anyone who looked at this unemotionally would say we're nuts to try for Fahim by busting down his door out in those woods. Suppose he has a few jihadis around as security? Us three guys against however many, and—face it, Jerry—you and the general are past it as combat Marines and *you* never were anyway. You zoomed around above the battlefield. Morales, although he shoots regularly at Quantico, hasn't handled a weapon in combat in what—twenty, twenty-five years? What's the shelf life of *his* close combat skills? Andy must be cursing his luck at drawing this assignment.

Shit, Jerry! What have you gotten yourself into? What have you gotten your boss into?

Aboard Southwest Airlines flight three fifty, Ray Morales pushed similar thoughts aside. I'm going to get this bastard or die trying. He has no clue we have him located. We'll hit the compound in the wee hours before dawn, the time when every sentry who ever lived struggles to stay alert. Thanks to my chat with Hadrab we know al-Wasari isolates himself in the A-frame; the poor slobs waiting to become martyrs are forbidden there unless invited. So he'll be alone. We'll bag him before the others have time to react.

Cabin crew were moving through the plane checking to be sure that seat backs and tray tables were "in their most uncomfortable position," as one had announced in the quirky Southwest style. Morales glanced at Andy, seated two rows behind across the aisle. The decision to fly commercial might have been unwise from Andy's viewpoint, but it was quick and left a fainter scent in Washington than pulling one of DHS's Lear 60s away from a scheduled run. *This has to be quick and quiet to work. And if it doesn't work? Well, I won't file a travel claim.* As the tires reunited with runway, the airplane jarred slightly, and Morales's lips twitched at his private joke.

After checking in at the Best Western Airport Inn, the three gathered in Thomas's room, where he had covered the bedspread and desktop with satellite photos and Forest Service maps. As they drank Miller and brainstormed, it was apparent to Morales that they didn't have enough information to make a plan for getting Fahim. The best they could create was a plan to make a plan. They would land in the meadow and do a sneak and peek of the compound in daylight, marking a route with chem-lights for guidance when they returned to get Fahim in the predawn darkness. Based on what they observed in daylight, they'd make their assault plan after returning to the meadow to wait for zero-dark-thirty. After dinner at Chapala's, which Morales was surprised to find met his Tex-Mex standards, they turned in. But Morales couldn't find sleep.

You're in over your head, Ray; you know that, don't you?

Not necessarily. We'll have surprise—al-Wasari has no idea we've found his hideout. He and whoever else is there will be asleep when we hit them. Well, maybe they'll have a night sentry, but I doubt it. This isn't a disciplined military outfit, so they wouldn't bother to post security unless they felt threatened. We know al-Wasari will be in the A-frame cabin and will be alone. We'll be inside and have him zip-tied before he knows what's up. Or I'll just shoot him. Unless al-Wasari is the luckiest man alive, we'll get him. Once we've done for al-Wasari, we've cut the legs from under the terror campaign. And that will earn all of us involved in Hadrab's interrogation a lot of forgiveness in the White House and on Capitol Hill.

* * *

The Pentagon

Eric Easterly closed the door of his SCIF, seated himself, and stared at the black STE unit on the table. Don't get this kid in trouble, he thought. Be very careful here. He slid his crypto-card into its slot and keyed Reddy's satellite phone number.

"Reddy."

"Commander, this is Easterly. These are my orders: Tell Hadrab you don't believe his story. We checked it out, and Morales was in Washington then, not Minneapolis. Be angry with this guy; intimidate him. Then throw him out and follow him. We want you to get a tracker on him somehow—think you can do that?"

"We'll figure out something, sir."

"We think Hadrab will go to Youssef al Wahdi, figuring that al-Wahdi will make a video of him telling his bullshit story and put it on the web with his other crap. The idea is, Hadrab leads us to al Wahdi, and we put a Hellfire through the roof of his hideout. With a little help from Hadrab, *Inspire* will lose its main man. You copy this, Commander?"

"Copy, sir. We've been after al-Wahdi a long time."

"OK, do it. Make your dad proud, son."

Easterly broke the connection and exhaled deeply. Not bad, he thought. Hadrab will go scuttling away to find an interested ear. Hopefully, he'll find al Wahdi, and we'll be able to track him there and kill them both. But even if that fails, I've kept him quiet for the several days I promised Ray.

* * *

Coeur d'Alene National Forest, Idaho

Fahim's ability to concentrate totally on a task set him apart in the often-erratic circles of the faithful bringing jihad to the world. He was a craftsman who never rushed the exacting work of constructing explosive vests or IEDs. Never had one of his creations failed to function perfectly. And unlike several less-disciplined bomb makers, he still had all his fingers and sight in both eyes.

Fahim stepped back from the workbench and began a final check of the last of three martyr vests he'd assembled since performing his morning prayers.

Americans are fools, he thought. Their stores sell me everything I need to destroy them except Semtex, and the Solano cartel brings that for me along with the drugs they supply to feed America's addictions.

The Cessna's raspy buzz reached Fahim's ears. He cocked his head, his hands ceasing their precise movements inside the ripstop black nylon vest spread out before him.

Airplane!

Downing his battery tester, Fahim opened the door of the shed and glanced hurriedly into the clearing where the two clueless shaheed had wandered that earlier day. It was empty.

Is it the same one? Airplane sounds the same, but that's not conclusive. Doesn't sound like it's coming toward me; seems to be off in the direction of that meadow. I'd better get a look.

Fahim hurried into the second outbuilding and emerged carrying his quad copter.

As the Cessna neared the meadow, Thomas wished he knew more about it. Not wanting to attract attention, he had made only two medium-altitude passes on his first visit. He had estimated then that there was room to roll out, and the grassy surface looked passable, but he wanted another look before committing.

The meadow was framed by tall evergreens, and he knew he'd have to descend quickly to touch down just beyond them. Thomas lined up, and just before clearing the trees, he cut power to idle, pushed full left rudder, and fed in right aileron. The Cessna, no longer in coordinated flight, dropped rapidly without gaining airspeed. At fifty feet he centered the flight controls, fed in power, and trimmed the nose up. Holding that altitude, he flew above the meadow, tall grasses beneath the Cessna rippling in its prop wash. As Thomas concentrated on flying the low pass, his passengers' eyes scoured the grassy surface passing them at sixty knots.

Feeling the controls mush, Thomas dropped the nose a bit and added power. The windshield seemed full of onrushing trees, their tops above the Cessna. Fighting back fear, he resisted the urge to yank the nose up and added more power. Its engine sound rising to an angry snarl, the Cessna gained vital airspeed, and he was able to pull up and clear the treetops.

Drawing a deep breath, Thomas said, "I didn't see any stumps or ditches; you guys see anything that could be a problem?"

No one had, so Thomas brought the Cessna around and lined up for his landing approach. Except for the mushing when he held just above stall speed, the Cessna had behaved well on the low pass, so Thomas flew a sideslip again.

Once past the trees and over the meadow again, the Cessna descended sharply, touching down in the tall grass with plenty of rollout ahead. The plane bounced and rattled over the surface.

The Cessna was rolling at forty-three knots when its nose wheel dropped into a small gully hidden by two-foot wheatgrass, blowing the tire and shock-loading the strut nearly to failure. In less time than it took Thomas's brain to evaluate that sound and jolt, the right landing gear struck the gully and crumpled. The Cessna dropped to the right and began rotating from the force on that wing, now dragging in the grass and mud while disintegrating with a sound like fingernails on a blackboard. The damaged forward wheel strut could hold no longer and snapped, dumping the aircraft's nose. During the one point eight seconds between the propeller's blades shearing off and the nose plunging into the meadow's grassy surface, the left and only remaining landing gear collapsed. The point of the propeller spinner assembly, forced by the remaining momentum of twenty-five hundred pounds of aircraft, men, and cargo, impaled the soft ground. The plane pivoted through the vertical and slammed onto its back with an end-of-the world sound. Thomas heard it but didn't notice because—up until the instant he lost consciousness—his brain was trying to process the disintegration of his expectations. It was during this violent flip that Andy's skull was crushed and Ray was ejected from the aircraft.

The wreckage skidded another ten feet and halted. Inside the cabin, which had been compressed to about three-quarters of its former height, Jerry Thomas hung limp and bloody, arms dangling, defying gravity because of his lap belt. Andy's corpse was crumpled on the roof that had become the cabin's floor, slashed by weapons and equipment that had been flung like shrapnel. The air reeked of gasoline, but none had splashed on the hot metal of the battered engine. A breeze was blowing across the meadow sufficient to disperse the vapors, so there was no fire.

Ray Morales, bloody and unconscious, lay about twenty yards from the engine, which emitted ticking sounds as its mangled innards cooled.

Chapter 62

Coeur d'Alene National Forest, Idaho

It was Reza who had seen the security camera. The three Iranians had been moving cautiously, parallel to a road once gravel, now mostly dirt and grass. Reza and Adel Ghorbani were spaced as far apart as possible without losing visual contact, the road between them an arrow pointing—they hoped—to their quarry, Fahim al-Wasari. Sirhan was to Ghorbani's right, keeping pace with him but barely in view.

Speaking to the others quietly by cell phone, Adel directed them to halt in place. After a few minutes he said, "We'll wait a little and see if that camera was being monitored. If nobody comes to investigate, we'll begin moving again."

Ghorbani knelt and took a few sips of water from his canteen. Might as well have something to eat, he thought. Can't tell when I'll have another chance. As he rummaged quietly in the bellows pocket of his camo trousers, he heard an engine. Freezing except for a slow turn of his head toward Reza, he then pointed to his ear. Reza nodded; he heard it too. The sound grew until Ghorbani identified it as a small airplane that seemed to be circling some distance away, beyond Reza.

Don't be distracted, thought Ghorbani; the issue for us right now is whether someone is coming this way after seeing us on camera. His eyes probed the road to his left and the woods in an arc across his line of advance.

Suddenly the airplane noise changed to a cacophony of grinding, rending metal that ceased as abruptly as it had begun.

They've crashed! Who were they? Why were they flying out here?

Twisting first toward Reza to his left, then Sirhan, Ghorbani saw them standing bolt upright, staring in the direction of the crash sounds. Urgently, he motioned Sirhan down, and he dropped immediately. For several seconds Reza faced away from Ghorbani, peering in the direction of the sound, and Ghorbani was painfully aware of how visible and distracted Reza was. Finally he turned and obeyed Ghorbani's emphatic signal, dropping to a knee.

Motioning to Sirhan, Ghorbani moved quietly toward the road. Halting in concealment, he looked and listened for about thirty seconds, then darted across. As Ghorbani made his way to Reza, Sirhan repeated his leader's maneuvers.

"No worries now about someone coming to look for us," said Ghorbani. "They'll concentrate on the crash. This is a good time for us to reconnoiter the compound." They leapfrogged parallel to the road, the lead man checking for cameras before moving, then motioning the others forward. Each time he spotted a camera, they diverted around it.

But they didn't spot them all. Silently, one lens reported their passage, but Fahim wasn't at his monitor screen.

Fahim heard the Cessna's death throes as he was preparing the quad copter. He's crashed! Whoever he is, he's crashed his plane. Praise to Allah that I have this to take a look quickly.

Careful, careful. Remember, small controller movements. He had nearly crashed the drone during his first flight by losing track of its altitude and direction of movement.

Warily Fahim increased power to the small drone's rotors, which lifted it upward, wobbling a bit but under control. As it rose above the trees, Fahim glanced at his video screen. The camera was working.

Where's the meadow from here? By trial and error Fahim set the drone on course in the direction of the crash. His airborne optics showed upthrusting branches pass beneath the little aircraft.

Wait! What's the range of my radio control system? And how much do the trees reduce it? Will I have any warning that it's reaching maximum or just suddenly lose control?

Fahim cautiously reduced the rotor pitch of the quad copter, slowing its travel away from him. Concentrating fiercely, he gradually attained a stable hover. Slowly, he increased power; the camera confirmed his bird was ascending.

There! The meadow in the distance. Fahim dialed the camera to maximum magnification, which caused the image to become grainy as well as larger.

It's not clear, but what I heard was certainly a crash, and the objects I see here don't look natural. This has to be wreckage.

Fahim commanded the camera to three-quarters magnification and was rewarded with a clearer image, within which the wreckage was unidentifiable objects lighter against the green grass. He watched for several minutes but saw no movement in the meadow.

His controller movements a bit more confident, Fahim set the drone on return course. It passed about one hundred fifty feet left of the Iranians, who failed to see it or notice its faint, insectile buzzing.

No movement, thought Fahim. So probably if anybody survived, they won't be a threat. But the crash itself is a threat. It's not as immediate as if the aircraft were burning, smoking, and maybe starting a fire in the meadow. That would bring the Forest Service in a hurry. But even so, at some point after that plane is overdue, a search will start. It may even have begun. The pilot might have gotten off a radio call as they went down. And don't planes have some sort of emergency beacon for crashes?

The quad copter's camera showed it was approaching a clearing; then Fahim saw himself, control box in hand. He brought the miniature aircraft down and cut the power.

What I just saw isn't good enough. I'm going to the meadow. There may be clues to what this flight was about and may be survivors. I must have a look before anyone comes to investigate.

Chapter 63

Supreme Command Bunker, Democratic People's Republic of Korea

"People of the Democratic People's Republic of Korea! We have been attacked from the south by the foolish and illegal Kang government clique and its American master. It is not enough that they have kept Korean families apart and repeatedly threatened us, clinging to the mangy fur of the American dog. Today they attacked us."

The stern visage of Field Marshal Young San-ho filled TV screens. It was noon in Korea, thirty minutes earlier in Beijing, and midnight in Washington.

"They will regret this! As I speak to you, our brave soldiers are driving nearer and nearer to Seoul. Our fierce pilots are hurling themselves at the pirates' aircraft and raining bombs on their soldiers and cities. Our navy is supreme. Our missiles crush cities.

"The putrid Kang government claims that our nation had President Gwon assassinated. That is a lie! They have forced an innocent North Korean, Chung Ma-ho, to falsely confess to the deed. They did this by threatening his dear sister, Chung Ma-eun. But I have rescued Chung Ma-eun, who is with me now with a message for her brother."

The camera's field widened to reveal a slender woman in a green dress sitting to Young's right.

"My dear brother, you were forced to confess to a terrible deed that I know you could never have done. You did this to protect me. But, as you can see, I am safe now in Pyongyang. Now you can tell the truth, that you are innocent and had nothing to do with this killing. Please, please, my brother, expose the lies of the Kang government."

The view contracted until only General Young San-ho was visible.

"For years," he said, "America has wanted to destroy the Democratic People's Republic. When President Gwon refused to do America's bidding, the Americans had him killed and replaced by their lapdog, Kang. They are now following a plan they practiced for fifty years, threatening us by what they call Exercise Team Spirit. We have warned many times that this would lead to war.

"We will defeat them both and at last unite all Koreans in the spirit of *Juche.* I expect that we will soon be joined in the skies and on land and sea by our Chinese elder cousins. Together we will crush the Americans and their stooges, the Kang regime. We will write another glorious chapter in the solidarity of the People's Republic of Korea and the People's Republic of China. We are inseparable and unconquerable!

"Death to Kang and Martin, dogs who eat their own filthy droppings."

* * *

Washington, DC

The Situation Room watch officer's voice broke the silence following Young's words: "That's all we have now, sir. We're bringing up Chinese military dispositions, and I'll be back to you with those shortly."

President Martin threw his ballpoint pen. It hit the mahogany table hard, then skittered to the edge and fell from view.

"What do I have to do to keep North Korea in its box? Kill another sixty thousand of them? Kill all of them? Damn that man!"

The others at the hour-old NSC meeting followed Martin's gaze toward Secretary of State Anne Battista.

"What do you say, Anne? Will the Chinese come in?"

"I spoke with Ambassador Caulfield a couple of hours ago when we first learned the North had come across the DMZ. He doesn't think the Chinese encouraged Young or knew his intention to attack in force. And my morning intel brief didn't report anything out of the ordinary with the Chinese military. But just now—"

Martin slapped his palm on the table. "Just now it's a new ball game," he said. "Young's put Ming on the spot, and there's a Party congress soon. Except for that, I'd be confident Ming wouldn't let himself be pushed into military action in Korea. But with it . . ." The president's voice trailed off; then his gaze selected General MacAdoo. "What about Pandora?"

MacAdoo's eyes widened; then he squared his shoulders and said, "Nothing yet, sir. And we should defer this discussion to a side meeting."

"Don't give me that classification mumbo jumbo, General! I'm authorizing a discussion here and now."

MacAdoo looked at Easterly, who leaned near the president's ear and said, "Sir this video link isn't cleared for compartmented intel. We must *not* discuss Pandora until the link's shut down."

Martin, flushing, nodded.

When the screens were blank, MacAdoo said, "Mr. President, Ma insists this attack is a surprise to China. He could be lying, but my hunch is he's not. He proposes that neither of us send forces into or over North Korea."

"What did you say to that, General?" said Martin.

"Sir," said Easterly, "Mac told him we currently had no forces in or over the DPRK but that, if the invasion continues, we may move north to cut their army's supply lines. That was the right answer."

"OK, that's our policy for now," said Martin. "But for how long? My administration mustn't be accused of failing to support our troops in combat."

"General Tedford's not asking for deeper strikes now, sir," said MacAdoo. "If he does, and you approve, we can begin them immediately."

"What about Pandora in that case?" said Martin.

"We tell Ma our planes are coming north, give him our northern limit line, and hopefully he'll keep his guys away from ours," said Easterly.

"All right," said Martin. "Mac, before we go back on the link, anything else you have to tell us about Ma and Chinese military plans?"

"No, sir. You know what I know."

"Well, keep it that way. Any developments from Pandora, you let me know right away!"

As the teleconference link was being restored, Easterly glanced at an email from his military assistant. He smiled as he read, "On-scene investigation confirms Wednesday's drone strike killed al-Wahdi and two unidentified men."

Martin glared at the DNI, seated three down from him on the left. "My administration is gonna get accused of another intelligence failure, Aaron. Why can't you guys be ahead of CNN once in a while?"

Aaron Hendricks wanted to say, "because you and Ming traded one lunatic dictator for another two years ago," but instead replied, "Because in this instance there were no strategic warning indicators. The DPRK's army has been massed just north of the DMZ for two years. They were already in position for a push south in force. We've been reporting that possibility for some time now. And the intent to invade was in the impenetrable mind of one man, Field Marshal Young San-ho."

Martin scowled, picked up another ballpoint, and began tapping on the table.

"And what about that woman's claim to be Chung's sister and that Kang used her to force her brother to make a false confession implicating North Korea?"

* * *

Near Beijing, People's Republic of China

"Damn, damn, damn!" Ming Liu, president of the People's Republic of China, leader of the Chinese Communist Party, and devoted gardener, threw down his hoe, startling the staffer who had delivered the news. He stood with hands on hips and let his gaze wander across his rows of lettuce, bok choy, tomatoes, squash, and kitchen herbs, trying to quell his rage at Young San-ho. His gaze also noted the arrival of a glistening black Mercedes and the young man who had popped out of the right front door and now held the rear door open for him. It beckoned like the dark mouth of an unexplored cave that he would now have to enter. He stalked toward it, removing his work gloves and stuffing them into the pockets of his Levi's.

Staring at him from the secure videoconference screen in the Mercedes was his minister of defense, Chen Shaoshi.

"President Ming, the People's Liberation Army stands ready. Although this is unexpected, if necessary we can quickly send fighters to protect Pyongyang."

"Would that be wise?"

"Sometimes it is wisdom to swallow bitter medicine quickly."

"Chen, you sound like a damn fortune cookie! Should we send fighters?"

Wide-eyed at Ming's unusual directness, Chen paused, then said, "In my opinion it would be unwise. Perhaps the assassination was a North Korean operation. If so, it may become necessary, but sending our forces to defend Young's regime against American and South Korean attacks that he brought on himself should be a last measure, not a first one."

"So you believe he had Gwon killed? Or is that woman right?"

"I well recall his arrogance when we met in Pyongyang, just days after we had supported his seizure of power and then saved him and all North Koreans from nuclear annihilation by the Americans. He acted as if he were doing China a favor by agreeing to rule a nation he could loot just as Kim did."

Chen continued: "I believe he has the arrogance and stupidity to send assassins after Gwon. But I haven't seen any clear evidence that he did. Chung Ma-ho could be lying about who bombed Gwon's car, as his sister just claimed, or could have been deceived himself."

"Where's our carrier now?" said Ming.

"In the South China Sea near the Paracels."

"Bring it into port immediately. It would be a tempting target for American submarines if we get sucked into this mess."

"But, sir, when in port it's an easy target for American missiles!"

"If the Americans attack one of our ports, we'll have a lot more to worry about than the loss of our carrier. Do it!"

Besides, thought Ming, having the *Liaoning* in port fits into the way out I'm beginning to see.

Chapter 64

Coeur d'Alene National Forest, Idaho

RAY MORALES HOBBLED THROUGH A stand of young larch trees, deeply shadowed by mature spruce above. He gazed ahead with just his right eye, the left one being covered in clotted blood, perhaps permanently sightless. His grass – and mud-stained clothing was torn in many places, particularly his right side, where rips in the fabric revealed bloody lacerations to his shoulder, hip, and knee. His right ear sagged, partially torn from his scalp. *What a fool I am! I was arrogant enough to think we could slip in here and nail the world's most wanted terrorist as if we were playing cops and robbers.*

Fahim strutted behind him, pistol in hand. "You're pathetic, Morales! One of your buddies may still be alive and I'll do for him when I'm done with you."

They walked under the gaze of perhaps a dozen pairs of eyes, most of them perched above.

One pair was human.

Adel Ghorbani, uncomfortably hidden in a hawthorn thicket to Morales's right, saw and heard the pair trudge past. Emerging quietly, he whispered into his cell phone, then clipped his AR-15 to his torso harness and began circling to get ahead of the prisoner and his guard.

Morales's right foot, the one with broken bones, snagged a vine, and he crashed to the ground. For a moment his world was nothing but pain, so much pain that he didn't even consider trying to hold back the scream that burst out of him.

"Screaming like a woman, Morales! Is that how the Marines do it?"

"Fuck you, raghead!"

In reply, Fahim launched a kick at Morales's right foot. Morales, with the slow-motion clarity he had experienced only in combat, realized this was his chance. The elusive demon who had haunted his dreams was in reach and off balance.

He grabbed al-Wasari's leg and yanked, tumbling his adversary beside him; then thrusting his uninjured left leg and levering with his arms, he flung his torso across Fahim and clutched the man's throat.

Fahim head-butted Morales, striking his left eye. Morales screamed and blood welled again. Scrambling out of reach, Fahim looked frantically left and right. He snatched his pistol from the dirt and aimed it at Morales. Fahim's chest heaved and his eyes flashed. He sized Morales up, and his trigger finger relaxed. After a moment, he spoke deliberately.

"All right, Morales. We have a change of plans. We're stopping right here, and here's what we're going to do. I'm going to put bullets in your shoulders and knees, so you won't be able to flail around as I open your throat. If I do it carefully, you won't bleed out too soon. After you've sucked air through that opening awhile, able to feel a symphony of pain, I'll open you up the rest of the way and expose your spine. Then I'll work my knife in and pry apart the vertebrae to cut off your head. That's probably when you'll snuff out, while it's still attached. And I'll get the whole thing on video and post it to show everyone that I am truly the greatest jihadi. Think about that while I'm gone."

Fahim shot Morales in the left foot and stood observing the effect. Satisfied that Morales couldn't escape, he left to fetch his beheading knife and video gear.

Morales lay on his back, breathing hoarsely, Fahim's words cutting through the fog of pain. He knew he could at most crawl, with no chance to get away before Fahim returned. He pictured Ali Hadrab twisting and shrieking on the blood-soaked gurney.

How could I have done that to another human being? And very soon someone who enjoys inflicting pain as much as Ruby will go to work on me.

Morales crossed himself and heard his quavering voice. "Hail Mary, full of grace, the Lord is with thee; blessed art thou amongst women, and blessed is the fruit of thy womb, Jesus. Holy Mary, Mother of God, pray for us sinners, now and at the hour of our death . . ."

Chapter 65

Coeur d'Alene National Forest, Idaho

Ray Morales lay on his back, covered in dirt, blood, and fear. They'll find the crash before long, he thought. Well, it's too late to help Jerry and Andy, and it'll be too late to help me. What a mess—this is just another of your boneheaded misjudgments, Morales. First with that terrorist, then Ella, now this. Would I have been able to regain Julie's trust? What will she think of me after this?

One part of his mind could sense the other part of it trying to flee from the horror it knew was coming. He drifted off in a fog of pain. Without warning he was above his body, looking down on it sprawled on the leaves, twigs, and decay of the forest floor.

He heard a voice, his own voice but strong and solid, no longer quavering: *Get it together, Marine. He's going to kill you, but you don't have to be his victim. He can kill you, but he can't beat you unless you let him. You're not helpless; stop acting like it. You can't run, but you can fight.*

Just as suddenly he was back in his battered body. I can still use my arms, he thought. Breathing raggedly, he patted his pockets, trying to recall their contents through the pain. His searching fingers brushed his belt buckle.

My belt, he thought. This buckle will do some damage if I catch him in the face with it. Pushing back the fog blurring his attention, Morales removed the belt with clumsy fingers. Mustering all his concentration, he lay the belt alongside his right leg, scattered forest debris over it, and grasped the end opposite the buckle.

His preparations made, Morales lay still, his fear pushed back a little by a determination to attack Fahim and by his adrenaline rush. As he lay there, a quality possessed by some humans since before the Vikings named it began to transform his fear into rage. Norse warriors called those with this quality *berserkers* because they fought in a crazed frenzy that was feared by even those brutal men. Feverishly, his heart pounding and adrenaline spiked, Morales awaited his chance to surprise Fahim.

Adel Ghorbani, who had doubled back upon hearing Morales scream, watched Fahim al-Wasari jog by his hiding place. When Fahim was several yards beyond him, Ghorbani stood and leveled a Glock 17 at his back, aimed between his shoulder blades.

"Al Wasari!"

Fahim, startled, spun around, his pistol coming up. Ghorbani double-tapped him neatly, piercing sternum and frontal lobe with nine-millimeter slugs. With no doubt that Fahim was dead, Ghorbani knelt and went through his pockets. His effort yielded a burner phone, car keys, a Montana driver's license in the name of Al Hassan bearing Fahim's photo, and a wad of cash. He buttoned the lot in the bellows pockets of his trousers and headed for Morales. Reza and Sirhan fell in alongside him, having killed the three would-be shaheed they found in the bunk house.

Ray heard gunshots and tensed. Still on his back, he contracted his stomach muscles and pulled his torso off the ground, aided with his forearms. Now able to see across his feet and to the edge of the clearing, he prayed Fahim would approach from that direction. Blood pounding in his ears, Ray readied himself to rip into Fahim's face with the swinging buckle and rattle him with a maniacal shout.

Suddenly a figure at Ray's feet loomed over him, having approached unseen from his right. Confusion pushed rage from his battered face at the sight of a bearded stranger in hunter's cammies with an assault rifle clipped to his chest. They stared at each other, Ray with the fierceness of a cornered badger, the stranger with calm curiosity.

"General Morales. I am General Adel Ghorbani of the Islamic Republic of Iran. You have heard my name before, perhaps? Maybe even you have seen my picture."

"You . . . are commander of . . . Quds Force," rasped Morales.

Ghorbani gave a bleak smile. "Correct.

"And I am the man who just saved you from a slow, horrible death. Fahim al-Wasari, or abu Shaheed as he styled himself or Al Hassan as his driver's license reads, is dead. I just shot him. I didn't do that to save you, General Morales. I did it for reasons of state."

Ghorbani unclipped his rifle, handing it and his pistol to Sirhan. As Reza covered Morales with his AR-15, Ghorbani lifted him into a sitting position against a tree. Morales groaned once but managed to keep silent otherwise.

"So now what, General Ghorbani? You've saved my life, but you're in America illegally, wanted by most of the security services in the Western world, and for all I know you're responsible for some of the shootings and bombings we've had."

Ghorbani chuckled. "Indeed, now what? Our file on you is correct. You never forget your duty, do you?"

Ghorbani's look turned stern. "Because I am what you just said, except the part about the attacks, perhaps I should shoot you before we leave. That way our presence here and our bringing justice—as you Americans say—to the man who destroyed Las Vegas would never be known. There would be no diplomatic protests, no presidential candidates demanding sanctions against Iran, no screaming for bombing."

Morales was silent.

"But for reasons I don't fully understand, I will not shoot you today. Perhaps it is out of the respect of one general for another, although I would shoot you in an instant if my mission required it."

"Reza," he said in Farsi, "come with me."

Ghorbani and Reza returned carrying Fahim's body. They laid it about fifteen feet from Morales.

"There. That's far enough away that the lack of powder burns will not be questioned."

Ghorbani placed his own pistol on the ground close to Morales but out of his reach and said, "This is the weapon that killed him."

Morales nodded.

"I suggest, General, that you struggled heroically with Fahim and managed to get to the pistol he dropped before he did. A man of your experience will have no difficulty imagining the details to support that story.

"And now, General, we say good-bye. Perhaps someday I will need your help. If that happens, I'm sure you will remember this day."

Ghorbani turned away, took a few steps, then turned back to Morales.

"You were fools to believe you could prevent us from having nuclear bombs. We are going to destroy the Jews and dominate the Arabs as we once did, in the days of Darius. Get used to it."

The three Iranians walked away, soon disappearing among the saplings and undergrowth.

Chapter 66

Beijing, People's Republic of China

"YOUNG SAN-HO HAS GIVEN US the opportunity to solve our Korea problem once and for all."

Ming studied the faces of the five men to whom he had just spoken and from whom he must have support at the next Party congress. One of them was his most likely opponent for the leadership.

Five unblinking stares; no one was giving anything away.

Not surprising, he thought. Each one is concerned first of all for himself, so each wonders whether I'm going down over this. And if so, whom I will try to drag with me? They're also wary because I called this meeting so rapidly they haven't had time to sound each other out. Each fears acting in isolation, of having the others turn on him as sharks sometimes decide which of their number to eat.

"We have one overriding interest in this affair: ending the war on our southern border as rapidly as possible," Ming said. "American soldiers are now in combat less than two hundred miles south of our border with North Korea; their aircraft are even closer. If this fighting continues, we'll be drawn in.

"This is not the time," he continued. "When we fight the Americans, it should be in the South China Sea after we have prepared and where we have vital interests, not in the miserable nation that huddles south of the Yalu River."

Ming noticed a slight nod from General Ma.

"North Korea has become a dagger pressed against China's side. Young's incredible miscalculation demonstrates beyond any doubt that we cannot allow him to remain in power. And there's no one else in Pyongyang who would be any less obstinate and stupid. We must bring that dynasty of fools to an end, smash the present system, and replace it with one that doesn't embarrass and endanger China."

They all agree, thought Ming, reading a slight relaxation in the posture of those around the table.

Zhou Yu, Party boss of Guangdong province, said, "I'm sure you already knew we all are in agreement that Korea has been a pain in China's ass and is now a threat. Do you have a proposal to present? And would it truly leave China better off?"

This is interesting, thought Ming. Zhou is making his move to become the leader of the five. That confirms it: he leans toward challenging me at the Party congress. And he thinks Korea may be his issue.

"I think we are all agreed that it wouldn't be in China's interest or the Party's to rule North Korea ourselves."

Ming observed a ripple of slight nods.

"And I think we also agree that China has made such great progress in economic development—and will under the Party's leadership continue that progress—that the prospect of a free-market economy throughout Korea is no longer unacceptable or even worrisome. We've grown much, much stronger in the past quarter century."

Seeing flickers of discomfort, Ming said, "It would be understandable to have some slight concerns about that. I myself do. But those concerns are far less than the concerns I have about continuing the present arrangement."

I think most of them are with me, thought Ming, so now I'll lay it out.

"The current crisis has created the opportunity to purge the North Korean ruling party and government, sweep them aside entirely, and take the bold steps that will at last give us stability and predictability throughout Korea.

"I will fly to Washington and use President Martin's panic about being sucked into another bloody war, his vanity about American leadership, and his presently perilous struggle to be reelected to maneuver him into proposing a summit to halt fighting and restore peace to Korea. As I did two years ago, I will use him as a tool to shape a solution favorable to China.

"At this summit will be Martin and me, plus Kang and Kato. The outcome will be a united Korean nation ruled from Seoul with the extraordinary costs of bringing the North into the twenty-first century underwritten by Japan, by Korea itself, and by America, with little or nothing from us. And China will be the main supplier of steel, concrete, and all else needed to do this.

"We will have an outcome that confers lasting benefits on China but that is paid for by others. And won't cost the life of a single Chinese soldier. This is an extraordinary opportunity that only we have been wise enough to see, and we're going to seize it."

Let's see what they do now, thought Ming. I didn't ask for a vote, but I might. Ma is with me because he doesn't want his precious PLA wounded by combat with the Americans before he believes they're ready. Wu and Gao are too cautious to buck me now; they will go along. I'd get three of the five at least.

What Zhou will do is the most interesting question. He won't want to call for a vote he will lose, because then he'll be on record as opposing a plan that may turn out to be a big win for China. But unless he raises some objection, he'll be part of this decision and won't be able to use it to attack me at the congress.

Zhou broke what seemed like a very long silence in the room: "Isn't this going to help Martin's reelection? Why would we do that?"

So that's his marker. Not much; he's just raising a side issue. This doesn't leave him in a strong position to second-guess me at the congress.

"Perhaps," said Ming, "but who can predict American politics?

"And remember that Martin was criticized severely two years ago for agreeing to bear some of the cost of assistance to Sinpo. Some of those supporting Rutherford now called him 'a stooge of the Chinese' then. He may actually lose some support for working with us again."

Ming looked around the table, letting silence hang. After about fifteen seconds he rose.

"Thank you for your support. I will fly to Washington."

Chapter 67

Supreme Command Bunker, Democratic People's Republic of Korea

Young San-ho paced his small office underneath Mount Jamo, emitting a stream of cigarette smoke. It's been two days, but the enemy hasn't offered a cease-fire to investigate the miserable woman's claim of her brother's innocence, he thought. Our wretched army is being destroyed, trapped north of Seoul in a box of enemy infantry and receiving tremendous blows from the air and from artillery.

But my soldiers inflicted great damage on Seoul before their artillery was destroyed or forced to pull back into our tunnels. Surely there are elements within the Kang clique who are desperate to save Seoul—but why are they powerless to call for a cease-fire? Doesn't Martin want to end this? Doesn't Ming?

If Martin and Ming want a cease-fire, they'll have one, even if the Kang gang doesn't want it. What would make the Chinese and the Americans want to end this immediately? Regardless of the wishes of the so-called Republic of Korea.

Nuclear weapons. Of course! If they believed I was about to launch a nuclear attack, they'd fall all over themselves to get a cease-fire. I don't have a nuclear weapon, but they can't be sure of that. I could have held one back two years ago. I was a fool not to do that, to hide a bomb in one of our secret caves where they'd never find it. But they don't know that.

If I *act* as if I have nukes and am preparing to use them, surely they won't take the chance that I'm bluffing. I'll demand a cease-fire be put in place, and they won't dare refuse me.

Elated, Young San-ho stormed into the command center, shouting for his staff to assemble.

* * *

Air Force One

"I think Ming wants to end this, fast," said Anne Battista to Eric Easterly in the senior staff cabin of the presidential Boeing 747 flying over the Pacific.

"But what if what he wants to do and what he is willing to pay the price of doing are different, Anne?"

"I think he's crossed that bridge. He's already paying a political price by asking for this meeting. If he were content with letting the fighting continue, we wouldn't be heading for Hawaii now. I don't think Ming wants a fight with us now, but if he did, Korea isn't the place. If he wanted to have a dustup, I think it would be in the South China Sea. He really wants to establish control over ships and aircraft passing through there."

She continued: "I think Young's move against the ROKs forced Ming to reexamine the basic premise of China's support of the DPRK. He looked hard at the dogma that the PRC can't stand to have a prosperous, independent Korea running north all the way to the Yalu and decided it wasn't right, or at least that it wouldn't be as bad as continuing to get whipsawed by standing up for North Korea's loony, frustrating leaders. So, if a reunified Korea is medicine he can swallow, why tolerate the DPRK any further? Surely, Young San-ho's move south is the last straw for China."

"So you think Ming's willing to dump Young and stay out while we whip his ass?"

Battista smiled. "Eric, you'd be a disaster as a diplomat, but, yes, that's what I think. But that still leaves a huge problem—for us, for Ming, for Kang—and for Kato, too: Who picks up the pieces? I'm betting not China. What Ming hopes to gain in return for enabling the reunification of Korea is a free ride when it comes to the hard work and huge cost of integrating the former DPRK into the ROK."

Battista's voice hardened. "Ming's not coming hat in hand. He's coming for a game of no-limit poker, knowing he's got to win big to keep his job."

The cabin phone chirped. "Yes, sir, Mr. President," said the Chief Master Sergeant who answered.

"Secretary Easterly, General MacAdoo, the president would like to see you."

MacAdoo, seated to Battista's left, closed the notebook he had been studying and followed Easterly forward, toward the presidential office cabin.

"Eric, Mac, have a seat," said the president. "Bart will be up momentarily on sivitz." Martin motioned toward the video screen to his left. "After we've done some private business, I'll bring in Win and Sam. The sergeant here will be glad to get you some refreshment."

"Nothing for me, Sarge," said MacAdoo.

"Me either," said Easterly, who was enjoying the smell of the cabin's new leather upholstery.

The familiar face of Chief of Staff Bart Guarini appeared on the screen, accompanied by a slight pop over the sound system.

"Hi, Bart," said the president. "Now that we've got you hooked in, let's get started. Mac, tell me about my nuclear options for North Korea. I have no intention of signing up to another bloody infantry war in Korea."

"Well, sir," said MacAdoo as he opened his notebook. "We have two North Korea options within the SIOP: a full lay down that will obliterate every city and significant military base and in the process destroy the regime and pretty much everyone else between the DMZ and the Yalu; and a decapitating strike that will take out Pyongyang and the regime's command bunker beneath Mount Jamo. Pyongyang would be leveled, ninety percent or more of its inhabitants killed, and those under Mount Jamo would be buried alive if not killed outright. And given a couple of hours to retarget, you could call an audible, and we could do some variations of those two preplanned strike packages."

Remembering Martin's agony over the Sinpo retaliatory strike two years ago, all three observed him closely. For a moment he hunched his shoulders as his eyes saw something far beyond his cabin in Air Force One. Then he straightened and said, "Probably I'll want the decapitating strike. I think that will do it—leaderless, the people of North Korea probably won't fight on. And I don't want to create a radioactive wasteland on Ming's doorstep because we need his cooperation to end this."

"I don't think you'll need nukes, sir," said MacAdoo. "We and the ROKs have control of the air above the battle space, the area between Seoul and Pyongyang. What aircraft the DPRK have left they've dispersed to hangars carved into mountains or are holding on the ground at Pyongyang's airport, figuring the city is off-limits, at least for now. General Tedford's troops and the ROK Army are holding north of Seoul. Some of those units have taken heavy casualties, but they've contained the North Korean thrust toward Seoul. We've fixed their army in place, and now we're going to kill it. Using air and artillery, we're carving it up like a Christmas goose."

"I'm glad to hear that, Mac," said Martin. "But I wanted to be clear on my SIOP options, just in case.

"Bart? Eric? Got anything to add before I bring in Win and Sam?"

"Yes, I do," said Bart Guarini. "Mac, do we still have some of those enhanced radiation bombs we used on Sinpo? I'm thinking, Mr. President, that you might consider those for Pyongyang. You may wish to leave the city itself mostly intact for postwar use."

MacAdoo flipped pages, then said, "Yes, sir. We've got about half a dozen of those W-70 ERWs."

"Good point, Bart. Mac, I want those available."

Martin segued: "Now, Win and Sam are joining. Nothing about this conversation to them."

Win Hernandez, who had been hustled to Vandenberg Air Force Base for the secure video teleconference, appeared on the split screen, followed in moments by Samantha Yu from the Situation Room.

"Win, how're we doing in California?" said Martin.

"I'd say better, Mr. President. This North Korean attack has gotten American's attention away from the terrorists, at least for the moment, and the press is playing the commander-in-chief, finger-on-the-button angle."

Win continued: "Your coming meeting with Ming has sidelined Rutherford. There's nothing negative he can say about it right now because most Americans don't want a war with North Korea and you're the one who can restore peace. Rutherford has little choice but to support your effort. Or, at least not attack it."

"Korea dominates the news cycle now," added Sam Wu. "The press is hounding Rutherford, trying for controversial sound bites. He's having a hard time deflecting them without sounding unconcerned or putting politics above national security."

"Mr. President, ladies and gentlemen," said Colonel Roberts on the intercom, "We're starting on our final into Hickam. We'll be on the ground in five minutes."

"Thanks for the update, Win and Sam."

As the bulky aircraft banked, Rick enjoyed his view of the startling purple-blue of the deep Pacific. Was there *ever, really* a time when politics stopped at the water's edge? he thought. I wish it were so; I wish we could come together for the good of the country. The very first time I boarded this plane, I thought we could do that. After nearly four years of riding this beast, I know we can't. Right now I'm glad of that, because I need to go on offense, find something to push terrorist attacks out of the news cycle. That's sad, but it's the truth. All the progress we've made in the first term goes out the window if Rutherford beats me.

And Ming is facing an election of sorts, too. He could be pushed out at the CCP congress. I hope he needs to stabilize Korea as much as I do!

Chapter 68

Aiea, Hawaii

Ming Liu tried to relax during the drive from Hickam Air Force Base to Camp Smith, but it was hard. He'd had little contact with Rick Martin over the two years since they had cooperated to remove the Kim family regime in North Korea.

I got the best of Martin then, thought Ming, although he surprised me with his toughness at the end. How did the experience of ordering a nuclear strike change him? How has he changed under the pressure of this Governor Rutherford's attacks? Is his vanity still a weakness?

The smell of flowers—plumeria, pikake, ginger—was strong in his first breath upon deplaning at Hickam, and that had helped calm him. But now he was sealed in a limo barging through heavy traffic shouldered aside by his police escort, and the perfumed air was only a memory.

It's a good sign, he thought, that Martin chose Hawaii in place of Washington for our meeting. It's good for me because it symbolizes meeting halfway, rather than China's leader rushing to the American capital for an audience with the president. I suppose he chose Hawaii to emphasize the U.S. military response to Young's stupid attack.

The car slowed and turned right off Halawa Heights Road. Ming's eyes caught sudden movement as General Ma returned the salute of a sentry as they cruised through the security post outside the headquarters of America's top commander in the Pacific.

"What do you make of the claim by that woman—Ma-eun, I think—whom Young San-ho put on TV?" said Rick Martin, leaning forward in a chair that was too low for his lanky frame.

"I haven't reached a firm conclusion yet," said Ming through his translator. "What do your analysts think?"

"They think they need more time and more information."

"Yes, that's the way of all intelligence analysts."

"Ming, I think her bona fides are beside the point right now. What's important for America and China is to get the fighting stopped, and her statement offers a reason for the ROK to accept a cease-fire. Until now there's been no way out, short of driving the North Koreans all the way to Pyongyang—a bloody struggle I presume we'd both like to avoid."

"We?" said Ming. "This is what the American and ROK militaries have been waiting for and practicing with your Team Spirit operations. You've finally gotten your chance to reunify Korea on your terms and to hell with China. Don't pretend otherwise!"

"Why did you ask for this meeting, Ming? Surely not just to repeat that false claim that Team Spirit is a threat to the North."

"I came to remind you, Rick, of China's two million soldiers. If we are not very careful, your allies will force American and Chinese soldiers to kill each other again."

Why is Ming being so obtuse? Maybe he's waiting for me to make a proposal so he can pick it apart. Damned if I'll give him that!

"I don't need reminding of the size of China's army. Do *you* need reminding about whose ally started this fight? After already having cost the United States a city by selling nuclear weapons to al Qaida. What are *you* prepared to do about Young San-ho?"

Ming squared his shoulders. "I might be prepared to help you solve that problem, if you went about it in a way not harmful to China."

Martin arched his eyebrows and raised his hands in a gesture that said, "And that would be?"

"Rick, who stands to benefit from a unified, stable Korea? The United States, the ROK, and Japan."

"Not to mention China and the miserable people of North Korea!" said Martin.

Ming's eyes flashed. "China? We'd be looking across the Yalu at U.S.

troops stationed in Korea through your treaty with the ROK. That's not of benefit to China. North Korea's people?" Ming shrugged. "I don't care what happens to them, so long as they don't try to enter China."

Martin's eyes bored into Ming's. "So what's your vision for solving this problem?"

"If China were to remove Young San-ho and everyone of any significance in the present ruling group, that would create an opportunity for you, wouldn't it? What would you do with that opportunity?"

What wouldn't *I do with it? I'd be the president who headed off a bloody war, freed twenty million North Koreans from serfdom and poverty, and paved the way for an economic boom in East Asia. I'd probably win the Nobel Peace Prize.*

And push past Rutherford in November.

"Ming, this is what I'd do with it . . ."

Chapter 69

Aiea, Hawaii

TWENTY MINUTES LATER THEY WERE joined by Ma, Chen, Easterly, Battista, and MacAdoo.

"With your permission, President Ming, I'll describe the main points of our agreement so our experts can work out the details."

At Ming's nod, Martin said, "We've agreed that Young and all the senior party cadre and military must be removed immediately, enabling America and China to work together, guiding the two Koreas into one state, whose first president will be Kang. The government of China will remove the North Korean leadership, maintain order within the former North Korea, and provide initial humanitarian relief. China will withdraw any military units that may be required in this first phase when requested by President Kang. President Ming and I are agreed that neither America nor China will maintain military bases in the new Korea north of the thirty-eighth parallel. We have also agreed that we will welcome the participation of Japan—"

A rap on the door briefly preceded its opening, interrupting Martin and attracting all eyes. Admiral Swafford entered.

"President Martin, President Ming, ladies and gentlemen—we've just received reconnaissance imaging of preparations for missile launch at North Korea's main missile testing sight, Sohae," said the admiral. "I've ordered continuous recce and intensive air – and space-based search for possible launch preparations elsewhere."

That son of a bitch! thought Martin. He turned to Ming. "You *did* remove all their nukes, didn't you?"

"Yes. Eight of them, isn't that right, Ma?"

MacAdoo noticed his counterpart's uneasiness as he said, "Yes, comrade Ming. You recall correctly."

"Sohae is in northwest North Korea, very close to your border, isn't it, General Ma?" said MacAdoo.

"The Reagan battle group is in the Yellow Sea. They could have bombs on target in less than two hours if I give the order now," said Admiral Swafford.

Martin, MacAdoo, and Easterly glared at Swafford, reminding her she was an interloper at this level.

"Admiral, General Ma and I will handle this!" said MacAdoo.

"Thank you very much, Admiral Swafford. You may return to your other duties," said Martin, turning his back on her.

After a whispered conference with Ming, Ma said, "We'll deal with Sohae. I'll return to our aircraft and issue the orders."

"Let me give you a lift, General," said MacAdoo, gesturing to the door.

"Could you give the two of us the room, please?" said Martin.

Ming lit a cigarette. Martin rubbed his temples and tried to ignore the pungent smoke. The two sat in silence until Ming said, "I don't know for sure that we got them all. There could have been one or two in one of their secret caves. Did you know that the Kims often killed the workmen to ensure secrecy?"

Martin said, "You should have looked. You should have checked every damn cave in the country!"

Ming shrugged. "That wasn't possible under the circumstances, Rick, and you know it!"

"China has gotten us into this situation. What is China prepared to do now?"

"Someday, perhaps not in our lifetimes, China will have had enough of American arrogance!" Pointing a finger at Martin, Ming said, "You don't dictate to me! Without my support for reunification, your army will be tied down in Korea for years."

He's right, thought Rick. I need him to clean house in North Korea. I need him to convince Kang that China won't interfere as he tries to reverse three generations of starvation and slavery in the North.

"I didn't mean it that way. I'm asking for your ideas on how to keep this thing from going nuclear."

A rap on the door was followed by the appearance of Anne Battista, who said, "Young San-ho has just broadcast a demand for putting a cease-fire in place. He said if his humanitarian offer isn't accepted, he will, quote, unleash the fires of hell on Seoul, unquote. Here are translations of his announcement." She handed a sheet of paper to each leader.

Ming scanned the Chinese translation, then wadded it up and threw it at the wall.

"I'm going to Pyongyang and show Young San-ho what the fires of hell actually look like!"

Brushing past Battista, he stalked through the doorway.

Catching Battista's eye, Martin winked.

Chapter 70

Chesapeake Bay, Maryland

"Coast Guard, Coast Guard, we need help."

"Vessel calling Coast Guard, this is Coast Guard Sector Maryland NCR, over."

"Yes, Coast Guard, I hear you."

"Vessel calling Coast Guard, what is the nature of your distress? Over."

"My father's having chest pains. He has nitro pills but forgot to bring them."

Petty Officer Aldridge, his spirits rising a little with the sun, got paper and pen ready.

"What's the name of your vessel, and what is your position? Over."

"The boat's called Angler Two, and we're near a big green buoy numbered eighty-one. Can you help us?"

"Angler Two, this is Coast Guard Sector Maryland NCR. We'll send a boat to you. What color and size is your boat?"

"It's not my boat. I don't know much about it. It's got gray sides and a white top."

Seeing Aldridge's interest, Big Nose said, "What's going on?"

"Somebody has a medical emergency, and Sector Maryland NCR is sending a boat."

"They anywhere near here?"

"Can I move over and look at the chartplotter?"

Big Nose grunted and motioned.

"Actually, the distress boat is near us." Aldridge pointed to the screen. "Look, there's green eighty-one, up ahead of the *Exxon Energy.*"

Big Nose looked alarmed. He grabbed the microphone and held it to the sailor's mouth. "Tell them this boat is near and you will help." He then laid the knife's blade against the sailor's throat.

After switching to an encrypted radio channel, Aldridge spoke, static masking the fear in his voice: "Coast Guard Sector Maryland NCR, this is Coast Guard four-five-one-one-two, over."

In the operations center all eyes turned to the radio speaker.

"One-one-two, this is Sector, over."

"Sector Maryland, one-one-two is conducting escort ops near the Angler Two's position. We will proceed to Angler Two and give assistance."

The radio operator looked at the watch officer, who nodded.

"One-one-two, Sector. Copy all. Make the initial assessment. If medevac is required, we'll send a boat from Station St. Inigoes. Sector out."

"How long until Atlantic City's helo gets there?" said a man with the four stripes of a captain on his sleeves.

"They estimate another forty-five minutes, sir," said the watch officer.

"How about the response boats from St. Inigoes and Crisfield?"

"About the same, sir," said the officer on watch. "Bad luck that the boats already out were patrolling up the Potomac and the Choptank."

"We need to do better than that! See if the navy at Pax River has a SAR helo on standby—if they're flying today, they do. And get me the base skipper on the phone."

"Coast Guard, Coast Guard. My father is bad off. We need help quick!"

"Tell them we're coming," said Big Nose, holding out the microphone. Aldridge quickly obeyed.

Big Nose motioned Aldridge toward the control console. "Get over there fast so that guy shuts up. Then tell your boss the man is improving; no need for another boat."

Responding to its water jet propulsion, the Coast Guard patrol boat leaped up on plane and shot north at nearly forty knots. Big Nose lurched backward but kept his feet. That gave Aldridge an idea.

Nearing the Angler Two, Aldridge cut speed to fifteen knots and approached the drifting boat at a shallow angle.

The Coast Guard boat closed the distance rapidly, its powerful diesel driving the water jet and thrumming like a swarm of bees. Aldridge and Big Nose saw a man on Angler Two's deck, aft of the cabin, waving his arms. Another was looking in their direction out the cabin door.

"Hey, don't smash into them!" said Big Nose, eyes wide.

"Don't worry. That's how we maneuver these boats because they have no rudders or keels; you have to keep them moving fast so you can steer with the thruster.

"I need your guys to go on deck and put lines over when I say to."

Aldridge saw confusion and alarm in the faces of the two men aboard Angler Two. The man on deck retreated to the far side of the boat and grabbed a handhold.

I've got no plan here, thought Aldridge. Maybe go overboard? These guys are gonna kill me anyway. I have to try something. If I can jump across, get to the throttle, and boogie while Big Nose is confused, maybe we can get off a call on channel sixteen; maybe the patrol boat from the LNG terminal will hear and can reach us in time. Maybe help is on the way from my duress signal.

Just as the boats' hulls were about to strike, Aldridge reversed the thrust on his boat's twin water jets and applied full power. When the boat had nearly halted he flipped a switch placing the controller in docking mode and pushed the joystick ninety degrees to the right, causing the twin jets to thrust the boat sideways into Angler Two.

Four-five-one-one-two lurched violently and leapt sideways, striking the fishing boat with a grinding crash. Big Nose lost his balance and toppled, swearing at Aldridge, who was grabbing a set of binoculars from its bracket.

The surprised Iranians aboard Angler Two recovered before the Somalis on the orange and gray Coast Guard boat. Suddenly, the man on Angler's deck was firing a pistol. The Somalis topside slumped, one tumbling overboard, the other clutching the Sampson post protruding from the foredeck, then buckling and going down.

As Big Nose tried to regain his feet, Aldridge swung the binoculars by their strap, smashing him full in the face. When the Somali's hands flew to his broken nose, Aldridge kicked him in the groin, then scrambled toward the fighting knife on the deck plates.

An Iranian Quds force commando burst into the deckhouse. Without a word he shot the two figures he saw there. After the hammer-blow sounds of an AR-15 in a confined space, silence reigned, broken only by the tinkling of spent cartridges rolling on deck and the crunch of glass underfoot as the Iranian left the deckhouse.

After a quick search of the Coast Guard boat, the Iranians hustled back aboard Angler Two, leaving Coast Guard four-five-one-one-two drifting in the light breeze, rocking gently in one-foot waves. Big Nose lay unmoving where he had fallen, his body beneath that of Petty Officer Aldridge.

Aldridge's view of Big Nose's shoulder and the gray, diamond-check pattern of the decking was fading. He knew he was dying.

I'm glad this doesn't hurt. And I'm glad I tried.

All life aboard extinguished, Coast Guard four-five-one-one-two moved southward on the ebb tide. As if in requiem, its radio speakers murmured the voices of mariners plying the bay:

"Do you mind if we meet on two, Captain?"

"I'll be just inside the green. See you on two."

"Security call. This is the tug Elizabeth Ann pushing a light barge, coming out of the C and D in about ten minutes."

"Harrington Harbor South, this is the sailing vessel Ladybug, over."

"Hurry, hurry! Get the signs in place," said Sahel. "We don't have much time before the Coast Guard gets worried and sends another boat."

Angler Two, now with a new identity, powered toward the *Exxon Energy.*

Aboard the huge ship, Tim Cook glanced cautiously around the bridge. There had been no threats or violence, at least on the ship's bridge, since the master had been slashed. Tim was less frightened now.

A shipping pilot meets many mariners and develops a knack for sizing them up. Working with a ship's master takes a certain deftness; after all, the pilot is telling the master what to do—and normally no one aboard does that. Reading people is a core skill for pilots.

After observing him for several hours, the pilot doubted that the pirate leader, whose name was Bobby Garst, had the master's ticket he claimed. Garst didn't have the presence of a ship's master, and Cook figured his claim of a master's license was probably a lie. He wondered what else that seemed to be in the pirate's favor was a lie. But the only thing that matters, Cook told himself, is that these guys have Uzis or something like that, and like to use their knives. That's all they need to control me.

Cook heard the rotor beats of one of the familiar orange Coast Guard helicopters. Hopefully, his eyes swept the bay ahead of the *Exxon Energy*, but the helo he saw was beelining south and paid no attention to the LNG tanker.

Hope of rescue faded as the helo disappeared. Cook's shoulders slumped.

But how does this end for us? We're not far from the LNG terminal near Calvert Cliffs. Why hijack the *Exxon Energy* if you're going to bring her to her destination? And if not to her destination—if the goal is to steal her or hold us for ransom—why keep heading north, toward the end of the Chesapeake? They could never get a ship this big out to ocean through the C & D Canal; they'd be trapped.

But what if . . . ? Cook didn't want to consider it, but his mind hurtled onward. Suppose this isn't piracy, but one of those terror attacks? Suppose this is another version of flying airplanes into buildings? Shocked, he recalled those fireballs.

"Hey, pilot! There's a boat headed our way. What do you know about it? And don't screw with me." Garst glared at Cook.

Cook looked where the pirate leader pointed. There was something lettered on the boat's deckhouse—could it be? But it was too distant for him to identify.

"OK if I take some binocs out and get a better view?" said Cook, pointing to a rectangular box mounted on the bulkhead.

After glancing inside the box, the leader motioned Cook over.

Glasses to his eyes, Cook saw a gray hull and white cabin with "PILOT" in black letters. *But there's no reason for another pilot to be assigned to this ship now. And I know all the pilot boats by sight—that's not one of them. Maybe it's full of SEALs!*

"It's a pilot boat," said Cook. "We're getting near the LNG terminal, and because it's tricky to moor there, the company uses a docking pilot."

Bobby Garst froze for a moment, then keyed his radio and issued orders.

Aboard the approaching boat, the Quds Force leader, Sahel, went through the plan again with six men crammed out of sight in the small deckhouse. After a round of nods he clapped Dalir on the shoulder, and Dalir sauntered through the door onto the open deck, glancing up at the towering ship rapidly filling his line of sight.

Dalir saw someone lowering the accommodation ladder, a long stairway slanting downward against the huge ship's hull from the main deck to the water's edge. He would climb that stairway, and that man would, he knew, check him out and shoot him if he wasn't convincing. Mumbling a prayer, he scrambled upward, keeping as close to the hull as he could. As he neared the top he saw, even farther above, a figure staring at him from the bridge wing.

"Hello. I'm Captain Ahmadi," said Dalir in American English.

His greeter said nothing, just stared at him.

"Say, can we swing by a head on the way to the bridge? I've really got to piss," said Dalir to the Somali pirate who had met him.

The man sent to vet him didn't move, so Dalir did, striding quickly away from the ship's rail toward a door in the deckhouse as if his bladder were about to burst. A glance revealed the watcher above had vanished.

The Somali rushed to him, and Dalir read confusion in his eyes; the man didn't know where the head was. Dalir took advantage of that confusion, whipping the blade from his arm sheath and slashing the pirate's face. When the pirate's hands flew to the bleeding gash and he froze, moaning, Dalir stepped behind him and drove the blade into his brainstem. It had been about forty-five seconds since he had reached the deck.

After looking upward to be sure the watcher hadn't returned, Dalir motioned to the boat below, and three men scrambled rapidly upward. A fourth, not as athletic, moved cautiously behind them. Sahel remained in the pilot boat.

Dalir glanced up at the bridge wing and to his left at a bright orange lifeboat, situated on a platform slightly taller than he.

That will do.

He dragged the Somali's body into the blind zone created by the lifeboat platform and saw that it offered a vantage point for directing his men. Drawing a pistol—an ancient .45 Colt model 1911 with serious stopping power—he moved to the rail. Alternating his gaze between the bridge wing above and the four men waiting on the accommodation ladder, he waved them upward, poised to shoot if a crew member appeared. The bridge wing was the only location from which those above could observe the ladder. As each of his followers scooted aboard, he waved them into concealment beneath the platform.

Dalir looked at his watch; about five minutes had passed since he was observed coming aboard by the watcher on the bridge wing. Those on the ship's bridge would soon become suspicious of the delay in his arrival there. No time for caution. He yanked the lever opening a door into the deckhouse and sprang through it, pistol ready.

He was alone in a brightly lit stairwell leading up, its rise interrupted by platforms at each level of the structure. Motioning to the others, Dalir started up, taking the treads two at a time. After charging up six levels, he was breathing heavily as he waited for the others. When three of the four had joined him, Dalir twisted the doorknob and sprang onto the bridge.

The next few seconds were all about reaction times, his and the pirates'. Dalir had shot three of the four in ski masks before Bobby Garst shot him. The next Iranian through the door dropped Garst, then put his back against the bulkhead and observed three men frozen in place as he swept his AR-15 barrel across them in turn. Each hostage was a finger twitch from death.

The stillness and silence of the figures in that tableau were broken by the ship's master, his left hand partly covered by a bloody bandage. "I am the master of the *Exxon Energy*," he said. "Who are you?"

"We are here for *them*," said the uninjured Iranian, whose name was Hadwin, motioning toward the sprawled pirates. "We will not harm you or your ship."

"So you say. In that case put away your guns," said the captain, finger pointing to Hadwin and the two Iranians who had entered as he spoke.

"You know what these men were going to do at Calvert Cliffs?"

"No."

"They were going to kill you, smash your ship into the LNG terminal, and go over the side into a boat, leaving behind timed devices to ignite your cargo. Have they set them yet?"

"I . . . I don't know."

"Well, you'd better find out. We're leaving now."

Hadwin motioned to his teammates, who picked up Dalir's body and carried it to the stairs. Before following them, Hadwin put a bullet in the head of each pirate.

Chapter 71

Chesapeake Bay, Maryland, Near Naval Air Station Patuxent River

"Corktip one-zero-one, Test. Proceed to item five."

"Roger, Test. Corktip one-zero-one commencing item five in three zero seconds."

Lieutenant Commander Kay Hutchins scanned her helmet-visor display in the F-35 she was piloting on yet another test of the new rotary missile rack. She glanced at her knee board and verified that item five was extension of the rack during a 4-g turn.

It's a great morning for flying! she thought, eyes feasting on the sparkling Chesapeake, fifteen thousand feet below her. Life doesn't get much better than flying the hottest fighter in the world on a sunny day with nobody shooting at you.

She caught the glint of the old target ship in the sun, run aground in the shallows near Bloodsworth Island, and turned her attention back to the test. Hutchins began a diving turn, tightening it until she reached 4 g.

"Extending in five . . . four . . . three . . . two . . . one. Extension initiated."

She felt a medium-strength buffet as the rack extended from the aircraft's bomb bay, but once it was fully in the slipstream, the flight control computer adjusted for the turbulence.

"Feels rock solid. No flight issues at full extension."

"Roger, one-zero-one. Report when ready for item six."

"Wilco."

Hutchins pulled out of the dive, the F-35 arcing up to fifteen thousand again.

Item six, launching an inert version of the Joint Air-to-Ground Missile, had been the subject of disagreement during mission planning. Kay felt the rack should be retracted after item five was completed so that item six would test the full cycle of deployment, launch, and retraction. But Flight Test had wanted to leave the rack extended between five and six so that they'd get a launch test even if it turned out there was a problem with the retraction mechanism.

Flight Test had won—no surprise to Hutchins. The program manager was hedging his bet, as always.

"Ready item six, Control."

"Roger, one-zero-one. Commence when range clearance verified."

A new voice spoke in her helmet: "Corktip one-zero-one, this is Range Control. You are cleared in hot, time two zero."

"Roger that, Range Control. One-zero-one commencing in five . . . four . . . three . . . two . . . one. Now."

Hutchins saw a flash as the inert test missile emerged into her field of view; immediately it became a bright dot receding from the aircraft as it streaked for the old Victory Ship at Mach six.

"Missile away, no issues." Hutchins pulled out and rode the thunder back toward fifteen thousand. Before she reached it, she heard Test in a new tone of voice.

"One-zero-one, knock it off, knock it off! Take angels one zero and vector zero one five."

"Wilco, Test. What's going on?"

"New mission. Search for a twenty-five to thirty-five-foot white boat with gray deckhouse, possibly with the word *pilot* on the side. The boat is wanted by law enforcement. Occupants are armed with automatic weapons and possibly Stingers."

"What are my ROE?"

"Use any means you have to stop the boat, one-zero-one."

"This is nuts, Test! I need some authentication."

"Flaming Hooker, this is Bandito, over."

Hutchins recognized the voice, a voice that had used her personal call sign and that of her squadron commander.

"Roger, Bandito. What's going on, Skipper?"

"The guys in that boat killed four Coasties. They've got a helo and some patrol boats after them. We've been invited to join the party. Do not endanger your aircraft, but short of that you are good to go with anything you can do to stop that boat."

"Roger that, Skipper."

"I say, again, do not endanger your aircraft. And keep an eye out for Coast Guard assets. Bandito, out."

Well, if that don't beat all, thought Hutchins. Navy—it's not just a job, it's an adventure.

Switching to Guard, Hutchins radioed, "Any Coast Guard aircraft, any Coast Guard aircraft, this is Corktip one-zero-one, over.

"Corktip, this is Coast Guard two-six-seven-zero, Jayhawk, over."

"Two-six-seven-zero, this is Corktip one-zero-one, Navy Foxtrot three five. I'm three one zero for thirty from Pax River at angels ten. Are you lookin' for a getaway boat?"

"I've found him, Corktip. He's headed your way. I'm at angels three in trail one-half mile. Be advised he has automatic weapons, over."

"Roger, Coast Guard . . . Ah, there you are. Break. Test, this is Corktip one-zero-one. Judy, I say again, Judy, over."

"Roger that, Corktip," said her controller, acknowledging that Hutchins had acquired the target and was attacking.

"Never mind the damn helo! It's not armed. We can make the pickup point before the boats catch us," shouted Saleh to his Quds Force commandos over the noise of the twin diesel engines.

The engines' roar was swallowed by another sound that seemed to shred the very walls of the boat's cabin, engulfing Angler Two from stern to bow like a gigantic wave. That gut-churning surprise was followed immediately by a thunderclap, the sonic boom of the F-35 that had passed down the boat's starboard side one hundred feet above the Chesapeake.

Hutchins pulled vertical to bleed off speed, then did a Split S and leveled again at eight thousand.

"Master Arm, on," she said to the fighter's weapons system computer.

Moments later Hutchins pressed her thumb against a red button on the fly-by-wire controller. A JAGM, blue-painted to indicate that its warhead contained no explosive, screamed toward her aim point. It smashed into the bay ahead of the boat, throwing a gout of water skyward.

The helmsman yanked the throttles to neutral, shouting, "That's it—we've got to surrender! That jet will blow us up on its next pass."

"Bullshit! Open those throttles or you'll die this instant!" All eyes turned to Saleh, braced against the cabin bulkhead, covering them with his pistol.

One of the men went for Saleh, who shot him without hesitation. Hurriedly, the helmsman rammed the throttles forward.

"Coast Guard two-six-seven-zero, Corktip. You're a SAR bird, right?"

"That's affirm, Corktip."

"Get ready for business. I'm putting a missile into that boat."

Gotta be careful, thought Hutchins. This is my last missile. If it misses, then all I've been doin' is puttin' on an air show. As the aircraft's combat system announced the target, she realized she was controlling her breathing as if she were on a pistol range.

Exhale, hold it, s q u e e z e. She pressed the button.

The last missile flashed into her view, darting toward the stern of Angler Two. When it hit, the boat's transom went under as if smashed by a giant fist. The forward three-quarters of the vessel, freed from the splintered stern, skidded along the surface until the inrushing bay claimed it. The bow tilted skyward, then slid backward and disappeared.

* * *

Yokohama, Japan

The two men held themselves proudly erect as they stood shoulder to shoulder on the tatami near the family shrine in Isoroku Kimura's incense-scented home. They wore uniforms of khaki, bearing the red collar tabs denoting infantry and the rank insignia of general officers. Each carried an officer's sword, suspended from a gleaming leather belt encircling his tunic, and wore the small, visored cap preferred by officers leading troops in the field. They faced a tripod-mounted video camera that recorded their three shouts of *banzai* and all that followed. Since it was no longer possible to atone the samurai way in public—another example of Nippon's degradation, thought Kimura—he insisted on the video record.

Facing the shrine, Kimura rang a small bell, bowed before his ancestors, clapped hands twice, and bowed again. He knew he had shamed them and shamed the man he thought of as his lord, by failing in his promise to restore Nippon's honor. The Divine Wind had fallen short, and there was only one honorable recourse for his samurai spirit.

Turning to face the camera, he read his death poem in the samurai way. He removed his hat, his sword belt, then his tunic, handing each to the Pilgrim. Finally he removed a white shirt, folding it carefully before passing it to his leader, leaving his trunk exposed except for his thousand-stitch *haramaki* bellyband of white cotton, worn for luck and the protection of the spirits. Reverently, he picked up the ritually purified *wakazashi*, the shorter of a samurai's two swords. Its razor-sharp blade glinted even in the softly lit room. He looked at the Pilgrim, who stood to his side and slightly behind, holding a *katana* overhead in a two-handed grip. Kimura held the other man's gaze for a few moments, then looked at his own belly. Holding the *wakazashi* in the prescribed two-handed grip, he drove it through the *haramaki* in the region of his left kidney and pulled the blade to his right. With a grunt, the Pilgrim swung his *katana*, which encountered Kimura's neck with a meaty crunch, slicing through flesh and into his spinal column.

Minutes later the Pilgrim gazed at Kimura's corpse on the blood-slick tatami, proud that Japan still produced true samurai and that his act of atonement would be viewed by his comrades. By this act, Kimura has saved the Kamikaze from disgrace, he thought.

Now I, myself, will prevent their defeat. Though unlikely, given the yakuza code, the men of Kamikaze who funded and directed President Gwon's death may eventually be identified. But Kimura was my only connection to them; I won't come under suspicion. This attempt to demonstrate that America cannot be relied upon has failed, but I will carry on the work. Untainted, I will gather an even more powerful group. And together we will restore Nippon to greatness, to her proper place among nations.

Chapter 72

Bethesda, Maryland

Ray Morales remembered his first impression upon regaining consciousness: crisp white sheets. Now, two weeks and three surgeries later, he sat up in bed in room six forty-two of Walter Reed National Military Medical Center, still on crisp white sheets, with two visitors. They were waiting for someone.

Julie Morales sat to her husband's right, looking possessive. Ella Martin stood across the room gazing out the window, her Secret Service agent outside the closed door. Her phone chirped and she glanced at Twitter.

> NK dictator dies in plane crash; China sending troops to maintain order in leaderless DPRK. Martin welcomes Chinese role.

A Secret Service agent knocked on the door to Morales's room, paused, then pulled it open for Senator Arlene Gustafson. The senator, her face registering surprise at what she deduced from the Secret Service presence, entered warily. Her eyes hardened as she saw Ella, who turned to her with a cool gaze.

"Thanks for coming, Senator," said Ray. "I asked you to swing by so we could correct the misimpression you got from the Camp David photo."

Gustafson's lips, which had been compressed to a scarlet line, became a spillway for her anger. "Misimpression, hell! You two were headed for the sack. Anyone would see that."

"I hope you didn't pay much for that picture, Arlene, because it's nothing," said Ella. "Just two old friends talking. I had a cold with a touch of laryngitis, so Ray was leaning closer to understand me."

"Don't give me that crap! You're lying! The picture has you dead to rights."

"Senator Gustafson, give it up," said Julie. "Whatever you thought you were going to gain from that picture, you're not going to get it. It's nothing. If you put your sad little fairy tale out there, Ella and I will go on every talk show in America to expose you as a fool and a charlatan!"

"I . . . I—" Gustafson turned away.

"But your trip isn't wasted, Senator," said Ray. "Please sit down." Gustafson spun to look at Morales, shaking her head. Hands on her hips, she said, "Say what you've got to say."

"I owe you an apology and my best efforts to right the wrong I did you years ago. I could have helped you get Matt into Arlington, but I refused. I was wrong. I was so angry at you that I didn't do my duty to a good Marine.

"Senator, I know I can't erase the pain I caused you, but I'm ready to give my strongest support if you petition the VA for an exception. Together, we can get your son where he belongs."

You're still a bastard, Morales! thought Gustafson. You're conveniently ignoring your refusal to intervene in Matt's discharge action. He'd be alive now if you had. That's never gonna change, but his burial can. So let's do it! But not quite the way you want, Morales.

"Thank you for this, Secretary Morales. I will greatly appreciate your support for my petition to have his discharge re-characterized as honorable. After that there'll be no question of his right to be in Arlington."

Arlene never lets up, thought Ray. But what do you expect? She's his mother. Maybe, just maybe, I was wrong to stand on duty, to dismiss the possibility of getting him by without the LTH. Maybe I used my duty as a shield, to push away the realization that an arbitrary date of repeal had placed Matt in an impossible situation. Somebody once said, "Nobody wants to die for a mistake." Maybe Sergeant Matt Gustafson died for my mistake. Lord knows I've been wrong a lot recently; maybe I was wrong then.

"I'll do that. Your petition will have my strongest support."

Morales held out his hand. "Thanks for coming over, Senator."

Chin jutting, Gustafson ignored his hand and said, "We're not done, Secretary Morales. Ali Hadrab—care to discuss?"

Ray stiffened and his features assumed the expression Julie called his "Marine face." He folded his hands carefully in his lap and said, "Senator, you're about to cross a serious classification line, and if you do, I'll have your ass, guaranteed! And your son will *never* join his buddies in Arlington."

Gustafson smirked. "I haven't crossed the line because I don't need to. Matt's going to be buried in Arlington, and that means you won't have to figure out how to explain Hadrab. My request to the VA will be messengered to you tomorrow. I believe we understand each other."

She strutted to the door, pushed it open, and disappeared.

Ella glanced at the door, then locked gazes with Ray and Julie. "Ray, whatever that's about, I don't want to know. My business with Gustafson is finished."

Pausing as she walked toward the door, Ella said softly, "Each of us made mistakes. I hope you and Julie don't think too harshly of me for mine."

Chapter 73

Bethesda, Maryland

"RAY, WHO *IS* THIS ALI Hadrab? Gustafson believes he's someone she can use to pressure you. I want to know what she meant and why you were so defensive."

"I wasn't defensive, Julie."

"The hell you weren't! You looked like she'd caught you out. What are you hiding from me?"

Ray rubbed his forehead, looking down at the bedsheets, his lips twisting in pain. Raising his gaze, he said, "Julie, I can't tell you that. I can never tell you the story of Ali Hadrab. It's classified way above top-secret SCI. All I can say is that we had an encounter, and it was crucial to putting Fahim out of business."

"Dammit, Ray! Your worst enemy, Arlene Gustafson, knows about Ali Hadrab, but you stonewall *me*? Is this going to be like your fling with Ella—others know but you won't tell *me*? Do you think you can repair our marriage while still keeping secrets?"

Ray rubbed his uninjured eye and looked away. Turning back to his wife, he patted the bed and said softly, "Julie, please . . . sit beside me."

She complied, settling close enough to smell his familiar scent and see pain, doubt, and even panic in his good eye.

"Julie . . . I had to do something terrible, something I never thought . . ." He took a deep breath. "And I got a good man killed and another really busted up because they trusted me and followed me on an arrogant, pigheaded scheme to capture Fahim. Someday . . . someday I swear I'll tell you about Ali Hadrab. But not now. Please accept that, Julie. Please help me"

For the first time in our relationship, she thought, my husband is asking me for help. This man, this good man, is hanging on by a thread. She squeezed his hand and nodded.

"Thank you, Julie," he said in a husky voice. She knew that now he would change the subject, but that wouldn't be a dismissal. He was deeply grateful and had done the thing that was hardest for him and most important to her: he had revealed his weakness and his need for her.

"Let's watch the president's news conference," said Ray, punching the remote. He moved carefully to his right, wincing with back pain, still unable to move his left leg normally, making room for Julie to settle in beside him. Holding hands, they leaned back on the raised bed and gazed at the screen.

"And so I think that through a combination of appropriate force and skillful diplomacy we have achieved a lasting, stable realignment of interests on the Korean peninsula," said President Martin into the forest of microphones, cameras, and smart phones pointed toward him. "This will not only halt the violence; it will also put China, the new Korean Republic—as they have decided to call themselves—Japan, and the nations of Southeast Asia on a path to increased economic growth and cooperation. I'll take your questions now."

Julie looked at Ray, eyebrows arched.

"So, is the president right, Ray?"

"At least for a while, Julie." He aimed the remote and raised the volume a bit as questions began.

"Mr. President, Governor Rutherford has said that you joined forces with China to pressure one of our oldest allies, the Republic of Korea, to accept an outcome the South Koreans didn't want and wouldn't have chosen."

"Helen, the governor is entitled to his opinion, but I believe he's dead wrong. Reunification has been the desire of the Korean people, South and North, ever since the country was divided in 1945. The Kang administration did what all truly democratic governments do: honor the will of the people. Yes, Kevin"

"Mr. President, how did you force President Ming to send bombers to destroy the North Korean missile launch site, Sohae, and then go on to dismantle the regime of Young San-ho?"

"Kevin, I didn't force President Ming to do either of those things. He came to Hawaii determined, as I was, to take the measures necessary to end the fighting in Korea. Young San-ho's preparations to escalate the conflict were detected while we were meeting. President Ming immediately decided to send aircraft to take out the missile pad before launch preparations could be completed. And let me say the cooperation between our two militaries has been smooth and effective. I find that an encouraging aspect, going forward. Yes, Kylie."

"Mr. President, a follow-up to the question about Chinese agreement to take down the regime. Senator Gustafson said in a statement yesterday that you, and I quote, foolishly and cravenly gave away our basing rights in Korea. What is your response to that statement?"

"Kylie, perhaps the senator didn't notice that China also agreed to forswear bases in the former North Korea. This was a fair trade. Fact is, we don't need bases in Korea anymore. We'd be wrapping them up anyway so that we could redeploy our forces to locations where they're truly needed. Your turn, Roger."

"Mr. President, one of your opponent's PACs released a statement charging that this was a manufactured crisis, intended to increase your support by drawing attention away from terrorism right here at home and giving you a chance to wave the American flag."

"The folks in that PAC may be surprised to learn that I agree with them—partially. This crisis was indeed manufactured, but not by my administration or my campaign. It was created by the assassination of South Korea's president and by the North's attack across the DMZ.

"Furthermore, to refer to American actions since the invasion of South Korea as 'flag waving' dishonors the sacrifice of the American and South Korean troops who held the invaders to a small incursion, giving diplomacy time to work. It also ignores the swift and courageous decisions made by our secretary of state and our secretary of defense, who made tough, correct calls when both time and information were in short supply.

"And you mentioned terrorism in America. That's another place the PAC got it wrong. Our battle against terrorism is succeeding. Mass killings have dropped to what is, unfortunately, their usual level. I am proud to be running on the record of this administration's campaign against terror. Yes, Frank."

"Mr. President, the NRA recently posted a statement crediting the 'good guys with guns' campaign with most of the success in the reduction of attacks. Governor Rutherford says he supported that campaign from the beginning, while you got involved late and grudgingly. And you vetoed the 'Good Sam' bill intended to protect those good guys. What do you say to the governor?"

Ray and Julie exchanged glances. "This will be interesting," she said.

"Frank, you've asked a hard question, one really impossible to answer from the facts alone. But the facts matter, so I'll start with those.

"It's true that the actions of armed citizens in schools, theaters, hospitals, sports events, and other venues brought down several shooters before the police reached the scene. But when we look at the toll from this violent episode that is now, thank God, behind us, the data show that a little over one-third of the dead and wounded were shot by good guys with guns. They were hit by bullets intended for terrorists. How are we to feel about those facts?

"Many people, including some loved ones of accidental shooting victims, regard the deaths and injuries as unavoidable casualties of war. Some of those families supported the Good Sam bill that Congress passed overriding my veto. This law grants immunity to those who mistakenly or unintentionally harm innocent bystanders during an active shooter event.

"But I felt—and so do many of the victims' families—that armed citizens should be held responsible for their actions just as police are. Rather than an assumption that there was no wrongdoing, each shooting should be investigated and shown to be unavoidable under the circumstances or prosecuted as manslaughter or murder. After all, it's not so long ago that Americans were marching in protest because they believed police were shooting people with impunity."

Suddenly, Ray punched the mute button, and the press conference became a pantomime. Julie sat up and assumed a cross-legged position on the bed facing her husband, who said, "Julie, what about us? Can you forgive me?" He straightened up against the pillows, sitting a little taller and crossing his arms.

No, she thought, not while you're keeping secrets. What else besides Ali Hadrab? But we've made a lot of progress today. And I do love this big lug.

"Not yet, Ray, but I'll probably get there. Ella and I had quite a talk while you were under. She insisted it was her doing; that she led you on. Should I believe her?"

Ray looked down at the bedsheets, where his right forefinger traced circles. After a moment he said, "It . . . was mutual. I could have said good night at the door to Aspen Lodge, but I didn't. I knew where it could be leading, and, at that moment, I wanted it."

"Wanted *it*, or wanted *her*, Ray?"

"Her."

Julie rose from the bed, her eyes searching her husband's as she stood beside him. "That hurts, Ray. It does." But being honest, she thought, admitting you aren't always in control, matters a lot. And so does all the good in our marriage, goodness that's still there.

"Ray, I knew I was marrying a big, dumb Marine. Falling in lust is part of the package."

She leaned down, sliding her right arm behind his head and kissing him deeply. As they kissed, her left hand found its target, and she felt him react.

Suddenly she stood up with a mischievous smile and said, "Well, gotta go now! But don't think you get off this easy. We'll resume this discussion when you get home, Marine."

As she closed the door, Julie heard her husband laughing.

Twenty minutes later Ray poked at the dinner just delivered from a cart of identical meals. I didn't tell her what I did to Hadrab. I couldn't . . . there'll be a right time, but now isn't it.

Bullshit, Morales! said the familiar voice in his head. *You were a coward not to tell her everything.*

Well, maybe. But I didn't know what to tell her, and I have the time to figure that out. What I did will remain secret. Regardless of how Bart and Eric feel, in the closing weeks of his reelection campaign the president won't rain on his own parade by admitting his secretary of homeland security went rogue. Hadrab was killed in the drone strike that took out al-Wahdi and a bunch of *Inspire*'s staff. Arlene Gustafson is suspicious but has no evidence. Andy is dead—because of my arrogance; another thing I'll have to answer for to God. That leaves only Jerry and the doc who helped me—they aren't gonna talk—plus Ruby, who will never leave that Supermax and never speak with anyone who doesn't already think she's crazy. I'm not gonna get called out but that doesn't mean what I did was right, was justified, and I don't know what to tell Julie about that.

Morales sighed. He swiveled the top of his bedside table to the side, adjusted the tilt of his hospital bed, and rearranged his pillows. He swung the tabletop back into position above his legs and took a bite of meat loaf. Not bad, he thought. It's hard to screw up meat loaf, even in a hospital.

So what are you going to do *about this mess you've created?*

First, I need to figure out how *I* feel about what I did. Then I'll be ready to tell Julie. It was illegal as hell. It was evil. But it led us to the bomber, and that saved lives. And it was my duty.

Knowing what you know now, would you do it again, Morales?

Ray Morales looked out the window. He heard Hadrab's scream. He saw the blood-spattered walls of Carlos Baker's high school. Again he lay on the forest floor, awaiting the bite of Fahim's beheading knife. Then he locked those memories away and thought about Adel Ghorbani and the Islamic Republic of Iran.

* * *

Qom, Islamic Republic of Iran

"Why didn't you kill him?"

Adel Ghorbani, notwithstanding the knot in his stomach, met the Supreme Leader's glare and held his eyes as he replied: "Because I realized he will be useful to us alive, and there was no need to kill him, Leader. Having General Morales in my debt could be very helpful. He's close to President Martin, who now will probably be reelected. Martin will be our main enemy for four more years. The Islamic Republic will be in danger from the Great Satan until we have nuclear warheads for our missiles. Then the Americans will be afraid to stop us. Now, they threaten our destiny and our republic itself."

"You should have killed him. But that is only a small failure. You prevented Fahim from an attack for which we would have borne the consequences. You are a man of sound judgment and resolute action. Adel Ghorbani, I am placing you in charge of our nuclear warhead program. I didn't agree with Khamenei and Rouhani when they accepted the nuclear deal with the infidels. To me, they are traitors!

"Now, they're gone. I am Supreme Leader. You will have all the resources at my command to breathe new life into our program. You are to restore the morale of our scientists and accelerate their efforts. I expect that Iran will take its proper place as a nuclear-armed nation within one year."

Smiling, Adel Ghorbani stood taller and saluted.

Afterword and Acknowledgements

I'm not surprised that, five years after the first *Code Word* thriller, North Korea remains dangerous. It is still "the foreign policy problem from Hell." I wrote in the afterword of the first book, *Code Word: Paternity,* that the then-new dictator, Kim Jong-un, might " . . . take North Korea in a different direction. But then again, perhaps not." Today, in 2017, we know that he did not. I'm dismayed to say that the danger at the heart of *Paternity,* Kim selling nuclear weapons to terrorists, has not receded. And even without nukes, terrorists of several stripes remain a danger. Especially if, as in the novel you've just finished, they purchase the support of international criminal networks and make common cause with those who would use violence against their fellow Americans for other purposes.

This second novel, beginning as it does in the circumstances established by the first, strays farther from the current reality of America's national security situation. But, as in the first book, I haven't given the hero any silver bullets, or made free with the politics or the likely foreign policy objectives of the nations of East Asia. I also drew on the considerable body of material documenting the views and rhetoric of extremist groups in America. If one grants the conclusion of the first book, the second, in taking it from there, hews closely to reality.

So many people to thank! My wife and boon companion, Janie. Fans of the first book; your words and actions encouraged me a great deal. My perceptive and thorough editor, Robert Brown, Jr. Men and women who know much more than I about aviation and medicine: Pilots John Dill and Phil Vittetoe, paramedic Susan Norton Kirby (my daughter), and critical-care nurses Heather Bernhard and Bobbi Bieler. Thanks for your patience and if I got any details wrong, that's on me. My intrepid Beta readers: Don Anthony, Sandra Bovee, Bud Cole, John Dill, Howard Eldredge, Phil Ferrara, Forrest Horton, Dennis Johnson, Maggie Kirby (my critical-care nurse granddaughter), Ed Linz, Nino Martini, Jim Mashburn, Phil Vittetoe, Doug Quelch, and Bill Waring. In a category by himself: Bob Bishop, who is not only in the Beta gang, but read the manuscript and offered comments *twice.* The members of The Guy's Book Club, to which I belong, whose comments about books far more distinguished than mine teach me something at every meeting. I hope they don't mind the use to which I put the club's name in *Code Word: Pandora.*

Rick Martin, Ming Liu, Ray Morales, and Adel Ghorbani will meet and struggle again in the third *Code Word* book, working title *Code Word: Persepolis.* And if you missed their first encounter, *Code Word: Paternity,* consider reading it now. You can sample the opening scenes by turning the page.

CODE WORD: PATERNITY

A PRESIDENTIAL THRILLER

Chapter 1

THE PRESIDENT OF THE UNITED States was sitting in a puddle. The south-east wind gusted and President Rick Martin happily steered up into the puff, his tiny sailboat heeling and accelerating immediately as the wind hit its green-striped sail. He straightened his legs, hooked his feet under the leeward gunwale, and hung his dripping butt over the side, counterbalancing the sail's pull so the boat wouldn't capsize. Rick shifted the tiller extension and the sheet into his left hand and reached out his right, fingers trailing in the bay.

He lost himself in the rippling sound and the slick, smooth sensations of the warm water streaming past the small Sunfish he was sailing at the mouth of the Gunpowder River where it meets the Chesapeake Bay. The sky was an inverted blue bowl, just darker than robin's egg at its zenith and milky around its rim. To the west a fringe of low white clouds curled around the horizon like the remains of a balding man's hair.

A bit over six feet tall and wiry—the build of a swimmer or runner—Rick Martin looked streamlined. His salt-and-pepper hair was graying at the temples, but his face was quite unlined, except when he smiled. After six months in office Rick still projected the optimism, lively intelligence, and likeability that had fueled his rise from Maryland congressman to president. He appreciated Camp David but favored another retreat from the pressures of office: the Chesapeake Bay. The VIP guest house at the military's Aberdeen Proving Ground made a perfect base for the sailing he loved.

He guided the boat, reflecting that sailing was one of the few things in his life that had purity and integrity. It's not that I expect politics to have either one, he thought. I take the hidden agendas and exaggerations and outright lies as they come and, let's be honest, do my share. But it's such a pleasure to enter a world, even a very limited world, where things are as they seem. The wind blows from where it blows—no man can control it or influence it. This little boat gives immediate and honest feedback.

Honesty . . . I should be grateful to Glenna Rogers. Had I beaten her back then for the Democratic nomination, I probably would've made the same mistakes she did as president. Those mistakes left her vulnerable as few first-term presidents have been, as Jimmy Carter was, and for the same reason: Most Americans don't like feeling that the country has been humiliated, and when that happens they hold the president responsible.

* * *

As Las Vegas receded at a mile a minute, Fahim fretted, the I-15 ahead of his car as crisp and stark as fresh black paint on the yellowish, desolate soil. There was nothing he could do now, so he should put it out of his mind. But he could no more ignore it than his tongue could ignore a bit of food between his teeth. He knew he was taking a chance, but he had backup. The young man driving the truck would get his wish for martyrdom in any case, although he didn't know about the timer or the bomb's secret. Fahim, who didn't want to be a martyr, had directed the man who did to press his button at 10:35 a.m.

Interrupting his drive to California at 10:25, Fahim pulled to the shoulder and sat in the air conditioner's blast, sweating anyway. The sweat overflowed the barriers of his eyebrows and stung his eyes, which matched the black color of his hair. He compared his worries to the opening night jitters of an actor playing the West End the first time. Thinking of London theater brought to mind his father, a university professor of history who disapproved of his violent embrace of the cause but was nonetheless willing to admit he was cultured—for an engineer. He smiled at the memory of their fond arguments, his wiry body relaxing slightly.

Waiting for the event that would henceforth define him, he muted his humanity, burying it beneath hatred. He remembered the tens of thousands of Muslims America had killed. He remembered the suffering of his own Palestinian brothers at the hands of the Israelis, who owed their existence to Americans. He remembered the humiliation of Muslims at Abu Ghraib prison. He remembered Guantánamo.

Suppose he failed? Some stupid oversight? The Sheikh's memory would be mocked instead of glorified. Heart pounding, he gripped the wheel as if crushing it would ensure success.

At 10:30 a flash brighter than Fahim had imagined stabbed his rear-view mirror, which he had set for night to protect his eyes. He cried out, mouth a rictus that was part astonishment, part orgasm, then slumped in release as triumph embraced him. I have just struck the mightiest blow ever against America!

And I am going to do it again.

* * *

The harsh sounds of jet skis and helicopter rotors were startling. Rick looked around and saw his secret service detail closing fast from their escort positions fifty yards away, followed by a small Coast Guard patrol boat. A familiar Marine helicopter was landing at the shoreline.

Agents surrounded his little sailboat. All but the one who spoke looked away, scanning for danger, hands on the waterproof bags he knew held weapons.

"Mr. President, there's a national security emergency and we need to get you to the helo! Get aboard behind me, please."

Feeling a stab in his stomach, but also a thrill, Martin clambered aboard, mind racing. Another Russian incursion into the Ukraine? Something involving Israel? Maybe Korea? Whatever it was, it might be his first crisis and he was secretly eager to tackle it, more than ready to be tested.

The crew chief jumped out of the helo—its rotors continuing to turn— trotted in a crouch to the president, and led him toward it. As if by magic the head of Martin's secret service detail, Wilson, appeared with a submachine gun and trailed him, followed by an officer carrying a briefcase. Rick moved to his familiar place, saw National Security Advisor John Dorn belted in nearby. The moment the president's soaking shorts squelched into his seat, the helo leaped skyward.

Martin, buckling his lap belt, looked at Dorn, saw his pale face, and said, "What!" in a sharp, flat voice that made it not a question, but a command.

"Sir, a nuclear bomb has exploded in Nevada, in or near Las Vegas! Because we haven't detected any missiles or unidentified military aircraft, we think it was a terrorist act. We have no communications—"

Dorn's lips kept forming words, but Martin's mind had stopped, like a sprinting soldier halted in mid-stride by a bullet. He sat back in his seat, folded his arms across his chest, and stared at the forward bulkhead. His gaze rested on the Great Seal of the President of the United States.

That's me.

He recalled, in a flash, his thoughts from many years past, thoughts that came immediately after he had once tumbled into a ravine, breaking an ankle while winter hiking alone in the wilderness during college: *Later this is really going to hurt, but right now you've got to put that away and figure out how to stay alive.*

Holding a satcom handset tightly to his ear against the chopper's noise, Martin asked General "Mac" MacAdoo, chairman of the JCS, "Do you have any doubt this was nuclear?"

MacAdoo responded from the Pentagon, "No sir! Two DSP satellites picked up a flash with the unique characteristics of a nuclear explosion. Besides, we have satellite imaging showing such destruction that it had to be a nuke, plus what they saw from Creech Air Force Base, about thirty-five miles away."

"Okay, Mac, but what's the chance that this was a ballistic missile attack and NORAD just missed it, somehow didn't detect a lone missile coming from an unexpected direction?"

"No chance, Mr. President. The old BMEWS radars might have missed one, the way you said, but now we have interlocking, multi-sensor coverage from six satellites. It's possible the warhead was put into Vegas using a short range missile, or an artillery tube, but if so the firing point had to be within the U.S., probably within the state. It's also possible it was aboard a commercial aircraft."

"I understand . . . thanks."

Martin hung up and looked numbly out the window.

Well, now it begins. Nuclear terrorism was a nightmare and now it's real and mine to deal with. How vulnerable is my administration: did we fail to connect the dots?

How do you deal with tens of thousands of bodies on a radioactive rubble pile?

Who did it?

Why Las Vegas?

What's next?

CPSIA information can be obtained
at www.ICGtesting.com
Printed in the USA
BVOW03s0711031217
501808BV00001B/94/P

9 780999 497609